Praise for Elizabeth Noble's *The Reading Group*

"A lively, witty novel that touches on themes of friendship and the redemptive power of art."

—Choice

"The ideal novel for social book babes. . . . Between them, these very different women learn to read between the line of life and fiction."

—YOU magazine

"Perfect stuff to chew on over a long night in."
—Daily Mail

"This is a real female-bonding novel in the very best sense; it's witty, pacy, and immediately engaging, with a careful balance of poignant and feel-good moments."

—Glamour (UK)

"It's impossible not to get sucked in."

—Daily Mirror

"A compelling read, with characters you'll really take to your heart."

—HEAT

About the Author

ELIZABETH NOBLE studied English language and literature at St. Edmund Hall, Oxford University, before working in British publishing for several years. *The Reading Group* is her first novel. She lives in Guildford, Surrey, with her husband and two daughters.

THE
READING
GROUP

THE
READING
GROUP

ELIZABETH NOBLE

Perennial

An Imprint of HarperCollins*Publishers*

DESIGNED BY PHILLIP MAZZONE

ISBN 0-7394-5540-0

For David and Sandy Noble,

my mum and dad

The real, hidden subject of a book group discussion is the book members themselves.

—MARGARET ATWOOD

ACKNOWLEDGMENTS

Thanks in vast quantities, are due to:

Stephanie Cabot, Sue Fletcher, Hazel Orme and all the great people at William Morris and Hodder & Stoughton who have helped the book get here.

In New York, Shana Kelly at William Morris, and the entire team at HarperCollins (most especially, my editor, Kate Travers, for being my champion and for the margaritas). Yvonne Temple and Katy Gibb, for taking control of everything else while I wrote it.

Dr. Nicola Barker, Katharine Livingstone, Ian Osborne and William Young for answering my daft questions without laughing.

David Young, who knows all the reasons why; Tallulah and Ottilie Young, for their insistence that writing a book is nowhere near as important as making fairy cakes and applying glittery nail polish; and to the rest of my big glorious family, for the Jubilee lunch and everything else besides.

My great friend Catherine Holmes, for planting the seed of the idea four years ago, and for her insights into "proper" reading groups.

And finally, my own, definitely "improper" reading group: Nicola, Kate, Maura, Jenny, Alison, and Kathryn, for providing suppers, support, inspiration, and even, occasionally, dialogue! And see . . . you're *not* in it . . .

THE BOOKS

THE CHARACTERS

Harriet   A thirty-something homemaker, and cofounder of
the Reading Group
Favorite book: *Gone with the Wind*

Tim: Harriet's husband, something big in finance
Favorite book: Michael Moore's ***Stupid White Men***
Josh: Harriet and Tim's eight-year-old son
Favorite book: *Harry Potter,* of course
Chloe: Harriet and Tim's four-year-old daughter
Favorite book: anything my daddy reads to me

Nicole   Harriet's best friend, and cofounder
Favorite book: *The Beautiful and the Damned*

Gavin: Nicole's husband, something in
advertising
Favorite book: *The Tipping Point,* by Malcolm
Gladwell
William and George: Nicole and Gavin's twin
sons, age eight
Favorite books: Stuff with ghosts or soldiers in it
Martha: Nicole and Gavin's daughter, age eight,
Chloe's best friend
Favorite book: *Olivia Saves the Circus*
Cecile: Their young French au pair
Favorite book: *Time Out Guide to London*

Polly   A forty-something paralegal secretary and single
parent
Favorite book: Magazines, to be truthful

Jack: Her new boyfriend, a solicitor in family law in his early fifties.
Favorite book: Anything by John Grisham
Cressida: Polly's twenty-year-old daughter from her first marriage, a student
Favorite book: Depends who's asking. Why do you want to know anyway?
Daniel: Cressida's fifteen-year-old brother
Favorite book: Prefers the Internet, but, if pushed, will read a sporting biography
Joe: Cressida's boyfriend, in his first year at University in Warwick.
Favorite book: and only book, right now: *Dummies Guide to Economics*
Dan: Polly's ex-husband, now remarried
Favorite book: *Fear and Loathing in Las Vegas*

Susan   Polly's old friend
Favorite book: *How to Eat,* by Nigella Lawson
Roger: Susan's husband, a GP
Favorite book: You can't beat a Nevil Shute—any of them.
Alex: Their elder son, away at University
Favorite book: *Catcher in the Rye*
Ed: Their younger son, also studying away from home
Favorite book: *To Kill a Mockingbird*
Alice: Susan's widowed mother
Favorite book: The Sunday funnies
Margaret: Susan's sister, who has been living in Australia for many years
Favorite book: *The Thorn Birds*

Clare   A midwife
Favorite book: Rough Guides and Lonely Planets
Elliot: Her husband
Favorite book: *The Red Badge of Courage*
Mary: Clare's mother, who works in Susan's curtain and upholstery business
Favorite book: A good Catherine Cookson

Clare watched as the young woman passed her in the corridor. First-timer, definitely: excitement and panic were etched on her pale face as she made her way slowly down the hall, dragging the IV on its wheels beside her, legs bent and shoulders hunched, shuffling in girlish slippers bought for this special day. Her glance at Clare said, "Help me. When will this be finished? When will he be here?" Probably came in half a centimeter dilated—when she'd fiddled with her TENS machine at home for a while, then called her mother and repacked the holdall with all the impossibly small, impossibly white sleep suits, scratch mittens and hats like egg cozies.

The double doors behind the woman swung open, and a big, dark man went to her, put one hand in hers, the other round her shoulder. He handled her gingerly. He was paler than she was. A Type X, Clare thought. They were copers, the strong ones. Type Ys barely made it through the epidurals without crying. They were a few decades too late—would have been happier pacing the corridor with a cigar behind each ear. Clare liked the Type Ys better.

Elliot was probably an X. Or maybe the hybrid: Y masquerading as X. They were okay unless things got scary. Who was she kidding? She had no idea which type he'd be. Not that it mattered. Not anymore.

The girl moaned, leant forward. Clare answered his imploring look. She never felt detached. Still, each story that played out, each life that started within these walls pulled her in. Still.

"Okay, hold on, let's give you a hand. What's your name?"

"Lynne."

"Okay, Lynne. We'll get you back to your room. You probably need a bit of a rest. Who's looking after you?"

A colleague appeared from behind the same double doors. "Sorry, Clare. Hang on, Lynne. We've got you. Got it from here, Clare. You're off, aren't you?"

"Yes."

"Have a good night, then."

"Cheers."

Tonight, thank God, she had a reason not to be at home, not to see Elliot. She'd probably be out again before he got back from college, and he'd be asleep by the time she made herself climb into bed beside him.

And that girl, Lynne, would be holding her baby in her arms.

7:20 P.M.

As usual Harriet climbed the stairs with a teetering pile of single socks, discarded sweaters, stray toys—the flotsam and jetsam of the day. Down was usually a mug or two, plastic cups found under beds, read newspapers and sticky plastic medicine spoons. Up, the aforementioned. Still, she supposed, with a fairly twisted smile, variety was the spice of life. Ha, ha. Domestic bliss reminded her of that silly film she'd seen once, *Groundhog Day*, where this guy was compelled to repeat the same day over and over again, never quite getting the girl because he couldn't change what happened. And slightly higher up the cultural scale, wasn't there that guy in mythology—Sissy something . . . Sisyphus, was it?—sentenced by the gods for some transgression to spend eternity pushing a boulder up a big hill only to watch it fall straight down again, and on, and on. At least pushing a big boulder up a hill would soon sort out these bat wings she was developing beneath her upper arms, Harriet thought. Sweeping the flipping kitchen floor four times, loading and unloading the washing machine three times and answering forty-two questions about why there aren't any more dinosaurs, and if there were, how big their poos would be, wasn't doing much for hers.

Upstairs, all was quiet for the first time since 6:00 a.m. Harriet followed the sound of Tim's voice to their bedroom. He was sitting on the sofa under the window, having been allowed by his kidnappers to remove his shoes and jacket, and loosen his tie. The children, damp and clean from their bath, were huddled, one under each arm, listening to their story. Tim was reading slowly, ascribing to each character his or her own voice, occasionally making animated gestures. Harriet felt a twinge of habitual guilt. She usually chose the shortest story and speed-read it: her children might be forgiven for thinking that every character in literature had been raised in the middle-class South, for all the effort she made with her inflection. Still, it was easier, wasn't it? Coming in at the end of the day, when the snot and the pasta sauce and the tears had been wiped away, and the fight over the toothbrushing, and the frantic shoving of toys into too-small cupboards had all been done. Easy to reward the exuberant greeting with warmth and affection and a story reading fit for Radio 4. The kids had spent their energy through the long day, and Harriet had absorbed it. Now the fight had gone out of them: they were passive, gentle. And she was catatonic.

Harriet hovered at the doorway, not wanting to go in and disturb the perfect tableau, the circle of love. Somehow, she didn't fit into these moments. Instead, she deposited her bundle on the guest bed and went into the bathroom. Studiously ignoring the bubble scum around the bath, the toothpaste squeezed carelessly across the washbasin tap, she poked ineffectually at her mad hair in the mirror and flicked some powder across her nose and chin. She hastily drew a line of lipstick on her upper lip, then rolled her lips together in concentration. (Not for her the liner-brush-blot prescribed by glossies she only saw every three months in the hairdresser's.)

Tim appeared in the doorway, carrying a slumped, sleepy Chloe. "Say 'Night-night, Mummy.'" Thumb firmly plugged in, Chloe waved her plastic beaker of warm milk vaguely in Harriet's direction.

"Night-night, sleep tight, darling." Harriet smiled.

Behind Tim, Josh asked, "Are you going out, Mummy?"

"Yes, I am, sweetheart. Daddy's going to look after you. I'll be home again later, though."

"Come and tuck me in when you get back? Even if it's really late? D'you promise you will?"

"Course I do, poppet. Give us a kiss before I go, though."

Harriet walked with her son down the landing and watched him climb into his low bunk.

"Daddy's coming back, Mum. Don't switch that light off. He promised he'd read me another chapter of *Harry Potter* when Chloe was in bed."

"Did he now? Two stories, indeed. Is Daddy trying to make me look bad?"

Her tone was light.

Suddenly Tim was behind her. "Couldn't if I tried." He kissed her cheek as he passed her in the doorway. "Now, remind me where we got to, Josh."

And they were quickly lost again in their reading. Tim looked up from the pages as he heard her turn, and winked good night at her.

Harriet's tread on the stairs was heavy. It's all so bloody perfect, she thought. Except that I really don't think I love him anymore. If I ever did.

7:25 P.M.

The mass of feeling sat just beneath Nicole's rib cage, as if her lungs had been folded into thirds at the base of her throat. It was a potent and complex emotional cocktail, part rage, part hurt, part frustration, part humiliation and, still, part suffocating love. Over the years the quantities of each had changed, but the result was the same. Almost overwhelming, drunken feeling.

She'd gone through the whole day in the closed-off state she had perfected. She had put it into the room in her mind with the padlock on it and not gone near it: opening it, and luxuriating in the feelings, would make functioning impossible. In that closed-off state, she was a dervish of control and efficiency. Dry cleaning and shoe repairs got dropped off; casseroles with interesting herbs were put in the Aga's slow oven; constructive play happened with the children; concise instructions were given to Cecile, the au pair.

And she looked great. Hair, makeup, figure, clothes: all as good as they always had been. Other women might tear out their hair at moments of crisis, but Nicole blow-dried hers into perfect waves. Only her heartbeat gave her away: like in that Edgar Allan Poe story, she was sure everyone she met, smiling benignly, must hear it, louder and louder, trying to get out.

She put the platter of crostini on the hall table and looked into the mirror. Downstairs it was quiet. One floor up Will, George and Martha were sound asleep, exhausted by swimming and soft play. From the top floor, where Cecile slept, Nicole could hear the soft beat of garage music being played behind a closed door, punctuated by excited French conversation. She must be on the phone (you don't say) to another member of the au pair Mafia, squealing about last night's adventures or plotting tomorrow's. These days, au pairs stayed in and babysat, then went out after you came home—"Oh, no, Mrs. Thomas, it no start, you know, really, until midnight." They could stay out until four, smoke forty cigarettes, sleep for two hours and still make animal shapes with Cheerios to persuade reluctant breakfasters to eat, smiling, at 7:00 a.m. It sometimes made Nicole feel 105 years old. Nicole liked Cecile, though. She was easy to have around, didn't need everything explained. And Nicole was pretty sure Cecile was knowingly impervious to Gavin's manifest charms, which, just now, suited her perfectly.

She stiffened as she heard his car outside, waited for the key in the lock. What to say? She had rehearsed all the different angles in the shower earlier, played out the fantasy of reacting as other women would. Although she knew that, when she saw him, she would be as she always was. How odd that this was a habit now, that this was a part of their life together. She had never thought it would be like this. That *she* would be like this.

God, he was beautiful. Those enormous, shining eyes: how could they not give away the secrets?

He smiled, then registered the tray of food, and that Nicole was in her coat and scarf. "Hello, darling. Sorry to be a bit late.

It's been a bitch of a day. What's this, then? Where are you off to?"
He leant in to kiss her.

Nicole swerved, left him pursing at air. "I'll be at Susan's, darling." She spat the last word, sarcasm heavy in the air. And that was the very best she could do. That, and a defiant slam of the door. Quickly. She didn't want him to see the food shaking on the plate in time with her arms.

7:30 P.M.

The ring was pretty well perfect. Big enough, but not flashy—some you saw were so obvious that the wearers might as well have taped facsimiles of their fiancés' black AmEx cards across their left hands. A modern setting, but not so trendy it would be the avocado bathroom suite of jewelry in ten years' time (presuming, against all the odds, that you were still wearing it). It was even the right stone for her—a ruby—and just about what she would have chosen for herself, if she'd been asked. Which would have been something of a shock, since the proposal had come more or less out of the blue. And pretty embarrassing, Polly figured, to peer into windows falling in love with the five-thousand-pound ring, wondering if *he* was looking at the five-hundred-pound one.

But, did the choice of the right ring make its giver the right man? Was it a sign? Or just down to good observation—even basic good taste? Could he have asked someone? Cressida? Suze? She thought it unlikely. That wasn't Jack's style. She bloody well hoped they would have warned her if they'd known it was coming. Although probably not. That wasn't really on. It looked pretty on her finger. She flexed her hand once more, moving the gem in and out of the light, then sniggered at her reflection in the dressing-table mirror and slipped it off. She pushed it between the folds of velvet, snapped the box shut and slid it back into her knicker drawer, hidden between party pants and period pants.

She opened her wardrobe, vaguely looking for a sloppy sweater she thought she might have shoved in there. Ah, my schizophrenic wardrobe: right side neat and tidy—"paralegal chic," she called it—with knee-length somber suits and court shoes, just as the partners of Smith, March and May liked them; the left was a Tracey Emin installation.

What kind of bride might she make? She'd always fancied red and plunging. Then again, you could wear that to any old Christmas party, while the white lace and butter-wouldn't-melt look wasn't one you could get away with very often. If they did it when it was cold, how about white lace underneath, and one of those fabulous velvet capes—in red, or maybe a deep forest green? Ooh, and beaded shoes.

Oh, for God's sake, Polly—Pollyanna, more like—aren't you a bit bloody old for this daydreaming? And shouldn't you be just a bit bloody wiser by now? One ring and one proposal, and you're sixteen again.

"Mum?"

Polly grabbed the moth-eaten sweater and pulled it over her head as she went out onto the landing.

"Mum? Is this for me?" It was Daniel, fresh from football practice, five foot ten of sweaty, spotty, starving fifteen-year-old, now foraging.

"Yes, love, microwave it—two minutes on high. And there's Christmas cake and mince pies for after."

Polly put her head round the door of the sitting room. Her daughter Cressida, arms hugging her knees, head against a cushion, was apparently transfixed by *EastEnders*.

"Cress, love, I'm at Susan's—do you remember? Shouldn't be late, though."

"Okay."

Charming, Polly thought. That girl is getting surly. What the hell am I doing, playing Brides upstairs with these two lumps down here to remind me who I am, where I've been and what I'm bad at?

What to say? What to answer? Yes? No? Would he settle for a "Maybe?"

7:35 P.M.

Five minutes later Cressida sat in the bathroom with her eyes screwed tight shut and made bargains with God. She didn't believe in God, but what the hell? She would, if only He would make it be negative.

How in hell had she got herself into this bloody mess?

If there was one thing Cressida hated, it was stereotyping and clichés. And here she was—twenty years old, loving her course and sure to get her pick of places to do her degree, which would open all kinds of doors, to a career she would love, people who would be fascinating, and freedom—about to become the most tired cliché in the book, like some effing Catherine Cookson heroine, caught and covered in shame. This couldn't happen. It just couldn't.

Ninety-nine percent accurate in one minute. She reread the instructions. The marketing speak was so carefully worded, aimed at both extremes of people taking the test: some wanted to see that blue line more than anything in the world; others would give their kidney for an empty window. She tried to imagine wanting a positive result, but it was too hard. Everything, and she meant everything, would have to be completely different. *She* would have to be different: a much, much older Cressida, with her two-foot-long hair cut into a sensible bob, her fashionable jeans swapped for grown-up clothes, the cigarettes and vodka a distant memory, with a CV that didn't stop after A levels. And there had to be a husband. On that point, at least, Cressida was weirdly old-fashioned. Now, none of the above was anywhere near happening. Particularly the cigarettes and vodka, she thought, remembering New Year's Day, when she had awoken unsure whether it was the pain in her head or the one in her throat that was going to kill her, but hoping that whichever it was would do it quickly. If there was a baby, it was bound to have two heads or something. Christ.

They'd always been dead careful—not that preventing pregnancy had been top of her list of priorities. She had been born in the eighties, after all—the AIDS decade. He was even the first—how tragic was that? A virgin at twenty.

Truthfully, though, her virginity hadn't weighed heavily on her, like it seemed to do on her mates. Several had apparently viewed their birthdays as deadlines: sixteen, do your GCSEs; seventeen, get a provisional driving license; eighteen, vote; any of the above, commence sex life with nearest nonrepulsive male. Not that Cressida was one of those Jesus freaks, taking the pledge until marriage. She sometimes thought she just hadn't fancied anyone enough. Or maybe she hadn't felt secure enough with any of the boys she'd gone out with. Doubtless a counselor would blame Dad: her trust in men had taken a battering when he had left Mum. Which was clearly bollocks, since they had pretty much left each other. Cressida didn't have a lot of patience with bleeding-heart divorce kids. She loved both her parents a lot—and a lot more apart. Dad was happy with Tina. Mum was happy on her own, maybe about to be a whole lot happier with Jack. "Worse things happen at sea," as Gran would say. Cressida didn't have any fears about the damage life had done to her heart. Look how it had soared when she met him! And she had been really glad that she hadn't been so close to anyone before—it had felt like a gift she had had for him, and she had been so thrilled, that first time, lying beside him afterward, that it had been him, that nothing could ever change how it was. Which wasn't to say it had been perfect, just that she was glad. Until now. Oh, no. Oh, no. Oh, no. It was a yes.

7:45 P.M.

Susan leant against the doorframe in satisfaction and exhaustion. Order had been restored in the living room—again. My God, Christmas makes a mess, she thought. You go completely crazy for the six weeks beforehand, shopping like a woman possessed and writing endless indecipherable lists. You treat the final trip to Sainsbury's like a military operation, complete with life-or-death missions—to get to the last fresh cranberries before the enemy in the twinset, to pile one more box of luxury crackers into the heaving trolley. You clean every surface in the house as though heart-bypass surgery was about to be performed on it, then fill them with sacred homemade angels and candlesticks. You religiously

follow *Good Housekeeping*'s "Tips for the Most Relaxed Christmas
Ever!," which actually almost kills you, but at least means that at
10:30 p.m. on Christmas Eve you can sit down with a glass of
(homemade, what else) eggnog and be the queen of all you sur-
vey. Three days later it's all over, leaving you with leftover turkey,
untouched Christmas cake and so much mess you feel as if
you've been occupied by a hostile army. But, oh, those three days:
they were the best in Susan's year. Roger and she, Alex and Ed,
and her mum, Alice. Just the five of them.

That was how Susan liked her house best. Her beautiful, good
boys asleep in their familiar rooms, Airfix models and school
sports trophies unchanged. Young, fun girlfriends, who made
them happy, asleep next door. Alice tucked beneath her own cro-
chet blankets in the old nursery beside Susan's room. And Roger
beside her—snoring gently, these days. Why did some women
complain that snoring drove them insane? She liked the rhyth-
mic purr, marking time through the night.

Susan put away the Dyson vacuum cleaner in the hall cupboard and took the last box of Christmas decorations to the upstairs landing—she would get Roger to do a loft trip after evening
surgery.

Alice appeared at the top of the stairs. She had seemed tired
this year, Susan had noticed. Bit off her food, too, although her
pleasure at being with her gorgeous grandsons had seemed undi-
minished. Still, she was glad she'd persuaded her mother to stay
on for a couple of weeks into the new year. "Let me wait on you,"
Susan had joked. Alice was in her seventies now, and it was nice
to have her there.

"All right, Mum?"

"Fine, love. I didn't sleep, just listened to a play on the radio
and rested my eyes awhile."

Susan smiled. Ah, yes, the eye resting of the elderly. Just like
children, they could never admit to being tired.

She glanced at the carriage clock on the sitting-room man-
telshelf. They'd all be here in twenty minutes or so. She'd meant
to get to some of those invoices in her office, but they would have
to wait. The run-up to Christmas was always busy in the workshop—people desperately wanted their curtains and soft furnish-

ings finished in time for Christmas, and Susan, with her own passion for the festivities, bent over backward to make everyone else's domestic dreams come true. Consequently, January was quiet, all billing and banking, no fun.

In the kitchen, she had laid places for Roger and Alice. Their supper was already made and covered neatly with cling film. It sat beside the oven, with a yellow Post-it note detailing the oven temperature and cooking time. She was looking forward to the reading group tonight. It would make a nice change. Her most recent experiments in organized social activities had proved unsuccessful: Keep Fit, with the ridiculously taut Teresa at the leisure center, had done little for her ample figure, still less for her bad back; French for Beginners at the local college had sent her to Paris on her wedding anniversary with unwarranted confidence and false bravado, but any self-belief had been dispatched by the snotty sales assistants and waiters.

Yes, it would be a good night, and she deserved a bit of something for herself.

7:50 P.M.

The silence in the house was stifling. Elliot dropped his keys noisily on the kitchen table and flicked absentmindedly through the day's post. Flyers, mostly, a gas bill . . . "Clare? Hello? I'm back . . ." He knew his wife was at home—her shift at the hospital had ended an hour before and her Metro was parked outside.

No answer. So, clearly today had been a bad day. Sad friendliness was a good day, indifference marked an average one. But when she ignored him, then became hostile, she'd had a bad one. Elliot scanned the room for evidence of today's trigger—there always was one. He looked back at the post: a card from neighbors on holiday at a family resort . . . No—of course. An invoice from Mr. Thompson, Harley Street. The end of the latest quest. Another dead end.

He climbed the stairs with a heavy tread, steeling himself to see his wife.

"Hi." As she heard him walk up the stairs she pushed the bathroom door closed against him—he caught a glimpse of her bare shoulder before he was barred. She had become like this gradually. Of course, she had been shy when they were first together, but they had been only fourteen, and even had there been the opportunity to see each other naked (which there certainly hadn't), it had all been so new, so timid. He always thought they'd been dead lucky. Together since the fourth year, all through O levels, A levels, her nursing degree, his teacher training. All their mates had played the field and suffered the heartbreak, humiliation and high drama of adolescence, but it had been different for Clare and Elliot. They had been at the core of a gang of lively teenagers, the fixed point on the compass.

It wasn't supposed to have turned into this, a sterile, empty, childless marriage. For five years they had been trying. It had been fun to start with, extrasexy to be making love with a baby in mind; he had felt fantastic lying there afterward, with his hand across Clare's belly, wondering if they had started something—someone. He'd had her all to himself for years and he was ready to share her; they were both excited. It hadn't taken long for her to fall pregnant the first time. And then, a few weeks further along, there had been the messy, miserable miscarriage. But that was okay, everyone said. "Of course you're sad, but it happens to so many people—really, you'll be fine next time." They were young; they cried together for the baby that would have been born in time for Christmas, and they moved on. Miles and miles on, until the couple they had been then was unrecognizable to both of them. Sixty months, five miscarriages (maybe more), dozens of tests, a seemingly endless procession of doctors, obstetricians, specialists. A calendar full of dates that celebrated nothing except what neither of them could forget.

Sometimes Elliot thought that Clare hated him nearly as much as she hated herself. And maybe more than she had ever loved him.

Clare came out of the bathroom, tightly wrapped in her terry dressing gown although it was only seven o'clock. She smiled weakly at Elliot, and he reached for her. A touch that he had learnt to make nonsexual, unthreatening. How he hated that: if

his fingers brushed her breast or rested on the curve of her buttocks, she shrugged them off as if they were red-hot, as if he was
a rapist. Now she let him touch her, but there was no response.

They hadn't kissed since before Christmas—not a proper kiss.
Christmas was always the worst time: the unbirthday of the first
unbaby. It was a time for family. This year Clare hadn't even
wrapped the impersonal shirt and tie she had bought him; she
had cooked salmon for Christmas lunch. Elliot's prettily wrapped
and beribboned jewelry box had sat by the fire like a reproach.
When she'd opened it, he hadn't been convinced she'd even seen
the bracelet. She hadn't worn it.

But still he tried. "Hard day, love?"

"It wasn't too bad, actually. Four women delivered, only one
had to go up for a Caesar. Three girls, one boy. Hannah, Victoria,
Liam and an undecided. One bloody annoying girl who had hers
on Monday ringing every five minutes for someone to pick up the
baby. And that supercilious resident's on holiday."

These details were delivered in a deadpan voice, with no eye
contact. As if I give a damn about all that, Elliot thought. She's
hiding in the details of the day. God forbid we should talk about
anything real. Aloud he said, "Speaking of holidays, Midge and
Paul's postcard makes me wonder if we should think about it. It's
a while since the Dordogne." That had been the holiday from
hell—he'd booked it as a surprise, got the dates wrong: one of the
black days had fallen right in the middle of the first week. Mind
you, it was getting pretty hard to find a fortnight that didn't have
a black day in it somewhere.

Clare turned to him, and he saw, for the first time, that her
eyes were red. "Maybe."

"We might be able to get a deal over Easter at a ski resort—
Austria, maybe. We've been talking about doing that for years."

They had never skied. In the first years they hadn't had the
money, more recently Clare had been worried about a fall, pregnant, unpregnant . . . she had climbed into her own invisible
petri dish.

"Oh, that's right," she snapped. "We can't have a baby, so let's
hit the slopes instead. Next best thing, really, a great holiday." She

didn't look at him as she furiously removed clothes from her drawers. She put on her knickers with her back to him, her dressing gown on so he couldn't see her. Punishment.

"Well, perhaps I'll pick up a brochure or two in town. Check that Internet site with the last-minute deals." Elliot's new tactic. To pretend that her responses were civil, interested. As though by carrying on regardless he could get her to give up this vendetta against him. And because Clare didn't have the energy to rail against him, today, at least, she was letting him carry on. In both their heads a tiny part of their brains insisted on imagining a holiday like the ones they used to have. They'd always been cheap packages to grottyish Mediterranean resorts, but they had been filled with laughter and love. Elliot and Clare, nut brown from afternoons under the sun, tired from making love all morning—always in the morning, when the brightness made the intimacy all the greater, when sex was open-eyed, as they gauged each other's responses and desires. Clare and Elliot, giggling from remembrances of tipsy evenings in the town, watching people not so lucky, not so in love, not so happy as they were. The memories played like 8-mm film, then spun off, back to reality. They hadn't had a holiday like that for four years. They never would again.

"I'm out tonight—it's on the calendar. There's pasta in the cupboard, and some leftover Bolognese from the weekend in the freezer. Just defrost it in the microwave," she said.

"Oh, yeah—it's that reading-group thing, isn't it? Did you read the book?"

"Of course. There wouldn't be much point in going if I hadn't, would there?"

"Is it any good?"

Clare looked up, considering both the question and Elliot's interest. The book had been good, brilliant, and she had read it in three nights, absorbed by the made-up lives of the pretend people. But Elliot's face, the handsome face that she had looked at for more than half of her life, gazed at her with only partial interest. He was so earnestly, so desperately trying to share with her, to keep the peace, to say the right thing. And she felt guilty, and irritated, and so, so hopeless.

It was like there were huge piles of rubble lying in the no-man's-land between them, the wreckage of previous battles, and she didn't have the energy to climb over them and wave her white flag. She was waving it, same as he was, but from the floor of a trench where he couldn't see it.

"It was okay," she said finally, "but I probably didn't understand it properly. I don't even know why I'm going. The others probably all went to university, probably all took notes. I bet I feel stupid. Probably won't go again."

"You're not stupid, Clare. You'll be fine. Who else'll be there?"

"You don't know them. It's at Susan's house."

"Ah, go on, it'll be fun. A bunch of women and a couple of bottles of wine—I bet you don't even talk about the book. Good old gossip, more like."

It'd been Clare's mum, Mary, who had asked Susan to include Clare. She'd thought it might help—about as much as a plaster would heal a gaping wound, Elliot thought, but he had given up offering opinions. For years, Mary and he had met for coffee once a week or so, first because they were worried about Clare, looking for ways to help, but now, Elliot knew, Mary was frightened for them both, Clare and himself. It had been Mary, articulating her fears for their marriage, who had made him think that maybe they couldn't survive this. These days, Elliot was sure that Mary met him as much as anything to make sure he was still there—as if over a skinny latte and an English breakfast tea her will and strength could keep them together, make Elliot stay for just six more days, a week at a time. So that, slowly, Mary herself had become part of the disease and not a part of the cure. She was helping to suffocate him.

Elliot pulled himself up off the bed. Wherever Clare was going, the relief of her absence would hit when the door closed behind her. He would put on the stereo, something loud and mindless, pour a big drink. And phone someone who made him feel good about himself.

"Whatever. Have a good time, Clare."

JANUARY
READING GROUP

HEARTBURN

Nora Ephron © 1983

"The pie I threw at Mark made a terrific mess, but a blue-berry pie would have been even better, since it would have permanently ruined his new blazer, the one he bought with Thelma."

Rachel Samstat is smart, successful, married to a high-flying Washington journalist . . . and devastated. She has discovered that her husband is having an affair with the lanky Thelma.

A delectable novel, fizzing with wisecracks and recipes, this is a roller-coaster of love, loss and—most satisfy-ingly—revenge.

So, did you choose this because it was a nice, skinny, hundred and seventy-eight pages, or 'cos you'd seen the film?"

"It's a film?"

"Yes, a gorgeous film. Jack Nicholson and Meryl Streep. Really sad."

"It's one of my all-time favorites. A desert-island movie."

"Neither, cheeky! Actually it was the recipes that got me hooked. The way they're all through the story—the woman, Rachel, she cooks these amazing-sounding things while her marriage is crumbling around her ears. Actually I made one, last week, the Key lime pie. It was delicious. But I think there's something really symbolic about the cooking. It's like even though she's this successful career woman in her own right, the cooking, the nurturing, that fundamental female thing is how she stays in control."

"Yes, she's into control, isn't she? There's that bit about making jokes of everything, and writing it down into a story that she can control. I suppose she means control what she shows of her pain."

"And she makes that epiphany, the pie scene, an exercise in the most public control."

"Yeah, but fundamentally she still isn't, is she? He's had the affair, he's still having the affair. She can't control that."

"Actually, I think she's a wimp. All those witticisms and clever put-downs don't change the fact that she stays with him, and keeps staying with him. Even when she leaves—running off to her father, incidentally, make of that what you will—she lets him come and get her, like a lamb. And the alarm bells don't even start ringing, you know, at that bit when he doesn't pay for her ticket on the shuttle. He's a shit."

"She's pregnant and in the kitchen most of the way through, that's true. Oh, isn't the bit where she has the baby sad?"

"Oh, yes, when she says, 'Tell me about when the first one (what's his name?) was born.' And then, when Nathaniel arrives and he's early, she says she can't blame him."

"Oh, yes, she says, 'Something was dying inside me, and he had to get out.'"

"I cried."

"But she loves him. Can't change that."

"Of course you can. You can remove yourself. Open the channels for healing. Shouldn't you always love yourself more?"

"She loves her children more. Maybe that's why she stays."

"No, I don't buy that. It's the States, for God's sake, in the seventies. Loads of people were divorced. It wasn't a stigma for kids anymore."

"Not a stigma, maybe, but certainly still a trauma."

"I don't think she stays for the kids. I think she wants it to work."

"There's a strange paradox, don't you think? She really wants him to love her, but she manages not to try to change to *make* him love her."

"It's not until the pie scene, though, that she realizes nothing she could change would make him love her."

"I don't agree with that thing it says on the cover, though. It isn't about revenge. She isn't looking for it, and she certainly doesn't get it. Isn't the pie-throwing scene more about drawing a line under it all? Like bursting her own bubble of naïveté? It's an act. It's action. That's the point—she is finally being proactive and not passive. There's the control. Not revenge."

"Didn't she write *Sleepless in Seattle*, too?"

"I'm amazed she still believed in love enough to write something so mushy and uncomplicated."

"But didn't you think that was Rachel's strength—that she carried on believing in love?"

"I think that Rachel's real strength was knowing Mark didn't love her, and being able to move on, even though she still loved him."

"Yeah, she leaves with this real optimism, doesn't she? She is *really* sad, and humiliated, and stuff, but she believes in a future. She does. Here, where she says, 'And then the dream breaks into a million tiny pieces. The dream dies. Which leaves you with a choice: you can settle for reality, or you can go off, like a fool, and dream another dream.'"

Nicole

The bouquet was so big Nicole couldn't see who was delivering it. The card had just the one word written on it—so big she could read it from the doorstep—"Sorry." It nestled harmlessly among the American Beauty roses.

She took the flowers roughly from the unsuspecting youth who proffered them and shut the door behind her with a brief, tight "Thanks."

The boy shuffled around momentarily on the step. He was new and unaccustomed to such a reception. Didn't all women want flowers? He shook his head, whistled and left.

Inside Nicole leant against the door, and a tiny, exhausted sob rose within her. For just a moment she let her head rest against the wood, closed her eyes and smelt the roses in her arms. Allowed herself to imagine that they weren't "sorry" roses. But only for a moment.

In her bright, TV-advert-spotless kitchen, she busied herself, expertly trimming the stems, blanching them in boiling water, adding bleach to the water in the three vases she needed to contain the roses. She did this well, as she did most things: rose clippings dispatched to a discreet bin, and glass mats produced from a drawer to protect highly polished wood surfaces from ring marks. One vase on the circular table in the galleried hall, another on the dining table, the last in the sitting room, next to the silver frames that documented their lives in photographs. Her parents in black and white, the twins in sun hats with ice cream beards, Martha as a newborn lying across the boys' podgy toddler legs, her mouth open in protest. And her and Gavin, on their wedding day. She placed the vase right next to that one. The bastard.

Nineteen ninety-two. May. Appropriately picturesque village church in the background, the door swathed in flowers. The bride, delicious and delirious in Amanda Wakeley; the groom, tall and proud in morning dress. Oh, and the look she's giving him: blindingly bright, stupidly in love. Princess Diana cow eyes. A smile that you knew had made her face ache.

The photograph stopped Nicole dead. Like a cheap special effect, the smart familiarity of the room spun and receded, and the memory of that day, those feelings, was sharp and real—she could almost smell them, sun-warmed, nervous and perfumed in that doorway. She had loved him so much, that day. On the way to the church, she had sat beside her father in the Daimler. He had taken her hand, saying solemnly, "I just want you to know, darling, if you're not completely sure, if you're having any doubts . . ." And she had turned to him, half laughing, half crying, uncomprehending. There could be no life without Gavin. To be his wife, to marry him was the only thing she wanted in all the world, the only thing she could do.

He had been the first guy to get to her. Adolescence had been the start of a fairly charmed life for Nicole. She was not the most gorgeous girl around, certainly: she had the good skin, even features, striking coloring and wavy hair of a naturally pretty girl who looked as good at breakfast as she had at dinner, and a flirtatious, easy, sparkly manner—the ingredient X that made her a much-sought-after prize at university. A boyfriend a year through the B.A. for which she didn't work very hard, plus the odd fill-in guy during vacations, and one or two impetuous one-night stands. Most of them had been more into her than she was into them. While never intentionally cruel, Nicole had had the laissez-faire air of the desirable—a girl who never worried about next Friday night.

She had arrived in London armed with an adequate degree, a sharp brain, a big debt and a newly formed determination to do well. It was pretty easy to make a splash in the lower ranks of the publishing house among the clichéd Surrey set, who were biding their time and waiting for husbands (the pretty ones) or juicy editorial projects (the plainer ones). Within four or five years she was a marketing manager with a salary that kept her in a nice flat in Battersea, with a couple of mates, in high-street suits (even the odd designer one in the sales), in a much-beloved lavender Citroën her parents had helped her to buy, and in her element. Work got her going in a way academia never had, and she was good at it. Fast-tracked by the company, who recognized the mix of ability, ambition and charm that earmarked the wunderkind, she took on new responsibilities with relish. In the early morning, when she caught sight of herself in the reflective escalator panels of the Northern Line, she liked the woman who stared back at her.

And then, on one of those mornings, she walked into Gavin Thomas.

She was undoubtedly ready—untouched by thunderbolts at twenty-six—to fall hard and fast, which was exactly what happened. In the boardroom Gavin was sitting between two colleagues when Nicole backed in one Wednesday, shunting the door open with her bottom, her arms full of files. His advertising agency was pitching for the campaign for a high-sales, high-maintenance sex-and-shopping novelist, the most important publication in Nicole's year. And the room became as empty as her head except for him the moment she saw him.

She'd had dishier men, that was undeniable. At the time she was dallying, ill-advisedly, with a tanned young travel writer her flatmates had swooned over. There's never much point in analyzing the magic: yes, he was handsome, and beautifully dressed, with huge, clean hands; his hair curled the right way across his forehead. Maybe it was the positively lascivious twinkle in his eye. Who knows? Whatever, it worked on her in a way nothing and no one ever had before.

Nicole couldn't remember what had transpired in the meeting, although the account had been Gavin's from the first moment. She couldn't even remember how, later that evening, they had ended up on one of the worn velvet sofas upstairs in Darcy's, getting drunk on red wine poured into fishbowl glasses, talking, talking, talking, leaning into each other. At some point she went, slightly wobbly, to the loo, and the woman in the mirror looked different.

She remembered every second of taking him back to her office, the two of them giggling conspiratorially as she punched in the security number of the back door, suddenly serious as he kissed her, crushingly, against the wall, then swept the Rolodex and her in-tray aside on her desk (all the while feeling very *9½ Weeks*), struggled with her tights. Him inside her. Later, he had put her into a taxi, given the driver a ten-pound note and kissed her nose. The gesture had seemed to her unbelievably tender and romantic. And life, as Nicole Ellis knew it, had changed forever.

Upstairs in her bedroom, Nicole took a dress, a beautifully simple shift, from where it had hung overnight on her wardrobe door and returned it to the garment bag, then hung it in the wardrobe next to the others that contained her corporate-wife clothes. The high-street suits were long gone, and these days, designer was for everyday. The closet was full of the right names, the perfect accessories, gorgeous shoes, right up to the minute, all in a perfect size ten (achieved with effort, every day). All clean, slightly fragranced with her signature scent, and set off with the immaculate modern face, Mayfair highlights and fashionable French manicure she was religious in maintaining. Every woman's dream. She remembered an old black-and-white film she'd seen, where a heartbroken girl cried with her maid as she flung fur coat after fur coat across a silk sofa. "I'm counting my blessings, Mammy, I'm counting my blessings."

The phone call brought her back into the present. She could tell from the digital set that it was Harriet, so she would answer it. Otherwise she would have let it ring: her best friend was the only person in the world she could talk to when she was in this mood.

"Hiya."

"What's wrong?" Harriet had radar, Nicole was sure of it. One word—or, rather, the tone in which it was spoken—was enough to alert her that something had happened. Or maybe, she thought ruefully, it was just that usually something was wrong.

"Was the opera *that* bad?" Harriet joked.

The day before yesterday Gavin had called midmorning, "reminding her"—in fact, telling her for the first time—that she was due, shimmering and engaging, in the company's box at Covent Garden by seven that evening for a performance of something ghastly and Wagnerian with some terminally dull lawyers. Cue some frantic scrambling for a babysitter—Harriet—it being the night of Cecile's English class, and a mad dash against the rush-hour traffic. They would both pretend that this was what had earned her the "sorry" roses. How she wished it was so: an administratively hopeless husband rewarding an ever-capable wife for her patience. They both knew, of course, that the flowers were for something else.

"The opera was every bit as awful as I knew it would be—even the set was dull, all gray and chalky. I wanted to lie down at the back of the box and die."

They both laughed. Their idea of what constituted having a good time was different in every way, but commiserating on corporate duties was one of their common grounds.

"Come on, though, Nic, I'm guessing Wagner isn't the only bloke who wrecked your evening. What was the problem? Nails the wrong color?"

No one else could get away with being as rude about Gavin as Harriet was. She and Nicole had known each other only a year before the gloves had come off and Harriet had confessed, drunk on baby-induced sleeplessness and Bacardi Breezers, that she couldn't stand Nicole's tall, handsome husband. Even as she had exhaled loudly and looked at her friend, Nicole wasn't outraged or pulling up her drawbridge: that was Harriet, and it was such a relief to know her.

"I met the someone else. The latest someone else."

"There? Who is she?"

"Charlotte Charles. One of last year's graduate intake. I saw her at the Christmas do. Gavin's standard issue—tall, legs up to there, hair made for tossing, tits, teeth and talk."

Nicole had walked into the box—just on time, deep breath at the door, big smile—straight into Gavin, who was standing leaning against the wall and over Charlotte Charles. Who, for her part, smiled impertinently up at him, breasts heaving ever so slightly, lips parted and wet. A pose that probably said to most, "Good colleagues, friendly, sharing a joke." To Nicole it had said, without doubt, "Gavin's latest screw." They were all much the same: fresh, somehow, reeking of eau d'ambition, success and savvy, which got him every time. Same as she had.

"Bastard. Are you sure?"

"Yup. Never knowingly overestimated, my husband. I can tell from the first moment. And then I just think back and, yes, the late evenings, the overnighters. If there was any doubt, there's the vast number of roses I'm staring at right now."

"Wanna leave? Spare room's made up." It was a joke between them, made often over the last two or three years. They both knew the answer: she didn't want to leave. She wanted it to be different. Damn it all, she still loved him so much. Harriet had almost given up preaching; settled for listening, loving and biting back as much as she could swallow.

"No, but I'll settle for a bottle of wine and girlie gossip. Let the fucker cook his own dinner and sort out the kids, shall I? That's a penance in itself."

"Too right! See you at eight? I'll send Tim to the pub or the driving range, or something."

"Thanks."

"Nic? I love ya."

Then the tears. Kindness did that. She tried to sound angry—tried even harder to feel it—because she was so fed up with hearing herself sound like such a pathetic doormat. But alone, in the quiet before the au pair brought the children home, she wasn't angry.

Harriet

Harriet put down the phone. She had been standing in her own front hall, gazing at one of the photo-montage boards she had hung up the stairs ("All the better to play happy families with, my dear"). It featured their two families—hers and Nicole's—on holiday the summer after their first babies had been born: Josh and the twins, William and George. They'd gone to Cornwall, rented a big, whitewashed cottage near the sea, been incredibly lucky with the weather (it had been a lovely summer, perfect for nursing newborns, 6:00 a.m. feeds with the windows open, bare arms and legs in the carry-cot). They all looked sleepily happy and proud, surrounded by the endless paraphernalia of affluent first-time parents.

It had been a great week, full of red wine, communally cooked pasta and catnaps. And we thought we all knew each other so well, thought Harriet. She remembered looking around at Tim, Nicole and Gavin one evening and thinking that they would be doing this, in different places, with more children—hopefully—but the four of them good friends, for years and years to come.

Theirs had been an instant, close friendship—of the kind made only in wartime and late pregnancy, Tim had joked. From the instant Nicole had flopped down gratefully beside her that winter on the enormous beanbag at the first antenatal class, smiling ruefully, Harriet had liked her. They were a motley crew, mostly with only their due dates in common, who had turned up to hear dubious words of wisdom that the dippy-hippie teacher, Erica, had to offer. She had sat in the lotus position ("Just because she's the only woman in the room who can," Nicole whispered) and pontificated about the virtues of dried fruit and isotonic drinks as aids to labor ("Gin 'n' tonic, please," Harriet whispered) before telling them, with just an undertone of smug cow, that she had delivered all five of her children under water at home, with the first four in attendance to help with the fifth. At that Harriet and Nicole had been united in eye-rolling horror.

The husbands, Tim and Gavin among them, had been sent to another room to discuss their own fears about the imminent arrivals. There, Tim had been asked to articulate Gavin's greatest fear, and vice versa. Tim's was "swapping my Z3 for a Volvo Estate" and Gavin's "Disneyland," which anointed them both with the mark of Cain, as far as Erica was concerned, but formed the beginning of a beautiful friendship between the pair.

The antenatal class had become the pub, become dinner, become daily phone calls between Nicole and Harriet, and long winter afternoons drinking hot chocolate (Harriet) and ginger tea (Nicole).

"I just don't think we have a future if you're going to sit there drinking that stuff and ignoring those double chocolate-chip muffins. This baby is two-thirds walnut layer cake already, and I've still got a month to go."

"Well, tough. I'm determined not to put on another pound, even for you. These twins can jolly well live off my hips for the last few weeks. I sat in the bath last night and just cried—it's never going to go back." The "it" in question was Nicole's stomach, which had grown vast, alarmingly protuberant, and taut. From the back, though, you couldn't even tell she was pregnant, and she looked beautiful in those fabulous French maternity clothes, which were actually designed to emphasize the bump. Harriet, on the other hand, might have been gestating in several parts of her body, and was truly fat from earlobes to ankles. Since the first trimester she had been reliant on M & S jumpers in size twenty-two, sobbing melodramatically and eating Toblerone whenever she read one of those helpful articles that suggested she "borrow shirts from your husband's wardrobe—he won't mind—and accessorize them with a colorful scarf." She'd outgrown Tim's stuff almost before she'd proudly shown him the blue line in the square window. Not that Tim had minded: he had been a sitcom husband, insisting from the first moment that she carry nothing heavier than a cup of tea and tackle no domestic task more taxing than flicking through catalogs of exquisite, outrageously expensive baby clothes. The fatter she got, the sweeter he was, the prouder, the more excited.

As much as Harriet envied Nicole her glamorous pregnancy shape, she didn't envy her Gavin, who was less indulgent. Although he, too, could hardly disguise his excitement, especially once they had established that the twins were boys, he was appreciably less entranced than Tim by his wife's changing shape. He was slightly impatient, even, about the process and its effect on Nicole. He snapped at her once, in a restaurant, the third time she had to nip to the loo. Harriet and Tim had exchanged a marital eyebrow, and she had been reminded, yet again, of how lucky she was.

Harriet and Nicole's areas of common ground were bigger than the babies they were about to have. They had grown up as only daughters of middle-class, conventional families, where the parents stayed married and celebrated silver wedding anniversaries with cruises in the Med. Both had been to university and had careers they loved—Harriet in advertising and Nicole in book publishing—which they were to put on hold to have the children, a decision that both excited and terrified them. And they saw in each other the friends they had hoped to find for the busy first years at home with the babies.

It was Harriet whom Nicole telephoned when her waters broke late in the evening six weeks before her due date: Gavin was away overnight, and although he took the first flight home that he could get the following morning, he missed it all. At the hospital the doctor had lost one twin's heartbeat and performed an emergency cesarean. Gavin's loss was their friendship's gain. Nicole had been terrified; but the panic had been brief. One minute the two women had been sitting, bump to bump, in the ward, waiting for the consultant to pronounce, joking about Lucozade. At the next, quiet but fast activity had kicked in. Harriet had found herself sitting beside an empty bed with Nicole's engagement ring in one hand and her contact lenses in the other. She stared hard into the diamond, blinking back tears of fear, for Nicole and herself, until a nurse stuck her head round the curtain and pronounced that the boys had been born, mother and babies doing well. So Harriet had got to practice on William and George.

Six weeks later, Nicole was one of baby Joshua's first visitors, arriving in Harriet's bedroom with a twin under each arm, a bottle of champagne in one hand. They had laid the three tiny boys side by side on the big bed, Josh in the middle, and become sentimental and squiffy on one glass each: pronouncing that in seventy-five years' time, when they were all little old men, they really would be able to say that they had known each other all of their lives.

God. Gavin was *such* a shit.

Harriet still remembered the shock of her first unpleasant discovery about Gavin. Joshua had been a few months old before she had finally lost enough weight to accept a lunch invitation to one of her old haunts—from a friend at the agency where she had worked. Lisa Clements was an incorrigible gossip, but nice with it, and Harriet had figured that of all the people she might have seen, Lisa would be the most efficient: she always knew everything that had happened to everyone—mostly before they did, since her best friend was PA to the human-resources director. Happily unmarried and drowning out her biological clock's ticking with the sound of her own laughter, Lisa had waited through a Caesar salad and glass of Chenin Blanc before she asked Harriet about "that lovely husband of yours and that perfect little baby—how old is he now, anyway?" The "he" was a brave guess; clearly the names of said husband and son were too much of a struggle. Afraid of appearing hopelessly pedestrian and suburban, Harriet had told her a couple of brief and, she hoped, amusing stories she had worked on during the train ride up to town, making mention of her good friends Nicole and Gavin. She was delighted to be able to slip in "You might know Gavin, actually, Lisa. He's a creative director at Clarke, Thomas and Keeble."

"Oh, my God. Know him? An awful lot of us 'know' him, if you catch my meaning."

Harriet, out of the loop for a few months, made a face that indicated she hadn't caught a thing.

"Serial shagger, darling! Sleeps with anything that stands still long enough. Famous for it. You know Anna Johnson, used to be with them, blond hair, never wears a bra . . . they had a thing. My friend Pam, at the media-buying agency . . . a gazillion graduate trainees, so they say. Oh, nameless, faceless many. I've always felt rather insulted that he hasn't made a move on me . . ."

Lisa had evidently been set to continue until she glanced at Harriet's face, became horribly frightened that there were going to be hormonal tears and went quiet. "Sorry, sweetie. Look, maybe he's changed. Fatherhood, and all that, does things to a bloke, don't they say?"

They skipped coffee. Lisa seemed pathetically keen to get back to some budget presentation, and Harriet's mouth was far too dry to talk.

Of course, after that everything had been different. She had gone home, unable to ring Nicole for what would have been their customary debrief, told Tim, then lain awake in bed, wide-eyed and furious.

Tim had been less shocked. "What a prick! I've never liked the way he eyes women up when we're out, gets chatting at the bar, but I didn't think he'd be stupid enough to do anything about it."

He squeezed her shoulder, then reached round to stroke the top of Joshua's head as his son lay cradled in Harriet's arms. "Who would risk all this?" And then, "Do you think Nic knows? Are you going to tell her?"

On this Harriet was clear: "Absolutely not. If she does know, and I don't think she can, what with the twins and things, but if she does and she hasn't told me, it's because she doesn't want to talk about it. And if she doesn't know, I can't be the one to tell her. If and when she needs us, we'll be here for her." She leant her head against his chest. "Won't we?"

"Always."

Always. Us. We. When was that? Just seven years ago. Or seven long years ago. She wasn't sure. She squeezed her eyes shut and imagined him as he had been then. Tall, strong, handsome, calm, kind. With a ready laugh that started in his eyes. An optimist, a gentleman, a thinker, but not a worrier. The perfect husband. An unbelievable father, who did night feeds as soon as Joshua, then Chloe had been weaned, winding them patiently as he swayed to Van Morrison downstairs in the sitting room. Who dropped to his knees, still in his suit, as soon as the front door closed behind him each evening to scoop both children into his arms and listened patiently to every tale of woe and triumph. Who brought her freesias every year on the anniversary of their first supper together. And most nights still held her face in his hands while he told her that he couldn't believe his luck, that he loved her dearly.

And what kind of husband was he now? Exactly the same, given the chance. Which he hadn't been lately. I'm the bolter, Harriet thought. I'm the one who's changed. I don't love him anymore. I made a mistake. I'm the bitch. But a bitch with a heap of housework to do. Harriet's inner Mrs. Mop sat down hard on her inner demons and got out the bleach. Something of a familiar pattern, these days: don't think about it, it might go away. Or maybe, she thought, I'll get an ulcer or spontaneously combust. But not this afternoon.

Surveying the chaos, she had to acknowledge that firing Tracey-the-cleaning-lady-from-hell had probably been a bit rash. Tracey might have had a penchant for *This Morning* and pushing dust under heavy pieces of furniture, but she had been better than nothing. The contents of the playroom had, as usual, flowed, like lava, throughout the house, and the naked Barbie dolls, stray pieces of jigsaw and forbidden balls of brown Play-Doh were an assault course on every carpet. Unfinished homework (Josh's) and rejected clothing (Chloe's) lay on the stairs. Bits of stray tinsel left over from the week before gave everything else, including the cat, who had clearly been rolling in it, a party atmosphere. Harriet picked up her almost cold coffee and dropped into the nearest armchair, neatly removing a piece of Lego as she did so. She started with the most appealing job: sorting the morning's post. She wasn't interested in the bills, but there might be the odd catalog among them.

At first she assumed that the white envelope with unfamiliar handwriting was a stray Christmas card from obscure relatives. When she felt the unmistakable thick card of an invitation she still wasn't excited: interesting people didn't have parties in January—they were in either Barbados, hibernation or rehab. It would be some terminally dull do organized by one of Tim's clients—not worth paying a sitter five pounds an hour. Suddenly Joshua was there, a freckly hurricane, followed swiftly by Chloe, three years his junior but intellectually his superior. At this stage in their childhood, when they were almost perpetually locked in a half nelson, that didn't shine through.

"Mum!" It was dragged out to last ten seconds. "Mum!" Repeated in case she tried to deny the charge. "I'm trying to watch *Bug's Life* and Chloe keeps turning it off."

"He's hidden the remote control, Mum, and I wanna watch *Sleeping Beauty*."

"But that's *soooo* drippy. *And* you've seen it about a million times." Then Joshua began, in an alarming falsetto, "I know you, I danced with you once upon a dream," pirouetting around the chair with Chloe's pigtail held high in his hand.

"*Aaagh,*" Chloe screamed.

"You two," Harriet began, in her best menacing-mummy voice, then looked down at the invitation in her hand. Quietly. "Joshua, please put *Sleeping Beauty* on in the playroom for your sister. Then you may watch *Bug's Life* in Mummy and Daddy's bed as long as you take your shoes off. I'll bring you some juice and sweeties in just a minute. Off you go, sweethearts." Which, of course, they did, somewhat flummoxed at their good fortune.

Very grand, thick cream card, luxuriously copperplate printing in which a couple she was sure she'd never heard of formally requested the pleasure of her and Tim's company

At the marriage of their daughter
Imogen Amelia
to
Mr. Charles Andrew Roebuck
at 4 p.m.
on Saturday 8 March 2002
at St. Mary's Parish Church, Dinton, Salisbury, Wiltshire,
and afterward at Chatterton House, Teffont Evias

And would they please RSVP to said strangers, in Debrett's approved etiquette fashion, purchase a practical yet stylish gift from the happy couple's list at the Conran Shop, lose that last stone they were still blaming on their four-year-old child, buy an expensive new outfit with matching hat and bag, follow the neat little map enclosed, arrive on time, sing hymns in tune or very quietly, not get drunk on the Laurent-Perrier and smile benevolently at the person they still thought of as the great love of their life as he promised to love another forever.

Would she hell! Harriet's heart had fallen onto the rug in front of her. He couldn't be in love with someone else. He didn't really love this Imogen Amelia (what an absurd name), and he sure as fuck couldn't be marrying her. Yes, all right, Harriet had moved on, she'd found someone else, she was married. But didn't Charles know that was a mistake? *He* wasn't supposed to go and do it too.

She hadn't seen Charles since she was pregnant with Chloe. That lunch had been a mistake. She had gone for a look that said "glowing with health, earth mother, look what you're missing, boy." But she had caught sight of herself in a shop window as she made her way to the restaurant and realized that the look she had achieved was more "auditioning for Moby-Dick; shoe in for the part." He'd just met Imogen, but that hadn't worried Harriet much—there'd been a few girls since her, but none had lasted long. Charles claimed he was enjoying his freedom (after so many years with her), but Harriet had understood that this was code for "no one compares to you." She'd heard from a mutual friend that Imogen was bossing him into moving away from his old friends, but she knew Charles wouldn't stand for that—self-determination was everything to a man like him: you couldn't pin him down. If he'd been going to settle down with anyone, it would have been her. This Imogen creature didn't stand a chance. Then she'd lost touch with the mutual friend and been left to speculate, but mostly to comfort herself with the thought that Charles would always regret her, like Willoughby in *Sense and Sensibility*. This was not right. Not right at all.

She ran upstairs to her en suite bathroom, kicked off her shoes, pulled her sweater over her head and jumped onto the scales. Shit. Right. Eight weeks. Two pounds a week. (Four pounds if she made that cabbage stuff Nicole sometimes ate for a few days.) Should shift a stone easily. In time to shop. For something with a lot of cleavage—in red. With extremely high heels. Harriet tucked the invitation under the pile of tummy-gripping knickers in her top drawer, fingers still shaking, and went downstairs to make herself a cup of the ginger tea she kept in stock for Nicole.

Polly

Polly had come straight from work to collect Susan. It was one of their regular nights at Café Uno—just the two of them. Four glasses of house red, two bowls of carbonara, a salad to share, and the world to set to rights.

They were school-gate friends, she and Susan. They'd met fifteen years ago, on the day when Cressida and Ed had started primary school. Susan was an old hand: Alex was in the year above. She'd been a lot slimmer then, but otherwise she was much the same. She'd been born thirty-five—that was what she said. She was one of those women who was attractive not because of what she wore or how groomed she was but because she gave off a kind of healthy happiness. Her wet-sand-colored hair—worn in a bob, despite Polly's best efforts—was thick and glossy, her cheeks always pink and her eyes sparkling. She looked happy because she was, apart from the normal worries and pressures of a working mum with two sons that occasionally assailed her. She never got stressed, she was organized to a fault and she was absurdly happy with her husband.

She had told Polly, once, that she hadn't found herself until she'd found him, which might have sounded a bit pathetic if it hadn't been Susan saying it. They'd met at some tennis house party or something, when Susan was ridiculously young. She'd known, she said, that he was "the one"—that mythical creature about whom the happily married go on ad nauseam if you let them—from the second round, after tea. Susan would never say, "from the moment I laid eyes on him"—far too dramatic! No, Roger had had to go through the first round and the strawberries-and-cream test before he passed muster. He'd taken her round the corner, behind the beech hedge, and kissed her "properly" while someone else called, "Game, set and match," on the other side. And so it was for them. They'd been together ever since.

Polly, who'd been more into kissing improperly, but who had nevertheless also married young (and, predictably, less successfully), was never entirely sure why they were friends or why Susan had approached her in the first place. Polly had been a mess back then. She'd let her wildly curly hair grow straight out from her head (à la *Crystal Tips and Alistair*) and worn those Katharine Hamnett slogan T-shirts. She'd have been a Greenham Common woman if she hadn't felt so passionately about Cressida. Susan probably thought Greenham Common was a garden center. But friends they had become, bonded by first-day nerves shared over a quick cup of tea that had lasted until lunchtime pickup, and friends they had stayed, all these years, although the kids had gone to different schools at eleven. The bond was strong enough by then, forged by fish fingers, discos, Casualty dashes, homework traumas, and all the good stuff you could squeeze in between if you talked fast enough. When Dan left, Susan had been brilliant: she'd taken Cressida and Daniel home night after night, given them their tea with her boys, while Polly and Dan had sorted things out. That first summer after he had gone she and Roger had invited Polly and the children to join them on their *gîte* holiday in the Dordogne. It was golden, the whole fortnight. The kids went caramel in the sun, building dens, swimming in the pool and recoiling in horror from the unpasteurized, cow-warm milk the farm delivered each morning. She had read and swum, cooked in the big, cool kitchen and begun to heal there. Roger and Susan were still so in love, but it didn't make her jealous: it made her believe. They would go off for walks, the two of them, leaving her to supervise the chaos, and come back hours later, sunburnt and smiling conspiratorially. Once, while she and Susan were preparing dinner, Susan raised her arms to reach something and grass fell out of her top. She blushed. "Been kissing 'properly,' have we?" Polly had teased her.

She loved her. And she knew that Susan loved her back. Soul mates, perhaps not. Touchstones, definitely. Best friends.

For the offices of Smith, March and May, Polly's appearance was smart and together, but her ancient Fiesta was the real her: newspapers, work documents, sweet wrappers, half-eaten bits of fruit, with the perfect ironic touch—a tiny aromatic fake fir tree on the rearview mirror, which was at least four years old and smelt faintly of cigarette smoke.

Now Susan cleared a space gingerly in the footwell with her shoe, swept the crumbs from the passenger seat onto the floor and sat down.

On the other side Polly jumped in, pulled on her seat belt, started the car and turned off Radio 4. "Guess what Santa brought me this year?"

"Diamonds, pearls—a dishwasher?"

"Close. Jack asked me to marry him. And it's a ruby, actually. We were washing up after Christmas lunch, so I was wearing a pink cracker hat, proving, at least, that love is blind."

"My God! Congratulations! I do mean congratulations, do I? You said yes?"

"I haven't said anything yet. When Dan asked me I said yes so fast he'd barely got the question out. Once bitten, and all that."

"But you're going to say yes? Eventually?"

"I don't know, Suze." Polly looked at her friend. "I love Jack. He's kind and funny, great with the kids, and he can cook and all that—perfect husband on paper—but he's also a slob, and indecisive, and too laid-back for his own damn good. And I've been on my own for a long time now. I'm not sure I want someone around all the time."

"You need a Woody and Mia arrangement—Jack should get a house across the road and visit on alternate nights."

Polly roared. "That'd be great until he ran off with Cress! No—but seriously, why wreck things? I'm not some ditzy twenty-year-old desperate for a husband."

"No," Susan said, slowly. "That's what you were when you said yes to Dan. This is different, surely."

"In some ways, yes. But marriage hasn't changed, has it? Right now I've got my independence, my own money, my own overdraft. I can drink Cointreau from a mug and watch Cary Grant movies all night in bed if I want to."

"Well, just so long as you've got good reasons for turning him down."

They had got out of the car now, just outside the restaurant, and Polly laughed as she pulled open the door, felt the basil-fragrant, warm air hit her face. "You know what I mean."

"I think you're just frightened. Scared of changing the status quo. You've become a control freak, that's all, after all that time being in charge. What do Cress and Daniel think about it?"

"I haven't told them. I think Daniel would like having him around. Not so sure about Cressida, though. To be honest, she hasn't been around much since she started this foundation course, which, by the way, she's loving. It's great to see her with so much enthusiasm. I think she's really found her thing, you know?"

"That's great. Sounds like Alex. I think Roger's unbelievably thrilled that he's so into medicine. But we're doing it again—talking about them and not about you. Cardinal sin of parenting."

"Oh, but they're so much more interesting than we are . . . they've got it all to do."

"Says Miss I've-just-had-a-proposal-and-wouldn't-I-make-a-lovely-spring-bride. How's that as a cure for empty-nest syndrome? And here's me, stuck in a rut with Roger after all these years."

"Humph."

They both laughed. Polly knew that Roger and Susan had a rock-solid marriage of the kind she envied, not because it had lasted so long—plenty of couples stayed together out of fear, habit, need, and celebrated their milestone anniversaries with pinched smiles and hollow speeches—but because with Roger and Susan it was this huge sense that they were always working together for the same things. Which wasn't dull, or staid, as she might once have thought: it was good, and real, and rare. And about as far removed from her first experience of marriage as it was possible to go.

She *had* married Dan on impulse: he had been drop-dead gorgeous in that totally arrogant way some young men have. Like Billy Bigelow in *Carousel*. A puffed-up peacock, her mother had called him. He was always broke, but Polly had been too drunk on the charm, the Babycham and the fantastic sex to notice that she was buying all the drinks. They had met at college in the late seventies, done the three Ds—demos, drugs and disco—together, had a fabulous time. Polly was away from her rather buttoned-up parents and their safe village, in London, the first in the family to get to university, and Dan had encapsulated everything she'd thought she wanted to be. He was lovely then, still was, as long as you didn't want too much from him—too much time, too much money, too much commitment. In 1982, when they got married, she'd been pregnant with Cressida. "Stupid girl," her mother had said. "You're going to miss it all now." At the time, of course, she'd thought her mother was the stupid one. What would she miss that mattered? Ha, ha. In an embarrassingly short time, she had found herself with two children, no husband, and a great new perspective on what she had missed. Dan was still around. After their divorce in 1986, he had married again, a drippy girl, Polly thought. Tina still hung on his every word, between keeping two jobs going to pay their mortgage. Fortunately there had been no more children.

Although Polly thought Dan was a lovely dad. It had driven her crazy in the early years—when she was slaving to keep them—that Dan would show up on Saturdays to do the fun bit: he'd take them to the pictures or for burgers or to fool around on Brighton Pier, then bring them home knackered and sick from candy floss to boring old Mum. But she had come to see that it was she, not he, who reaped the rewards of all that effort, and although they loved their dad—while respectfully having no time for Tina—it was to her that they came with their triumphs and problems, their dilemmas and funny ways. They were *her* kids, and she was fierce about them. Dan had had to take second place, and to his credit, he accepted that role gracefully.

So, marriage was on the cards again after nearly fifteen years on her own—which was three times as long as she'd been married in the first place. Not that Jack was Dan, although they had some of the same characteristics: Polly had learnt to recognize her weaknesses, even if she still gave in to them.

Susan smiled at her benevolently—as if I was her daughter, Polly thought. She's enjoying this: she thinks I'm going to say yes because she's an eternal optimist. She believes in love and marriage and happy-ever-after and all of those things I know don't really exist. Christ, she's the matrimonial equivalent of an evangelical friend gone mad. Any minute now she's going to say how happy I'd be if I opened my heart and let Jack in.

"Okay, okay, so it's a definite maybe. Can we leave it at that? Right now the only question that I'm giving an 'I will' to is 'Do you want wine?'"

"This is a good thing, honey. Honestly it is."

Polly made a sick noise, pulled a face, and Susan admitted defeat (for the time being). "Yes, yes, of course. Wine."

A glass and a salad later, they were talking about the reading group.

"It was a bit weird at first, sure, but I really enjoyed myself."

"I can't remember the last time I was in a room where I didn't know everyone inside out. Well, that's not true, of course. There's work stuff and things I go to with Jack and for the kids. But then you don't really *talk* to people, do you? It's usually all hairdresser-level chat, small talk. It isn't terribly British to start talking about serious stuff."

"Didn't feel too touchy-feely, though, did it, because it was all about the book, sort of? Like that makes it safe to talk about bigger things, puts it in a comfortable context."

"Maybe. I did worry, though, about whether we weren't being clever enough. A girl at work goes to one that sounds terribly intellectual. All plot and themes and irony and device, she goes on about. Sounded a bit over my head."

"I reckon we might get more ambitious as we go along. We're bound to be sussing each other out to start with."

"I suppose. Anyway, the real meat is more interesting. Do you really think someone like . . . oh, I don't know, D. H. Lawrence sat down with a list of his themes and his 'devices' or d'you think he sat down and wrote a bloody good story straight from the heart? Although, I'd have thought *Lady Chatterley's Lover* came straight from somewhere a bit further south."

"If that's the level of insightful comment we can expect from you, Polly Bradford, I don't think this thing will ever get off the ground."

"I liked the women, though. Interesting bunch. What do you know about Clare? She was pretty quiet, I thought."

"Her mum, Mary, works with me. You've met her at ours, I'm sure. It was Mary's idea—I asked her if she'd like to come, but it's not her kind of thing. She thought Clare would enjoy it, though. She's worried about her. Really worried."

"Why?"

"Can't have a baby, apparently. They've been trying for years. It seems that getting pregnant isn't the problem, more staying pregnant. Almost like her body is allergic to being that way. Or to her husband."

"God, how awful. I can't imagine that. Got pregnant with my two practically as soon as I lay down."

"I know. She had that kind of sad look about her, don't you think? I've never met her husband—I think he works at the college, something in administration. Mary says he's really nice. They're starting to feel the cracks, though, apparently."

"No wonder. Christ, didn't Clare say she was a midwife? Having to work with pregnant women and new mothers every day—it's like a sick joke. I'm surprised she sticks it. Can't they do anything?"

Susan's phone rang. She'd only started using a mobile in the last year or so—it was useful for work. Normally she didn't keep it on in the evening, but today she'd forgotten to switch it off. Mouthing "sorry" to Polly, she answered: "Hello, darling? Everything okay?"

"Fine, love, or at least I hope so. Is your mother with you?"

"No. I left her at Mabel's this afternoon and told her you'd pick her up after early-evening surgery. I thought you'd both have been back by now. I was sure I reminded you this morning."

"You did, and that's exactly what I thought, but when I got to Mabel's she said Alice had left—she was going to walk over to the surgery, wanted some fresh air or something. I thought maybe you'd had a change of heart and taken her along with you."

"No. Where are you now?" Something like panic rose in Susan's stomach.

"Well, I came home to see if somehow Mabel had got the wrong end of the stick and Alice had caught the bus back here or something, but she's not here."

"Oh, God. What should we do?" Susan's mind was racing now. She knew Alice had had her thick herringbone coat with her, but what about her gloves, her hat, her scarf? She couldn't remember checking when they had left. She'd probably thought they were unnecessary—Alice was only going to Mabel's and from there straight into Roger's warm car, then home. What if she'd fallen and was lying somewhere on the cold, hard ground?

At the other end of the line, Roger read her mind: "I've been back and traced the route from Mabel's to the surgery—it's only about five hundred yards—and there's no sign of her. Can you think of anyone she might have bumped into who would have taken her back to their place?"

"Not really—not after dark. Oh, Roger, I don't know what to do."

"I think I'd better call the police. Do you think you— Oh, hang on, that's the doorbell. It'll be her, love. Hold on a minute."

For a few long seconds Susan listened to Roger's muffled voice, straining to hear Alice's higher tones. Then he was back.

"Suze? It's a policeman. Don't worry—they've got her. She was lost or something. Look, why don't you stay with Polly? I'll get to the bottom of it and tuck her up on the sofa. You can talk to her yourself when you get back. You won't be late, will you?"

"Oh, I'm coming now. That's scared the life out of me. I won't be able to relax until I've seen her." She pulled a face at Polly, who smiled back and raised her hand to attract the waiter.

After Susan had gone, Polly took her charge card out of her wallet to pay, then fiddled with her naked ring finger. She let her mind meander back to Christmas morning. Jack had stayed over, for the first time, on Christmas Eve. They'd slept all night together before—he had taken her on a weekend trip to Edinburgh—but never in her house, not with the kids there. Cressida had suggested it. "Go on, Mum. What's the big deal? Me and Daniel both know what's going on." Then, in a mockingly stern parody of Polly, "'We'd rather you were sleeping together somewhere safe than up to God knows what God knows where. At least this way we'll know where you are.'" Daniel had sniggered. "And we like Jack, don't we, Danny? He's a good bloke. What's the point of sending him home sober at midnight so he can get up and come back in the morning?"

A few weeks earlier Polly had broached the subject of Jack spending Christmas Day with them. Since Dan had left, the three of them had always celebrated Christmas alone—Polly had figured that making Christmas happy for the children proved she was a success as a single parent. Both Cressida and Daniel had leapt at the chance—almost insultingly keen for company, Polly considered. "We're not kids anymore, you know." My God, didn't she know it?

So her children had persuaded her to ask Jack to stay over, and they had woken up together, in a chaste bed ("Get off, you old devil, the kids might hear," Polly had giggled), faces close together on the pillows to whisper "Merry Christmas" and smile conspiratorially at each other. They'd had a golden day. Jack had bought champagne, and they had drunk it round the tree, with smoked-salmon sandwiches, as Cressida and Daniel opened their presents, both suddenly childish again amidst piles of paper and discarded packaging, exclaiming at their booty. Later, liberated by Jack from the duty of mother-sitting, they went out before Christmas dinner: Cressida to the pub with her crowd and her boyfriend Joe, and Daniel, armed with his latest PlayStation game, to his friend Pete's house, where Christmas *Top of the Pops* was not forbidden. Polly and Jack had gone to bed and made slow, gentle love.

Much later, when the kids were flopped on the sofa in front of the obligatory Christmas blockbuster with a family box of Quality Street, Jack said, "Come on, woman, let's get this washing up done. I can't stand weepies. Bring back *The Morecambe and Wise Christmas Special*, I say. Angela Rippon in fishnets—now *that's* what Santa ordered!"

Cressida threw a cushion at him. "Dirty old man!"

In the kitchen he slid his arms round her waist as she stood over the sink, rinsing glasses. "I really love you, Polly Bradford." He hadn't said that before. The hairs on Polly's neck stood up. "Marry me." It didn't sound like a question. Her heart did double time, and she was glad he couldn't see her face. Was he serious?

Jack must have felt her stiffen with shock, because he took away his arms and picked up a glass, which he dried slowly and carefully. Polly spun around and flicked him across the arm with a tea towel. "Marry you? And you with an Angela Rippon fetish? You must be joking. You'd have me reading the headlines during sex." She looked at him, her smile tinged with a desperate plea. *Don't make me answer that. Not today.*

Jack took his cue. He grabbed her flicking arm, pulled her closer and began to tickle her armpit. "Go on, hurt me again! Be very, very strict with me, Miss Rippon. Please!"

In bed that night, Polly was half asleep, with Jack's whole length warming her back and his arm heavy across her, when he said again, "I mean it, Polly. Marry me. This is what I want. You and me. It's good. I'm happy. And you are too."

"Oh, Jack, of course I am. It's just—"

Jack pressed his arm against her chest. "Ssh. I'm not asking for an answer tonight. Just think about it. Please."

She ran her hand down to his and held it, squeezed once. Within minutes his breathing had changed: he was asleep. It took Polly a lot longer.

Eight mornings later, on January 2, her car was covered in a thick layer of ice; Polly stomped inside to retrieve the deicer spray from the hall cupboard. Beside it lay a small, royal blue leather box on top of a plain brown luggage label on which Jack had written, Alice in Wonderland–like, WEAR ME.

When Polly got home Jack was asleep in an armchair. She leant over the back and kissed his nose. He started awake, and the newspaper he had been reading fell from his lap. His half-moon reading glasses had slid low down his nose. "Christ, Jack. You just need *The Archers Omnibus* on the radio, a pair of fingerless gloves and a box of snuff, and you'll be everyone's picture of the average pensioner."

"Can't a fellow fall asleep at his hearth after a hard day's grind without being ridiculed?"

"One, it's *my* hearth. Two, you're a solicitor, not a coal miner. Three, you're meant to be in charge of my kids. Where are they?"

"No one's actually been in charge of your kids since, oh, about 1993, my sweet. Cressida's off with Joe, I think, said something about a new band playing at the union. And Daniel, riveted though he undoubtedly was by my company, went to bed about half an hour ago. Geography test tomorrow, you know."

"I do know—they may be latchkey kids, but they're well-quizzed ones. He told me this morning. Did you make them some supper?"

"Bought fish and chips. Did have a stinker of a day, as it goes. Some twisted individuals going ten rounds over the custody of their kids."

"Oh, darling, I'm sorry. That sounds a bit grim. Want to talk about it?"

"Not really. I'd rather not let them into this house. Jinxes." He stood up and folded her into an embrace. "Besides, I'd much rather hear what you ladies got up to."

"It was me and Suze at the Caffé Uno, Jack, not an Ann Summers party."

"Never underestimate the fascination that girlie gossip holds for men, Pauline Bradford. I learnt everything I know about women from eavesdropping."

"Pity you didn't do more, then, isn't it?" Polly laughed.

"Oi!" Jack pinched her bottom.

"Actually, hold on, I just want to give Susie a ring. She had to go early. Something about Alice . . . won't be a minute. Do you love me enough to make me a cup of tea?"

"Susan? It's Poll. I thought I'd check on Alice. Is everything okay?"

"I wish I knew. It's Mum. She's had a funny turn."

"Is she there? With you now?"

"She's on the sofa, with a hot toddy, wondering what all the fuss was about. She wandered off, you see, from Mabel's. The police found her—our address was in her handbag, so they brought her home."

"What was she doing?"

"She told them she was going home. They asked her where to. She said sixty-eight Eaton Close. That's what's so weird. It was where she and Dad lived after the war. Where Margaret and I were born. She moved out years ago, after Dad died."

"God."

"She said the strangest thing when I was tucking her up on the sofa. She said Dad would be worrying about her."

"Oh, Susan. Oh dear. What does Roger say?"

"He says we've got to get her checked out. Could be all sorts of things, something or nothing. He says she's slowing down a bit. But Poll, she's only seventy-one. That's not old, these days."

Susan sounded tearful. Polly wanted to tell her that she was sure it was nothing, but she couldn't. It didn't sound like nothing. "Call me, will you, Susie, when you've taken her somewhere? Promise? And try not to worry."

"I'd better get back to her. I will call. Thanks for ringing."

She told Jack what Susan had said while he finished making her tea. She leant against the kitchen unit watching him squeeze the tea bag, making it as strong as he knew she liked it, and stir in the milk.

"Why don't you pop over and see her tomorrow?" he asked. "It doesn't sound good, though, does it?"

"No. Susan adores Alice. I've always been a bit jealous of what the two of them have—my mother was Watford's answer to Joan Crawford. God knows what she'd do without her."

"It's the cycle of life, isn't it? Mother, daughter, mother. She's got Roger and the boys. And you. I just hope if it *is* serious that it isn't one of those long-drawn-out nightmares. So undignified, and so hideous for the family to have to watch. It's weird, though, isn't it, her going back to the sixties. It happened to my dad. He was alive and well, and living in North Africa with his fellow Desert Rats, but it was actually 1985, and he hadn't been further than Brittany for forty years. One doctor told us that sometimes, when that happens, you go back to the time in your life when you were happiest. Great compliment to Alice's husband, I'd say, for her to return to when they were together. Amazing thing, the brain." He put the milk back into the fridge. "So, Ms. Bradford, which time would you go back to? Hm?"

Polly smiled. She'd had a lot of good times. And some really cruddy ones. But she wasn't chasing better ones anymore, she realized. She was contented. That was a good feeling. Comfortable. That was pretty nice too. Safe. Who wouldn't want to be? And, she thought, watching his long back busy at the sink, more than a little in love. "I reckon it would have to be 2002. That's a bloody good year so far. Jack?"

"Digestive biscuit?"

"I will marry you. I will. Yes."

The expression on Jack's face when he swung round made her feel fantastic. Imagine making someone so happy with just one word. He punched the air in a gesture of triumph. "*Yeeesss!*"

Cressida

"What's wrong, Cress?" Joe shouted, against the extraordinary noise of the band on stage behind them. She'd been in the loo for ages, and now she was back she looked really weird, like she'd been crying, or had had a bad fright. "Something happened?"

Cressida shook her head furiously. Then, leaning right into him, she shouted in his ear, "Outta here," turned and pulled him toward the illuminated exit sign. It took a couple of minutes to get through the crowd, but she held tight to his hand all the while. Outside they leant against the wall, drawing in deep breaths of the fresh air, letting their ears become accustomed to the relative quiet.

"You okay, Cress? You look a bit funny."

"I didn't like the crowd much—or the band. That lead singer thinks he's Kurt Cobain but he sounds more like Danny in the bath. Actually, Danny's better than that. What an ego!"

"Yeah, well, I'd had enough too. Let's go and get a drink."

Cressida looked at him. "I don't really fancy one."

"I know what I fancy." Joe leant into her, kissed her earlobe. His hand went round her back, pulling her hips toward him. He moved his mouth to hers. Cressida stood back and pulled her jacket tightly round her, hands retracted within the sleeves. She jumped softly from foot to foot. "Not here, Joe. It's bloody cold, apart from anything else."

"We could go back to mine, then. Mum and Dad are out. Show you my etchings?" He ran his hand over her bottom.

"Oh, Joe, is that all you can think about?" Her tone was harsh, exasperated.

"Sorry! What's wrong? You know that's not true, Cress, but I'm going back to Warwick on Sunday, and I thought, you know . . . It's just that we haven't spent much time alone since I got back from uni. Is something up? What have I done?"

Cressida gazed squarely at him. He looked hurt, and somehow younger. When she spoke again, her tone was softer. "Nothing, Joe. You're right, I'm sorry. It's me. What a cow. Time of the month, I expect. Look, I just want to go home, be where other people are not. Grab an early night. Okay?"

Joe was off the hook. He smiled, linked arms with the girl he had loved since he was fourteen and pulled her down the street. "Right you are. Home, James, and don't spare the horses. And we don't have to speak all the way, m'lady."

Later, as she fumbled to find the key in her jeans pocket, he pulled her round to look at him under the light by her front door. "Cress? Everything is okay, isn't it?"

"Oh, Joe, of course it is. Why all this heavy stuff now? This isn't like you. Got a guilty conscience or something?"

Joe rubbed his sweater angrily across his face. "Not me. What about you?" It stood, the question that was really an accusation, in the cold air between them. It *had* been tough, that first term away from her. University was all new, terrifying but wonderful. They'd been a couple in the sixth form, gone through the exams together and stuff, pored over the admissions forms, laughed at each other's personal statements, and daydreamed. Joe thought she was crazy when she decided to stay at home for her course—they'd had a big row, and he'd accused her of being a coward. They'd made up, of course, in the alcohol-hazed summer after A levels: Cressida had promised she'd come to Warwick—be the sad girlfriend from home cramping his style at the freshers' disco. He'd said that he'd be proud of her, that everyone would recognize her from the pictures on his notice board. Joe had imagined the two of them in his small room, in his narrow bed, what might happen with their parents far away. Maybe she would finally let him make love to her, and they could be as close as he wanted them to be. But she hadn't come. All term she'd made plans and canceled them—she wasn't feeling well, she had this huge project to hand in by Tuesday that she hadn't started, Mum wanted her to go somewhere. Joe's mate on the same corridor had joked that Joe had an imaginary girlfriend.

That pretty girl, Issie, from his Wednesday tutorial, with whom he had coffee every week after class, had suggested gently that maybe separation had broken the spell for Cressida. Her sister, she said, had been engaged to her policeman boyfriend when she started her first year at college: she had dumped him after two weeks and an encounter with the captain of rugby. Cressida hadn't dumped him. She always sounded so sorry, so gentle, when she broke the news that she wasn't coming. She told him how much she was looking forward to seeing him at Christmas. How nice it would be to have the old gang back from the four corners of the country. That she still loved him. Or maybe she had let him tell her that he still loved her. He couldn't remember now. But Joe was worried. Christmas had been and gone, New Year's too, and he was off tomorrow, back for the spring term. A whole term gone, and now a whole holiday. They hadn't made love. They hadn't even spent a whole evening alone together. And now he had asked her if she had something to hide. And she wasn't answering. She was looking at him, and her eyes were full of tears. And she wasn't answering.

Oh, Christ.

"Christ, Cress, *what*? Just say it."

Cressida shook her head at him. "Not now, Joe. It's nothing. Don't be silly. You're leaving tomorrow. Don't do this now."

Joe felt a shaft of terror, then exhaustion. He knew what was coming. He even sort of knew why—he wasn't an idiot, and he understood that a long-distance relationship was always an outside bet. He knew that he could make her tell him what was wrong, that it wasn't the same anymore, that it was over, best this way, and that they'd had a lovely time and been really good for each other . . . Perhaps he'd known that for weeks. They would go in, and make a hot drink, and talk for hours, and cry and hold each other, and mourn the inevitable passing of their young love. A tiny part of him, deep down, knew that he would be okay. He imagined himself recounting what had happened over coffee with Issie back in Warwick. But, right now, he didn't have the energy for the death dance with Cressida. More than anything else he wanted to be inside, alone, not looking at her face. With huge will, Joe kissed her cheek, one hand resting briefly in her curly hair. "Yep, you're right. You take care. I'll see you soon. 'Bye, Cress." And he was off.

"'Bye, Joe." They'd made no arrangements to meet in the morning, and Cressida knew he wouldn't call, that this was it. She wasn't relieved at being let off the hook of explanation. She felt like a shit. But she had barely a thought in her head to spare for Joe.

Nicole

Two-thirty a.m. The sheets on Gavin's side of the bed were cold. Nicole rolled onto them for some relief. She had been lying, hot and bothered, on her side for hours. There'd been a message, left beside the phone in faltering English by Cecile. "Mr. Thomas work late. Maybe not come home." An hour or so later Gavin had rung.

"Darling! Did you get the flowers?"

"Yes. They're indescribably lovely. Thank you."

"Nic, don't be like that."

"Like what?"

"All cold and frosty with me. I really am sorry, you know. About the opera."

"Yes. Where are you?"

"I'm not going to make it back, babe, I'm afraid. The creatives have been having terrible trouble with a pitch they're doing at the end of the week. They needed me. Had to roll up my sleeves and get the old juices going. Quite good fun, actually."

"I'm sure."

Gavin appeared to ignore the sarcasm in her voice. "We're going to grab a bite now, give it one more good going-over, and then I'll bed down at the club."

No wonder he was so bloody good at his job, Nicole thought bitterly. He spoke in double entendres even when he wasn't trying to. She'd given up trying to second-guess him. He might even have been telling the truth. Then again, the flowing juices, bites, going-overs and bedding down might have nothing to do with winning some detergent account. She used to check up, phoning his club very early with some important question about the house or the kids, or try to catch him out with carefully orchestrated small-talk questions over supper. She used to make love to him the night after he had been away. Why? To see if he was still interested? If he had learnt any new tricks, had enough energy? Or was it to prove that she was better than anyone he might have been with? That she still knew better than any one-night stand or office fling where to touch him, exactly how hard and just how long? She wasn't sure how much longer she could keep trying.

"Whatever you like."

"Thanks, sweets. You're a brick. I'll make it up to you at the weekend. Promise. Why don't you book a sitter for Saturday? I'll take you out for dinner. Your choice."

"Okay." Nicole hated herself for looking forward to it, but she knew she would. She'd see if Cressida was free to sit. Maybe get her hair and nails done on Friday afternoon. Choose somewhere candlelit, wear something beautiful, and let him talk his way back into her heart and her bed. Like she always did.

"Good night, darling."

"Night."

A few nights later, Nicole was reapplying a deep red shade of lipstick to her mouth in the soft, flattering lights in the ladies' at one of her favorite restaurants.

By the time she got back to the table Gavin had refilled her glass with glorious Viognier—her favorite. It was the wine they had drunk at their wedding breakfast, no less. She had to hand it to him: he was pressing all the right buttons tonight. Trouble was, she kept score only as far as the starters. By the time the waitress put her main course in front of her, she was once again a fully paid-up member of the Gavin fan club. A sliver of her own conscience stood next to her, taking in the low, silky dress, the cleavage dusted with shimmer, and shook its head. *Encore une fois*, it said. Been to this movie. But the lion's share of her was loving being this way again.

"Are you trying to get me drunk?" she asked.

"No, you're no use to me drunk. I just want you relaxed enough to enjoy the rest of the evening." Gavin put his hand on her knee under the table, stroked a feather of sensation along her thigh. He hadn't touched her like that for days. Hadn't dared to. "All of it."

"What did you have in mind?" She was flirting now, brazen. He laid his lips against her cheek. "Oh, just about anything you like, Nicole." He sat up suddenly. "But first, my darling, I have a plan to share with you. I've been busy figuring out how to make it up to you, all these late nights and weekends I've been doing lately."

Gavin shorthand again. Nicole stiffened as resentment threatened to flood back. But straightaway he put his hand into his inside jacket pocket, pulled out British Airways tickets and dropped them beside her plate. Nicole picked them up eagerly, pulled open the top one. Venice. Venice. "It's all arranged for

April. I've spoken to your mother, and she'll have the kids for the weekend. I even braved Harriet, and she says no problem with the school run and stuff." (What she had actually said to Gavin was, "I should think so too. Hope it's the Danieli. And with a lengthy excursion to Gucci planned." And to Tim, "Talk about putting a Band-Aid on a gaping wound, the prick!") "The au pair'll be there. I think I've thought of everything. I want to spoil us, take us back to the Danieli. Not so bloody hot this time, I hope." Gavin had found Venice, their honeymoon destination, smelly, overrun with clicking Japanese tourists and not a little dull. For Nicole it represented the Narnia days of her marriage. Hot, certainly, requiring regular pit stops for Bellini and Campari soda on their voyage of discovery of that exquisite city. Steamy in their suite every afternoon. And cooler in the evenings, over those long, languid suppers and strolls and once, when she'd begged, a gondola ride—they'd lain back against red velvet heart-shaped cushions and kissed themselves dizzy.

"Gavin! That's brilliant! Perfect. Thank you!"

He looked suddenly serious, sincere. "I do love you, you know that, don't you, Nic?"

She threw her arms round his neck, whispered into his ear: "I know. You're forgiven. Let's go home."

The next morning, after the school drop, she was still humming with pleasure when she met Harriet at Starbucks. At the front of the queue, listening to Harriet bleating about some parent-teacher meeting, she ordered their usual. "Tall skinny Americano with a poppy seed muffin, and a mocha latte with whipped cream and a chocolate muffin. Cheers."

"Uh-uh," Harriet interjected. "A tea for me, please, no milk. And forget the muffin."

Nicole looked at her in surprise. "Your body a temple today, then?"

"Not just today, all frigging spring," Harriet spat as they settled into the velvet sofa.

"Tell me more."

"Not yet. I want to hear about you first. What gives with Gavin the Grot? Did he tell you about the major sucking-up trip he's got planned for you?"

"Oh, Harriet, you are bad. Suppose he hadn't?"

"Excuse me, lady, but since I knew he was taking you to Chez Gaston last night—ordering Viognier, I daresay—I figured he'd have the holiday as a dessert chaser, just to clinch the deal."

"I've got to stop telling you things. You know altogether too much about me." Nicole laughed ruefully. "What deal?"

"You know, the takeover of the marital bed, the merger with the other occupant, the reacquisition of the wife's adoration. None of which will have been nearly hostile enough, if you ask me."

"Which I didn't."

"Don't get sulky with me, Nic. And don't try to deny it. You've got that shagged-until-five-minutes-before-the-alarm-went-off look about you—and on a school night!" Nicole looked at her sheepishly. "Look, this is no surprise—this is the pattern of your mania. I simply reserve the right, as your best friend and the smarter half of our partnership, to remind you of what a complete idiot you are."

"Listen, I'm not going to spout any of that it's-different-this-time stuff—"

"Good—you'll sound like one of those desperate women on *Trisha*."

"It's just . . . well, you know, really. He's my Achilles' heel. I love him." It was said in the tone of Nancy in *Oliver*.

"Oh, don't feel bad." Harriet squeezed Nicole's arm. "You and a gazillion other women throughout history. I know you can't help it. I may hate it, but I do get it. Honestly. So . . . Venice. He must be *really* sorry this time."

"I think so." Harriet threw her a sharp glance. "Okay, okay, well, I don't care. We had an absolutely magical, orgasmically wonderful, gorgeously romantic time the last time we were there."

"Nic, everyone has an absolutely magical, orgasmically wonderful, gorgeously romantic time on honeymoon. Even Tim and I had our moments on St. Lucia."

"Yeah, but have you ever been back? Re-created the recipe?"

"You know we haven't. Can't see it happening, somehow. Right now I wouldn't want to go on a day trip to Brighton with Tim—he's driving me mad."

"Well, I'm going to try. Get us—I'm married to Don Juan but holding on to girlish hope even though it flies in the face of all reason. You're married to Mr. bloody Darcy, and you're not happy either. What's the poor sod done now?" Nicole loved Tim almost as much as Harriet despised Gavin.

"Oh, he hasn't done anything wrong. Of course not. How could he? It's me, really. And this." She pulled the invitation out of her bag and watched as Nicole read it.

The canceled chocolate muffin immediately fell into place. "Oh, hon." They held hands, briefly, there on the sofa together.

Nicole knew all about Charles, of course. On one of those long afternoons together in the park, years ago when the babies used to sleep for three hours after a feed, they had played the deepest-secrets-truest-loves game. They both had pretty short scorecards. Nicole was married to the love of her life, and Charles had been the love of Harriet's. She loved Tim, Nicole knew she did. When they had first been friends, and Nicole had first understood about Charles and Tim, she had kept her fingers crossed that Harriet would fall in love with Tim. That the babies—how good he was with them, the family they were crafting—would tip the balance and turn love into being properly "in love." But when she looked at herself, and the stupid, crazy, desperate way she felt about Gavin, she knew that Harriet wouldn't find that next to an Aga or over her baby's sweet-smelling head. Charles had been It, as Gavin was It. Although over the years Nicole had wished that Gavin had got away from her, or that she was married to her own Tim. A calmer, gentler love had its appeal, especially in the bad times.

But this invitation, this declaration of Charles's intentions, so stark in black, embossed text, she knew how much it had to hurt.

Clare

Clare switched off the soap opera she hadn't really been watching and put the sandwich she hadn't really been eating into the fridge. Then she looked at the clock. If Elliot wasn't back by now he was staying away on purpose until she had left for her night shift. Neither pleased at avoiding *him* nor angry because he was avoiding *her*, she collected her bag from the hall cupboard and left, switching off the last light behind her. Elliot would come back to a dark, empty house. Leaving the light on in the front window, as she would have done once, felt like too much of a welcome.

It was as if the nurse inside her, the observer, had climbed out and sat beside her on the passenger seat of the car to watch her flick on the heating to defrost the windscreen and push in the cassette. She told her that nonchalance was the scariest thing, the last stop on the road to clinical depression, and willed her to feel. Driving along the elevated highway, Clare thought, at the bend where she always thought this, What if I didn't turn the wheel, just let the car go straight? What if I did that? Straight over, into the road below?

But Clare didn't want to die. She just wanted something to change. She wanted to *feel*. She'd be all right when she got to the labor ward, which was her favorite. When well-meaning people, with their relentless, invasive questions, discovered that she couldn't have a baby, they invariably said, "And you a midwife. How sad for you, all those babies." But it wasn't often like that. Sometimes, when it was quiet at night on the postnatal ward, it was. The hospital maintained an old-fashioned night nursery, where mums who had had cesareans, or second-time mums who wanted to grab a precious night's uninterrupted sleep, could park their plastic cribs with their precious cargo. Then, if there was time between new admissions and answering bells, Clare would sometimes take a newborn, bathe her, really properly, sometimes cut her tiny, sharp fingernails or toenails, and dress her carefully in a white bodysuit, scratch mittens and a hand-knitted cardigan the mother had packed with such hope and excitement weeks earlier. Then she would hold her, swaddled, and rock in the chair in the corner of the night nursery, rock the rest of the room away. That made her ache, especially when the fiercely possessive new mother would come, anxious for her baby, breasts swollen and painful, muscles sore from delivery, smiling with gratitude as she staked her claim.

The labor ward was different. There, women needed her, and she was good at caring for them. She knew how to do this.

She had recognized Harriet at once the other night at the reading group. It happened to Clare all the time, walking around town—she had delivered a lot of babies. Harriet had joked that she probably didn't recognize her with her knickers on, but Clare remembered everything: that it had been a longish but straightforward labor, that the baby had been a girl, called Chloe, weighing seven pounds or so and with long feet, born almost at sunrise. And Harriet had remembered her, too. That she'd been kind, encouraging and strong. That she herself had been beastly, noisy, rather wimpish and particularly grateful to the little dark-haired girl who had stayed on after her shift to be with her at the end. There was a picture of Clare in their family album, all in white, holding a tiny, red-faced, newborn Chloe in a white blanket, competently on the upturned palm of one hand, leant in on her, and another at the head of the bed next to Harriet. "It's a weird relationship," Harriet had said. "We were each other's entire universe for about six hours, and then we would never ordinarily meet again." Clare liked it that way. Mostly.

Tonight a woman called Maria was delivering her first baby. Clare had met her a few times at the clinic, liked her, knew that she was terrified. Maria's husband, Ian, was clutching a bag of boiled sweets he had taken from a large rucksack—clearly packed to his wife's specifications: Clare could see a tape recorder and a cassette, whose case carried handwritten notes—music they wanted to give birth to. No doubt there would be aromatherapy candles and a vial of arnica among the rest. One look at Maria's face told Clare that labor had progressed to a stage where all that careful planning had been forgotten. The young woman grabbed her hand as she approached the bed. "I think I'm ready for an epidural now. Really. Please. I don't want to do this anymore. Please."

Clare heard the underlying hysteria and fear in her polite voice. "Hello, Maria. Now, we'd better just have a look at you, see if this baby's planning on making an appearance tonight." She brought her face close to Maria's, put a hand on her shoulder. "Don't panic. I'm here, and I'll stay with you, however long it takes. You're going to have a beautiful, healthy baby safe in your arms just as soon as he's ready. You can do this. I know I can—this will be my hundred and fiftieth baby. I'm good!" Maria smiled weakly. "Let's have a look, and then we can have a chat about what you want to do. Okay?"

Elliot

Elliot flicked the switch on his computer, pulled his jacket off the back of his chair, rubbed one eye and stretched both arms skyward. A long day of looking at the screen. Mostly Elliot's days were fairly sociable—a steady stream of kids and mature students through the office with inquiries, bantering lunch with a colleague, meetings—but he was working on a data document that was due at the end of the week, and he'd been shut behind his partition door since 8:45 a.m. He had had only a tuna-mayonnaise sandwich and an argumentative phone call with the local garage about his car's service to break the monotony. He hated days like this had been. He was only too aware that, lately, he had had most of his human contact from colleagues. Clare showed him so little kindness and warmth, and he couldn't reach her. Friends were harder and harder to be with: the ones with kids were impossible; the ones without didn't want to be with them anyway. Christ, he and Clare didn't want to be with themselves.

Outside it was freezing cold, so Elliot turned up his collar and hunched his shoulders against the wind as he scanned the parking bays for his car. He should have gone home earlier. Clare would have been there.

On the other side of the car park, a bunch of kids pulled open the double doors of the pub: warm golden light and the sounds of music, shouted conversations and clinking glasses spilt out into the dark evening. It was a great pub, pulling in a mixed crowd of students, workers from the nearby office blocks and anachronistic regulars, who sat in jealously guarded seats at the bar and treated the youngsters like the cabaret, nursing pints in their own tankards, which were stored on hooks next to rows of alcopops.

Staffed by rowdy Australians and Kiwis, it was noisy, smoky—and real.

Elliot opened the car, threw his briefcase onto the backseat, locked up again and set off, hands pushed deep into pockets. He'd take an hour of the comfort of strangers.

Brightly colored chalk on the board by the door announced that this was karaoke night, and Elliot almost turned away, but a burst of raucous applause and wolf whistling was irresistible. Three girls had taken to the stage and were listening, hands round their microphones, to the introduction of their song. And there she was, watching them. They must be friends of hers. As they massacred the first line, they warmed to their disco-diva task, and their performance became a magnet for the crowd. Elliot couldn't take his eyes off her. She was so . . . beautiful. So free and young. Her hips swayed in low, wide corduroy trousers, and above them the gem in her navel sparkled under the lights. As her friends finished, bowing theatrically and hugging each other, she saw him at the edge of the stage, and her smile changed. It was just for him, that look. It gave her pleasure to see him.

Not pain.

She inclined her head toward the door and whispered to her friends.

When she came out, wrapped in a huge woolly sweater, he was waiting down the alley at the side of the pub. "Hello, you," she said and kissed him deeply, her arms round his neck, fingers in his hair.

Elliot held on to her. "Hello, me."

Harriet

Harriet couldn't sleep. At 3:00 a.m. she gave up, tied her enormous white toweling robe round her and padded along the corridor to look at her children. Joshua was spread-eagled like a starfish, duvet pushed down to the last fifth of the bed, palms open, vulnerable in sleep as only a child can be. Harriet covered him lightly with the duvet, but he shrugged it off again. Chloe was facedown, right on the edge of her bed, with one arm hanging almost to the floor. She smiled and curled one arm round her mummy's neck in her sleep as Harriet moved her toward the wall. She plugged her thumb back in and nestled down. She smelt like an angel.

Downstairs, Harriet flicked the switch on the kettle for a mug of tea and resisted the temptations of the biscuit barrel. She'd been on this bloody diet for a whole week now. This morning the scales had shown a gratifying three-pound drop, which had strengthened her resolve. Now, instead of chocolate biscuits, she would treat herself to a nostalgia fest. Harriet often sent herself back to the summer of 1988—when she couldn't sleep, when the kids were driving her barmy in traffic jams, when she was swimming. She'd been doing it more and more often lately.

She had been nineteen, a perfect size ten, for the first and last time in her life, slimmed out of her puppy fat by a year of self-catering in university halls. She was also very brown, and lying naked in the middle of a very white bed, with very white muslin curtains billowing at French windows. Beyond, the Mediterranean sky was an exquisite azure blue. Just recovering from the aftershocks of her first orgasm—which had been rather wonderful and totally surprising—and looking into the eyes of the man she knew without question was the great passion of her life. Charles Roebuck. History, third year. Very blond, incredibly sexy and heart-stoppingly beautiful.

About ten of them had taken bucket-shop flights to Athens and a ten-hour ferry from Piraeus harbor in the summer after her first year at Durham, for three weeks' camping on a beach on Ios, that year's designated party island. Charles had been a friend of a friend, admired only from afar, and occasionally followed to the college laundry, until after one tequila too many Harriet's friend Amanda had suddenly been sharing a tent with his friend Dominic. Charles and Harriet were left sitting shyly at the campsite's all-night coffee bar, chatting over the noises emitting from under canvas all around them. By the eighth night a spirit of if-you-can't-beat-'em had clearly come over Charles: he had led an awestruck Harriet into her tent, and they had kissed until she thought she would liquefy and flow away down the beach. The next morning, when they were awoken by the heat, making them sweat in their nylon love nest, it being already close to ninety degrees outside, Charles had smiled down at her stubble-rashed face and said: "I think if we're going to take this any further, we'd better book ourselves a room at that hotel down the end of the beach and do it properly, don't you?" Sir Galahad could not have had a bigger fan.

He announced their decision to upgrade over breakfast, and among much whooping and phwoaring, they tripped off to the relative Nirvana of a hot shower, their own loo and room service. Oh, and that bed. Which was where Charles finally showed her what all the fuss was about. She'd had other lovers, of course. A couple in the sixth form, one ill-advised drunken liaison with the captain of cricket, and a drippy English undergraduate who had sent her a poem on Valentine's Day. But Charles was the first man who had, in the nicest possible way, screwed her brains out. She'd thought she wouldn't be able to walk afterward, her legs felt so shaky.

On an impulse she went to the dresser cupboard and pulled out one of her old college photograph albums. Most of the pages had been pillaged by the kids, and photos were missing or shoved back in the wrong order, so a handful fell out as she carried it to the kitchen table. On the top was one of her and Charles, sitting with a bottle of beer each, raised in a toast, his arm casually around her shoulders. There was another of them at the college summer ball the next year. That was the first time he'd told her he loved her, which sealed her fate. She'd been wearing his dinner jacket—it was about three in the morning, and the college lawn was littered with party detritus and exhausted bodies, bedraggled now in prized gowns and rented suits.

That night she had been emotional: he had finished his degree and was off to a lucrative management-consultancy job in London, and she was afraid. Afraid because she loved him so much that she thought her ribs might crack, and although they had had this brilliant, amazing year, of sex, parties, working side by side in the library and more sex, he had never told her he loved her, and so she figured he didn't. But that night he had. He had told her he loved her. And that he wanted her to come down every weekend to his new flat, to stay in his life. That they could make a long-distance relationship work, easy. And that she was beautiful. Then they went back to his room, and lay down naked on his narrow single bed, with the noise of the ball shrieking and throbbing around them, and he told her again that he loved her. He said it once with each long, slow thrust inside her, and when he came his eyes were full of tears, and he said it one last time, his lips against hers, so that the breath of the words was hot inside her mouth. And she knew that, whatever happened afterward, when she lay on her deathbed that was the moment she would remember at the last.

Ha, ha. Harriet smiled at the memory of herself at twenty. Of course, that didn't stay true—not when you'd held your own babies in your arms: they were everything. But just imagine the feeling if they'd been Charles's babies, not Tim's.

Suddenly angry, with herself, with Tim and most especially with Charles, Harriet slammed the album shut, shoved it back into the dresser and went to do the ironing in the utility room. Better not waste that energy.

She'd polished off most of the basket when Tim appeared. "Cup of tea?"

His calmness irritated her anew. Why the hell isn't he asking me why I'm doing the ironing at four o'clock in the morning? she thought. That's just not normal. "Thanks. I'll be in in a moment."

Tim flicked the switch on the kettle. He put tea bags into mugs and took milk from the fridge. He tried not to look at the invitation on the shelf. He'd seen it a few days ago, when he'd come in from work, and he'd felt the old fear seep back into him. He'd rushed home and changed out of his "worky stuff," as Chloe called it, in time for stories. There was a big deal brewing at the moment, and when it went to due diligence in a couple of months he would have to miss a few chapters. While he had to admit that the bonus, if he pulled it off, would be nice—take the heat off the school fees for a few years, certainly—he didn't relish the idea of time away from the three of them. Chloe had insinuated herself under his arm. She didn't really understand *Harry Potter*. She liked *Milly-Molly-Mandy*, but Mummy had read that to her earlier, she told him, while Joshua was on a submarine secret mission in the bath, and she was quite happy, snuggled into Daddy, smelling his familiar smell, listening to the lilt of his voice, while Joshua listened from under the other arm. She felt safest with Daddy between them.

It had been a strange afternoon, Chloe had confided. Mummy, who was normally terribly firm about that sort of thing, had allowed them to gorge themselves senseless on sweets, watch videos *and* have Nutella sandwiches for tea. And Joshua had had to remind her himself that he hadn't done his reading homework. This he helpfully did fifteen minutes before bedtime, but even that didn't earn him the telling off he could normally have expected. Mummy was definitely in a funny mood, Chloe had said, with her lovely, solemn face, to her daddy while he was changing.

"Oh, darling girl, Mummy's just busy—trying to find enough room on the sofa for our bottoms, after you two have been making a mess all day. Anyway, what videos did you watch? And what sweeties did you eat? Not the chocolate gingers Father Christmas brought me, I hope,'cos then I'd have to tickle you." And he advanced toward her, mock-menacing, fingers wriggling. Chloe shrieked with delighted terror and shimmied under the duvet as her father fell on her, growling.

But he had noticed it too: Mummy *was* in a funny mood. Was it the invitation? Or was it the conversation they had had over New Year's? Or, rather, the conversation he had tried to have. He'd been a bit tipsy, a bit brave, he supposed. And she had looked so lovely. He never got tired of looking at her face—warm, soft and animated. And listening to her—he loved to listen when she was on form, as she had been that night—when she made other people laugh. He had felt proud and contented and, yes, a little bit tipsy and, yes, more than a little bit randy. And he'd whispered to her that maybe this year was the year to have another baby, someone in the family should be born in the twenty-first century. Maybe even starting tonight. Harriet had looked at him blankly, then turned and walked away. Ended up on the other side of the room, with ten people between them, for "Auld Lang Syne." *Should* old acquaintance be forgot?

Susan

Susan shivered in her car. She turned the key far enough in the ignition to switch on the heating and sat, arms folded, staring at the house ahead, waiting for the warm air to come through. It was called The Cedars. She had the brochure on the passenger seat beside her. It was full of marketing-speak about trying to walk the thin line between comforting and patronizing. And probably failing. The Cedars, it said, was "a dignified, caring environment, in which those elderly loved ones who can no longer care for themselves are nurtured, physically and emotionally, in an atmosphere both relaxing and stimulating, leaving their relatives free from worry." Free from guilt, Susan thought. That was the point. A gardener makes the flower beds pretty, they stick a few prints on the wall, and let you bring your own portable television, so that your children can park you here and bugger off back to their own lives without feeling too bad about themselves.

I can't do it to her.

Roger said it wasn't going to get any better. TIAs, they were called, transient ischemic attacks. Little strokes in Alice's brain stem, each one killing off a part of what made her herself. Alice would *hate* that: she'd much rather have a big, dramatic one that ended it all in a minute. The first one had damaged her memory. Like watching episodes of a drama series in the wrong order, her life was rearranging itself in her brain. She was younger, she was married. So where was he, and who were these other people? She was starting to treat Roger as if he was her doctor, not her son-in-law of some quarter century. She called him "dear." She wandered around Susan's living room looking blankly at photographs—Susan's wedding day, the boys as babies, as gangly school sports stars, herself as an elderly woman. Susan was clinging to the fact that she still knew her, never missed a beat before calling her Susie.

But Roger, pragmatic and loving, kept telling her that she had to accept it—that this, too, would change—and that Susan couldn't expect to cope with it on her own for much longer. For the first time in her marriage, Susan was willing Alice to side with her against Roger. She knew he was right, but still she implored Alice, with her eyes, her voice, to prove him wrong, to come back to them, or at least not to get any worse.

And now there had been this stupid milk incident. She was almost angry with her mother for failing. Alice had burnt herself on boiling milk: milk that she'd put on the stove, let boil, then poured, messily, across the back of her left hand, making an angry red patch over the liver spots and wrinkles. It wasn't healing very well because she was old.

Susan was angry with herself as well. I'm in my forties, she told herself. I have grown-up children of my own. I have Roger. My dad died long ago. I should be ready for this. This shouldn't be the apocalyptic, terrifying thing it is. Maybe it was just the home. They hadn't had to do this with Dad. He'd just died. Here one day, then dead. Susan remembered crying at the kitchen table in the early hours of one morning, then going back to bed and sleeping, long and sound. He had been her dad, a great dad, and she had loved him, and now he was dead. And somehow that hadn't been too hard. There'd been Alice to care for, of course, and a funeral to arrange. (Which was amazingly like a wedding, when you were in charge of it. You had to choose the color of the flowers and you have to have a view on the lining of the coffin, and whether it would be vol-au-vents or sandwiches afterward. And, yes, you drank sherry, whiskey and tea instead of champagne. And people at the wake were self-conscious when they laughed and expressed pleasure at seeing old friends. But, essentially, it was pretty much the same. Except that a life had ended instead of beginning.) But somehow, all that admin and all those good-innings, full-and-happy-life and bosom-of-his-family clichés she kept hearing made it kind of okay. Throughout, inside her own head, Dad had stayed the old man he had become. That was how she saw him: he was the boys' grandad.

With Alice, it was different in almost every way. There was no funeral to organize, for a start. Instead there was this coffin of a rest home to consider. No clean break, rather a slow decline to anticipate. But the weirdest thing, which kept tears in Susan's eyes, and a big stone on her chest, was that every time she closed her eyes and thought of Alice, she was young again. Alice was dark-haired, not gray; vital, not frail; laughing, not confused. Her eyes were bright and mischievous, not milky and vague. She was Susan's mum. The mum who had been known to wake up on glorious June mornings, declare it was far too nice for school and take Susan and Margaret to Brighton on the bus for a shimmering day on the beach. The woman whose worst threat was that she would show her knickers on the main road in front of their friends (she had done it once to prove she would), who was brilliant at making fancy-dress costumes for summer fêtes and school shows out of scarves, silver paper and papier-mâché. Who always said she'd leave Dad if Paul McCartney ever asked her, and read them Georgette Heyer novels at bedtime.

That was the mum she didn't want to say good-bye to. Not now, not yet, and definitely not here.

FEBRUARY
READING GROUP

I CAPTURE THE CASTLE

DODIE SMITH © (1948)

"I write this sitting in the kitchen sink" is the first line of a novel about love, sibling rivalry and a bohemian existence in a crumbling castle in the middle of nowhere. Cassandra Mortmain's journal records her fadingly glamorous stepmother, Topaz, her beautiful, wistful older sister, Rose, and the man to whom all three of them owe their isolation and their poverty: Father. I Capture the Castle has inspired writers as diverse as Armistead Maupin and Joanna Trollope, and remains a classic tale of the triumph of youthful naïveté over middle-aged cynicism.

Nicole and Harriet were in Harriet's kitchen. Harriet was slicing the two quiches Nicole had brought; Nicole was making a salad dressing, whisking vinegar, whole-grain mustard and sugar into olive oil in a jug. The other women were next door, and their lively chatter filtered through the open doors. Everyone had loved this month's book, and there had been no awkward pauses. Spines were well-broken, yellow Post-it notes and folded down corners had marked favorite passages and the characters had come alive in their discussion. Now it was time to eat.

"So, I'm seriously thinking about it. I think maybe it's the right time for us. Thought I might persuade you and Tim to join us, keep the symmetry going?"

Nicole's attempt at a light, flippant tone fell on stony ground. Harriet snorted. "Forget that, for a start. This isn't about me and Tim. You're insane. *How Not to Improve the Woeful State of Your Marriage*, chapter three, paragraph eight. How could you even think about pulling a stunt like that?"

"I wish I hadn't told you."

Harriet recognized that Nicole was in defensive withdrawal. Carrying on now would represent what Tim called "entering the discomfort zone." But what kind of friend would she be if she didn't? Every inch of her knew this was a disastrous idea. "Yes, but you did, didn't you? You can't expect me not to react. I'm sorry if it's not what you were expecting."

"Not expecting, just hoping."

And the doe eyes weren't going to work either. "Nic, having another baby isn't going to make Gavin faithful. It didn't with the twins and it didn't with Martha. That's the reality, and I know it hurts you. What on earth makes you think it would be different this time?"

They were whispering, hissing, really. This wasn't the time. Which is probably, Harriet thought, exactly why Nicole chose now to tell me.

Polly appeared in the doorway. "Need any help, you two?"

"No, thanks, Polly." Nicole smiled. "It's all ready."

Polly wandered back into the living room, calling, "Supper's served."

"It's not a stunt." Nicole was close by Harriet's ear now. "I'm not playing games. That's his department."

"Exactly. You need a game plan, and you need it not to be this."

"When I was fifteen I thought this was the best book ever written. It was so romantic, so intimate, literally like reading someone's diary. All that unrequited love . . ."

"Did it translate to adulthood, though?"

"When I asked for it at the library, they got it from the young-adult section."

"Misclassification. Well, it could be either, I suppose. I remember Cressida reading it when she was about that age, fourteen or so, and loving it. She said I should read it then, but I didn't fancy it."

"It absolutely did translate. I read it exactly like I was Cassandra again. The adult women, apart from Topaz, the stepmother, are so sterile and unappealing and world-weary in contrast to her—it's like escapism. She's got such a strong narrative voice that you can't help but get caught up in her enthusiasm, her passion, her drama."

"Yeah, and believe again, sort of. Do you remember what we were talking about when we did *Heartburn*? How her dreams were still intact, even after all the shit she went through with her husband? Well, I thought Cassandra was like she might have been, Rachel—before she got her heart broken."

"But if she's so young, so naïve and inexperienced, how can

you really learn anything from what she writes? I mean, she doesn't see the world how it really is, does she? She's writing, quite literally, in the proverbial ivory tower."

"Nothing very ivory about it. She's dealing with poverty, with her sister and her father, who is at best unstable."

"And she still has some of the most lucid thoughts in the whole book. Look at the way she sorts her father out, how she deals with the Stephen situation. Look at the appeal she has for the adults in the book—Simon joining in with her summer-solstice ritual, all of that. Oh, and the conversations with Miss Blossom, the dressmaker's dummy."

"And she still thinks you can make something happen by wanting it badly enough." Nicole looked straight at Harriet.

"But look how that backfires on her. She can't make Rose love Simon, and Rose can't make *herself* love Simon, when she really loves Neil. And no amount of scheming on Cassandra's part can change that."

"She isn't scheming, surely. She's trying to make something happy that she thinks is what everyone else wants. She's a crowd-pleaser, at the end of the day, isn't she?"

"But what happens happens anyway, doesn't it? Was always going to. I actually thought that Rose was the most interesting— she felt trapped by her gender, her circumstances, that the only way out of a life of destitution and dullness was to marry some-one. Someone with enough money to pay for a different life."

"It was, in those days, wasn't it? A girl didn't have options, not like now."

"Is now really so very different?"

"Don't be ridiculous. Of course. We all have options. There's no excuse now just to settle for something."

Nicole stood up abruptly. "Susan's brought something totally wicked-looking for dessert. I'll get it, if someone gives me a hand to clear these plates." Her mouth was set in a hard line, and she wouldn't meet Harriet's eye.

Clare stood up quietly. "I'll help."

Harriet closed her copy of *I Capture the Castle* and laid it be-side her place mat.

Polly and Cressida

It wasn't that Cressida was locked away in the bathroom for hours every morning, heaving theatrically. Or that she was wearing her baggiest jumpers. Or eating lots, or eating nothing. It started out as a feeling. Cressida had changed since Christmas. At first Polly, typical single mother, had looked to herself for the blame. Maybe Cressida *wasn't* as happy as she had seemed about Polly accepting Jack's proposal. Perhaps she found it embarrassing, inappropriate, to watch the two of them together. Maybe it was strange having a man who wasn't your father at home all the time. She was as sure as she could be—and she had thought about it, which made her feel horrid—that Jack's behavior toward Cressida was everything it should be and nothing it shouldn't. Could Dan be putting on pressure in some way? It didn't seem likely: it wasn't his style. Perhaps the Joe thing had run its course and she wasn't sure how to tell him it was over—Polly couldn't imagine it was the other way round. Not college, surely . . . Cressida loved the course.

But something wasn't right. And, frankly, Polly was a bit fed up with it. Cressida was too bloody old for a teenage funny-five-minutes. She'd been a pretty easy kid at fifteen, sixteen, seventeen, but Polly had no intention of putting up with a late adolescence. By nature Polly was confrontational about problems: festering, sulking and petulance were a cancer to her—eating away at her family's equilibrium.

But, lately, Cressida had put quite a lot of effort into dodging what would obviously be a difficult conversation. So, that afternoon, as she put away the Sainsbury's shop (for probably the millionth time, she reflected, squashing tins of beans into the too full larder cupboard), Polly was feeling frustrated and not a little hurt. She'd tried that morning, she really had. Over breakfast she'd said, "I've a free day today. Daniel's at Dad's and Jack's sorting out some stuff at his place. How about coming to Kingston shopping with me? We haven't done that since before Christmas. Just the two of us. We could even have a laugh in the Bentalls bridal department. I can just see you in a peacock blue taffeta job. And I promise to try on the most hideous dress you can find, just for your amusement. Mind you, they'd think I was the mother of the bride, I suppose."

"Can't, Mum. Sorry. I've promised someone. See you." And she'd been gone, quick as that.

Bentalls bridal department wasn't so enticing on her own, and Susan was busy with Alice, so she'd taken a deep breath and tackled the supermarket. The worst thing about working full-time was having to negotiate the aisles and tempers on Saturday morning with the rest of the world. No, take that back. The worst thing about shopping was having to put it away.

Polly staggered upstairs under the weight of loo rolls, shampoo, a deodorant for Daniel and a month's supply of tampons. She opened the cupboard on top of the water tank, and attempted to push everything in. She was moving last summer's now defunct factor 15 to one side when she noticed something. Every month she bought two boxes of Lil-lets, super for herself and regular for Cress. Her own last month's box was nearly empty. Cressida had one, two, three unopened boxes. Polly had been buying and putting them away without noticing.

She opened the door to Cressida's bedroom, feeling strangely guilty. She was often in the room, sitting on the edge of the bed, watching her daughter brush the fabulous hair she'd inherited from her dad, listening to stories about student friends, collecting the dirty laundry that both kids left moldering on the floor. But it was an unspoken rule that she didn't go into their bedrooms when they weren't there, as they didn't come into hers.

Ostensibly everything was as usual: a funny mixture of little girl and lovely young woman. It was a room on the cusp, with teddies still squashed at one end of the bed, ill at ease with the CDs, makeup and tiny underwear strewn elsewhere. The mirror was framed with snapshots of friends, smiling brazenly to the camera. Cards—birthday, Valentine, silly sorrys—stood on the desk among the papers. And the two big, black art folders Polly had given her for Christmas were leaning against a chest of drawers, one spilling out something vibrantly colored. On the dressing table there was an aerosol deodorant, a tub of hair wax and a bottle of the "grown-up" perfume Dan had given her every year on her birthday since she was thirteen. ("You're a young woman now. About time you stopped smelling like sweaty socks at a bonfire.") No tampons.

Polly was anxious now, and that made her do something she would normally have recoiled from. Leaning over Cressida's desk, she opened the black plastic diary that lay there. It was marked with a bright pink ribbon that declared the diary's owner to be a "groovy chick."

And it almost jumped off the page at her: the telephone number of the family-planning clinic at college, circled in red, on a date sometime in the second week of January.

A couple of hours later the house was in darkness when Cressida's key turned in the lock. Earlier, Polly had made two calls: to Dan, "Can you keep Daniel with you tonight? Something's come up and I need a bit of time to sort it out. . . . No, thanks, love, it'll be fine . . . just hang on to Danny for me. . . . You, too. Bye." To Jack, "I need to take a rain check on the cinema tonight. I think Cress might be in trouble and I want to talk to her about it. . . . Can I tell you later? . . . Thanks, sweetheart. . . . Yes, I'll call you in the morning. I love you too. Night." Then she sat and waited.

"Mum?"

"I'm in here."

Cressida went straight to the lamp and switched it on. "What are you doing in the dark? Where's Danny—and Jack?" She saw her mother's face. Started to speak, then just sat down, heavily, on the edge of the sofa, opposite Polly.

"Cress, don't you think it's about time you told me?"

The relief in Cressida's shoulders, in the sob that escaped before she buried her face in her hands, covered with stretched jumper, shocked Polly. The distance she had aimed to keep between them for this conversation was suddenly too far, and she was across the room, pulling her daughter's lovely head onto her own chest, murmuring as though Cress were a baby. "There, there. Ssh."

Long minutes of silence later, Cressida asked, "How did you guess?"

"Oh, darling, I've known for a few weeks that something was wrong. I've only just today concentrated on working out what it might be. I'm sorry—have I been too far up my own bum since this wedding business?"

"Oh, Mum, don't *you* say sorry. Typical! I'm the one who's stuffed up, and you're the one apologizing. I didn't want you to know. I thought I could sort it out on my own, but it's got away from me. It's all too big, you know?" More tears.

Polly cuddled her a bit more, then sat up and pushed her hair behind her ears. "Let's be very British and have a cup of tea with sugar. Got us through the war, you know." Cressida smiled weakly.

Later, in the kitchen, Polly thought she had better be practical. "Darling, how far along do you think you might be?" God, saying that was scary—made it real.

"About three months, I guess. I must have been—you know—before Christmas, but I didn't know until January. You know I've always been a bit late, and I suppose I didn't think about it, what with everything that was going on . . ." Her voice trailed off. "And we were careful. We were, Mum, honest."

"Oh, love, it happens. I'm sure you were." Polly felt sick, and stupid. She always told people, like a mantra, "We're so close, Cressida and I, more like sisters, really. I was so young when she was born, you see." She didn't even know Cressida and Joe had been sleeping together. Not for sure. In fact, she had thought Cressida would be bound to talk to her about it if she was thinking of doing it. At the very least she had believed she would recognize the change in her if she had slept with Joe. To be honest, she had seen their relationship as a cushion between Cressida and the big, bad world of sex—the two of them had been together so long, and there was something so comfortable, sexless somehow, about them that Polly had believed Cressida would be chaste for a while longer. "Have you been to see anyone? A doctor? Someone at college?"

"No. I couldn't face that, Mum. If I'd gone to the surgery, Roger might have seen me, and then he'd have told Susan and it might have got back to you. I got the number of the clinic at college, but I lost my nerve. I can't believe I've been so thick. I'm probably too late to do anything about it now."

Is that what she wants? Polly thought. Thank God. An abortion had to be the best way—Christ, wasn't it the only way? Cressida had it all in front of her. She couldn't give it up now.

But suddenly Polly was twenty-one again, sitting in the front room, twanging nervously at the stretchy, olive green cover of the three-piece suite, listening to her mother ranting: "How could you be so stupid, Poll? Did I teach you nothing? Your father and I have slaved for years, gone without, never thought about ourselves, to put you through school, college. The world was your bloody oyster—you could have been anything you wanted. Why, for Christ's sake, would you choose a life like I've had, choose all this instead of something better? This wasn't supposed to happen to you." Throwing her arms out expansively in the small room.

Polly had never before heard such venom and rage in her mother's voice. It was the first time she had seen that her mother was unhappy. The contempt she had felt for her own life was staggering when she gave it vent.

Cressida was blowing her nose loudly. She looked pale and very young. More tears were welling in her red-rimmed eyes, and Polly saw that her nails were badly bitten. Not now, she told herself. There's time for all this. She did a quick calculation in her head. If Cress hadn't suspected anything until New Year's, she must be eleven or twelve weeks. There was time to make it all right. Polly knew instinctively that tonight was not the time to force Cressida to become an adult, responsible and efficient. She must let her be a child while Polly was her mother. Just as she had always been, even when her own mother was pouring scorn on that role all those years ago. It hurt to think that her baby had been struggling on her own with this secret for weeks. Her poor, poor baby.

"What does Joe think?" she ventured. It was hard to picture the lad as a tower of strength and support.

"Joe doesn't know"—Cressida sat upright—"and I don't want him to."

"But, Cress, sweetheart, he—"

"No, Mum. Promise me. I don't want to tell him, and I don't want you to either. Promise. Please? Mum? Please?" More sobs, big, long, loud.

"Okay, baby, okay, baby." Polly rocked Cressida gently.

Hours later, Cressida had fallen asleep on the sofa, and she was curled up now in its feathery depths like a baby. My baby, Polly thought, as she laid a plaid blanket gently over her, tucking a rogue curl back from her face.

In the kitchen, she poured a glass of wine, drank deeply from it and leant against the sink. She looked at the phone—suddenly felt hugely lonely and scared. She wanted Jack.

He answered after four rings. He sounded sleepy.

"It's me. Did I wake you, sweetheart?"

"You did, as it happens, but it's fine. I'm in my armchair, as usual, so it's just as well. Maybe I am a sad old git, after all. What's going on? Things sounded a bit odd when you rang earlier. Did you get to the bottom of it?"

"Oh, Jack." Polly started to cry softly.

For a couple of minutes, Jack murmured to her, stroking her down the phone with his calm, strong voice. Then he said, "Darling, do you want me to come over? I could be there in just a while."

She loved that about him: no explanation required, just a promise to be with her. But it wasn't a good idea. "No, Jack. No, thanks. It's Cressida. Oh, God, Jack, she's pregnant."

"Whoa! Christ."

"Exactly. You can't be any more shocked than I was. I knew something was up—you and I both did—but the penny only dropped this afternoon. And I had it out with her this evening."

"Where is she?" Jack sounded worried.

"Here. She's had a good cry, and she's fallen asleep. I think she's relieved to have it out in the open. She's known for a few weeks, and the poor kid's obviously been scared to death. I feel so stupid, Jack. I had no idea."

"You're not stupid, love. How could you have known? I didn't even know Cress and Joe were at it."

"Neither did I, Jack. Neither did I." Polly leant her head against the wall, with the phone cradled against her shoulder. She felt old.

Susan

Roger had a late surgery, so Susan and Alice had eaten together at the kitchen table. Now they were in the living room, one at each end of the deep sofa. Susan was trying to read *Atonement*. She'd got only halfway, and the meeting was next week. But she couldn't concentrate. She was watching her mum. Alice was supposedly reading a color supplement from one of the Sunday papers, which went largely ignored on Sundays but spent the week on the coffee table. This one had a feature on Robert De Niro, who was promoting some film or other. No chance of getting Roger to that—he had a pathological dislike of the actor and any film he was in. Susan didn't know why—she didn't think Roger really did, either.

Alice was holding the magazine upside down. Susan turned it round for her.

"Oh, thank you, dear." But now that it was the right way up, she still wasn't reading it, although she had her glasses on. She hadn't turned a page in ten minutes, and now that Susan looked at her, she could see that she was staring into the middle distance. "Not in the mood for reading tonight, Mum?"

"Oh, yes, dear, very interesting."

"You're not reading it, though, Mum."

"Oh. I'm not?" It was a question.

"Are you tired?"

"Me, dear? No, no. You go off to bed, though, if you like. I'll wait for your dad."

Roger had told her there wasn't any point in arguing, or correcting her, because Alice's short-term memory made it impossible for her to hold on to whatever you told her. But Susan couldn't do that. It felt like surrendering.

"Dad's not coming home, Mum. Roger is coming home." She spoke slowly, and she held Alice's hand as though it might help.

"Oh, Roger, of course. Silly me. Lovely boy, Roger. A lovely boy."

"He is, Mum. Not so much a boy, these days, though. Do you remember? We've been married for years—it'll be twenty-five next April."

"Twenty-five years?" Alice said slowly, working the words

around her mouth. Her eyes were blank. "A happy marriage is a wondrous thing." She sounded as if she was reciting poetry, or sermonizing. "We had the very happiest, your dad and me."

"I know you did, Mum. Would you like me to get you the album, so you can look at some pictures of Dad?"

Now she smiled at Susan, all maternal and warm. "No, dear, there's no need for that. I've got it all locked away up here." She pointed at her temple, where the hair was thinning, yellow-white. Then she tapped her forehead sagely a couple of times. "You don't need pictures, if you've a fine memory." She was still for a moment, then nodded again, as if she had completed the inventory of her mind and was satisfied.

She leant over suddenly and kissed Susan's cheek. Her cheek was cool and powdery. "You're a good girl, Susan. We were so lucky to get you. So lucky."

That made it harder. "I wanted to talk to you about something, Mum." I'm going to put you in a home. I can't cope with you, and everybody tells me I mustn't try, so I'm going to get rid of you.

"Lovely, darling. Let's just have a nice cup of tea, shall we? I'll make it." She started to get up.

"No, Mum, you sit down. I'll get it."

"You're an angel. You do that, and then we'll have that chat."

When she came back with two mugs, Alice had turned the television on and was staring straight through a documentary about insects. The volume was at its highest level. Susan took the remote control and turned off the sound. "We were going to talk, Mum? Can I switch it off?"

"Oh, no, darling. Your father will love this—he's mad on this sort of thing. He'll be home any minute." She took her tea and patted Susan's hand gently, dismissively, never taking her eyes off the screen.

MARCH
READING GROUP

ATONEMENT

IAN McEwan © 2001

On the hottest day of the summer of 1935, thirteen-year-old Briony Tallis sees her older sister, Cecilia, strip off her clothes and plunge into the fountain in the garden of their country house. Watching Cecilia is Robbie Turner, a childhood friend who, along with Briony's sister, has recently graduated from Cambridge.

By the end of that day the lives of all three will have been changed forever. Robbie and Cecilia will have crossed a boundary they had never before dared to approach, and will have become victims of the younger girl's scheming imagination. And Briony will have committed a dreadful crime, the guilt for which will color her entire life.

Atonement is Ian McEwan's finest achievement. Brilliant and utterly enthralling in its depiction of childhood, love and war, England and class, the novel is at its center a profound—and profoundly moving—exploration of shame and forgiveness and the difficulty of absolution.

"What are you making that face for?"

"What face?"

"That 'I hated it' face."

"Oh, God, I'm not, am I?"

A chorus of "Yes" rippled good-naturedly round the sofas.

"You made that face about all the books I suggested!"

"I just didn't fancy any of them. Sorry." Harriet made a self-deprecating face.

"Can you remember the last book you really liked?"

"Yep. *Heartburn*. Loved it. And *I Capture the Castle*."

"Do you know why?"

"Actually"—Harriet shuffled her book and her notebook, tapping the edges like an orderly secretary after a meeting—"I think I do."

Clare loved it when the book group took this turn—it was usually Harriet who started it. She didn't like talking about this bit or that bit of a book—she was still afraid she might say something stupid or just wrong, or have missed something through reading too quickly. The others seemed to have read so much more of this stuff than she had. Really, she wasn't much of a reader. She had devoured the Sue Barton series—*Student Nurse, District Nurse*, that lot—when she was a kid, and she remembered one of the girls at school bringing in her mother's copy of *Lace*, by Shirley Conran, when they were all about twelve, and reading them the rude bits. After the goldfish scene Susie Atterbury had burst into tears and had to lie down in the sickroom. Clare had quite liked it. When she was training at St. Thomas,' the flat had been full of magazines (and policemen from the station in Lambeth—Sue

Barton might have bagged a doctor, but most nurses seemed to end up with PCs): light relief after textbooks and wards. Thick, glossy novels had been reserved for holidays.

Elliot was the reader. He browsed in Waterstone's for his books while she was more of a Tesco shopper—chuck in the new one by so-and-so, with its pretty pastel cover, next to the *petits pois* and the *fromage frais*. In recent years she'd had a go at a few of Elliot's. She hadn't been able to make sense of *Captain Corelli's Mandolin*. Elliot said it reminded him of Dickens, with all its characters and subplots. Clare just felt, each time she picked it up, as though she'd missed a chunk—the text escaped her. It made you look clever, though, so she'd held it up across her chest beside the pool on that holiday they'd had in Cyprus in 1996; she'd had her sunglasses on and dozed off behind them. Elliot got cross with her. It was affected, he said, this feigning of ignorance. He called her Uriah Heep (who the hell was he?) because he said she always offered an opinion apologetically about politics, literature and big things, as if she was unworthy. She was just as clever as him, he said, and most other people.

She wasn't sure that was true—but she was feeling braver, here, in this group. They were so nice. She liked Harriet best, though. Harriet was funny and rude, and Clare had this secret theory that when she hadn't finished the book, or had read it too fast to talk about details, she just thought up this big debate you could have about something in it and steered the discussion that way. Clare thought that was clever. Maybe that was what she was doing now.

"Come on, then, Professor, let's have it." Nicole was smiling at Harriet.

"I don't think I like books written by men."

Polly laughed. "Well, that's most of the literature of the last two thousand years wiped out, then. Let's piss off home."

"Hang on, hang on. There's more." Harriet wasn't defensive, and this wasn't one of her planned diversions. She'd read every word of *Atonement*, which had left her grumpy and dissatisfied. "It's about how you read. And why. And we're all different."

Nicole poured herself another glass of wine. "Christ, she's getting deep. Anyone?" She waved the bottle.

Susan sat forward. "What do you mean, Harriet?"

"Okay. I've got a mythical hour—no, a morning—with nothing to do but read, right?" Some snorting around the coffee table. "And I'm offered either the new Penny Vincenzi or the new Ian McEwan. I'm going to take the new Vincenzi every time, aren't I? I've always been that way, even when I was a student. Now, I've always thought that that was because it was less demanding. You'd have to think less, that it was less clever. And, to an extent, I've always been happy with that diagnosis—that I would rather read a woman's saga than a man's intellectual novel because it was easier. But now"—and here her tone was Agatha Christie's Miss Marple revealing a red herring—"now I realize that it is because I *care* so much more about the characters women create. And if I don't *care*, really *care*, by about page fifty, forget it. I can read it, most of the time I can understand it, but so what? Who cares?" Harriet finished with a flourish.

Clare was nodding: Nicole was shaking her head.

Susan spoke first, choosing her words carefully. "I think you have something there. But I have to tell you that I think you're quite wrong about the male-female divide. Look at . . . D. H. Lawrence, Thomas Hardy—Shakespeare, dare I say it? Dripping with emotion. Total wets, the lot of them."

"Historical novelists. Aha. Completely different. That's why I don't want to do the classics. Life was so different. Everything was different. I'm talking about modern writers."

"But I like reading classical stuff for exactly those reasons. I like to learn about things—I want to feel like I've learnt something when I get to the end of a book, not like I've been put through an emotional mangle. I can watch *Oprah* on satellite if I want that." This was Nicole. No surprises there, then, thought Harriet. It was always about control with Nic. "Or ring Harriet!"

"I agree with Harriet," Polly chimed in. "Think about the books you've loved, loved, loved over the years, whether they're literature or not. *Jane Eyre*? *Rebecca*?"

"*A Woman of Substance*." Clare was warming to Harriet and Polly's theme, so much so that she didn't feel nervous about offering up Barbara Taylor Bradford.

Polly was exultant. "Exactly. Big, fat, wonderful book. I can still remember their names. Emma, Paul, Blackie. And it must be—what?—twenty years since I read it. You just didn't want it to end."

"But they wouldn't be much good for a reading group, would they?" Nicole said. "However much you loved them, what would we talk about? You need something more complicated, something with 'themes' and 'issues.'"

Harriet was still thinking about men. "Men are emotionally retarded writers. Not all of them, but a lot. They've got the imagination and creativity to come up with plots and stuff, but the feeling is all missing. Like *Atonement*. Cold, just cold."

"Don't you think that maybe the whole point of 'literature,' if that's what you want to call it, is that the emotion *is* there, but below the surface, between the lines, hidden in the language and the action, and you put it in yourself. You personalize it with your own experience. Maybe?" Susan looked at them.

"I suppose." Harriet mulled over the thought.

"Yes, I agree with you, Susan. The trouble with you lot"—Nicole gestured at Harriet, Polly and Clare—"is that you want all the work done for you. Like there's a recipe for heartstring tugging, and you want every author to follow it."

"That's not fair. I just want to care."

"Me too."

"And you didn't? About this lot?"

"Not really." Harriet shrugged. "They annoyed me."

Polly laughed. "At least that's an emotional response, of sorts."

"Well, honestly, *what* atonement? Typical Catholic. As long as you feel sorry, tell God you're sorry, that's enough. You don't actually have to make everything okay in the real world. She doesn't atone at all. I don't buy it." Harriet was stroppy now. Happy, interested and stroppy. The others enjoyed her like this. Nicole liked to take a position—she took on Harriet most frequently. But Polly was getting braver, too. Susan sometimes got left behind, thinking too carefully about Harriet's throwaway remarks. And Clare was happy more often than not just to listen. Her book was always well-thumbed, and Harriet, next to her, saw notes written, corners turned down. She hoped Clare's confidence would grow in time. The group needed everyone to contribute—a silent person was audience, not cast, and inhibited the rest of them. She knew Clare was thinking things that were worth saying.

"I just think you have a much more black-and-white idea about guilt and remorse. You want her stoned in the street before you believe she's sorry," Nicole said. "You're obviously not happy that she's clearly going to be full of regret and remorse for the rest of her life."

"Remorse is one thing. Guilt's another. I'm talking about the book's own title. Doesn't 'atonement' mean 'making up for?'"

"It does. And she's trying."

Harriet harrumphed. She wasn't sure anymore whether they were talking about Briony or Gavin. She might be more prepared to forgive Briony.

The debate raged for another hour or so, across dinner and coffee. It was loud, full of unfinished sentences and eager butting in. The conversation flew, like the workings of a pinball machine, between Catholicism, Harriet's diatribe against male writers, Susan's assertion that she did, indeed, care horribly about Briony and Cecilia, Nicole's enthusiasm for McEwan's atmospheric sociological history and how good Polly's tarte tatin was.

"Look, here, page three hundred and two. 'Everything she did not wish to confront was also missing from her novella—and was necessary to it. What was she to do now? It was not the backbone of a story that she lacked. It was backbone.' I rest my case." Harriet, the natural, if slightly despotic leader, closed her copy dramatically. "Whose turn is it to choose next month?"

"I think it's me, isn't it?" Susan said.

"No pressure, now, Susan. Just don't choose anything by a man, or a Catholic, or anything that isn't positively reeking of sentiment!"

"How about *Love Story*?" She wasn't serious.

"Aha!" Polly shouted theatrically. "I think you'll find that was written by a man. The soppiest book *ever*!"

Harriet laughed. "Okay, okay—you got me."

"I'd already chosen, I'm afraid." Susan pulled a book out of her bag. "Roddy Doyle—*The Woman Who Walked into Doors*. I got this from the library."

Harriet was impressed—she never made it past the children's

section, with its primary-colored sofas, and its endless supply of lift-the-flap books with the flaps missing.

"It's been out a couple of years, I think," Susan went on, "so you should be able to buy it in paperback. I was quite interested in the subject—it's about wife beating."

"Something you want to tell us?" They weren't serious. Roger seemed pretty much dream-husband material—if a bit dull, Nicole thought.

Susan giggled. "I haven't read anything of his before. Have any of you?"

They hadn't, but they had all seen and enjoyed the film *The Commitments*.

Nicole found herself humming "Try a Little Tenderness" in the car on the way home.

Harriet

Harriet looked at herself hard in the mirror. Service stations on motorways were not great places to appraise your appearance—the lights were bluey white and far too bright, and the mirrors did you no favors at all. So, although you knew you looked better in reality, your self-esteem suffered untold damage. She remembered reading somewhere that Liz Hurley recommended plucking your eyebrows in first-class airplane loos because of the quality of light in them. (Was it darker in Economy?) She ought to try it on the M3 in the restroom at a service area. The undereye concealer wasn't quite covering the bags left from Chloe's week of "hacking-cough-need-juice-pink-medicine-and-a-cuggle-Mumma" nights. The lip liner, which the much-pierced man in the exclusive shop had told her would change her life, had indeed stood the test of time—well, an hour, anyway—but the lip gloss hadn't: it gave her mouth the appearance of an unfinished cartoon. Her Bridget Jones knickers were holding her tummy in, all right, but were pushing it back out again at midthigh. Still, there was half a stone or so less of her, thanks to the diet that had gone from an indulgent "I'll cut out crisps and biscuits, I've got eight weeks to go" to a rather more desperate "If I don't eat for the next seventy-two hours *and* drink ten pints of water I'll do it," and the label in her suit said size twelve. Harriet was so proud of herself that she'd considered wearing it label side out. Not for the first time she wished she could be more like Nicole, who always looked as if she'd just walked out of the salon, hair, face, nails, clothes always just right. Harriet always looked as if she was on her way in: too little hair, too much bosom, not enough polish but plenty of shine. It was a pretty suit, though, and Harriet had to admit that even in this ghastly light it was a gorgeous color—just the right shade for her eyes and skin. Of course Nicole had chosen it, marching authoritatively around the department store, dismissing all Harriet's own selections—"Too fancy, they'll think you're the cake!" "Only if you're planning to stand up and sing 'It Should Have Been Me!'" "Pleeease—are you a bridesmaid?" She felt . . . classy. Successful. Tearful.

Back in the foyer, Tim was easy to spot among the crowd—conspicuous, even, in his morning suit. Why did he have to come in with me? I'm not Chloe, for God's sake, Harriet thought crossly. He looks a prat. He'll get knifed if he's not careful, looking like that.

Clearly today was a day on which Tim could do nothing right. He had taken Josh and Chloe to his mother's first thing this morning, remembering their swimmers *and* armbands. He had stayed out of the bathroom while she busied herself in it, had taken the car to be washed so that it shone, and picked up pretty buttonholes for both of them from the florist on the corner. A white rose for himself, freesias for her. Bit pointed, that, Harriet thought. If he were a dog he'd have weeed on me to mark me out. One tiny bit of her tried to remind the rest that it couldn't be easy for Tim, taking her to Charles's wedding. The two men had met once, years ago, and these days Charles was almost never mentioned, certainly not by Harriet. But, still, she hadn't made much of a secret of her feelings. For heaven's sake, Tim had been around at the beginning—he was a volunteer: he'd known what he was letting himself in for, hadn't he?

The first time she'd met him she'd almost flung herself into his arms. She and Charles had had the most terrible fight, and she'd been lying alone—a bit chilly—drama queen style, on the hall carpet in the flat she and Amanda had shared in Wimbledon, sobbing and waiting for his return, his abject apology. At the sound of the doorbell, she'd jumped up, checked that her face looked attractively ravaged by misery and thrown open the door to feel the full force of Charles's guilt and affection. Instead she got Tim, sober-suited, straight-faced and horrified, looking for his colleague Amanda, with whom he had agreed to play squash that evening. Tim had been instantly sympathetic, melted by the sight of her disheveled sadness, which, though definitely hammed up for effect, was undoubtedly genuine. Harriet had been mortified, and far too miffed that he wasn't Charles to take much notice of him.

Story of their life, really, Harriet supposed, as she watched him perusing the newspaper headlines.

"You really do look very pretty, Harry," Tim said, as they set off west again. "That color is beautiful on you. I'm proud to be with you." And he took his hand off the gearstick and placed it across her own, which was lying in her lap. "They've been pretty lucky with the weather, haven't they?"

The previous week had been miserable, gray and drizzly. But this morning was of the kind you must have imagined when you planned a wedding for March—bright blue sky, not too cold.

Christ, we're actually talking about the weather, Harriet thought. How totally scintillating. To Tim she murmured that, yes, it was a nice morning, then switched on the radio. Whitney Houston was belting out "I Will Always Love You." Not good. Not even with waterproof mascara. Charles had given her a Walkman for Christmas one year. With a tape in it. Of "their" songs. Not all quite as hackneyed and clichéd as Whitney's, but few that could have been more tear-jerking this morning. Over to Radio 4, and something less emotive, in clipped BBC English. It was going to be a long day.

Hideous traffic on the A343 meant that Tim and Harriet arrived flustered—just what she hadn't wanted—and feeling for all the world like Hugh Grant in *Four Weddings and a Funeral*, with the bridal Rolls-Royce hard on their heels for the last mile to the irritatingly perfect church in the chocolate-box quaint village where butter-wouldn't-melt Imogen must have grown up. Yuck.

They slid into pews halfway back, aisle seats, just as the music started. Something very trad but not, heaven forbid, the Bridal March. Everyone stood up, and Harriet saw Charles square his shoulders and make a quarter turn to watch his bride. She felt as though a physical blow had landed on her. Her heart was pounding, her breath caught in her mouth, her palms were moist. She put her hand on the pew in front to steady herself. Charles. Charles.

He didn't see her. His eyes bored into the approaching Imogen. Who had not even had the decency to wear a meringue with bitching potential for bitter ex-girlfriends. She was looking, as brides should, her best. Not catwalk material, but no jodhpur thighs either, Harriet was forced to admit. She looked, well, nice. Smiley. Warm. And totally smitten with her groom. Harriet's mother loved two things best—apart, Harriet hoped, from her family: musical films, and Christopher Plummer. Nineteen sixty-five was thus an extremely good year for her, marrying, as it did, Plummer and the excruciatingness that was *The Sound of Music*. "'Edelweiss,'" Harriet used to say. "Need I say more?" Harriet's family was forced to watch the film every time it was shown, until the video release, after which her mother was happy to watch it alone, often. And every time, after Julie Andrews had triumphed over the scheming society babe and caught her captain, Harriet's mother cried real tears during the wedding scene and said, "Fancy having that waiting at the bottom of the aisle for you!" *That* was how Imogen looked—like Harriet's mother would have looked if she was tripping down the church toward Christopher Plummer. Harriet could understand why.

Throughout the ceremony she made a serious study of her hands. Every time she looked up she could feel Tim's eyes on her, his concern always palpable. Which made it worse. It seemed to take ages. Our wedding took all of ten minutes, Harriet thought, even on island time. Suddenly she felt as if saying all those words, singing those hymns and having loads of acquaintances there in hats made this wedding more important. As if not doing it made her marriage a bit of a fraud. Like it was no wonder it wasn't working.

She hadn't felt that way in 1993, when she had married Tim.

But maybe even then she'd known it was a second-choice marriage to a second-choice husband so had deliberately settled on a second-choice wedding. No, surely that wasn't true. She had loved Tim. She was sure she had. They'd gone to St. Lucia, just the two of them, had planned the wedding for the second week—long enough to get a license and a tan for the photographs, with time for a honeymoon afterward. Her mother had gone mad, although Harriet was secretly sure that her father was relieved at being saved the expense of a traditional, full-monty wedding. Then it had seemed to her like a great adventure, something a bit different.

A few nights before she'd left, Harriet had got drunk with Amanda, cried a bit about Charles, then protested, slurring, that she did "really love Tim, honest." Drunk though she might have been, Harriet remembered to this day what Amanda had said: "Bollocks! You know what this is. It's one of two things. One: (waving her thumb) you're playing a really stupid game of Call My Bluff with Charles, which, I ought to tell you, you've lost. He isn't going to be climbing out of the surf in Paradise to raise an objection, you know. Or two: (shoving up what she thought was two fingers, although she couldn't be sure) this is a Musical Chairs wedding."

"What the hell is that?"

"You're afraid that the music's stopped and you're going to be stuck on your own, so you're grabbing the nearest chair. Which is ridiculous, since you're only twenty—what—twenty-five. But that's what I reckon."

"You can shove your stupid amateur psychology, you drunk cow," Harriet had spat at her friend. "We'll be fine, you wait and see." But she had never forgotten it. Maybe that was why it had been St. Lucia. Like it was a secret, or something. It was a bit funny, actually, getting married on the beach. Harriet's view, throughout the most important ceremony of her life, was of an impossibly pert pair of male buttocks, neatly dissected by a black strip of thong. At the time it had made her giggle uncontrollably—the hotel's luxury portfolio of ten photographs all showed her looking a bit sweaty in her not entirely appropriate wedding dress and laughing. Tim looked impossibly proud. St. Lucia hadn't been his ideal, but he had hugged her close and said they could be married anywhere, he didn't care, as long as she was there and she said yes . . .

And then it was done. All those beautiful words had been said, the register had been signed, to the strains of something tasteful, and Charles and Imogen were heading straight for her, with huge smiles. Friends and family were mouthing to Imogen, "You look beautiful" and "Well done, darling." She had her arm through Charles's—he had put his left hand across to grab her fingers and was squeezing so hard that his knuckles were white. He would have been nervous, she realized. He hated public speaking or being the center of attention. As they passed, he turned and looked straight at her, smiling. Harriet waited for a wink, a change in the smile, something to pass across his face, but he carried on, the same expression for the dowager aunt figure in the pew behind, the slightly shocked look of unseeing joy to which everyone was being treated. He hadn't really seen her.

Outside the church, Harriet didn't want to stand around in the customary predrink, let's-pretend-the-photo-bit-is-interesting limbo, watching Charles watch Imogen. "Come on, Tim, let's find the hotel. I'm dying for a pee—must be all that coffee I drank this morning."

"Okay, sweetheart." Tim wanted to get her away to where she could have some peace before the ordeal of the reception. It must be bloody odd for her, he told himself. She and Charles were together for a longish time—she must know all these relatives and people. He wished again that they hadn't been invited to the godforsaken wedding. It just stirred up all those old feelings. For Harriet and for Tim. Why did there have to be this ridiculous pretense at civility and friendship? Once, Harriet had really loved Charles, and he, fool that he must have been, hadn't realized what a wondrous thing he had, and had broken her heart. Left her the wreck that Tim had found. So lucky for him. He thought he'd probably been in love with her from the first day. He'd never believed anyone who said that before. And certainly, on that evening when he'd gone to Amanda's flat, he hadn't been expecting the flood of feeling he'd experienced for the crazy-looking, puffy-eyed girl who had let him in. He had wanted to pick her up and take her away and make her safe and make her happy. He *still* wanted to do that. Especially this morning. But he knew Harriet well enough to grasp that today, of all days, she needed him to keep his distance.

Harriet had to drink a glass of champagne very fast before she could collect herself. Then she grabbed a second from a passing silver tray and joined the long queue for the receiving line. She was well into the third before she reached the bridal party. She issued a suitably effusive remark to the smart couple who were obviously Imogen's parents (still married, of course), then moved on to Charles's father, a twinkly-eyed, gentle man of whom she'd always been fond. When she and Charles broke up that last time, he'd written to her, a sweet note saying that he would miss their talks and walks and that he knew she would make some lucky fellow a wonderful, funny wife, and what a pity it wasn't foolish old Charles. He kissed her on both cheeks, held her shoulders and told her she looked good enough to eat. To Tim he said simply, "Lucky chap!" Charles's mother was considerably less warm—no doubt she thought it was highly inappropriate, not to say messy, to include ex-girlfriends in the proceedings, particularly girls who had been so . . . highly strung, shall we say? as Harriet. "Such a shame you weren't able to bring the children, dear. It would have been lovely to meet them." You're not convincing me, you dessicated old bat, Harriet thought from behind her best smile. Tim nudged her gently forward and launched a brief charm offensive on Charles's mother. Imogen, engaged in a giggly chat with a woman in front, was holding up her dress at the front to reveal her shoes, and Harriet found herself looking up at Charles.

"Hats! It's really, really lovely to see you. You look wonderful. Motherhood and country air agree with you. Thanks so much for coming. We were so thrilled you could make it." Ouch at that "we." Did his hand linger a little too long in hers? Was his smile regretful? Lascivious? Private? Not a bit of it. "Tim, old chap! Good to see you. Thanks so much for coming!" And on he went.

Tim saw that Charles had caught the longing in Harriet's eyes. Longing and three glasses of champagne. Agreed with him, for once, that control had to be exerted over her. He reached across her to shake the groom's hand, giving her no opportunity to linger.

Well, fuck him then, Harriet thought, moving reluctantly away into the marquee. Fuck him. And fuck Tim. Why couldn't he have stayed away? Is that why they invited me? So that Charles could be all smug and happy and rub my face in it just one more time? Did he not do a good enough job of it last time? She wished fervently that she was anywhere else in the world. Had she imagined what they had had between them? Day-dreamed it all into something it never was? No, she bloody well hadn't. Charles ignoring it couldn't change the past. It was hers, his and hers, whatever he did. She *knew*.

Harriet moved toward a waiter for yet another glass of champagne. They had been in Imogen's home, with its enormous hall, sweeping staircase and serious art, barely twenty minutes and the first three glasses hadn't caught up with her, but she could feel bubbles in her legs, and in her fingers.

"Hats? Hats!" Her old university name again. Jesus, if this place was going to be full of alumni she might as well go home now. She was not up for a cozy trip down Memory Lane. She turned and looked into the chest of a very big man. "Remember me? Nick?"

Remember him? Oh, yes, she remembered him, all right . . . Nick had been one of Charles's closest friends at university. They were united by a love of beer, rugby and pretty girls, and a loathing of economics lectures. Harriet had always thought he was handsome, in a von Trapp family, blond and blue-eyed way, but thick, and a bit of a shit. A friend of hers, whose name she couldn't remember now, had been hopelessly in love with him, and he had treated her pretty shoddily—all over her like a (stubble) rash when he was pissed and she happened to be about, then dismissive and high-handed the next day. Stupid girl, Harriet had thought, to make an idiot of herself like that, but even she had had to admit he had a bit of something about him. He'd been on Ios that summer with Charles, Dominic, Amanda and the others, and he was cute, good fun. She hadn't seen him for years, but she thought he was "something in the City."

Oh, yes, she tuned in to Tim's polite small talk, he was a

broker—Tim appeared to have heard of his firm—and "having quite a good time of it right now, actually. Easy come, easy go, and all that." All what? City talk bored the pants off Harriet. She understood shockingly little about finance (she always declined the "check balance" button on the cashpoint machine—if it let you have money it was good, if not, bad, that was all you needed to know) and even less about what men like Tim and, apparently, Nick did. While the men chatted easily, she looked Nick up and down. She'd forgotten how tall he was, and how cute. Had he always had that dusting of freckles across his nose that made his eyes seem even bluer? Had he worn his hair shorter in college? She remembered slightly juglike ears, but they were not in evidence today, hidden by hair that curled over them, in a not quite girlie way that she liked. He looked sort of rich—it was a Hermès tie, she knew, and a Jaeger-LeCoultre watch. No wedding ring. Big hands. As she continued her appraisal down to his shoes, Harriet felt a bit dizzy, and by the time she focused on the black lace-ups her head had fallen forward to rest on Nick's suit. Tim put his arm round her shoulders, righting her as subtly as he could. He was saying, "Two, a girl and a boy . . . ," but Nick wasn't listening: he was smiling—naughtily, Harriet thought—right at her. The pig.

Susan

When the alarm went off at five-fifteen, Roger rolled over and took Susan in his arms. "Morning, darling."

"Mmm. No, it's not." Susan opened one reluctant eye, closed it again. She had been dreading today. She leant back into Roger's warmth.

Roger gave her a squeeze, rolled once more and got out of bed. "You jump into a quick shower and I'll make you a nice cup of tea."

He returned as she was pulling on her clothes with tea for both of them, and a piece of buttered toast. "Are you certain you want to face her yourself? I could come, you know. Might not even miss the start of surgery—I just checked on Ceefax and the flight's on time. If the traffic's not too bad we could be back by eight-thirty." He sat down.

"No, but thanks. It was my decision about Mum, and I've got to sort it out with Maggie."

"All right, darling. You do it your way. But I'm telling you now that if she gives you a hard time she'll have me to deal with. I'm not having her swan in after all these years and start throwing her weight around. It's just not on."

Susan looked at her husband's face. Normally so gentle, it was tight with anger. Her hero. What would she ever do without him? She picked up her handbag from the chair by her side of the bed, bent down and kissed his forehead. "Look, this is bound to be hard for her too. Let's get her home, and then we can talk properly. She probably isn't as cross as she sounded on the phone. She's had time to get used to the idea—to see the sense in it."

"You have rather more faith in her better nature than I do."

"She's my sister."

"I know." His forehead crinkled. "I'm just not having her have a go at you. That's all."

"Understood, Sir Galahad. Now, why don't you curl up and go back to sleep? You've another good hour at least."

"No, I'm awake now. I think I'll potter about a bit—pay some bills."

"Okay. I'll see you tonight. We'll have dinner, the three of us. Better make it an early one—Maggie'll be tired after the flight."

Susan looked around her, taking in the real-life soap operas going on at every corner. She loved airports because they were places full of expectation and excitement. And she especially loved the drama of long-haul terminals, like this one. A British Airways Sydney flight coming into a Heathrow dawn was one of the most emotional: families meeting after months, years apart; anxious parents waiting for grubby, backpacking teenagers, as she had waited last year for Edward—who, much to his chagrin, had been wheeled off by ground crew with his ankle heavily bandaged: he had joked ruefully that he'd escaped his heroic outback journey unscathed only to trip ignominiously over his shoelace on a Melbourne street the night before his plane took off. Susan remembered how she had stood on the highest step she could find, tears close after her son's six-month absence, and how her heart had stopped at the sight of the wheelchair, until she'd seen Ed's face, the familiar twinkling smile. She had exhaled a tremendous breath that, she later realized, she'd been holding since he had gone away from her.

Next to her on the metal rail was an elderly couple, waiting, they had told Susan, for a daughter they hadn't seen in ten years, and the two grandchildren they had never laid eyes on. The woman was bobbing with anticipation, and Susan's eyes filled when two little blond heads ducked under the rail, reaching for people they had seen only in photographs. Above them the father clung to his daughter. Her tanned, strong-looking body made him seem frailer still. Pull yourself together, Susan, she told herself. She had been in a bit of a state lately, with all this Mum stuff going on. It reminded her of how she had reacted when the boys were born: everything hit you harder when you were newly delivered—the news was sadder, even the adverts were sadder, as if you had been peeled and now all your emotions and nerves were closer to the surface. And it was the same now, every time she thought about Alice in that place . . .

And then Margaret was at the rail.

"Hello, Maggie."

"Hello, Suze."

No hugging across the rail. They walked together, on either side of it, avoiding the humanity piled all around them, and met at the end in an awkward embrace, Margaret one-armed as she held her bag beside her.

"Here, let me help you with that." Susan took it. "We're in the short-stay—just over here. Good flight?"

"Under the circumstances? It was okay." Margaret's voice was flat, almost expressionless. Susan's spirits sank even lower. This was not going to be easy. She wished now, as she set off towards the car park, Margaret following, that she had accepted Roger's offer to come with her.

. . .

Margaret had never been an easy person to love, even harder to like. Although they were close in age, with Margaret just a year older, they had always lacked the closeness Susan had envied in other siblings. People seldom made the connection that they were related. Physically they were dissimilar—Margaret looked more like their mother: there had been a picture at home, when they were little, an old-fashioned, formal one of Alice, aged about four, in a high-backed chair with her brother Alexander standing stiffly beside her. She looked just like Margaret in it, with the clear, blue eyes so distinctive even in a black-and-white photograph. Susan's eyes were brown. But for all that they looked alike, Margaret and her mother were of different temperaments: Alice was gentle and calm, Margaret rough and excitable. While Alice and Susan loved to sit at the table to draw elaborate, fanciful scenes with stories woven into the pictures, Margaret longed to climb and rampage in the garden, throwing conkers at far-off birds and digging muddily in the vegetable patch their father had made for them in the corner of his own. If Maggie was jealous of Alice and Susan's closeness, she gave little indication of it as a child, treating them with disinterest and, even, disdain. She was always amazingly self-contained. Every day when Alice collected them from the village school and they walked the half mile or so home across the common, she proffered two hands to her daughters, but only one was taken. So she and Susan walked together, Susan spilling out all the minutiae of her day, while Margaret zigzagged endlessly across their path, waiting for her mother only at the big road they must cross halfway home. At night they slept together, in narrow twin beds, with a tall chest of drawers between them, so they could hear but not see each other in the dusky landing light. But it seemed to Susan that Margaret always went straight to sleep after their mother had read to them; she never seemed to want to talk.

And that was how it was between them, through school and on, until the day Margaret had come home with Greg, a young man unknown to them. Susan and Roger had been courting for almost a year by then, and Roger had become a regular fixture at Sunday lunch, ambling to the pub for a pint with Susan's dad while Alice and Susan peeled carrots and laid the table in the dining room. Margaret, who was living in a flat with a girlfriend, and working as a receptionist in one of the big, new office blocks on the edge of town, missed three out of four of the once-sacred weekly family roasts. But one Sunday she telephoned and said she would be there, and could she bring a friend?

Greg had filled the house with his tanned bulk and his deep, Australian voice. They had met at a party, Margaret said, a few months ago. Greg had asked her to marry him, and she had told him she would. Greg, momentarily shamed by Margaret's father's expression, added, "If that's all right with you, sir?" his voice lifting in a question at the end of that and every sentence. They were going to marry over there, as soon as it could be arranged. Perhaps just have a party here, for the family, before they left. Nothing too fancy. And there were photographs of the farm, acre upon acre, sheep upon sheep, and a bronzed, weather-beaten group beside a farmhouse—a handful of women and children and about a dozen men, all big and brown like Greg. "So much space, Mum," Margaret had said, her eyes wide. "Hard work, for sure, but . . . I just know it's the place for me. And he's the one." She seemed happier than Susan had ever known her.

After they had gone, Susan's mum and dad sat side by side in their armchairs, facing out into the garden they loved, while Susan and Roger washed up in the kitchen.

"Christ, Susie, your sister never ceases to amaze me." Roger and Margaret were not friendly. When she wasn't ignoring him, Maggie goaded him, half laughing at his earnestness and solidness. She made it clear that while he might do for Susie, he was far too pedestrian and dull for her to bother with. Susan was only worried about how her sister's bombshell would affect her parents.

"I know Margaret's been gone from here for a while now, and they're not particularly close, but Australia? That's half a world away. And to get married over there too—they know Mum and Dad can't possibly make the journey, even if they had the money, which I doubt they do, now that Dad's retired. They've never been further than Malta."

"That, my dear, is the whole point, I'm sure. She won't want them there. Margaret has always behaved as though she's trying to punish them for something—God knows what—but this is just another score for her."

"Oh, Roger, that's a bit deep, don't you think? I reckon it's just selfishness—she hasn't thought it through. This Greg bloke has turned her head, made her forget where she comes from because she's so excited about where she's going. I'm sure she'll change her mind, get married here, at least—let Dad give her away, and let Mum fuss around with a dress."

"I bet you she doesn't." He kissed her ear. "Still, your mum's got you, hasn't she? I think there's the distinct possibility of another wedding around here before too long, don't you?" Susan's cheeks pinked, and she stared harder at the roasting tin she was scrubbing, smiling to herself.

Half an hour later, when they had finished and taken in a fresh pot of tea, Alice's eyes were puffy from crying, but both her parents were quiet, resigned. Susan always wondered what they had said, how they had felt about her sister's announcement, but it was something they kept to themselves. Alice said only, "She's always wanted adventure, that one. I'm happy it's found her."

Margaret hadn't changed her mind. Three months later she was gone. That same month Roger asked Susan's father for permission to marry her, and when it was granted, joyously, he had proposed and been accepted. Six months after that they were married, on a blustery spring day. Alice got to make her plans, and Susan's dad got his proud walk down the aisle. Margaret sent a telegram, but was too busy on the farm, with the harvest, she said, to make the long journey home for the wedding.

Clare and Elliot

There were no lights on when Elliot got home. Clare's car wasn't there. And the front door was double-locked. He didn't realize until he got upstairs that she had gone. Not out, but away. She'd left him. Strange, really, that there should be so few things downstairs that she needed. As if she was living in a B and B. The living room, the kitchen, the hallway were all exactly the same. The words of a Philip Larkin poem he had once read swam round his head as he wandered, vaguely dazed, from room to room: "left, shaped in the comfort of the last to go." Only it hadn't been shaped to Clare's comfort. She had left barely a dent in the fabric of the home they had shared. Her bathroom shelf had been emptied of the utilitarian toiletries she used, her toothbrush was gone from the mug suspended next to the washbasin, her side of the wardrobe was empty. He assumed the drawers were, too, but he didn't check. She had left the box of tissues on her side of the bed. The next month's reading-group book choice was gone, but the picture of the two of them, taken in the glare of the Mediterranean sun, was still there. It was stupid, he thought, how quiet the house felt, because she had never made any noise when she was in it. But, as though her things had somehow contributed to the ambient noise, it was quieter, hollowish, without them.

Elliot didn't know what to feel. If you could experience desolation, loneliness and fear at the same time as relief and a kind of excitement, then that was what he felt, but he knew that didn't make any sense. Mind you, what did anymore? He felt guilty, too, that it had had to be Clare who made this dramatic gesture, Clare who had underscored the hopelessness of their situation and been the first to do something about it. And angry, as well, that her action had made him the coward, the ostrich.

He knew where she was, of course. Her mum and dad lived five minutes away in the home where Clare had grown up; they hadn't changed her bedroom since she left.

Elliot picked up the phone, then put it down again. He wanted to hear it from her, watch her face while she said it, not have information about himself and his life filtered through her parents.

Clare's father let him in, holding the door wide open. His face was contorted with paradox: he had so much to say to Elliot and knew that there was nothing *to* say.

Clare was sitting with her mother on the sofa. She was holding a tumbler of whiskey, Dutch courage. Mary got up, squeezed Clare's hand and came toward Elliot. She smiled at him sadly. "Are you okay?"

"I'm okay, Mary."

She enclosed him in a hug, and then she was gone, the door was closed and he was alone with Clare. She was the first to speak, and she launched in, as though the conversation had already been started and she was picking it up in the middle. And, of course, it had been going on in their heads for months. But it was still surreal to hear the words.

"I'm just fed up with being so bloody sad all the time, and everything about home . . . and you"—Elliot winced—"makes it worse. I can't do it anymore, not right now."

There was possibility, in those last words, hope. Elliot didn't know whether he wanted it to flicker on in his head or not, but at that moment, it made it possible for him to leave. It wasn't forever.

"I know. Me too," he said. "I'll be at home, if you need me. Any time."

Clare smiled, grateful to him for making it easy. "I know."

He didn't speak to Mary, or to Clare's father, although he knew he could have done. They didn't know what he was doing, they didn't blame him. They wanted to help, he knew. They just couldn't.

What now?

Harriet and Nicole

They called it synchronized shopping, and they did it most Mondays after the school run. They met in the supermarket coffee shop for a weekend debrief, then took their trolleys to opposite ends, Nicole to bread and pastries, Harriet to fruit and veg. They met in the middle, criticized the contents of each other's trolley ("That's not cheese, it's yellow plastic." "Put those *back*!" "How can you feed your children on those?") and again in the queue. Some mornings the coffee-shop bit took hours, and the shopping had to be done trolley-dash style, in fifteen minutes. This was one such morning. It had taken two coffees so far for Harriet to relate every dreadful detail of the wedding.

"It was just awful. Awful. I was such a prat."

"Oh, come on, it doesn't sound like you were *that* bad. I'm sure

I've seen you a lot worse—what about that quiz night at school last year?"

"Nic, I fell on someone. Fell. A more than averagely dishy man, as it happens."

"You didn't fall, you leant. Besides, you could have thrown up on his shoes. Now that *would* have been shaming."

"Yup. It would have been even more humiliating. Just."

"I'm sure that no one took any notice. Half of them were probably just as drunk as you. I always get sozzled at weddings—it's all that waiting around for the bloody photographs to be taken with the champagne on tap."

"And that's almost the worst part of all. No one *did* take any notice. At all. Except this Nick bloke, I s'pose. And I think he just found me faintly ridiculous."

"Well, sod him for a start. You'll probably never see him again. And as for anyone else, what on earth were you expecting? A starring role in the speeches? To get up and do the first dance with Charles?"

"No, no, no! Don't *you* make fun of me as well. I'm in no fit state to retaliate."

"I'm not, Harry, honestly." Nicole smiled. "Look, you've done it now, he's off the shelf, you've got your 'closure.' You were never going to have the time of your life, were you? That's not why exes get invited to weddings. You were there for Charles to prove that he's oh-so-mature and well-adjusted, and such a great guy that even his ex-girlfriends want to be in his life, and for this Imogen person to prove that she's secure and you're no threat, and to make sure you get that message. Which, I assume, you got loud and clear. All you can do now is just let go of it. Don't think about it anymore."

"Easier said than done. I wish we hadn't gone, I really do."

"You do not! I know you better than that. You had to see how it had turned out. It just wasn't quite how you'd hoped. Although the wedding invitation would have been a big clue for most of us . . ." And she was smiling wryly again.

Harriet smiled back. "Okay. But I don't know how to explain it. I wanted . . . I wanted some indication, however tiny, from him, that what we had wasn't nothing. That he remembered it. Cherished it, even. Like I do."

"Sweetheart, I'm sure he does. But that wasn't the time or the place, was it? Really—come on. Why does it still matter so much? After all this time?'

And the question hung in Harriet's mind all the way round Waitrose. Good point. Why did it still matter so bloody much?

As she pushed the trolley absently down the drinks aisle, Nicole was relieved to be with Harriet. She missed her when things were off track between them. Things had been a bit difficult since she had told Harriet about her . . . Plan sounded too calculating: it was a dream, really, a lovely daydream. Nicole was convinced that she and Gavin should have another baby, with his eyes and her hair, and tiny fingers and toes. Harriet thought she was an idiot, and had told her so. That was the trouble with having a best friend: honesty sometimes made it hard. She wanted to be told she was right. Harriet had said, "You don't want me to lie to you, do you? If I really think this is a mistake, I have to tell you so. You see that, don't you?" Nicole didn't want to see it, and didn't want to hear it. Didn't want her bubble burst. So it was good to have the wedding and this ex to talk about. Harriet had been wallowing and self-absorbed—her feelings mitigated only by how funny she was when she told the sorry stories. At the end she had been too wrapped up in it to ask, "What's going on with you, then?" as she would normally. Maybe, Nicole thought, she doesn't want to talk about it either. But not talking about it wasn't going to change her mind any more than talking about it had done.

Besides, Gavin was being great. Best behavior, Harriet called it. And it followed the pattern: Gavin had been caught out so Gavin felt bad (and Nicole still believed that he genuinely regretted it, that his behavior was more addict than adulterer), had behaved ever since like a model husband. Part of Nicole despised herself for having the strength to recognize and acknowledge that the pattern existed but being so weak that she still fell for it. But she wasn't falling for it, she was jumping into it. Each time, and there had been several in their marriage, she thought about not having him back, played out in her head how the conversation would go. She'd pack a bag of his things and leave it on the doorstep. She'd show up at his office and tell everyone what he had been up to. She'd change the locks, slam the phone down, see a lawyer and present him with papers. But she didn't really believe she would ever do any of those things. Nicole—passionately, desperately—wanted her marriage and her family to work. She loved Gavin in a way she knew she could never love anyone else. Unlike Harriet, apparently, she felt certain that no other love, past or future, could ever measure up to the highs in hers for Gavin. That was why Venice was so perfect. It represented, in its few square miles, the very highest point. Going there together now should bring back all those honeymoon feelings, which would be reinforced by what had come since: three children, a home, a life together. Even Nicole's forgiveness should make it stronger.

She remembered one night best of all. They had been drinking red wine from huge glasses and listening to k.d. lang with only the light of a fire. They were lying together—making love had been for earlier, and would be for later, long into the night and through to the morning. This was better, closer. This meant more. For now they were lying like spoons against cushions, listening to the deep, longing voice on the stereo, silent except for the visceral sounds their bodies made. Nicole had felt complete happiness and oneness with him, and she had always reasoned, and believed, that she could not have felt that unless he, too, was feeling it. He was—she knew he was. And if you had felt that with someone, even only once, could it ever go away? Wasn't it too strong? Stories like this one were the medicine Nicole took to cure herself. She played the tapes in her mind until the other pictures went away.

That was why she didn't want to listen to Harriet, who would dilute everything. There was a woman they both knew who had had a daughter in school. She was a single parent, and the girl was the product of a liaison, still ongoing, with a married man who clearly had no intention of leaving his wife and family. Harriet and Nicole had learnt this at a drunken potluck supper a couple of terms ago. She was a quiet woman, always rushing to work and not dawdling to gossip in the car park, and the story spilt from her like a boil being lanced, full of love and hate, fear and defiance. Afterward Harriet had declared her insane and taken a position of logic ("She's wasting her life, waiting for a train that's never coming into the station—we're none of us getting more attractive, just nearer the pavement") and righteous indignation ("There are just so many victims in a setup like that, and she's not one of them! I'm surprised at you, of all people, being on her side!"). But Nicole felt she understood. Love did that, to people it shouldn't and to people you wouldn't think it could. Gavin's conquests just fucked him, like he just fucked them. This was different. This was sad. She had made overtures of friendship to the woman, but she had snapped shut, appalled by her own indiscretion, and moved her child to a different school at the end of term.

At the weekend, Gavin had taken the kids, early, to the soft-play center in town (a major concession, since he hated the sock smell, sticky floor and glass-shattering decibels). Before they left he had brought her toast and tea on a tray, with the newspaper. When the door had closed behind them, laughing and shouting together, Nicole had reached into her bedside drawer and pulled out the Rough Guide to Venice. Inside, marking the chapter on restaurants (where those that she and Gavin had visited on honeymoon were circled, then ticked in red after they had been booked) was a thin notebook with a list of what she was packing. In the margin, next to "beaded top and matching wrap," was a doodle of dates and numbers. Her cycle. Gavin could not have planned it better if he had tried. Even Nicole couldn't quite bring herself to believe it was a sign that she should get pregnant. But it wouldn't hurt . . .

Cressida

"Cressida Bradford."

The nurse had a dead kind face, really motherly. It was a relief to be called in—physically, because she had drunk six glasses of lukewarm water and was desperate for a pee, and otherwise because it was unnerving to be alone in that waiting area. Everyone else, it seemed, had someone with them, from the shy-looking couple with shiny gold wedding rings to the loud, cross-looking woman with the huge belly whose rather small husband was on a constant march up and down the corridor with two other children.

Perhaps being by yourself was okay. Mum had nagged to come along with her, but Cressida was aware that this would label her a "silly pregnant girl." She was going for "independent, freethinking woman." *He* didn't even know she was here, didn't know anything yet, and Polly just worried.

"Right, Cressida—great name, by the way."

"Thanks."

"Right, up here you pop. Top up, bottoms down—Here, tuck this tissue inside your knickers to keep the goo off them. That's it. Radiographer will be right with you. First time?" Cressida nodded, and the nurse squeezed her shoulder gently. "Don't worry—nothing to it." And off she breezed.

Worried? Huh? Cressida wondered how many people lay on this couch and felt as she did. Probably more than you think, she reprimanded herself. You're not the only idiot in the world. She knew, thought she knew—no, *really* knew—that she couldn't "kill it": the thought of lying there while someone scraped out a real human life was untenable, however she might defend it for others. Beyond that, who knew? Keep it? Keep it how? Live at home with Mum and Jack, give up college? Live with the father, playing at happy families, be a wife, a mother? At twenty? Live alone, struggling?

Or give it away? Suddenly Cressida saw herself in every film she'd ever seen on the subject, a tortured middle-aged woman—Julie Walters or Alison Steadman—and snapped her mind back into the present. One thing at a time. Just see how this goes.

Cressida didn't know what to expect when the radiographer came and the cold jelly was smeared across her still flat stomach ("You might want to take that navel ring out at some point, Cressida. You may find it uncomfortable as the pregnancy progresses." It seemed surreal to look down at the dip of her tummy, hammocklike with her jutting hip bones at either end, and imagine it pushing out and round—curious and horrible and exciting all at once) and the thing that looked like what they scan food with at the supermarket was pressed onto her full bladder. When the whooshing gray swirl of her blood gave way to the kidney bean of her baby, its heart blinking at her, tears came instantly into her eyes. What she saw, she knew at once, was life. What she felt was amazed, fascinated. It was mad that this thing—this *person*—should be inside her. What she said was: "Hello, baby." And what she wanted was someone's hand to hold, someone to see it with her. Cressida wanted her mum.

Polly

Polly pummeled the cushions until dust exhaled through the fabric. She straightened the magazines and books, lined up all the remote controls—including the one that had been down the side of the sofa for weeks—on top of the television and Flashed away the smelly rings left by milk bottles on the shelf in the fridge. That was how agitated she was.

Perhaps she should have argued more when Cressida had said she didn't want her at the hospital. Or just turned up in the waiting room—surely Cressida wouldn't have sent her away? Well, not the old Cressida. The new, pregnant Cressida was an unpredictable force—sometimes like a tiny child, wanting to curl up beside Polly and be held, and at others so spiky and hard that Polly couldn't get near her. She was so determined to cope, yet so clearly unable to. It made Polly unutterably sad. Cressida shouldn't be doing this, not yet. Life should be about which band to see, and which boy to go with. Those decisions, those dilemmas, not life-and-death ones. Polly wanted to be in charge of Cressida's life now more than ever before. She wanted to be responsible for making the decisions. Earlier in the week they had had the most spectacular row. Polly had tried to be decisive, stern even: she didn't want Cressida to go for the scan, she wanted to call Joe's mum round and discuss it together. She wanted Cressida, she told her, to have an abortion and put it all behind her. Get on with the foundation course, get her degree, kiss lots of toads and find a handsome prince. Be free.

"But, Mum, how can you, of all people, tell me that? How can you? You weren't much older than I am when you had me. Do you hate your life so much? Was it so awful?"

"I was young, yes, but I was married. I had a husband, a home, support." She realized as she said it that it wasn't true. Her mum's you've-made-your-bed-now-lie-in-it attitude had been hard to take, and Dan had been next to useless. It hadn't been much of a home, and she knew now that it hadn't been much of a marriage. She disliked herself for falling back on clichés and rhetoric, for reinventing her own history. But she knew that it was worth it, if only she could make up Cressida's mind the right way.

And then the wheels had turned in Cressida's mind and her angry voice had become calmer, scarier. "Do you mean you wish you hadn't had me? That you'd got rid of me?"

"Cressida, that's not fair. You're here, you're my daughter, and I love you."

"I didn't ask you that, Mum. I know all that and I won't let you hide behind it. I asked you to tell me the truth about then, about how your life turned out because you didn't get rid of me."

Polly didn't answer.

"Come on, Mum." Cressida's voice was getting louder. She had smelt her mother's fear, and this baby was no longer what they were talking about. "Do you wish you'd had an abortion? Tell me, Mum?"

Polly's eyes were full of tears. She couldn't tell the lie that she desperately wanted to tell.

"No. Not for a second. Not for anything. You are, you were, you and Daniel, you always will be, the very best thing that ever happened to me. Regretting that would make the whole of my life a sham."

And the *but* that said, "I want more for you than I had myself," that said, "I want to protect you from some of what I had to go through"—that *but* was left unsaid.

They'd fought about Joe, too. Polly wanted to talk to him. She was angry that Joe had gone back to Warwick, and that he wasn't going through any of this with Cressida. She wanted to know how he felt.

On that point, more than on any other, Cressida was emphatic and, from her face, impervious to persuasion. Polly daren't go behind her back. "He is not to know. You've no right to tell him, Mum. None at all."

Nothing had worked. Polly had tried to say that he should face up to his responsibilities, that he shouldn't get away with this scot-free. When that hadn't got through, she had appealed, "Doesn't he have a right to know? Is it really up to you to make a decision about a child that belongs to both of you?"

That had been a mistake, which had caused Cressida's anger to flare again. "Oh, I see. Five minutes ago you couldn't even bring yourself to call it a child, you were so desperate for me get rid of it. Now it's a child. It's Joe's child, if you please, now that it suits you. Christ, Mum, it's got nothing to do with Joe, okay?" She had said that before. "It's my problem, and I'll deal with it, okay?" (No, not okay, Polly thought. Not remotely okay.) And then: "If you tell him, I'll leave. I'll just go, and you won't know where, and you won't find me."

That threat had chilled Polly. Jack had said she'd never follow it through: "Where would she go, for God's sake? It's adolescent angst, Poll. A bit of melodrama. That's all." Jack thought she shouldn't tell Joe, or his mum. "It's not your news, love."

Polly looked at him, and for the first time he seemed like the man he really was, a man who hadn't had a child. Who couldn't understand. She cried at Susan's kitchen table when she told her what he had said. "It *is* my news. She's my little girl. I'm being shut out and Jack thinks that's fine."

"He doesn't think it's fine, Poll, he's just looking out for you."

"But he doesn't understand, Suze. He can't."

So they were all going through this half experience on parallel lines that almost never crossed. Polly was exhausted by the effort of trying to be the parent Cressida needed her to be. She was building a wall against Jack—punishing him, she supposed, for not being Cressida's father or anyone else's. She was trying to cushion Daniel from everything. Susan was doing her best, but she had her own hands full with Alice and Margaret.

And now she was straightening cushions on an already tidy sofa, waiting for Cressida to come home from the hospital. She should have been there: this was a crunch point—it had to be. The jury was out, and waiting for the verdict was unbearable.

Harriet

He was *definitely* playing footsie with her. The first time she had thought it was just an accident. Now she was sure it wasn't. And she wasn't going to stop him. Giddy wasn't in it. Harriet was a different woman. It wouldn't even be true to say that she was like she used to be—she wasn't sure that she had ever been like this.

In her first year at college there had been a girl, Lucy, wildly beautiful with long, thick, dark hair and jade green contact lenses, who used to hold court atop the college bar late at night in an antique brocade gentleman's dressing gown. Harriet was being like *her*. Wanton and free, amoral, desirable, risqué, and . . . it was delicious. Frumpy, stuffy old Harriet had stayed at home, and this new creature had caught the ten-seventeen to Waterloo to engage in frankly lascivious behavior in a smart hotel brasserie. The mere presence of beds a few meters above her head was filling the air with possibilities. (Although, of course, she couldn't possibly sleep with him in daylight—God, no. Blackout blinds, a sliver of moon and preferably a power cut were essential for that progression.) But she was thinking about it. A lot.

It had started a couple of weeks after the wedding. Harriet had steadfastly refused to think about the entire bloody day: the warm, loving, yet amusing speeches, the tables of identikit glamorous guests, the flipping croquembouche cake, the tasteful string quartet, which gave way to the nostalgic and groovy Dexy's Midnight Runners type disco, the bride's perfect Armani going-away suit, the Aston Martin leaving for the sodding safari honeymoon . . . the silently disapproving Tim and the spinning hotel room. Oh, and the hangover. Too much. Too bloody much. For the first week the humiliation had been her first thought on waking and her last before falling asleep. By the second week she had resolved to forget about it. So she wasn't best pleased when the phone rang and she heard Nick's voice.

"Hats?" Yuck—that name again. "It's me. Nick." And when Harriet didn't reply: "From the wedding? I mean, I know you were pissed, but please don't break my heart by saying you don't remember."

"I was not pissed. I was tired. I had been up all night with one of my kids, dreadfully poorly, if you must know."

"Sorry, Hats. Haven't got any myself. Shouldn't have presumed. Yes, of course. Tired. Is the little darling . . . better now?" Harriet could imagine the twinkle in his eye, and hear the amusement in his voice. Nick knew exactly what state she had been in that day—and why.

He was ringing, apparently, to see if she was going to some reunion set up by their university. She wasn't. She'd known nothing about it. She never discovered if a reunion was really planned.

By then she was too flattered by his call to care. Nick Mallory had tracked her down.

And then Nick Mallory had pursued her. By phone. He learnt her habits—when she was on the school run, when she worked out (well, she'd told him she went to the gym: if he chose to imagine her working up a sweat on the treadmill in a skimpy leotard rather than reading *The Sun* over a full-fat caffé latte in the lounge *at* the gym, then why should she disabuse him of an idea that clearly gave him pleasure?), and he called her from work, once or twice a week at first, then almost daily.

He showed no interest in Tim, because Harriet didn't let him. She sidelined him, so that to Nick he would appear little more than a flatmate. Which didn't excuse Nick's caddish behavior, Harriet thought. But, still, she was being a cow. She knew she was. She most especially knew because she hadn't told Nicole what she was up to. Couldn't face it, really. Nicole felt like her conscience, perched on one shoulder. Odd that it wasn't Tim on her shoulder, reminding her of her obligations, her vows, her family. She had done well in shutting him out of her head. And, anyway, she wasn't doing anything wrong, was she? It was just lunch with an old friend.

Wrong. She actually fancied him rotten. Mainly, she'd admitted, at least to herself, because he was making it perfectly plain that he fancied *her* rotten. Cor! What an aphrodisiac *that* was.

"So, Harriet"—even the way he said her name, now that he was using it, was sexy—"what have you got to say for yourself? I've bought you this scandalously expensive lunch, which, incidentally, you've hardly touched"—oh, joy, the loss of appetite. That never happened—"and been extravagantly complimentary to you while you've pushed it around the plate and insulted me in return."

That was true. She had teased him mercilessly about the old days, the conquests and even the jug ears. She had loved doing it. And he had loved her doing it, except, possibly, the bit about the ears. Achilles' ears, she thought.

"You can afford it," she said now. "Weren't you just telling me about that huge bonus you've pulled off and this bachelor shag pad you've bought, and the cars, and the villa at Le Saint-Géran you're booking? I know all about you City highfliers."

"Aren't you forgetting that you're married to one?"

It was the first time he had mentioned Tim all through lunch. Harriet had a brief vision of Judas, but she looked at her watch— it had already struck twelve.

"Hardly. Tim's an analyst, not a broker."

"Ah, yes, the serious bit. Those boys earn a fair old whack. I've asked around"—golly, he was curious about her—"and your old man is a seriously rated bloke." Was he? Harriet had had no idea. "He's got some pretty serious irons in the fire, I hear." (Stop saying serious. Point taken, okay.)

She shrugged. Nick leant in, eyes focused a few inches south of her chin. "Not very sexy, though, is it? It doesn't get the old blood pumping in quite the same way, does it?"

Harriet was reasonably sure they were no longer discussing the relative merits of brokers' and analysts' careers.

He smelt nice. A few brown hairs curled at the edge of his crisp, white, professionally laundered shirt, which was open at the neck. The skin beneath was brown—genuine winter sun. "What you overgrown boys get up to in your oversize playpens with your electronic gadgets and your massive . . . *egos* does very little for my blood pressure either way, actually."

Nick laughed. And then, with his head cocked as though she were a sculpture he was appraising, he said, "I'd forgotten how much fun you were."

Harriet had forgotten too, but she enjoyed being reminded.

Nick raised a hand for the bill. While he signed the credit card slip, Harriet glanced down at her watch. Three o'clock. She'd promised the sitter she'd be back by four, and now she was going to be late. The homely, rotund Mrs. Cartwright had assured her that time was of no relevance to her. "Never you mind, my dear. As long as I'm back to give Mr. Cartwright his tea by seven, it's fine. I can sort the little ones out if you get held up, what with those rotten trains and all." Mrs. Cartwright would probably have felt differently about the whole business had she known that, instead of a cozy girls' lunch with a spot of shopping in John Lewis, Harriet had been planning a liaison with an old . . . well, if not a flame then certainly a match. Mrs. Cartwright took a dim view of such things, especially when they happened on *Coronation Street*. Which was why Harriet had promised four o'clock. Going home to Mrs. Cartwright was the married woman's equivalent of a St. Trinian's girl having to slip in after curfew past Matron. She wanted to do it with an if not completely clear then just slightly smudged conscience.

Outside, on the pavement, she looked about her for a black cab. There were none. She turned to check in the opposite direction, and he was close—way too close. He put his hand behind her neck, under her hair, brought her face to his. Harriet hadn't kissed a man apart from Tim for years—hadn't kissed *him* properly for months—and this was a full-on, end-of-the-school-disco when the Spandau Ballet twelve-inch of "True" is playing and your dad's outside in the car park snog. Isn't it funny how we're all so much better at kissing if that's all we're going to do? she thought. Once second and third bases, and even home runs, are on the cards, you start racing through the first. Which, she was now remembering, was a mistake. Yummy. She was responding to his kiss in an appropriately Barbara Cartland manner. Heart?

Pounding. Knees? Weak. Pulse? Racing. Plus all the other bits of her that Barbara had left out. All in perfect working order.

He broke off. "Mmm. I wish I'd done that years ago." And kissed her again, pressing her to him with his other hand at the small of her back. He tasted of tobacco and garlic. And he tasted, despite the three-course lunch, very hungry.

APRIL
READING GROUP

THE WOMAN WHO
WALKED INTO DOORS

RODDY DOYLE © 1996

I swooned the first time I saw Charlo. I actually did. I didn't faint or fall on the floor but my legs went rubbery on me and I giggled. I suddenly knew that I had lungs because they were empty and collapsing.

R ing 'em up, and cancel."
"I will not."
"Why not?"

"For starters, I like them. I look forward to my reading group. I enjoy it."

"More than you enjoy this?" He nudged her again with his hips.

Not more than this, no, Polly acknowledged. This was pretty good. Daniel was out: it was Thursday, so he was at football training and he'd yelled something back over his shoulder at her this morning about going to Ben's afterward. She didn't know where Cressida was: she was so scratchy, Polly hadn't dared ask what her plans were. Jack and Susan had both told her she needed to be patient, give her space. Anyway, she didn't have the energy for more arguments.

She'd come home from work to an empty, slightly lonely house, no lights on, no Radio 1 blaring. Ten minutes later Jack had been at the front door, with a bottle of red, and ten minutes after that they were naked in her bed, two navy suits with white shirts lying together on the floor, instantly forgotten along with office concerns.

"We're more like a pair of desperate teenagers than a respectable middle-aged couple, grabbing time alone together around your two's busy schedules," Jack had said, in mock-complaint.

Polly, laughing, hit him. "I am not middle-aged."

He held her to him, flattening her breasts against him, then grabbed the duvet and pulled it up to their shoulders. "You feel pretty good, for an old bird."

She rubbed her cheek against his chest affectionately. She loved lying like that. "You too, for an old git." They were quiet, languorous, for a minute. "Besides, you like doing it in the afternoon."

He chuckled. "I can't deny it. It feels kind of naughty."

It felt kind of wonderful, lying there with him. Peaceful. The evenings were getting lighter, and warmer. She hadn't closed her bedroom curtains, and the sky was a wonderful color. She felt loved and desired and, she realized, looked after. She hadn't felt that way for a long time before Jack: she had almost made herself believe she didn't need to.

"Come on, get up. They'll be here in a bit. Danny and Cress might be even sooner."

Jack stirred reluctantly, kissed the top of her head and slapped her bottom playfully. "I've every right to be here, enjoying my fiancée."

"Not on a reading-group night you haven't. What are you going to do with yourself tonight?"

With affected melancholy, Jack began to dress. "Go back to my empty house, eat a TV dinner, I suppose. I'm taking my wine home with me, incidentally. I don't know, a guy comes round with a bottle of wine, gets stripped off, used, abused and thrown out again before he's even had a glass."

She rubbed his head as she passed him at the foot of the bed. "You'll live."

They talked while they got dressed. Sex with Jack was bloody fantastic, but chatting while you got dressed, not minding if you looked a bit ungainly as you put your feet into your knickers or had to yank a bit on your zip was pretty marvelous too.

"Are you going to tell your friends tonight?"

"About Cress? No. Suze knows already, of course, but not the others." She saw the question in Jack's face. "It's not that I'm ashamed of her, just that, well, there's nothing to tell, is there, yet? No story, I mean. I can't just say, 'My daughter's pregnant.' People expect details. What's she going to do, that kind of thing. I don't know, do I?" she finished bleakly.

Jack kissed her softly, tucking a curl behind one ear. "So don't tell them. No need, tonight." She stood still, with her arms by her sides; she looked so young to him in this light. He held her to him gently. "It's going to be all right, you know."

She wanted to believe him. "Promise?"

"Promise." They stood that way for ages, half dressed, his arms round her in the fading light.

"I think she is definitely the most vivid, most extraordinary woman character I can ever remember reading. Paula Spencer. She's an alcoholic, she's an abused wife, she's a mother—she's unbelievable."

"Now, here's a question for you, Harry . . . How do you explain a man writing that?"

"I can't. I kept thinking that all the way through. How could a man know those things, understand those feelings?"

"Totally. And so sad. I read the whole thing in an evening, with this incredible ache across my chest. It's the saddest, saddest story."

"It sort of made my head ache, too. She jumps about all over the place—it was really hard to get the time sequence right—the dialogue is difficult to keep up with, and she repeats herself, all the time."

"She's disoriented, isn't she? She's drunk, and she's grieving, and she's trying to put the story together."

"I thought it was like an epic poem. The repetition and stuff were just part of that. It's a monologue. I found myself saying bits of it out loud to myself, in this dodgy Dublin accent."

"Me too."

"I thought there was too much swearing. I'm a bit of a puritan for that. I can't watch a film, either, if it's the F-word and the C-word all the time. It gets in the way for me."

"Oh, I just forgot about that after a while. It's just how Paula speaks, isn't it?"

"I think the reviewer, the one they quote on the cover, is wrong. He says it's a 'loveless marriage.' I thought it was anything but. That's the real sadness of it. She'd have walked years ago, if she hadn't still loved him."

"I think it's brilliant, the way it makes you understand her love for him and then puts it against a backdrop of abuse. It's totally instant and physical and all-consuming, her love for Charlo, isn't it?"

"Even though in the eyes of the world he's nothing special—and, in fact, his death, as a failed kidnapper in a bungled raid, a masked buffoon, underlines that, doesn't it?"

"But at the dance, when she's watching him, and she says about him smoking—'He took the fag from his mouth—I could feel the lip coming part of the way before letting go'—that chemical reaction. And on their honeymoon, discovering sex, really, really wanting him. It puts the abuse in such a brilliant context. I don't think I've ever got so close to understanding how women stay with men who abuse them as I did reading this."

"Yeah, she keeps on saying it, doesn't she? That he loves her, loved her right until the end."

"How could you love someone and give them a choice—left or right—as to which of your little fingers they would break?"

"Or believe someone who loved you could do that to you, to anyone?"

"It's the worthlessness she feels. That's what got me. Even in her cleaning job. She breaks her back, cleaning these offices all night, and she says she's 'a vital cog in the machine, and none of the other cogs have even seen me.'"

"And about the alcoholism, she says, 'I've never admitted it to anyone. (No one would want to know.)' That's tragic, isn't it?"

"And the beatings . . . when she's in church and at the shops with all those horrible injuries, 'Ask me ask me ask me. Broken nose, loose teeth, cracked ribs.' It's like she's invisible or something."

"Didn't you think it was interesting that the final straw for her was when she thought he was going to go for her daughter? She never worked up the courage to do anything about him when it was just her—it was only when she thought one of her kids was in danger that she finally stopped the cycle, the one that had started in her own home."

. . .

Susan was helping Polly stack the dishwasher. clare was in the bathroom. Harriet smiled at Nicole. "Makes Gavin look like a dream husband, doesn't he, that Charlo?"

"Stop it." Nicole wasn't angry, but sometimes she was more in the mood to knock him than she was tonight. She poured another glass of wine—Harriet was driving her home and Gavin was away tonight—what did it matter? Soon she would be dry for nine months: better make the most of it now.

She'd been thinking about him, though, reading the book. He'd never laid a hand on her, of course—he was nothing like the character Paula described. It wasn't that. It was more to do with the way Paula tried to carry on believing the best, that he loved her, that he was sorry. When she talked about keeping the house and the kids spotless, about putting on lipstick, it was "to prove to him. I was worth it, worth loving." Was that what Nicole was doing? And the way he looked at her, after he'd hit her, like he was sorry and like he did love her—the look that made it possible for you to believe, and keep believing, and for the cycle to continue. That *was* the same, however much she wanted not to think so. And the hurt. Paula said that she had "holes in her heart that never stop killing" her. Nicole had those holes.

It wasn't going to end like that for her, though. She wasn't going to throw Gavin out. She wouldn't need to. It wouldn't come to that.

"Can I give you a ride home?" Susan offered. Clare's car was in the garage.

Clare shook her head. "No, don't worry. I'll catch the bus. It goes from the end of the road."

"Bus?" As far as Harriet was concerned, Clare might as well have said "rocket." She hadn't been on a bus for years. If you couldn't get there practically as the crow flew in a four-wheel drive, she had no interest in going.

"Don't be daft." Susan was being bossy now. "It's no trouble, honestly."

"Thanks, then," Clare mumbled, into her coat collar.

She's a funny one, Harriet thought. She gets pretty animated when we're talking about a book, and she can couch her opinions and thoughts in the abstract, but then goes quiet again. Prefers to listen.

They said good night to the others, and Clare followed Susan to her car a little way up the road.

It wasn't until Susan had started the engine and indicated to pull out that Clare said, "I'm not going home. I'm staying at Mum's tonight. Dad's away, you see, and I said I'd keep her company." It all came out in one breath.

Mary hadn't said anything about being on her own, but something in the tilt of Clare's head stopped Susan questioning her. She drove on in silence for a few minutes, but silence wasn't a natural state for Susan, and she dredged around for something to say. "It was good this month, wasn't it? We seem to be really finding our stride."

Clare nodded. "I really liked the book. *Liked* isn't the right word, I suppose, but I'm glad I read it."

"Me too. Another world. Makes you think." Susan shuddered. "I wasn't sure what I'd make of the reading group, when Harriet first suggested it. I suppose I didn't think I'd be any good at it. Never was much good at school, not at English anyway."

"I wasn't either. I thought everyone would be dead clever, and that I wouldn't have anything to say." She smiled at Susan now. "I only came because Mum made me," she confessed. "Ridiculous, isn't it? A grown woman doing what she's told by her mum."

"I'm still telling my two what to do—trying to, at least."

Clare didn't know how much Susan knew about her, how much Mary had told her. "It's just that, well, you probably know how much Mum does for me, and I think she . . . Well, I just did it to make her happy. She thinks having an outside interest will make things easier for me."

"Hopes, not thinks. I think your mum just wants you to . . ." Susan didn't know how to finish the sentence. Wants you to have the baby you want. Wants it so bad for her that she'd carry it herself if she could.

"I know. . . . She wants me to keep busy. She's been brilliant. That's why I came—it was something I could do for her."

"I'm glad you did."

"Me too." Clare dug her hands deep down in her pockets and smiled broadly.

She seems so young, Susan thought. Younger even than Ed and Alex. Infertility was clearly one of those things, like cancer, a cheating husband or a parent with Alzheimer's, to be whispered about, not referred to overtly.

She wanted to talk to Clare about it, but she knew she had no right. She had two gorgeous, strapping sons. Why would Clare want to talk to her?

Cressida and Polly

Cressida hadn't shown anyone the picture they had given her at the hospital. She kept it in her wallet, under her student-union card. The name BRADFORD was written in black type along the side of the scan that stuck out above the plastic of the card—every time she looked at it she felt affirmed. BRADFORD. BABY BRADFORD.

Now it was time to talk to Polly. It was a Saturday: Jack had taken Daniel to the football, so it was just the two of them at home. Polly had been up for some time and doubtless thought that Cressida was still asleep, head under the duvet. Instead she was fully dressed, sitting on the edge of her bed with the scan image in her hand. She ran one finger speculatively across it, slipped it into the back pocket of her jeans and went to face her mother.

Downstairs, Polly heard Cressida moving about and poured another mug of coffee from the cafetière. She was desperate for a conversation but determined not to let it show. "Good morning, darling. You're up."

"Morning, Mum." Cressida sat down in front of the mug Polly had put for her on the kitchen table. "Can we talk?"

"Of course, sweetheart."

"By which I mean to say, can *I* talk? I've been doing a lot of thinking, and I've got some stuff sorted out in my head, and I just want to tell you. I don't want to fight, I really couldn't bear it. So can I talk, and can you listen?"

Polly was impressed by her calm, and could see that Cressida had put a lot of thought into that speech. "Okay." Anyway, she had no choice—her daughter was holding all the cards. Jack had made her see that.

"Right. First of all, I wanted you to know that I'm pretty sure Joe and I have split up."

Polly was shocked. It was not what she had been expecting to hear.

"Things haven't been going well the whole time he's been in Warwick, and when he came home at Christmas, well, things had just changed between us. I suppose it was bound to happen, with him going off and starting this whole new life and everything."

She looked at Polly, must have seen the question in her face, but couldn't bring herself to hold the gaze while she answered: "No, it's nothing like that—he hasn't met anyone else."

As she said it she realized two things: first that she had no idea whether he had met anyone else or not, and second, that she really hoped he had. Someone nice and simple.

"It had just run its course, that's all. I think it fizzled out, and I think we both admitted it, that last night before he went back. I haven't spoken to him since."

Polly didn't know what to think. Was that why Cressida was so desperate for him not to know? Was she afraid he would think she was trying to trap him? She hadn't thought that might be it, although of course, now, it made perfect sense—this happened to most kids their age, didn't it, when they went off to college? Poor Cress. Polly wondered if she had done the right thing in encouraging her daughter to stay at home when all her mates were leaving for their new lives. Had she just been selfish?

Cressida was still talking: "And I'm okay about that. Really I am."

"Good." Polly leant across and touched Cressida's arm. "I'm sorry about that, love."

"It's okay." A deep breath. "And the second thing, well, I've decided to keep it. I'm going to have this baby." She was looking not at Polly when she said it but at the pine table. Now she raised her head, looked straight at her mother. Her voice was stronger than she felt. "Whatever you say, Mum, I'm going to have this baby. Don't ask me why. I just think it's the only option I have. I've thought about the others, believe me, and this is the only one that feels right. And it would be easier, and nicer, if you were on my side. So, please, be on my side, Mum?"

It was a question.

What could she say? Polly looked at the girl-woman sitting across from her, and a montage of memories passed through her mind. All the times she'd been on Cressida's side. The colic nights of pacing and pacifying, the first day at school, concerts and sports days, when she was passed over for party invitations, or had spots, and when the friendships and exams came out right. All those times. Where else could she be but on Cressida's side? She nodded and got up. She needed to be touching her now. Mother and child. And child. She folded her in a hug that lasted for ages. When they broke apart, both wet-eyed, Polly realized that a stillness, a sort of peacefulness, had descended on them that had been missing since she'd found out about the baby. That phase was over.

Now Cressida pulled the scan picture out of her pocket and proffered it. Polly took it and realized that, for the first time, she was looking at her grandchild. This was her baby's baby. It was scary, and it was not what was supposed to happen, but here it was anyway.

"Oh!" was all she could say.

"I know," Cressida said. And so the new phase began.

Dear Joe

I am so very sorry about Christmas. I know things were rubbish between us, and I owed you an explanation, for lots of things. I was a coward for not talking to you then, and maybe I am a coward for writing to you now. But I can't come to Warwick—it would be too weird, and I'm sure it's the last thing you want, or it will be after you've read this.

I'm not writing this to hurt you. Please don't think that. I want you to know, from me, not from anyone else, what's going on with me. But it will hurt you, I know. And I'm sorry for that.

I'm pregnant, Joe, about four months. You don't know the father, I promise you don't. I don't know if that helps. I was seeing him last term, while you were at Warwick. That's why I didn't come up and visit you. I shouldn't have done it, not behind your back, and I won't blame you if you never want to talk to me again. I suppose I thought you might finish with me, once you got there and met a whole new crowd. That would have been easier, in a way. I'll always be ashamed for having done this to you—I hope it's not like me, but I suppose it must be. I think I love him, the father. I did love you, I loved you for years, since we were kids. But maybe that's the whole point—maybe what we had was never meant to be a grown-up thing. I'll always love you, although I know that's a trite thing to say and you probably think it's bollocks. But I will. You made being a teenager great for me. This probably sounds awful, but I'm glad we never had sex. What we had was brilliant without that. Do you know what I mean? Look, I don't know what's going to happen with this guy. I just do know that I can't get rid of the baby, or give it away or anything. I'm going to have it, and look after it. I don't expect you to care, and that's fair enough.

And I don't blame you for whatever horrible things you think or say about me. I just wanted to tell you myself. And I just want you to be okay. I'm sorry, Joe, about everything.

Maybe I'll see you again sometime, when you're home. I hope so, but I understand if you don't want to.

Lots of love
Cressida
xx

Joe shoved the letter into his coat pocket. He berated himself for opening it in the porter's lodge. He ought to have known it was a Dear John, after the Christmas thing, although he could never have guessed how devastating its contents would be. It was just that he'd seen the envelope, and her handwriting, in that silly jade green ink she insisted on using, and he'd been so pleased.

Bloody, bloody hell. It was so enormous he didn't know which bit of the news to grab on to first. She'd been seeing someone else. She'd been sleeping with him. That hurt more than Joe had ever been hurt. He had always thought that that would be him, that they would do that together. Hours and hours they'd spent kissing, clothing askew, on each other's sofas, on park benches, at the cinema, stopping short, although it had half killed them both. Cressida always said she wanted it to be special and deliberate, not clandestine and furtive. In a bed, she said: "In a bed we're allowed to be in, in a place we choose to be, when it's right." And he'd respected that. He'd waited. There were boys, he knew loads of them, who wouldn't have bothered. Joe could have had sex with someone else. But he never had. He wanted to make love with Cressida. And he could wait. It caused him acute pain to realize that someone else must have been more special to her. Someone else had been right, and she had chosen his bed. He closed his eyes against the image of her, naked, her skin against that of a faceless man, who wasn't him, but he couldn't make it go away.

And pregnant. Oh, my God. That he could not grasp. Two minutes ago Cressida had been a virgin. Now she was going to have a baby. Someone else's baby. It was too big for his head to hold.

Christ, don't let me cry here. A few yards away the rugby team were tossing a ball around. In front of him a couple of pretty second-year girls were chatting. Not in front of everyone. Joe hauled on his backpack and dug his fingers, white-knuckled, in his palms. Let me get back to my room first, he pleaded with himself. Across here, in this door, up here. Why was he so shocked? He had known things weren't going well—he had even begun to consider what it would be like not to be with her and to be with someone else—someone here. He had imagined having a girlfriend he could see every day, in Grumpy John's at the union, at lectures. He took the stairs two at a time, head down, not stopping until he got to the third floor. Nearly there. People had propped open their doors with chairs, and someone had a radio on. A couple of the girls he shared the kitchen with were dancing in front of the toaster when he went past. One was Issie. "Hiya, Joe. Want some toast?"

"I'm fine."

She came up to him, looked at him hard. "You're not, though, are you?" She put her hand on his arm. That felt better than being alone in his room.

He could talk to Issie. He *wanted* to talk to her. Out here, he trusted himself only to shake his head.

"Here." She steered him through her door, and shut it behind them.

Margaret and Alice

The brochures for The Cedars were on the coffee table. Susan had been showing them to her sister, telling her about the other homes she had seen and what she'd liked about this one. She was putting a brave face on it. It had big rooms and high ceilings, she said, a gorgeous view across open fields, and Alice had a room that got the sun most of the day. She hadn't told Margaret how she had cried in the car after she'd visited it. How she had wondered whether it would be kinder to go home and put a pillow over Alice's face than leave her in there. How tiny Alice had looked the day she had moved in, confused and disoriented. And how Susan had come home and sobbed for ages on Roger's chest, blurting that she was a rotten daughter, that she should keep Alice at home.

Roger, always kind, sad, too, for Alice, kept telling her, "You can't. However much you want to, you can't give her the care she needs now. And they can. Please, my love, believe me. This is the only thing you can do for Alice now." She didn't tell Margaret that, either.

"I'll go tomorrow," Margaret said. "That's what I came for, after all."

"Fine. I'm not too busy at work just now so I'll come with you."

"I'd rather go by myself, thanks. Roger said I could borrow the car, didn't he?"

"Yes, of course, but—"

"No buts, Susan. Look, you took the decision to do this to Mum. The least you can do is let me form my own opinion of the place."

That was it. Susan had had enough. She let her sister have it—weeks' and weeks' worth of emotion. "I've had just about enough of this."

Margaret seemed momentarily shocked into submission by Susan's demeanor. "How dare you swan in here and start accusing me? I haven't *done* anything to Mum except the only thing I could do. I can't look after her at home, Maggie. I have Roger and the boys and the business. I have a whole life. Just like you. Mum is sick, Maggie. The old Mum you remember is gone. And that hurts and I miss her and I wish she was still here. But I've had to get used to it, and so will you."

Margaret was quiet, and Susan realized she hadn't seen her sister like this before. When she had gone to Australia, Susan had been the passive, quiet one, but motherhood, work and life had made her tougher. Getting used to what had happened to Alice had made her stronger still—until Margaret had hurled these allegations at her.

She tried to calm herself, to explain it the way Roger had to her. "Look, Maggie, the first couple of strokes changed her. Her memory started to go and she did things like forget she'd put the gas ring on, go out without her coat—things like that. We could cope with that. I've always loved having Mum around, and that stuff wasn't a big deal. Although keeping an eye on her all the time was hard work. But I did it. The big stroke, the one she had the day I called you, when we weren't sure that she'd live, changed everything. She's like a baby. What memory she does have is all warped and out of sync. Sometimes it's the nineteen forties, sometimes I'm *her* mum, sometimes she doesn't know Roger. She needs help to feed herself, wash, use the loo. I can't do it, Maggie, and I won't."

"It's what she did for us, isn't it?"

"Oh, for God's sake, don't be so bloody pious. You think you're immune to all this, don't you? That you can just fly in, tell me what a mess I'm making of it all, then go back to your perfect husband and your perfect life. It doesn't work that way, Maggie. Sorry."

Margaret stood up, signaling an end to the conversation. Susan wanted to hit her. "I'll go tomorrow." Christ, she was infuriating.

At the door, she turned round. "And just for the record, Susan, Greg and I split up ten years ago. He left me for one of my best friends. They'd been having an affair for seven years before that. You don't know as much about my 'perfect life' as you think you do." Then she was gone.

And whose fault is that? Susan thought, as she lay back against the sofa cushion.

The room Margaret was shown into by the vast, bustling care assistant was big, with high ceilings and sash windows. It needed repainting, and the furniture didn't go with it—cheap pine stuff made for box houses on estates: the top of the wardrobe was some inches below the picture rail, and the matching dressing table and two chests of drawers were similarly out of proportion. It all looked vaguely absurd, like children's furniture in an adult room. Only the bed was big, wide and high, white metal, with rails and a red call button twined round the head. Alice had her own bathroom, with a white rail next to the toilet, and along the bath. There was a big cork notice board, on which Susan had pinned smiling pictures of her and Roger, the boys, one of Margaret and Greg on the farm. Margaret was struck by how young she looked in it. There were more pictures on the chest of drawers: Susan in her wedding dress, the boys on child-sized tractors, taken at a long-ago county fair. Above Alice's bed was a picture taken of her and Dad, their fortieth wedding anniversary, his arm proudly round her shoulders. Margaret didn't like pictures of dead people, but she supposed Alice wanted it there. She didn't like the smell either—the watery-cabbage smell of school dinners, and the sharp odor of urine. The whole place filled her with disgust. The patronizing staff, speaking in absurdly loud, slow sentences, made her bristle. And as for the lounge she had passed, well! Each high-backed velour armchair held a tiny ancient person, staring through milky eyes at some inane daytime gardening program on the vast television, probably sitting in their own excrement, waiting . . . God knows what for. There had been a grandchild, or great-grandchild, in the lounge when she passed, screaming to be picked up, terrified, almost certainly, of the old women with paper-thin skin, curled, gnarled fingers and contorted, toothless smiles.

Here, now, in the relative normality of Alice's room, Margaret fought for control of her revulsion, and her urge to bolt. Thank Christ she had insisted on coming alone. For just a second she felt something like pity for Susan—she had been facing this almost daily. Just as quickly, it was quashed. It was Susan who had put their mother in here.

"Here we are now, Alice, a surprise for you. It's your daughter, come all the way from Australia. What do you think about that, then?"

Shut up, shut up, Margaret thought. She sounds like a children's librarian reading a fairy story to toddlers.

And there was Alice. And Margaret was looking at her for the first time in maybe ten years.

What she saw shocked her. Alice was an old lady. She seemed inches shorter. Her shoulders were rounded, and she had an osteoporotic hump at the base of her neck. Her hair was thinner and messy, parted on the opposite side from the one she had always chosen, and through it Margaret could see pink scalp. She couldn't remember seeing her mother without lipstick before— the same Rimmel shade throughout her life—but now her lips were thin, pale and dry. Her cardigan was buttoned up wrongly, and there were crumbs on it.

"Susan?"

"No, Alice. Remember we told you? Not Susan, it's *Margaret*, come from Australia."

Margaret couldn't take that voice anymore. "Thanks. Look, I've got it from here. Perhaps I will have that cup of tea your colleague offered me, after all." Anything to get her out of here.

But as she moved forward to take her mother's arm, Alice looked longingly at the lumpen girl, alarmed.

"It's okay, Mum. I've got you."

Still, Alice seemed confused.

"It's Margaret, Mum. I've flown over from Sydney. Remember?"

The girl was going now. She whispered over Alice's head, "She might not—We're having a bit of trouble with her today." Like a puppy they were trying to house-train.

Margaret nodded, tight-lipped, and the girl was gone. She pulled Alice forward into the room and settled her in her armchair, pushing the wheeling table aside. She took the photograph of her and Greg off the notice board and held it out to Alice. "You know, Mum—Margaret. I married Greg and we went back to Australia, where he was from, more than twenty years ago, now."

"Twenty years?" Alice looked up. "Margaret, yes." She said the name slowly, deliberately.

"That's right. Margaret. How are you, Mum?" She put an arm round Alice, disturbed that her mother didn't smell familiar. Was that just the passage of time?

"Margaret," Alice repeated. "Come back to us at last. All the way from Australia. Your dad will be so pleased to see you. When he gets back from playing golf."

"Golf?"

"Oh, yes, dear. It's all he does since he retired, you know. Eighteen holes, most days. I'm a grass widow, you know." And she chuckled quietly.

Margaret felt ill-equipped to deal with this. She almost wanted the lumpen girl to come back. "Mum? Dad's dead. He died eight years ago. I'm so sorry, Mum."

"Dead, you say? Dad? Oh, no!" And Alice was crying, real tears of loss.

Susan had said that Mum's short-term memory couldn't cope with that news anymore. Every time she heard it, it was new and he had just died. "I don't tell her anymore, Maggie," she had said. "What's the point of putting her through it every time? Let her believe he's out there playing golf."

"That's ridiculous," Margaret had said. "You can't treat her that way." But as she sat holding Alice's small hand, she wished she had listened.

Cressida

She'd never been here before. Never wanted to—had not wanted to admit she was curious. But now here she was. And, like most things lately, she wasn't reacting like she thought she would.

He'd been quiet after he'd picked her up, and he'd driven with her hand under his on the gearstick. She hadn't wanted to ask why they had come here. Sometimes he was quiet like this, and she had learnt, even in the short time they had been seeing each other, that what he wanted from her was comfort, not questions, touching, not talking. At these times she felt as if it was she who was the older one—he could be almost childlike in the simplicity of his needs. And afterward, after she had held him, made love to him, he was different—happy and calm. Funny, too, and interesting.

He'd opened the door with the key in the wrong hand, fumbling, muttering swearwords under his breath, against her neck, as he held her tightly with the other. He was always passionate, always made her feel that he wanted her, but there was a real urgency in him tonight. He seemed almost desperate.

He had made love to her in the living room, on the sofa, on the floor, in the dark—only an orange glow from the street lighting them through the voile curtains. He told her she looked beautiful in that light, perfect and glowing. He traced her mouth with one finger. He moved body, arms, legs, turning them and watching them as they caught the light, following his stare with fingers, lips, as if her body was a thing of wonder to him. He had more time to watch her now, and he luxuriated in it. His lovemaking was extravagant, somehow, and indulgent. He was making her feel like a goddess, like a precious thing. She had loved sex with him before, but this felt like they had moved on to a different level. Like he knew.

What fears Cressida might have had about telling him seemed silly now. He felt tuned in, as if his body knew what she was going to tell him before she had got the words out. At once it felt like a gift.

When they had finished, and their breathing had steadied, and he had pulled a blanket round them where they lay together on the floor, and he had spread his palm, fingers wide, on her smooth, naked belly, she told him: "Elliot, I'm pregnant."

They had met on her first day at college. It had begun not with violin solos and electricity but with a random act of kindness. Cressida was lost and late. Elliot was passing and showed her where to go. That afternoon, once again in the right place at the right time, he held open the door as she labored through it with a big art folder, a rucksack and a couple of hefty library books. "How did it go?"

Cressida was startled by his familiar tone—that morning she had been too nervous and anxious to take in his face or his voice.

"We met this morning," he told her.

"Oh, yeah, sorry. I was a bit . . ."

"I know. I was, when I started."

"But you're not . . ." Elliot didn't look like a student. He was older than she, ten years or so, she thought. And he wasn't dressed in the uniform of every other man within two hundred yards. He looked nice, though.

"Studying here? No, no. I wish! I work in administration. Been here about eight years now."

"Right."

"Right. Well, can you manage that lot from here?"

"Yeah, thanks. And thanks for this morning. I wasn't very organized, I'm afraid. Forgotten all that stuff over the summer. It would have been really embarrassing to be any later than I already was."

"You're welcome."

"'Bye."

"Yeah,'bye."

Five minutes later, he pulled up alongside her in a small red Mazda, as she stopped for the second time to switch her possessions from one arm to the other in an effort to make the load more comfortable. "Look, I'm not being funny but it's going to take you forever, and I can't bear to see you struggling while I sit here in isolated splendor. Can I give you a ride somewhere? I'm heading to the top end of town."

His face was open and friendly. He didn't look like a weirdo, and he worked at the college. And Cressida's arms were aching.

"That would be brilliant. I live on Rosedale Road. D'you know it?"

"Sure do. No problem." And Elliot jumped out to open the passenger door, took her things and put them on the backseat. He seemed so pleased she had said yes. Before he closed the door for her, he said, "I'm Elliot, by the way. Elliot Richards."

"Cressida Bradford." And she beamed at him.

And that was when Elliot had first felt it, suddenly and powerfully, as if he wanted always and only to be in the headlight-bright beam of this girl's carefree smile.

Of course for Cressida it had taken weeks longer. College was so different from the sixth form, full of new people, and the work was so much more interesting than A levels had been. She was horrified, when she stopped to think about it, which wasn't very often, by how little she missed Joe. But she told herself it must be the same for him—more so, with living away from home as well.

She saw plenty of Elliot, chatting in the corridors, or out on the grass in the autumn sunshine. Several times he offered her a lift home, and once or twice, when she wasn't going to the pub with her new mates or meeting Polly, she accepted. One morning he even picked her up at the bus stop.

She liked talking to him: he was funny, told irreverent stories about the lecturers and tutors. She had briefly wondered whether it was all right to spend time with him. But he wasn't a teacher and she wasn't a kid, so what harm could there be in it? But to Cressida, for the first few weeks, he was just one of the new faces in the new crowd. That was all.

She wasn't thinking anything when, one day, the traffic was awful, and he pulled into a pub car park. "Sod that, if we're going to be late, we may as well get out, have a drink and get going again when it's a bit quieter. What do you reckon?"

Quite right. Pubs were a pivotal part of Cressida's college life. She had made almost all her new friends in smoky rooms that smelt of beer where you had to shout to make yourself heard over the trivia machine, the landlord's dodgy CD collection and whichever fight or football match was on the big TV screen.

They talked until the pub shut. Cressida felt herself sparkling. There was suddenly so much to say. They talked about films, the news, art, Cressida's dad and Elliot's parents, about perfect holidays, first records, fantasy dinner parties and . . . everything. They listened to each other, talked over each other, laughed at each other. Liked each other.

Later that night, when Elliot had dropped her off, and Cressida had let herself into the house, she had met Polly in the hall, on her way to bed with a mug of tea. Spontaneously she gave her mum a bear hug. When Polly pulled away, laughing, she said, "I can't tell you how nice it is to see you so happy, love. It's the best thing you've ever done, isn't it, this college course?"

"I think it is, Mum. You're right."

Cressida had found it difficult to go to sleep that night.

She was half expecting to see him at the bus stop the next morning, and she was not disappointed. He leant over and opened the door from the inside.

"Hiya!" she said.

But his face was serious. "What have you got on this morning? Fancy going somewhere first, for a coffee or breakfast or something? I want to talk to you."

"Nothing until ten-thirty, really—I was going to do some reading in the library. Sure, why not?"

Over a toasted tea cake and a huge mug of builder's tea, Elliot took a deep breath and began. "Look, I had a really good time last night . . ."

Oh, God, Cressida thought, he's going to tell me that fraternization between staff and students isn't allowed. We've been breaking the rules.

"I loved being with you. Last night, you know, in the pub. I want to see you more," he said.

Cressida waited for the "but." It came.

"But there's something I need to tell you first. And you probably won't want to see me when I've told you."

Now he was scaring her. "What?"

"I'm married."

"You're what?" No ring. No mention. No photograph on his desk.

"I've been married for ten years."

"Oh."

Elliot carried on with his explanation, looking down at his plate, carefully laying out the facts—his dark confession. "My wife is called Clare. She's a midwife, up at the County."

"Right."

"We've been together since we were kids, really."

Cressida pushed back her chair. "Well, okay. Thanks for telling me. Don't know why you didn't before, really. Or why you are now, for that matter. It's not like we've done anything wrong. Just had a couple of drinks. And a chat." It didn't feel like that, though. She felt like she'd been kicked. And she quite wanted to kick him back. She stood up.

"Listen, don't go, please. I want to tell you about it. We're . . . things aren't great . . . we can't . . ."

"Oh, Elliot, please." Her tone was scathing. "Don't turn into Mr. My Wife Doesn't Understand Me. I think you're better than that, and I know I am. I'll see you." She turned toward the door.

"Cressida, hang on—" He was pulling money out of his pocket. "Please, just let me talk to you about this."

"Nothing to talk about, Elliot. Like I said, I'll see you around." And she was gone.

She didn't see him around for a couple of weeks, almost long enough for her to stop half looking for him. Almost long enough for her to stop thinking about him when she dressed in the morning, wondering if he'd like this sweater, that hairstyle.

She was in a pub one night, karaoke night, with a crowd. One of the guys, a cocksure South African called Rowan, was flirting with her, buying her drinks. She was almost falling for it, too. She let him request a song for them, laughed at the hysteria their crowd generated when their names were called out—"Christ, get a load of these two, Cressida and Rowan—bloody hell, they sound posh. Come on up, you two, you've requested a snazzy little number from *Grease*. Remember this one, 'You're the One That I Want?' Olivia Newton-John in those skintight black trousers. Give it up for Cressida and Rowan . . ."

Rowan, who was a handsome brute, pulled her onto the stage, assumed a John Travolta swagger and began to sing.

"I've got chills, they're multiplying, and I'm losing control."

Cressida glanced away from the autocue—and saw Elliot, standing apart from the crowd, smiling at her. She felt an almost irresistible urge to go to him.

She finished the song, refused to comply with her companion's lurid dance moves and slipped off the stage, leaving Rowan Travolta to soak up the applause.

They talked, then, in his car. It was getting colder outside, and he had to put the heating on, so the windows steamed up. Elliot talked. And Elliot cried. And he said that he hated himself, his life and his weakness. But that she had to believe this had never happened to him before. He didn't know whether it was because he'd given up on him and Clare, reached the end of his tether, or whether it was just that she was so lovely. But he couldn't help it. He hadn't meant to come tonight, just as he hadn't been at the bus stop, or on campus. He had tried to stay away. But he needed to be where she was—God, he must sound pathetic, but even if nothing happened between them, could she not hate him, not judge him, not never let him be where she was.

And so it had begun. Cressida couldn't quite believe that she was doing it. She could hear Polly's voice—"Did I not teach you more sense than that?" She had watched her own parents' marriage fall apart. And part of her hated how weak she was—but a much bigger part had taken over. She told herself all sorts of things. It was amazing how you could make things sound okay, justify your behavior, make it possible to live with yourself. She wasn't cheating on Clare, Elliot was. She wasn't cheating on Joe—who knew what he might be up to at Warwick? Elliot and Clare were married in name only. Elliot couldn't leave her when she was so sad. All the clichés, and all the lies suddenly sounded believable. For a few days, a week or so, after that time outside the pub, whenever they met, they talked about Clare and Elliot. He told her everything: about the babies they'd lost, the treatment, and further back than that, about when they had been Cressida's age, and how simple it had all been then. And Cressida knew that what he saw in her was the people they had been, before life got so messed up for them. She was the blank canvas they had been before they got all Jackson Pollocked by life.

And when the talking part was over, and she thought she understood, Cressida went home alone one night and made her decision. She was going to do it anyway: she was going to be involved with Elliot.

The next time they met they made love. They parked his car, took a blanket from the boot and walked for twenty minutes or so without talking. Then they took off some of each other's clothes and lay down together. The watery sun was warm on their skin.

Cressida was nineteen years old, and it was her first time. And it was what she wanted. In unspoken agreement, they never talked about Clare again.

And now she had told him. She had tried not to think about how incredibly potent this information would be for Elliot, because to do so would be to acknowledge Clare and the tragedy of her childlessness, and she didn't want to do that, not now.

But as soon as she had said it, lying here in Clare's barren house, it hit her. He didn't speak. His first reaction had been to snatch away his hand from her stomach, as though it was red-hot, and to sit up. He propped his elbows on his knees and hid his face in his hands. He looked vulnerable, naked, like that. His skin was so pale under his arms that it looked almost translucent, and she could see the blue veins beneath the skin. She didn't know what he was thinking. For the first time it felt cold on the floor, and a bit uncomfortable. She pulled herself up and sat beside him, careful not to touch him, although she wanted to reach out.

When Elliot lifted his face, it was wet with tears. He was laughing and crying and shaking his head all at once. He still hadn't spoken, but now he pulled her onto his lap and cradled her in his arms.

Nicole and Gavin

Venice was surely the most amazing city in the world. The sight that greeted you when your water taxi rounded the last bend in the lagoon was the most delightful thing she had ever seen. She'd been to Venice in the summer, when it was overcrowded and whiffy; she'd been in the depths of winter, InterRailing when she was a student and it was so cold that you felt your feet might shatter if you stepped too hard on the pavement. But spring was definitely her favorite time. This morning the sky was a perfect blue, and the water was just lapping against the pavement. Nicole laughed.

Five minutes earlier she and Gavin had been entangled in a white linen sheet sideways across their mammoth hotel bed. She had just given him, if she said so herself, a hell of a good time, and she was lying back against the pillows, her hair tangled, the sheet covering one breast, triumphant. Gavin looked at her, then jumped off the bed. "I want a picture of you, looking just like that. Don't move."

He grabbed the camera.

Nicole giggled. "You what?"

"I want to remember you with that cat-that-got-the-cream expression on your face." He clicked. The flash made her blink.

"I reckon this is how all the artists got their best pictures, don't you? Leonardo probably gave the Mona Lisa a jolly good seeing-to just before he painted her."

"Interesting theory . . . What do you think Munch did?"

"Rogered them senseless."

They were both laughing now.

"Or Picasso!"

"Now you're really getting kinky."

He was still holding the camera. "No, not good enough . . ." And now he was jumping into his trousers, no underpants, pulling a sweater over his head. "I need to capture the location as well. You"—and he pulled at her arms—"come and stand here, just like that, perfect, and wait there just a minute, just as you are." And off he rushed with the camera.

So now here she was, naked but for a sheet, hair all over the place, standing at the window just above the *a* in Danieli, in the foot-high gold letters on the hotel wall. And down there on the pavement was Gavin, looking similarly tousled but very tall, almost lost in a crowd of Japanese tourists, taking her photograph.

This weekend was turning out to be everything she had wanted. Gavin was back, they were back. And it was just as funny, and as close, and as sexy and as right as it always had been.

It felt to Nicole as if her marriage was a roller coaster, a white-knuckle ride. Here, at the top, the moments were perfect, and you could never remember how sudden, swift and petrifying the drops were. If you could, you'd never get back on the ride for a second turn. At the top, you'd say anything was worth it for the view, and the way your heart soared, and when you were at the bottom you'd do anything to be on the carousel instead. Nicole was sure she'd stolen that metaphor from a film, but it was exactly right. And, oh, how she was enjoying this ride. Maybe there would be no drop around the corner this time.

She lay down on the bed to wait for Gavin's return, put both hands on her stomach and wondered if she was pregnant already . . . she squeezed her eyes shut in a silent wish. The first time, with the twins, she had felt she knew the minute it happened. Gavin had laughed when she said so, told her she was confused by the quality of his lovemaking. But a couple of weeks later, before she had reason to do a test, he had watched her one morning walk naked across their bedroom, and he had known it too. "You're pregnant!" he had said. And she knew she was. Even though she had joked with him that he was just trying to tell her she was getting fat, they had both felt it.

She couldn't have said the same with Martha—she had been exhausted by the incessant demands of two small boys (and one big one). She was too exhausted to plan a seduction, let alone a pregnancy and, apparently, far too exhausted to take her mini contraceptive pill at the same time each day. The twins weren't even two when she became pregnant, and she would have liked to have waited a little longer.

Gavin, in alpha-male style, was terribly proud of her fecundity—or, rather, his ability to make her pregnant, chemical intervention notwithstanding. He deflected all her worries about not being able to cope. "Look, sweetheart, we'll just hire people. I'm doing well at the firm, so we can afford it. Stop worrying, be a lady of leisure, for God's sake. Be a cottage industry." And he made her hire someone to do the cleaning and the ironing, and to look after the children, and she learnt to be a lady of leisure—and that he thought she should be grateful that he paid, uncomplainingly, for all of these blessings. But, still, she looked at Martha and the boys, and she felt guilty. Especially about Martha: the boys had each other, but she worried that she hadn't spent enough time with her daughter.

Harriet pooh-poohed that. "Cut yourself some slack, for Chrissakes. Those children adore you. You're the original yummy mummy, all slim and glamorous, and quality time–ish. Why should you feel so damn guilty because you get someone else to do the Play-Doh and the snot? Madonna's never changed a nappy in her life, but do you think her kids are going to hold it against her?" Harriet was a fount of knowledge when it came to showbiz trivia, and fond of using celebrity examples to justify civilian acts.

Gavin was even less patient about her guilt. "Don't you dare stop going to the gym because you think the boys need you. What they need is a mother their friends all fancy when they're in senior school."

At the book club last month they had got onto the subject of mothers feeling guilt and mothers condemning their children to repeat their own lives. They had all agreed that guilt and worry came with your milk, and stayed. Polly had looked at the young mothers and said, "And, believe me, the older they get, the worse it is." A cheering thought.

This time might be different, though, Nicole thought. The boys and Martha were at school. She had more time, felt more confident about how to be a mother, less tired. This baby could be perfect for all of them. Martha would love it—she was passionate about Baby Annabelle, a battered plastic doll who had to go everywhere with her own miniature equipment—what fun she would have with the real thing. And Gavin loved his kids. She knew that. Whatever else those other women gave him, she was the only one who had ever given him a child. That title was hers and hers alone.

Gavin ran in, pulled off his sweater and jumped at her. "What more can a man ask? A hot woman in a warm bed! Got the energy for one more before lunch?"

"You'd better make it a quickie—you've promised me a Bellini at Harry's Bar."

He looked at her in mock anger. "I, Mrs. Thomas, do not do 'quickies.' I am strictly a quality and quantity man, I'm afraid."

"Well"—he was kissing her ear, exactly as she liked it—"I suppose Harry could wait."

Gavin groaned. "Yes, I think he fucking well can."

Later that afternoon they phoned the kids on his mobile from St. Mark's Square. Martha wanted to know about the pigeons, George whether they were bored of looking at churches, and William whether they had bought him a present and if he and his brother were allowed to watch *Buffy the Vampire Slayer* before bed.

"No, we jolly well haven't. And, no, you jolly well can't, cheeky devil. Go on then, ten minutes. But then straight to bed, no nonsense. You promise?" Gavin laughed. "I love you too. Give each other big kisses from both of us. See you Sunday. Bye-bye."

"They sound fine, don't they?" Nicole asked, as he put an arm round her and they started walking.

"Yes, mother hen." He kissed her cheek. "You're a great mum, you know?"

She didn't remember him saying that before. She crossed her fingers in her pocket, made her mantra wish again. Please let me be pregnant. Please.

Harriet and Tim

Harriet had been trying to hide it, even though he would of course see it eventually. He had usually showered, dressed and gone while she was still in bed, propped against pillows, drinking tea he made for her, and the children, usually Chloe first, the early bird, then Joshua, woken unwillingly by the noise of the house coming to life, would have crawled in beside her to watch cartoons as he left. Not this morning, though: he had an early appointment in the center of town with their accountants, some pension thing or other, he had told Harriet, although she had forgotten, and so he could hang around, drop Josh at school for her.

When she remembered it now it irritated her, as everything about him did. She could hear the low hum of Radio 4's *Today* program from his shower room, its somber tones fighting with the talking badger the kids were watching. Even his own tea, next to hers on the bedside table, got up her nose: he usually grabbed a coffee at the station. The reality was that she liked him being gone. She was happy to deal with his washing and his dry cleaning, his shoe repairs, and his paperwork, and even his phone calls home during the day. She just wasn't happy with him here in the flesh. Poor sod. She knew it was rotten, but she couldn't help it. And now he was going to see it. Six nights running she'd gone to bed in her knickers, which, these days, was not unusual, so he hadn't spotted it then.

The novelty of Daddy being home at this time had roused Chloe and won out over the television. She had sat on the deep windowsill and watched him shave, and now she was "helping" him get dressed, asserting with all the fervor a four-year-old can muster that, yes, the pink tie was the only choice. Her fringe was growing out and, in the early morning, before the tangles had been teased out and the hair elastic eased in, she had to tip her head right back to see out. Tim disappeared, came back with a hairband from her bedroom, got down to her level and pushed it gently behind her ears, stopping to kiss her nose. Then he folded her into a lung-flattening squeeze.

"What have you lot got planned for today, then?"

"Same old same old," Harriet muttered grumpily. "Two school runs, a ballet class, a big food shop, oh, and some laundry—five loads or so, just for fun."

Tim looked like she'd smacked him. The implication was so clearly that all this domesticity was his fault. He was not foolish enough to suggest that she get some more help—he had learnt that Harriet wasn't interested in solutions, although he would gladly employ a whole army to relieve her if he might get back the sparkly, funny girl he'd married as a result. He was afraid—no, he knew—that the housework, and the child care and the other things she moaned about weren't what she wanted to change. And that was not a place he wanted to go. So he said, "Sorry, love. I should have remembered." Answer the unspoken accusation. He turned to Chloe. "Ballet today, is it, darling? Are you going to wear your blue or your pink for Miss Polly?"

"Pink. Pink. Pink." Chloe pirouetted, her standard response to every question.

"What about you, Joshie? Football training after school today, is it?"

Josh answered without turning his head from the television. "Yeah. Mr. Cuthbert said he might give me a go in midfield this week."

"Great. Good job we had that practice in the park at the weekend. You give him what for!"

Josh smiled. "Yeah, I will. Thanks, Dad."

Then Tim turned to watch Harriet on her way to the bathroom. He loved watching how she walked. The extra weight she was carrying only made her more desirable—her bum wiggled. It always had.

Chloe's had the same lines in miniature. He loved that, the way Chloe's bum proved she was Harriet's daughter—he was forever looking at his kids to see himself—those genetic characteristics that stamped Joshua and Chloe undeniably, publicly as his. Harriet didn't like him watching her, though. Not anymore. She made him feel like a bit of a pervert sometimes. "You're sex-mad, you are." She said that every time he tried to initiate something between them. Or "You must be joking, mate. After the day I've had?" When she did submit, and that was what it felt like, never like she really, really wanted to, she always made him switch off the lights. She said she didn't want him to see her wobbly bits. He thought maybe she didn't want him to see her eyes. Once he'd run his hand across her face, in the middle of it, wanting to be tender, and they'd been screwed tight shut.

Then he saw the tattoo. Left cheek, bottom right. Just inside where underwear would go. He could see the faint, browny white line from where her swimsuit had ended last summer, and it was on the white. It was a small, pretty butterfly, black in outline, with just blue and green, stained-glass shades with the tiny wings. It had healed completely—she must have had it a week.

Suddenly Tim felt sick. He saw Harriet watching him. She stuck her chin up, defiant, but there was a tremor in her voice as she said, "I got it last week. Some guy in Kingston did it for me. He was recommended. All clean needles and everything—they're not like they used to be, these places. All government-controlled and everything. Tattoos are popular now, loads of people are getting them."

Actually a tattoo hadn't been her first choice. She'd wanted a navel ring—she thought they looked stunning. But a frank session in front of their mirror had convinced her that a jewel in her navel, stretched strange by pregnancy, flanked by two silver stretch marks and dimpled with wobbly flesh, would (a) be very hard to find anyway, and (b) make people feel sick. So a tattoo it had been, the butterfly. And wasn't that what she was doing—coming out of the chrysalis, finding her beautiful wings? Actually it was the prettiest design the guy had on the wall. Even Harriet thought the little devil was tacky. She didn't want some Beckhamesque Celtic or Oriental symbol that purported to mean "love and eternal peace" but might just as likely say "kick me here." The dove was cute, but an extra stone in weight could easily turn it into an albatross (around your ass, not your neck) or a pelican. The weight thing could have been avoided by putting it on her ankle or shoulder, but she couldn't imagine crossing her legs at parents' evening or ever again wearing something strapless to one of Nicole's pompous charity-type dos with one there. So bum it was. And she was bloody pleased with it—it made her feel naughty and empowered—although it had hurt like buggery and, on the humiliation scale, ranked right up there with cervical smears. Although they were not, in her experience, performed by exceptionally good-looking, snake-hipped men called Troy. Troy, the tattoo "artiste," had worn a very tight T-shirt proclaiming that he "doesn't play well with others," which Harriet did not for one minute believe, and had referred to her bum as a "great canvas," which Harriet had thought was quite possibly the nicest thing anyone had ever said about it.

It had all been worth it. Even though Tim's face was making her feel less like a Spice Girl and more like Delilah by the minute. Well, she wasn't going to think about it. It was her bum; to graffiti or not to graffiti it was entirely up to her. It didn't mean anything, did it, anyway?

Did he have to stand there looking all bruised? Tim stirred himself, looking at the kids, who were absorbed in Naomi the Origami Queen. "Fair enough." He came closer, bent down. Harriet made herself stand still. "I quite like it, actually. Suits you."

Which was the biggest lie he had ever told her.

All day, through the meeting at Baker Tilly, in the first-class compartment of the train, across *The Times* leader page, at a sober lunch in Corney & Barrow, against the screen of his computer and even superimposed over the image of his smiling family, gilt-edged security in their frame on his desk, a tiny butterfly laughed scornfully at him.

Harriet and Nick

It was uncomfortable holding a mobile phone under your ear and against your shoulder. Last year, in her stocking, Tim had given her a hands-free unit for it, "so you can talk to Nicole for eighteen hours a day, instead of the sixteen you currently manage," but she knew that he knew she talked on the phone in the car on the school run, and she figured he was worried about Joshua and Chloe. Not that she used it. People wandering around apparently talking to themselves looked like care-in-the-community candidates. Or like ball-breaking career women still cherishing the dialogue from *Wall Street*. Not that she would pass for a career woman, ball-breaking or not, in a mac with a greasy handprint down one side and what looked suspiciously like snot on the other shoulder. She looked every inch the harassed young mother. Except that she wasn't in the yogurt section of the supermarket, she was in the lingerie department at John Lewis, oh yes, where she was looking for underwear to dispel the image of the mac. Not the sensible nonwired items in the color they laughingly called "flesh," or the big pants that weren't supposed to show under trousers, but the stuff with brand names that suggested sex—Passionata, Silhouette, Fantasie, Rigby & Peller. Well, perhaps Rigby didn't exactly suggest sex, but my God the knickers did. Well, okay, that particular pair of knickers was actually just three bits of lace sewn together, and suggested yeast infection, but you get the picture.

Harriet was shopping for sin, and she was on the phone to Nick, having a conversation that she would later describe to herself in the Dear Diary internal monologue she had been forced to adopt since Nicole had made her feelings on the subject known as strictly X-rated.

"Oooh," Nick was saying, in a not at all Jack from *Will & Grace* way. "Tell me more."

"Black?"

"Black's good. Black and small."

"Lacy."

"Lacy's good. Transparent's better."

It was a whole new world. Boyfriends before Tim hadn't taken much notice, they were usually in a rush to get it off you. Except for one who'd clearly seen too many Sharon Stone films and liked her to start the evening with nothing on underneath. Oh, and one who, again, was clearly under some celluloid influence and had ripped a pair of pants off her—which, since they had been new, and not cheap, had proved not erotic but extremely irritating. Charlie hadn't been averse to a bit of a floor show but was just as happy to jump her straight after hockey training in her sweaty gray gear. Tim had always liked her naked. Or in white cotton. But best naked. Nick clearly liked things a little different—she got the feeling nippleless and crotchless might be right up his street, although she drew the line at those. Silly.

"Shut up, you dirty sod." Harriet had seen the tiny, clenched saleswoman eyeing her distastefully. "What are you calling me for?"

"You know what."

She did indeed. "I've told you. No."

"I heard the words, but I didn't believe them. I can also hear the longing in your voice—to say yes."

"You are one arrogant bastard, Nick. Do you know that?"

"Oh, yes. So remind me, then, why not?"

"I cannot come away with you. I am a married woman. With children. And a life."

"Great! So there's a husband to look after the children while you come away with me. And it's not so much of a life that you haven't been seeing me for weeks now."

"Seeing you is one thing. Going away for a weekend is another altogether." Which it was. So far there had been laughing and kissing, and last week, what might be described as fondling, but a weekend meant bed and sex. Scary, and exciting and . . . scary and . . . exciting.

"Which is why I want to do it. Come on, Hats, you know you want it."

His pantomime City-boy lines didn't grate. She was feeling persuaded.

"I know you. I remember how . . . resourceful you can be. You can make this happen. If you want to."

He didn't know her, of course. That was the whole point. She hadn't ever thought of herself as particularly resourceful and wasn't sure what student endeavor he was referring to, if any. But she could make it happen. She'd figured all that out ages ago. She had a friend in Norfolk, Sally, who had been trying to get her to come and visit for ages. She and Tim had avoided it because Sally's kids were much older than Josh and Chloe. And obnoxious. And because Sally had cream linen furniture. And Tim hated her husband, Ian, who was a pompous git in property development, whose opening conversational gambit with anyone he ever met was "What's your gaff worth, then?" She could say she was giving in to Sally. Agreeing to meet her somewhere, maybe a health farm. No danger whatsoever of Tim ringing Ian to check. And the beauty of mobiles was that you never had to give contact numbers—you were your own destination. Oh, yes, she'd thought about it. "Why should I?"

"Because you want to find out what it would be like. Because you're tired of kissing me standing up in doorways. Because you're dying to show me that butterfly you told me about."

And the killer blow. "Because you're terrified that your life is passing you by and you haven't taken a risk for years. Because you're bored. Oh, and because I'm as horny as hell."

Harriet couldn't help laughing. Arrogant, but accurate. "I'll see what I can do." And she hung up. Which she thought was pretty cool.

Polly and Jack

Jack had left a message on the machine. "I'm running late, love. Could you bear to find your own way to the restaurant and I'll meet you there? Take your reading-club book,'cos I might be five minutes late—I've only just got out of this blessed meeting, and I've got some things on my desk that won't wait until tomorrow. I'll see you there. Looking forward to it, I really am. Love you."

Actually Polly was quite pleased. It would make it more of a date, arriving separately. She pulled at her hair in the hall mirror. She'd better go and make herself presentable. Even better than presentable would be good: she wanted tonight to be lovely.

They hadn't been out for dinner alone since February, Polly thought. They'd gone out, of course, foursomes, a couple of parties and a gruesome Sunday lunch at Susan's with that sour-faced sister of hers, to a few loud and mindless films at the cinema with Daniel, but not on a proper date. Not for ages. She knew she'd been taking him for granted. That was the paradox: they were a young couple but trapped in middle-aged lives, dealing with the problems of young-adult children before they'd even married. Her young-adult child, to be accurate: he hadn't dumped any emotional baggage on her doorstep—it was all one-way traffic. The joys of the modern family unit.

She'd read an article in the paper at the weekend, some smug television personality on her second marriage, writing about taking her kids into her new relationship. "He knew the score from the start," she wrote. "We came as a job lot." The new man in question had been quick to add, obsequiously, "It wasn't a struggle, I loved the boys almost from day one." Well, newsflash to perfect people from TV land: a job lot was a struggle for everyone. And there are different kinds of love: you could never love a child who didn't belong to you with the same visceral fervor you felt for your own child. If you hadn't had your own child, like Mr. Smug TV, or Jack, you didn't understand that love, not properly. Polly decided that the best you could hope for was to fall in love with your stepchild, which was easier if it was a Mark-Lester-in-*Oliver* look-alike, much harder if it was a spotty youth on the cusp of adolescence, and even more so if you were talking about a beautiful young woman. A pregnant beautiful young woman.

She'd been pushing him away a bit, she knew, partly because she was so used to coping on her own, so that it had become, if not quite a reflex, a point of honor to do so. And partly because she felt so protective of Cressida, but partly, too, because she felt he didn't entirely understand how it felt. He'd been trying, God knew, and he'd been a hero with Daniel, as good as taking over the practical side of his life—the football practices, the weekend matches. With Cressida he'd been gentle: without initiating a conversation with her about it, he'd treated her with something like tenderness. It was over Cressida that things between Jack and Polly had become strained. He'd said all along, prefaced every conversation by saying, that as he wasn't Cressida's father he couldn't understand exactly what she was feeling. Then he'd told Polly some truths, objective, impartial, observational truths, like it not being her right to tell Joe or his mum. That was what had made her cross, if she was honest. She didn't always want to hear sense. Sometimes she just wanted support; a comforting "there there." Men wanted to find solutions, make things okay. Jack knew she was strong, and probably thought comfort was patronizing. She didn't always have the energy left, after Cressida, to explain to him what she needed, just resented him for not giving it to her automatically.

He was still fantastic, still far and away the best man she knew. And Dan's reaction to Cressida's predicament had cast Jack in an even more glowing light. Polly had gone to tell him one evening at Cressida's request—she wasn't frightened of what he would say, she had said, just felt stupid and embarrassed.

Dan's first response had been arm gestures and swearing, and Tina had calmed him down with murmurs and strokes. Polly watched in something like fascination—how one man could choose two such different wives still amazed her. It was so clear to her now, though, that Tina was exactly what he had needed all along. No wonder their own marriage hadn't lasted. It never stood a chance!

When he had calmed down, she had found herself taking

Cressida's speaking part in a repetition of all the conversations the two of them had already had. Then he had said she had to have an abortion. She couldn't have a kid. What about the studying? What did Joe have to say for himself? Defending Cressida's decision was a useful exercise: it made sense when you said it out loud. It sounded reasonable. Dan had retreated into self-pity—his party trick. Why hadn't Cressida come and told him herself? He'd been a good dad, hadn't he? He'd always been there for her.

At that point Tina had stepped in. "Come on, Dan, imagine how hard it would be to tell you this. She probably knew you'd go off at half cock. She knew it would hurt you, upset you. I think she did the right thing, sending Polly. Give you a chance to calm down before you meet up with her. Get it into perspective. Get over the shock."

This was the longest speech Polly had ever heard Tina make, and she was grateful to her.

Jack had even told Danny himself. They had asked him to, of course. He would never have presumed. Danny was completely revolted by that sort of thing just now. Cressida being pregnant was irrefutable proof that Cressida was having sex. Bad enough that Jack and Mum were at it, but Cressida as well? It was all too much. So they reckoned it might come better from Jack. And it seemed it had. One morning, after Jack had picked up Danny from football training, Danny had come into the kitchen, swallowed at the sight of his sister and then, on his way past to the fridge, given her a half hug half swipe, his face lost for just a second in her neck. "All right, ugly?" he said, and then necked a bottle of milk straight down.

Later, when the kids had gone upstairs to their respective pits, Jack had smiled at Polly. "That was a beautiful moment, don't you think?"

"Oh yes, Kodak quality." Polly had smiled back.

"I think he thought I was going to tell him you were pregnant, so it was probably a relief when it turned out to be Cressida. I guess a niece or nephew is at least more palatable than a brother or sister."

She slid her arm around his waist. "Thanks, Jack."

"All part of the service."

You see, he was so good at that. At making her feel safe and like she was part of a team, like she didn't have to be responsible for every little thing on her own.

In the restaurant, she ordered a gin and tonic and some sparkling water, and sat back to read a few pages of *Guppies for Tea*, this month's choice. It was beautifully written—Polly could hardly believe that the author, Marika Cobbold, could write so well in her second language—but it wasn't a very comfortable read. Not for someone staring down the barrel of old age and, most especially she imagined, not for Susan. She wondered if it had been a tactless choice—Clare had suggested it months ago after she had talked about it to someone on the ward, and it had come up on the list for this month. Susan had been at the meeting, and she hadn't seemed to balk, but then, Polly reasoned, she wouldn't. Susan was a coper, a doer, a stoic. It was probably only Roger who knew the full picture, but Polly thought she saw more than most. Susan hadn't talked much about Alice these last few weeks since Margaret had left. She had always managed to turn their conversations to Cressida and the baby. When Polly tried to return to Alice, Susan looked sad. "Cressida has choices, Poll—there's so much more to talk about. Mum has no choices, and neither did Roger and I. What can you say?" And then the shrug, and the faraway look.

She'd been with Susan, once, to where Alice was—Susan went every day, sometimes more than once. It hadn't seemed so bad to Polly—or not as bad as Margaret would have had you believe: it was clean, there were nice prints on the walls, and silk flower displays in all the communal rooms. They'd turned up at lunchtime, daft really, and that hadn't been too nice—dozens of old people sitting in silence, dribbling soup down themselves, with one poor woman sobbing for her Colin. The private patients sat at tables with linen cloths. How absurd. As if age and ill health hadn't completely leveled the playing field.

But she, Polly, was seeing it objectively: this new, disheveled, empty-eyed Alice was Susan's mum, and that must be dreadful.

They had rescued her from an unappetizing plate of something indeterminate with custard and taken her back to her room. Polly had gone through all the motions, chatting to an uncomprehending Alice about Cressida, Daniel and Jack. She left out the baby but told Alice about the wedding.

"Getting married?" Alice asked incredulously, looking first at Polly and then, puzzled, at Susan.

Polly and Susan laughed.

"Yep, I guess getting her head round that one is a bit of a challenge." Susan snorted.

"Oy, it's not that hilarious. I'm only forty-four, for Chrissakes."

Alice smiled at them indulgently, as if they were teenagers laughing at boys. "You young things! We'd better start saving coupons then. In such a hurry, you young people are."

They giggled again. "If only the kids could hear her call us that!" Susan said. She combed Alice's hair gently while they talked on, and Alice sat still, eyes closed, enjoying her daughter's touch.

Afterward, Susan linked arms with Polly on the way out, past manicured flower beds, to the car. The giggling turned into a swallowed sob, as giggling is often wont to do. "Thanks for coming, Poll. That was great. You're good at this sort of thing. Until today I hadn't seen her smile since she went in there."

"You're welcome. Any time. Honestly." Polly took a deep breath. "Suze?"

"Yes?"

"Roger and I were talking, a few days back. He's worried about you, hon. He thinks you're up here too much and it's making you too tired."

Susan stiffened, but did not take her arm away. "She's my mum, Polly."

"I know, I know. Really I do, and so does Rog. It's just"—this wasn't easy to say—"well, if she doesn't understand time so well anymore, and she doesn't really know if you've been or not, do you really need to put yourself through it so often? Couldn't you give yourself a bit of a breather?"

Now Susan did take away her arm. "She's my mum, Poll." Again. "You don't just think I'm going up there for her, do you?"

Jack was a noisy bugger—as soon as the door of the restaurant opened she knew it was him. Loud apologies to someone he'd jostled, asking for her, so sorry to be late, got held up, and then he was there, a light sheen of sweat, a briefcase, a jacket over his arm and a redundant umbrella—the big corporate kind.

He was a nice-looking man, with a big, smiley face. Polly felt a stab of possessive pride.

"Hello, darling. Sorry I'm late. Get my message?"

"Yeah, no problem. I've been reading."

"Good, good. Good?"

"Well, to be honest, I've been thinking about Susan and Alice. That's sort of what the book is about."

"Right." Jack grimaced. "Heavy stuff?"

"A bit."

Jack pulled it from her, slipped a card advertising the restaurant in at her page, snapped it shut and slid it into her open bag on the floor beside them.

"Right, well, that's enough of that, then. Tonight, Mrs. Soon-to-Be-Fitzgerald, is declared a nonmisery evening. I've got you all to myself, for once, and I'm banning all talk of Cressida and Daniel and, for that matter, Susan and Alice, much as we may love them all. I want to have a lighthearted, delightful, possibly drunken meal with my gorgeous and, may I say, terribly sexy fiancée." He gave the old-fashioned word resonance and gravitas. How could she help but love him? That was absolutely what he deserved. He kissed her hand with a flourish.

The waiter appeared. "To drink, sir?"

She raised her glass. "I'm on gin."

"Bugger that, mother's ruin. I'm not having you sniveling over your tiramisu. A bottle of champagne, please. Two glasses." He handed the gin and tonic to the waiter. "And you may take that."

"Certainly, sir." The waiter was smiling, enjoying Jack's theatrical style.

Jack was reaching into his briefcase. "And I've brought just the thing to get the conversation going."

Polly started to laugh. He was holding up an ancient, well-thumbed copy of *You & Your Wedding*, obviously stolen from some reception area.

Three hours, two bottles and a great deal of sniggering later, after Jack had forbidden her to wear at least three-quarters of the dresses advertised but marked with a Biro the lingerie he favored; after a heated debate on the honeymoon, and an agreement that, yes, he would look an idiot in morning dress, they had arrived at a date. He had watched her face as she calculated months, and raised a hand imperiously. "Aha. Now, over most things you and your gal pals will have total control. This decision, along with the wine, I claim as my own." He had already done the counting. "I have always wanted a Christmas bride. How about it?"

She had never loved him more.

Susan and Mary

Roman blinds were boring to make. You had to concentrate because the sewing was fiddly, and there were all those lengths of cord. Also, you didn't make so much money with blinds: on curtains there was more to be made on the fabric, which they bought at trade and sold on at a small profit—unless Susan took a liking to a client who had her heart set on something she couldn't afford. Sometimes it was nice to see the delight when you offered to pass on the trade discount. Soft-furnishing Santa.

Susan liked swags best, with their yards and yards of soft fabric. Not in her home, of course—dust traps! To look at, she preferred blinds, clean, simple and, in the right material, stunning, maybe with a pelmet or a lambrequin if the window or the room's décor could take it.

Thank God for Mary, who liked making blinds. That was one of the reasons she made such a good companion in the workroom. She also made wicked flapjack, which she brought in every Monday, and shared Susan's passion for Radio 4, which played all day long while they worked. It was so much more interesting than gossip. Mary had been with Susan for fifteen years or so—

Susan had forced her to come out for lunch about six months ago when she'd realized it was their anniversary. This morning they'd both been doing what they did best. Susan spent a couple of hours helping a rich young banker's wife go through the books for an extensive selection of magnolia linens at a hundred pounds per meter, trying to decide which one was just perfect for the enormous Georgian windows in her new home. By the time she left, on a cloud of Chanel, with a dozen swatches to show her decorator, Mary had sewn and threaded three plaid roman blinds for a new kitchen.

"Brilliant! They look great. I'll drop them off this afternoon on my way to see Mum. Henry's going round to fix the poles in the morning." Henry was their token male, an ex-accountant who had chucked it all in when his youngest child left home. Now he hung poles and ratchets for their customers, and occasionally offered harassed housewives advice on paying their nanny's tax and National Insurance. "Did you get anywhere with Lady Bountiful?" This was Susan and Mary's private name for the girl who'd just been in. They had done rooms in the new family seat before and were quietly amused by her grandiose schemes and less authentic accent—Susan thought they were probably dreams she'd been working on since childhood in her single-bedroom in Balham.

"Who can tell? I don't know why she doesn't just bring the bloody decorator here—it'd save us a fortune in samples, and anyway, it's pretty obvious it's what he says that goes." She reasoned Lady Bountiful's taste inclined more naturally toward the brighter chenilles and velvets than toward the earthy, natural shades fashion demanded. "Bodily fluid colors," Mary called them. "Fancy a coffee? Let's eat lunch outside—it's gorgeous, the first hot day we've had this year."

The workshop was part of a collective that took up two of the three vast barns attached to an old farmhouse, whose present owner kept the third as an art studio from which he ran watercolor courses in the summer. Mary and Susan shared with an upholsterer and a cabinetmaker. The barns were set at the end of a steep track two or three miles off the road, and they had a spectacular view over the valley behind. Just being here made Susan feel calm.

Outside they sat together, sipping coffee and eating their sandwiches. The sun was warm on their necks.

"Clare asked me to tell you she won't be coming to your reading club this week. She's sorry but she can't make it."

"That's a shame. We'll miss her. She's really come out of herself, you know. She reads the books with a very different perspective from the rest of us—she has lots of interesting things to say. She isn't ill, I hope?"

"No, nothing like that." Mary sighed. "You may as well know, she's left Elliot. Moved back in with me and her dad, a few weeks back."

"Oh, Mary, I'm so sorry. I had no idea."

"No, well, you know me—I don't like to talk too much about these things. She seemed to be enjoying the group, too. Always been a bit of a bookworm. When she was a little girl I used to have to get books out of the library in threes and fours for her, she devoured them so fast. *A Tree Grows in Brooklyn* was one of her favorites. And *Rebecca*—she loved that." Susan remembered that Clare had suggested it. "Clever little girl she was—her teachers said she could have gone to university if she'd wanted to. She never did, though. She always had her heart set on training as a nurse, then as a midwife. That—and Elliot—was all she ever wanted."

They both knew it wasn't true. She had wanted so much more than that. As if acknowledging this, Mary went on, "I read in the papers sometimes, you know, those stories about women who have babies for their daughters who can't. I'd have done that, but I'm too old. We waited too long to have her ourselves. It took me years to fall with her. Now I've been through the change, you see. I'd've done anything else, if I could. We both would. Reg said he'd sell the house to pay for treatment if there was anything they could do, but there isn't. These days, we think doctors and money are the answer to every problem, but there are some who just aren't meant to have children of their own, and she's one of them, my little girl."

Mary wasn't the kind of woman to invite physical contact, and Susan didn't know what to say. Eventually she said, "Do you think they might get back together? There's no one else involved, is there?"

"I don't think so, not like that. No one real." Mary turned to look at her. "That house is haunted, I think. *They're* haunted—by the ghosts of all the babies they've lost, the life they wanted." She shook herself, as though she'd said something stupid. "I thought keeping them together was the best thing I could do for her. I thought that in time they'd heal each other, that they'd learn to have a happy life together without children. They were so happy, you remember?'

Susan did, vaguely. She remembered them one day, years ago, when Elliot and Clare were still teenagers, buzzing about in the workshop. They'd gone outside, and he'd been chasing her, laughing. He caught her eventually, held her shoulders while he hooked her legs with his foot so that they fell together to the ground. He'd smoothed back her hair behind her ears and kissed her, his hands on her cheeks. Then she remembered Mary coming in with wedding photographs, hundreds of them, it had seemed, Clare dazed with happiness as she gazed up at her new husband.

"Yes, I remember."

"But that's not right either anymore. Home is the best place for her just now, and for me. I want her with me. I need to take care of her."

That was it, wasn't it, Susan supposed. The steel ribbons that bind us—Mary and Clare, me and Mum, Polly and Cressida, Cressida and her unborn baby. Harriet and Nicole and their children. Me and my glorious boys. Clare would never have that.

Mary shrugged. "Ah, well, this won't get the work done, will it? I'm off back to it. Thanks for the coffee, and the shoulder."

"That's okay. I'm sorry, Mary. Send Clare our love. Tell her she's welcome back at the reading club as soon as she's feeling up to it. I'll let you know what the next book is, and then she can decide."

"Cheers, Susan. She'd like that, I'm sure."

Susan had watched Mary, all the rest of the afternoon, but she'd closed back off again, as quickly as she had opened outside on the bench.

Cressida

What a stinking irony. Four months ago she had been going to the loo praying to see blood in her knickers, on the toilet roll. Now she'd been through all this shit, the scan, the fights with Mum, the breakup with Joe, telling Elliot, and at the end of it she'd made up her mind, and nearly everyone else's, and she had been starting to feel almost good. And now there was blood.

What could it mean? Everything had been going the way it was meant to with the baby. She certainly felt pregnant. Her boobs were enormous, and her hipster trousers were starting to be uncomfortable—she'd had to abandon the black ones already. Her hair was thick, and those last few spots had gone, and she was peeing for England. So far, so textbook pregnancy. She'd been reading her book, the one Mum had bought her, *What 'to Expect When You're Expecting*—a corny-looking tome, with some pregnant woman in a Laura Ashley smock sitting in a rocking chair, that had turned out to be a brilliant reference tool—checking off her "symptoms" each week, looking at the pictures of the baby. Although she'd stuck a bloody great paper clip on the chapters on delivery. Not right now, thank you very much. It was in, and it would be coming out, and that was all she needed to know at this stage. The midwife she'd seen at the hospital had said young mums usually had an easier time of it in labor than older ones, "like shelling peas," she said, which was scant comfort; babies' head, mummy's bits—you figure it out. When she was in town, she looked with new curiosity at the young mums she passed. They'd done it, and they could still walk. Some of them could still wear hipster trousers. How bad could it be?

She had spent hours looking at herself naked in her bedroom mirror, turning this way and that, watching the subtle but inexorable changes in her body. Sometimes, fully dressed, she had shoved a cushion up her top and clutched melodramatically at the small of her back, trying to imagine how she would look nearer the time. She'd copied down a few numbers off the board in the obstetrics department—she particularly fancied a yoga class she'd seen advertised there: it sounded like a chilled-out way to get ready for the birth. "Dunk Your Bump" at the local pool sounded quite fun, if you could get your head round the idea of appearing in front of the hunky lifeguards looking like Moby Dick with varicose veins.

That was the trouble. Once you had made the decision to keep the baby, your mind raced on ahead, through the pregnancy, into infancy and way beyond. You found yourself daydreaming about the craziest things: what it would be, what you would do together, what it would like and not like. Cressida was sure the baby was a boy, her imagination was always working in powder blue, she didn't know why. She'd been doodling in class the other day, a list of boys' names.

She couldn't be losing it now. Please.

She stood up, did up her trousers, flushed the loo and went out onto the landing. "Mum!"

Polly came to the bottom of the stairs, alerted by Cressida's desperate tone. "What's the matter, love?"

Cressida started to cry. "I'm bleeding, Mum."

"Right." Polly leapt up the stairs two at a time. "Don't worry, darling. Let's get you lying down." She guided Cressida to her bed. "How much blood, sweetheart? Just drops or a trickle? Does it hurt? Are you feeling okay?"

"Drops, just drops, I think, on my underwear. There's no pain at all." She clutched at Polly's arm, her face ashen. "Mum, what does it mean? Am I losing the baby?"

Polly had picked up the phone and was dialing. "Of course not, sweetheart. Lie still, try to stay calm. I'm calling Roger."

She sat down beside Cressida as the phone rang at Susan's house. Sunday afternoon. Please God, let him be there.

He was. He reacted with his usual capable, calm kindness. "You've got her up on the bed, have you? Right, make her a cup of tea, with some sugar in it, and one for yourself. I'll be right round. Don't worry, Polly, this isn't unusual. She's probably perfectly all right."

Cressida didn't want Polly to leave her to make tea. "Don't go, Mum. Please stay with me."

They wanted to be together much more than either of them wanted a cup of tea with sugar in it. Polly held her daughter, stroking her hair, murmuring that it would be okay, that Roger was on his way, that she wasn't to worry. All the time her mind was racing. Surely Cressida couldn't be miscarrying, not now, not after all this. Her daughter's fear communicated itself to her, and she took deep breaths of her own. Not the baby. Not now. She didn't know who she was most afraid for, the baby, Cressida or herself. Scraped knees she could deal with, broken hearts she could try. Losing a baby you wanted—she wasn't equipped to deal with that. It wasn't fair for Cressida to experience a tragedy that she herself hadn't been through—how could she offer comfort, how could she understand, how could she make it better? To have to watch your own child wild-eyed with fear and be unable to help was horrible.

When the bell rang Polly leapt up and ran downstairs. Roger smiled at her briefly, reassuringly, then went straight upstairs. "She's in my room, Roger."

Susan had come with him, and she folded her friend in a bear hug in the hallway.

"Thanks for coming so quickly," Polly said.

"Don't be daft. Leave Roger with her for a minute or two, while we make a drink."

Polly looked up the stairs, unsure.

"It's probably nothing." Susan had had a fair amount of experience, married to a GP. "There are lots of reasons why a woman bleeds at this stage. The baby is usually fine." She smiled at her friend. "And the mother is always fine."

Roger explained it to her the same way. He said he'd booked Cressida in for a scan at the hospital tomorrow morning, but that it was purely a precaution. He didn't think there was anything to worry about, although it might be best if Cressida stayed in bed today, and had a rest after her fright.

Polly was surprised by how overwhelmingly relieved she felt—for all of them. After Roger and Susan had left, Cressida fell asleep. It was childish, Polly thought, having complete faith in the doctor. If he said it would be all right, it must be so. For a long while, Polly sat and watched her, until she felt herself calm down again. Not once today had she thought it might be for the best if Cressida lost the baby. Not once had the thought even occurred to her. She wanted her to keep it.

Elliot

Elliot couldn't concentrate. Not on his computer screen. Not on the earnest student sitting across from him asking about renting flats near the campus. And not, apparently, on shaving: he had cut himself twice this morning and had had to drive in with those ridiculous dots of tissue paper stuck to his chin and neck. That was because he couldn't look at his own reflection without remembering, and remembering made him a useless fool. Cressida was pregnant. She was going to have a baby. His baby. He was going to have a baby.

It was surreal. He was reacting to the news on so many different levels, both obvious and totally left field.

He knew it sounded stupid, but he had been so shocked. While sex with Clare was always about babies—or at least it had been for these last years—the possibility of a baby had never entered his head when he was making love to Cressida. They hadn't talked about contraception—if he'd thought about it at all, and he was ashamed to say he hadn't, he'd have assumed she was taking the pill or something. But pregnancy, babies, hadn't encroached. It had been pure, somehow, the sex between them: about two people who fancied each other rotten giving each other pleasure, making each other feel good and wanted. There was a fantastic freedom in that: it wasn't weighed down by the framework of their lives, routine or sadness. He couldn't remember loving sex as much before. Cressida's virginity had been exciting to him, and he'd wanted to get it right for her. She told him, after that first time, shyly, that he had, that she was glad she had waited for him.

Now he felt puffed with pride at his own virility; at once it became obvious to him how totally emasculating it had been to be unable to perform that one simple function. He and Clare had known for a long time that the physical problem lay with her, not him, but it must have tainted his idea of his masculinity anyway. Like in some stupid way his sperm should have been able to overcome whatever obstacles Clare's body put in their way in their rabid determination to reproduce. He knew it sounded silly, even within his own head, but he felt sort of studly—he couldn't deny it.

And suddenly the lights had come on in the corridor in his brain that he had long since locked up: Elliot as a dad. He had made those longings go away so that he had more room to deal with the idea of Clare not being a mum. He would say to people, when they asked, "It's not so much me, you see, it's Clare who feels it the most. All girls want to be mums, don't they? Starts with the dolls, I suppose, and then their mates have them, and then . . . It's Clare it's most awful for. I'm all right." And so it had been, for so long that he had pretty much believed it. But it wasn't true. From the moment Cressida had told him, he had been running home movies in his head—swinging a baby onto his shoulder, podgy fingers pulling his hair, tickling to illicit giggles, kicking a ball, checking the little one before he went to sleep. Damn right he had wanted all of that. Damn right he'd been angry with Clare, not because she couldn't give it to him—he knew he hadn't for one second blamed her for that—but because she'd never lived with his pain the way he had lived with hers. The balance had all gone.

He'd have to tell her. It wasn't so much that he owed her, it was just that he couldn't hear anyone but himself say the words. Mary or Reg would do it, he knew, but it had to be him. Not yet, though. He didn't want to see her face with the news reflected in it. He was still loving seeing his own in the mirror with that news in his eyes, and Cressida's, so beautiful, when she'd told him. He hadn't been able to say much then, he'd been so shocked and so pleased and so moved. She had just held him—she was good at that—and not asked anything of him.

MAY
READING GROUP

GUPPIES FOR TEA

MARIKA COBBOLD © 1993

Amelia Lindsay is an exceptional young woman. She shares her days between a grandmother whom she loves, a mother whom she tolerates with patient fortitude and Gerald. They had fallen in love two years earlier, when he was in his artistic phase, and had begged her to move in with him. Now (no longer in his artistic phase), he is showing signs of irritation.

And suddenly Selma, the talented and much-beloved grandmother, has become old. As life—and Gerald—begins to collapse all around Amelia, she is determined that the one person who will not fade is Selma. Fighting a one-woman battle against Cherryfield retirement home, Gerald's defection and her mother's obsession with germs, Amelia finds herself capable of plots, diversions and friendships she has never imagined before.

Harriet had left the door on the latch, so Polly let herself in and followed the sound of laughter into the kitchen. She loved all of Harriet's house but especially this room, with its vast scrubbed-pine table (which she imagined Harriet had ordered prescrubbed, since she did not seem the rubber gloves and scrubbing brush sort), the mandatory Aga (in hot pink; a heinous crime against country kitchens, but very Harriet), and the big American fridge-freezer covered with her children's vivid artwork. Today a cardboard and Bubble Wrap jellyfish hung menacingly from the light fixture above the table. The whole effect was warmly chaotic, like Harriet herself, and it was a comforting place to be.

Nicole, out of place in immaculate cream linen, was at the French windows with a spritzer in her hand. Susan was crouching down, deep in conversation with Chloe, while Harriet smiled at her daughter, pride and affection dancing across her face. Chloe, hair damp at the edges, resplendent in Barbie pajamas, was solemnly showing Susan the toes on her left foot, on which she had noticed recently that the third curled naturally under the second.

"That's just the way you're made, isn't it?" Susan was almost whispering, conspiratorially.

"That's the way God made me," Chloe countered, triumphantly.

Harriet rolled her eyes. "We're going through a pious phase, I'm afraid."

Chloe knew when she was being condescended to. She turned

in mock rage to her mother, hands on hips, and said, "It is, Mummy. They said so at school."

Harriet nodded. "Absolutely, darling. Quite right. Now you've had your juice, off to bed with you."

Instead Chloe turned back to Susan. "Does God have toes? Do you think they're bent a bit, like mine?"

"Chloe! Enough! You'd better ask your teacher in the morning—she's the expert." Harriet steered her toward the door by the shoulders. "Say good night to everyone. Hiya, Polly, wine's on the table. Chloe?"

"Good night, everyone."

They chorused back, and Chloe was gone.

"She's gorgeous." Susan turned to Polly, who was pouring herself a large glass of white. "Okay?"

"Fine. Sorry I'm late. I see I'm not the last—Clare's not here yet?"

"Ah, I've got news."

Harriet came back in. Chloe had slipped gratefully into bed, and her eyes had closed as her head touched the pillow. "What news?"

"She's not coming this month. She asked her mum to let me know."

"Is she ill?"

"Not exactly. She's left her husband, gone back to her parents. I suppose she doesn't feel up to explanations just yet. I gather it's pretty recent."

"Poor Clare."

"That's awful. Do you know why?"

"I think it's all to do with not being able to have a baby. Mary thinks it's ruined everything. Such a shame—they hadn't been married all that long." Susan held up her hands. "I guess none of us knows how it feels to go through that."

Nicole was stroking her belly, almost unconsciously, still flat and taut under the linen. Friday. She could take a test on Friday. She was sure now, though. If she concentrated she could visualize the cells multiplying inside her, fizzing with life.

"I wonder why they didn't think about things like adoption, long-term fostering?" This was Polly.

"I think for some people it's just not the same, is it? Besides, we don't know her husband. We don't know how important it may or may not have been to him to have a baby. It might have been all too one-sided. It just isn't the be-all and end-all for everyone, is it?"

"It was for me." Harriet was looking at the paraphernalia of her own children. "I've always known I wanted them. I used to think that if I got to be forty and hadn't found someone, I'd have just gone and got myself pregnant. Being a mother was really all I was ever certain about."

"Not me. I was more the Paula Yates school of motherhood. I saw babies as a gift I could give Gavin, something that would bind us in this unique, private world. Like fecundity was a sort of blessing on our marriage. I never thought much about babies until I met him." She saw Harriet was looking at her thoughtfully and added, "Of course, the minute they were born, I adored them completely in their own right."

"I know that." Harriet was speaking directly to her, quiet and amused.

"I never thought much about it at all," Susan said, smiling. "You young ones"—Harriet and Nicole smirked—"analyze everything. Roger and I just did what everyone else was doing. We met, fell in love, got married, and as soon as we'd saved enough for me to give up work, I came off the pill and we had the boys."

"Me too. More or less. I mean Dan and I met, fell into something—bed and lust, perhaps, more than love. Of course, we didn't do the getting-married bit until later . . . but basically the same. I think women our age just expected it."

"There must have been some who were infertile, though. It isn't a new thing."

"Not new, no. And of course there were. But we didn't dwell on it in the same way, somehow. IVF wasn't around—Louise Brown had only just been born when we had Cress and Ed, hadn't she, Suze? Different times."

"I think, sometimes, that it's the trying to get pregnant that causes the problems for people like Clare and her husband as much as the not achieving it. All those injections and scans and 'Quick, quick, do it right now.' It must be awful." Susan shook her head.

"She's not gone for good, though, has she?" Harriet asked.

"I don't think so. It was just a bit soon."

"Hope so. I like her." They all nodded.

After *Atonement*, they had decided each should explain her choice. Since Clare wasn't there, Susan spoke first: they all looked at her expectantly, recognizing that Clare's choice must have affected her more than them. "Well, as you all know, it's pretty relevant to me just now. It's about a young girl whose grandmother is in a home like Mum. Only it's about a lot more as well—her romance with this deeply selfish man falls apart on her at the same time, and she's got a mother with obsessive-compulsive disorder, so she's pretty much up against it. But I mostly related to it because of the grandmother."

"Did you like it?"

"I loved it. I thought it was brilliant."

"Anyone hate it?" Harriet interrupted. She liked to know. They all shook their heads.

Susan continued: "It was hard to read, for me. So much of what goes on in the home rang true about Mum. I cried a lot. Some of the stories about how humiliating it is to be treated that way—like having all your nice clothes taken away because you're incontinent, things like that. I related to Amelia a lot. That bit where she comes home from a particularly depressing day and wants to make a special dinner for Gerald, with champagne and lovemaking—she wants to celebrate life. I got that absolutely. That's exactly how I feel every time I come away from Mum's place. Like I have to make the most of every minute until I'm in there myself. And you feel bad for feeling good that it isn't you."

"She says, doesn't she, somewhere near the end, that she wonders 'why what is right and what is kind so often seem to be quite different things?'"

"And the impulse she has, to take her away, and let her die at home—not that it is her home anymore—I understand that completely. Not that Mum's dying, but I do get flashes with her, moments when I can't believe what they tell me, that she doesn't know what's happening to her, and that's really painful. I'm lucky.

The grandmother in the book is always begging to be taken home. Mum has never once asked. I don't think I could bear it. I'd probably do exactly what Amelia does and discharge her."

"You'd have to hide her from Roger." Polly smiled. "It was a bit convenient, wasn't it, that she managed to die at home just before the police arrived to throw them out? That end bit was farcical."

"Yeah," Harriet answered, "but it's a story, isn't it? It wouldn't make such a good book if she took six chapters to fade away, and you only got a death rattle at the end. I loved her sitting up and saying, 'Bugger the pills,' just before she died at the end."

"One bit was interesting, I thought," Nicole said. "When Amelia says that she thinks God has 'read her heart's desire, but through a mirror, and given her Selma,' she's saying—a bit like you, Harry—that she's got this incredible urge to nurture but it's got all twisted, and she's ended up with a geriatric baby. In the end, it's all she's got—the old boyfriend leaves her, the new one goes too, in a way, her mum is a waste of space, so caring for Selma is pretty much all she has."

"Which is different from me, I suppose," Susan acknowledged. "I have Roger and the boys, and my work. She's a bit of a flop everywhere else, isn't she? I suppose that's age. Selma's her grandmother, not her mother—that's probably one of the reasons the author put in an extra generation."

"I used to think, though," Harriet said, "that when you were married, with a family of your own, in your thirties, that you would be ready, somehow, to lose your parents, lose your mum. I'm not ready. She doesn't live nearby, I don't see her all the time, and she doesn't know everything that's going on with me, but I am so not ready to lose her. I just need to know she's there. I could cry just thinking about it now." She looked over at Susan, who was fighting back tears. "God, sorry, Suze. What an idiot."

"It's okay." Susan blew her nose, wiped her eyes. "Well, look, I'm in my forties. I'll be a grandmother, maybe, in a few years. I've lost her already, to all intents and purposes. And I'm not ready either." Harriet reached across and laid her hand on Susan's.

Polly was flicking through the book. "Here. One of them says, Henry, I think, 'When someone you love, dies, it's as if they leave you with half shares of your life together. The person you were in their eyes dies with them.' Isn't that the point? Isn't our mother the most important part of how we become who we are, and therefore the hardest to let go?"

"I thought the Amelia-Gerald stuff was incredibly good. I wasn't expecting that."

"She had a brilliant way of describing anger, like lava."

"And she makes you feel how hurt Amelia is. It's incredibly poignant, I think, her making an effort to look good for him because she senses that it's over but it isn't quite, officially over yet, and she thinks she should keep going."

"There's an awful lot of lipstick and scent. All the women use it as a shield. And a comforter."

"Who doesn't?"

"When she finds him shagging his secretary in the chair— that's brilliant. And the way she describes Clarissa trying to get her knickers back on with dignity!"

"Can you imagine!"

"I can't imagine being cool enough to say—what is it she says when she catches them? 'I didn't know you were home,' something like that?"

"No, or cool enough to drive his car into the front room."

"She's pretty wise about relationships, isn't she?" Harriet was piling up the plates slowly. "That bit where she says you should judge a relationship's success not on how often you made love but on how much you talked in restaurants. That was spot on for me."

"Me too. I don't even want to make love unless there's been talking in the restaurant first."

"Poor Jack! Do you mean he's got to buy you dinner every time he wants to get his leg over?"

"I'm speaking metaphorically, of course. Women have to be seduced from the head down, don't we?"

"Absolutely!"

"Can't remember. I've been married for twenty-four years, remember!" Susan laughed.

Polly winked at her. "Rubbish. You probably get more than the rest of us put together. Harriet and Nicole are exhausted young mothers, I've got a live-out lover. I reckon you and Roger are the ones having all the fun."

Harriet was sure she was blushing. She was remembering how Nick's mouth and hands had felt on her, and thinking about the weekend away to which she had just persuaded Tim to agree. He had smiled at her when she asked. Said of course she must go, that it would be great for her to see her friend without him and the kids along. She had wished he'd sulked. Still, every second she was alone she was screening it in her head, imagining herself, like Jane Seymour in a *Hello!* photo shoot, floating in a gauzy dress across a sun-dappled lawn into the arms of a handsome stranger, who was going to kiss her *that way* again. And again. She got up, took the plates to the sink and rinsed them with her back to Nicole. Then she scooped up Josh's games shirt from the top of the Aga, lifted one of the lids and put the huge, heavy kettle on the hot plate. "Coffee, anyone, or are we all on the peppermint tea this evening?"

"How's Cressida getting on?" The book bit was finished now. They were drinking their tea. Harriet had heard Tim come in about half an hour ago, and she sensed that the other women were getting ready to leave. She didn't want them to go.

Susan heard Harriet ask the question and stopped listening to Nicole, who was asking her something about making a blind for a funny-shaped window. It was a bit like being a doctor and having inexplicable rashes shown to you at dinner parties. She'd drawn it in pink crayon on the back of one of Chloe's rainbow paintings—Harriet hadn't been able to find any other paper.

Polly took a deep breath and held her mug tightly between her two hands. "Pregnant."

"Christ."

"Since Clare's not here, it's probably a good time to tell you two. Susan knows already. I've sort of been dreading having to tell you with her here, you know?"

Nicole knew exactly.

"She's about five months. She didn't tell me"—Polly forgave herself that little white lie—"until February, bless her. She was terrified—she must have forgotten that people in glass houses shouldn't throw stones." Polly smiled wryly. "I was only a couple of years older when I got pregnant with her."

Five months. Harriet's mind was racing ahead. Poor girl. She still remembered vividly a scare she'd had at about the same age. She'd sat in the university toilet, waiting silently for the result, and it had felt like the white breeze-block walls and ceiling were slowly coming down on her. They'd been watching *Neighbours* in the junior common room next door, and she had heard the theme tune through the wall as she sat there. All those idiotic fantasies she'd had about having Charles's baby had evaporated. But she'd been lucky—stupid, but lucky. Five months. She must be intending to keep it. "What's she going to do?"

"Keep it." Polly seemed so calm: how did she manage that? "We've been through it a million times over the last few weeks. She's made up her own mind. She's been extraordinarily self-possessed about it since I found out. Went for the scan on her own and everything."

"That must have been hard for you."

"Of course. She's my baby. However old they get, you still think of them that way, and you want to protect them, don't you, Suze?"

"Totally. And throttle them!"

"Protect and throttle. That sounds familiar," Nicole said.

"Well, it doesn't change much, believe me." Polly smiled. "My baby she might be, but she's also twenty years old, and I don't have a great deal of choice but to go along with what she decides. And she's decided she wants to keep this baby. I wasn't sure I believed her at first—I was afraid she might be caught up in it, not thinking straight, you know? But she had a scare last week, some breakthrough bleeding, nothing serious—and everything's fine—but we weren't sure for a few hours, and she was terrified of losing it. I could see it in her face." Next to Polly, Susan nodded.

"What about the father?"

"Joe? He's out of the picture, I think. He's at Warwick—they've hardly seen each other since he went. It was basically a sixth-form thing that wasn't going to last, she says. They were taking very different directions."

"But he knows?"

"I don't know. She hasn't said."

"Hasn't he got a right to know?" Nicole was asking.

Polly felt suddenly protective, and her response sounded crosser than she meant it to. "I don't know if he has, not with things the way they are between them. That has to be Cress's decision. I'm sure she'll do the right thing. She's got a lot on her plate at the moment."

"Of course. I didn't mean . . ." Nicole was instantly apologetic.

"I know. Sorry. It's okay. Don't mind me, I'm practicing being defensive." She and Susan exchanged a look.

"And how do you feel about it all?"

Harriet's face was kind, but Polly couldn't give a simple answer: bewildered, scared, excited, disappointed, powerless, proud? She shrugged, noncommittally. "I'm her mum. I love her."

Susan

"Margaret? It's me, Susan."

"Susan? What's happened?"

"Oh, don't worry—I'm sorry, I didn't mean to scare you. Everything's okay."

Margaret didn't fill the space, echoing on the line.

"It's just, well, I've seen Mum today, and I wanted to tell you about the visit."

"What about it?"

Maybe this hadn't been a good idea. She'd called on impulse— Alice had made her feel so close to her own childhood that she'd missed her sister. She had wanted to draw her back into the memories she and Alice had shared. "She was incredibly lucid, the best I've seen her for months. She seemed really, really well. She knew exactly who I was, who you were, and it was lovely. She was talking about when we were little girls."

"What about it? I don't understand what you're saying, Susan."

Come on, Maggie, come on. Don't freeze me out. "Well, she was just, you know, reminiscing. She made me remember when we were little girls, playing out on that low wall at the front of the house—doctors and nurses, shopkeepers. She was talking about when we made all the other kids on the street be patients. You remember? I just wanted you to share it."

"Susan." Margaret's tone wasn't angry: she was firm, sensible and more than a little patronizing. "You obviously don't remember it any better than she does. We weren't the Waltons. We fought all the time, and we liked doing different things."

"Yes, I know. She remembered that too. But we were sisters, Maggie. All sisters do that, don't they?"

Margaret didn't answer, and Susan felt stupid. "It was just, well, it was lovely to hear her sounding like her old self. That's all. I thought you might want to hear that."

"There's no point, though, is there? She isn't her old self, is she? You could go back in there today and find that she thinks you're one of the staff."

The noble experiment had failed. Margaret was even jealous of the one hour of pleasure Susan and Alice had shared in the midst of weeks of misery.

She cut her losses. "You're right. Silly." She searched around for a legitimate reason for the call. "I thought you should know, too, that Mum's friend Mabel died a couple of months ago."

"I never met a Mabel."

"I know. I just thought Mum might have written to you about her or something. They'd been pretty close for a few years now—they were both widowed at about the same time. Anyway, she died, poor old thing."

"I'm sorry." Margaret sounded as if she couldn't care less.

Susan couldn't bear to be on the phone a second longer. "So, I'd better go. It's peak time and everything. You keeping well?"

"I'm fine. Thanks for calling."

"I'll give your love to Mum, shall I, when I see her tomorrow?"

"If you like. If you think she'll know who you mean."

Susan wasn't going to rise to it, not today. Today she was happy—she'd snatched a bit of Alice back from the abyss, and even Margaret wasn't going to ruin that for her. "I will. Just in case. 'Bye."

"Good bye, Susan."

Clare

The ward was always quiet when they lost a baby. Somehow the news, or a shadow of it on the faces of the midwives, communicated itself to other patients, the lucky ones. They sent their visitors away quickly, feeling guilty about the flowers and balloons. They tried to keep their babies quiet, often wiping hormonal tears onto the blankets they were swaddled in, as though the noise of their own newborns was an affront. Clare didn't think it was: she felt, when she was with parents going through it, that they had already switched off from the rest of the world for a while. One had said to her, "Makes no difference to me what's going on out there. Why shouldn't I be glad they've got their babies? It doesn't change things for us either way," which made a lot of sense to her. Fortunately, it didn't happen often. Nine times out of ten they were born amidst drama that lived forever in the minds and stories of their parents, but didn't cause a wrinkle on the labor ward. Sometimes there were problems for her calmly, efficiently to solve. A baby might stop breathing for a minute or two and need suction to bring it back, spluttering almost indignantly. It might be yellow and spend a few days under the sun lamp, or have sticky eyes, or a low Apgar at birth that needed watching for a couple of days. And so she suctioned, and she pricked, and she cleaned carefully with cotton buds, and she comforted the mothers who couldn't bear their babies being fiddled with, and she sent them home, in brand-new car seats nervously fitted. When it did happen, there wasn't much to do. That was what made it so hard. You cleared away the mess of delivery, you helped to dress the baby, took photos, if they wanted—they kept a camera on the ward specially. (It didn't get used for the live babies, whose dads picked up film or disposable cameras in the lobby, where they also bought the pink or blue flower arrangements, Milk Tray and phone cards.) You guarded their privacy fiercely, made them tea for as long as they wanted it. And that was all.

Not today. This dead baby had a twin who was very much alive, and parents whose emotions had been macheted in an instant. Two boys, one so much bigger and stronger. His father held him, both of them crying for comfort that was not forthcoming. The little one was with his mother, who had dressed him in the sparkling white Babygro with blue bears embroidered on the front that matched his brother's. She'd put on the hat, too, "to keep your little head warm," she had said. She was rocking him now, trying to pass a lifetime of love and care into his little body even though he was beyond feeling it.

She looked up at Clare. Her eyes were dry and empty. Clare knew she was stronger now than she would be again for weeks, anesthetized by shock and pain. "We've chosen the names—we knew they were boys months ago. Matthew and James. Good, solid names, we thought. Matt and Jamie. Sound like good mates, don't they?" She looked down at the still baby in her arms. "I never worked out how we were gonna choose which was which." She glanced at her husband, whose tears streamed down, incapable of speech. "We'd have just waited, I suppose, a few hours—see how we felt then, see if one of them looked more like a James or a Matthew." She smiled a grim, self-deprecating smile, but now her voice broke. "I think we'll call this one James. That was my favorite, you know, of the two. That seems fairest."

Clare squeezed her hand. "All right." But suddenly she needed to be gone. She nodded at the nurse to take her place by the bed and said, "I'll be right back, I'm just going to check on that doctor."

Out in the corridor she wept, because there were some feelings she was glad she would never experience.

Harriet

There was that lovely bit in *Bridget Jones* (film, not book) where Renée Zellweger is driving off with Hugh Grant, in his sports car, up an incredibly straight road to a country-house weekend of boating and (anal, apparently—since when did the ordinary stuff, done properly, of course, get so dull?) sex. She's congratulating herself on being the woman she has always fantasized about being. Harriet had loved that film and especially that bit—the heroine being unshackled from her spinsterhood.

Her dirty weekend with Nick hadn't started like that. Bloody BJ—who never did anything but moan about her single status— hadn't had to cope with the lead-weight guilt that an adulteress must carry around. Tim had agreed with cheerful alacrity to a weekend with her long-lost friend Sally (good idea, you should have a break from the kids) and had happily set about filling the two days when she would be away—"We'll have great fun, won't we, you two?"—and the three had been huddled, like Macbeth's witches, over the kitchen table for days, planning trips to the Science Museum, the cinema and the dreaded Leisure Lagoon (twelve inches of water the temperature—and basic chemistry— of wee, full of fat parents and their whinging offspring, surrounded by white rapids and terrifying waterslides inhabited by whippet-thin, body-hairless youths sniggering at the fat parents in the middle and largely ignoring the "no heavy petting" signs). Not for the first time, Harriet felt that they might prefer it if their father took care of them every day.

She was cross when she got into the car that Saturday morning—cross because they weren't sorry she was going and no one had cried, or clung limpetlike to her leg, and crosser still with herself for being cross about it. Chloe had had a bad night, with a bed-wetting episode at midnight followed by a more-juice session at two and, the final straw, the bad-dream debacle at four. Permitted then, for sheer persistence, to climb into her parents' bed, she had assumed the position she reserved for Mummy and Daddy's bed—the thrashing starfish—and fallen into a deep, if mobile sleep. Normally Harriet loved having the kids in bed— they smelt so good, and they breathed so peacefully, and you could stroke their faces or their baby-soft hair without them swatting away your hand. You could look at them in the light from the landing and try to imagine their grown-up faces, and who they would marry and what they would be. Sometimes they would hold your hand and squeeze back, or nod their heads, from far away, when you asked them if they loved you. Sometimes, though, eight hours of uninterrupted sleep was better.

And this had been one of those times. Alone in the bathroom—at least that was possible with Chloe comatose next door—Harriet examined the dark circles under her eyes. She'd been to The Clinic, a beauty parlor although its silly name suggested STD treatment, but it was close, and the girls knew her now, and there was a limit to the number of people you were happy to show your excess thigh hair and cork-tile heels to, so to The Clinic she went; there she had had her legs and bikini line waxed—what was the point in buying expensive pants if it looked like they were being worn by the missing link? She'd had her feet done, too, but drawn the line at a fake tan—Tim would surely have thought it odd for a night away with an old school friend. When she looked at herself in the mirror now, though, she realized it had been a mistake: she was pale, not at all sexy and possibly a little frightened.

Three hours, a hundred miles and several inches of tinted moisturizer later, she was feeling better, and slightly Renée Zellwegerish. She had promised herself she wouldn't think about Tim, Josh or Chloe from the second she pulled out of the drive until the second she turned back into it, although she had also promised she would call them on Saturday evening before bed, which might prove a challenge. Heading vaguely in the direction she had told Tim she was going—as though geography would be his prime concern in the event of his catching her out—she had chosen, and Nick had booked, a pretty red-brick Georgian hotel, set in a few acres of formal gardens (good, she thought, for Jane Austenesque flirtation) and parkland (for the more D.H. Lawrence moments of the weekend). The sun was bright and the sky very blue—you could tell yourself, if you were searching for justification, that the gods were smiling on you. She recognized the personalized number plate of Nick's Audi TT, and her heart raced—he was here first. That was flattering.

He wasn't, as she might have hoped, hopping from foot to foot in Reception, with a plaid blanket over his arm and a champagne lunch hamper in the other, or behind a broadsheet in the spacious lounge, checking the cricket scores to still his racing pulse. "Mr. Mallory . . ." Was that a judgmental pause there?—don't be silly, she told herself—these people are trained not to raise an eyebrow if you get it on at the front desk with a complete stranger. Discretion costs, and Nick's paying. ". . . has already gone up to the room, ma'am. Suite five, at the top of this flight of stairs, first on the left. If you would be kind enough to leave your car keys, I'll have someone bring up your luggage directly." Harriet hoped the someone wouldn't notice that the car was full of dried clementine peel and sweet wrappers.

She counted fifteen stairs, wide and expensively carpeted, like the ones Vivien Leigh falls down, lies across and gets carried up in *Gone With the Wind*. She didn't think she'd have been more nervous walking the Green Mile. Except she truly felt, or told herself at least, that she was walking not toward death but headlong at life. Not a life with Nick—even Harriet wasn't that naïve—but life in its most capital-L sense, full of experience, emotion, fun and . . . all the things she was now almost sure a life with Tim did not offer.

She walked up them as slowly as she dared, under the gaze of the reception staff, so that she wouldn't be any more breathless at the top than she had started out at the bottom. Knocked at the door, quietly. Nick answered straightaway. She realized she hadn't seen him in an open-necked shirt since university: at the wedding, and at their weekly trysts, he had always been smartly dressed—he looked more handsome buttoned up, she thought.

He pulled her into the room and kicked the door shut. "Well, hello! What's a naughty girl like you doing in a nice place like this?" He didn't give her the chance to answer. His marvelous mouth came down on hers, and he was kissing her, as wonderfully as he had all the other times, his hands pulling her bum up into him. He'd been looking forward to seeing her—that was perfectly obvious.

She drew back, hands pushing his chest. Surely there were things to say. "You made good time." Scintillating.

"Yeah, got away early. Couldn't sleep, thinking about you." He kissed her again.

"They're—they're bringing up my luggage in a minute."

"Oh, no, they're not." Nick broke away from her. He took the Do Not Disturb sign off the inside of the door and slipped it on the outside. "That should make things clear." He smiled.

Harriet was suddenly nervous. It was only eleven-forty-five in the morning, and she felt embarrassed by the sign. She wasn't sure she'd be able to face the staff at lunch. She saw a bottle of champagne resting in an ice bucket on the desk, two graceful glasses next to it. "Oh, Nick, champagne. That's sweet of you. Let's open it."

"In a while. I'm not thirsty." He was back at her side. "Look at you," he said. "Gorgeous dress, sweetheart." And he was pushing her backward, nudging her with his knees, and his shoulders, toward the bed. "You look good enough to eat. In fact"—now she was sitting on the bed, on the satin cover, and he was pushing her down, gently but firmly, with one hand on her shoulder—"I think that's exactly what I'm going to do . . ." He was on his knees at the foot of the bed, between her legs, and his big hands were pushing up her skirt, feeling at each hip for the elastic of her underwear. He was looking. It was broad daylight. He groaned appreciatively. "I see you took my advice about the underwear. Very nice." And then he wasn't talking anymore, just moaning a bit.

Harriet closed her eyes, but her body was stiff and she couldn't relax, so she opened them again and looked at the ceiling, with its ornate rose. His hands were under her knees, trying to move them further apart. Evidently he felt how tense she was because he raised his head. "Relax, Hats. Let me do this. Believe me, I'm very good at it."

That was it for Harriet. He might have an A+ on his sexual CV for this particular thing, and he could keep doing it until he got a permanent crick in his neck, but he wouldn't get anywhere with her—not like this. Where was the kissing? The gorgeous, deep, forbidden kissing of doorways, cabs and station platforms. She had imagined him making slow, tender love to her here, free of clothes, responsibilities and an audience, with lots and lots of the kissing. She had dreamt of a slow, sexy buildup—a long, boozy lunch, and a walk in that beautiful sunshine, in those gardens. When they'd talked and held hands and laughed and done all of those things, they'd come back here, pull off each other's clothes (it would be dark by then, and dark was essential to Harriet's grand plan) and bring each other to a succession of majestic orgasms (all simultaneous, of course), each one reminiscent of waves crashing on beaches and orchestras reaching crescendo and making them sob with its perfection.

No, no, no. All this "I'm so desperate to possess you I have to put my head up your skirt in the first three minutes and act out the Kama Sutra in the first hour" might be designed to flatter, she supposed, but it wasn't doing anything for her.

She pushed his head away and sat up, smoothing her skirt with both hands and wriggling as her displaced underwear cut into her. She tried to laugh. "Hey, not so fast. I don't charge by the hour, you know."

Nick's expression was sulky as he got to his feet. "This place bloody well does, though." He ran his hand through his hair and went for the champagne. Harriet sat redundantly on the bed, wondering what to say next. He passed her a full glass and drank his own in one irritable gulp. Clearly he wasn't used to rejection. A couple of minutes passed while she sipped at the champagne on the bed, embarrassed, and looked at his angry back. He looked out of the window. It was very, very quiet.

"I'm going to check out the gym. I'll see you later." And he left, before she had thought of what to say or how to say it.

She wanted not to be in the room, too—if she could face walking back past Reception. God, she felt like an idiot, like a precocious schoolgirl whose playground bravado has taken her way out of her depth with the big boys. Nick wasn't interested in her sensibilities, was he? Why had she ever thought he would be? He was only interested in getting his leg over. If he wanted entanglement of the psychological, not carnal kind, he would find it with someone altogether less complicated and more toned.

She did her best to float down the stairs, smiling at the girls behind the desk, who took little notice of her, and went out into the gardens, which were still very pretty and child-free (always welcome, even in times of emotional distress), although they lacked the throbbing, fecund quality she had imagined in them earlier. She sat on a bench with a view and tried to look happy and attractive, independent yet approachable, to see if that made her feel better. On the whole, it didn't. By the time he found her there, an hour later, Nick had recovered his composure. "Sorry, I was a bit of a bull in a china shop. Didn't mean to be. Can I help it if you drive me wild?" And he smiled his sideways City-boy smile at her.

She forgave him. "And sulky?"

"And sulky. Sorry."

"I'm a bit out of practice," she confided, "that's all. I haven't been seduced in a hotel for, ooh, well, forever, really."

"That is a travesty and a waste."

He was sweet. Cheeky and opportunistic and vaguely amoral, but sweet with it. She hadn't been entirely wrong about him. "I think I was just expecting—"

"To be romanced a bit?"

"Well, yes. Just a bit." Harriet felt sheepish. "I'm pathetic, aren't I? A pathetic housewife trying to inject a bit of Barbara Cartland into her life."

"No. You're lovely." Nick took her hand and squeezed it. "To be honest, the girls I usually take to places like this are gagging for it—they're the kind you meet in bars and clubs, see you've got a bit of cash, think you're quite good-looking, I suppose. They've usually got their hand in your fly while you're tipping the porter."

And she'd worried about what they might think of her. "I must seem incredibly prudish."

Nick looked at her. "You seem incredibly nice. You always were. I'm a bastard. Don't know what the hell I was playing at."

"Nice? Euk. What's that expression about damning with faint praise?"

"No," he said firmly, turning her face gently toward his with one finger. "Too nice for this and definitely too nice for me. But enough of this bollocks. If word gets out that I have a softer side, and that a woman has failed to succumb to my considerable bed-room charms, I shall be laughed out of the Square Mile." He stood up. "You wanted gardens, I shall give you gardens." And with a Raleighesque gesture, he swept the moment aside.

It was no good, though. The gardens were beautiful, and the sun was warm; lunch was delicious and so was Nick. They lay down on the grass in the late afternoon, holding each other, but the kisses were no longer thrilling and Harriet didn't want more. She tried to get the feeling back, but the moment had passed up there in the bedroom, under her skirt. It had stopped being a game, and Nick had stopped being a one-dimensional player in it, and Harriet had stopped being a woman who could lie and cheat on her husband, whether she loved him or not. She felt foolish and tearful. "I can't do it," she confessed.

"I know that." He kept an arm round her shoulder.

"I'm sorry, Nick, I've been a terrible pricktease."

"My prick and I will survive—we probably had it coming." He smiled and took a deep breath that raised her head where it lay on his chest. "I think it's me who should be sorry. I think you were a bit vulnerable when we met up again and I took advantage."

She propped herself on her elbow so that she could see his face. "When did you get so sensitive? I don't remember you that way at college."

"I think it only happened a couple of hours ago, actually. God, you've probably ruined me for one-night stands. I'll probably be married within the year. Will you come and get drunk at my wedding in a very short skirt?" The twinkly boy was back.

She used the elbow to dig him in the ribs. "I bloody well will not! That's what got me into this mess in the first place. I'm staying well clear. I'm going home to put my head down."

"You shouldn't do that, you know—stay with him, if you're not happy. Not for the kids or the lifestyle or any of that crap. You've changed, Hats—you'd lost your sparkle when I saw you at Charlie's do. You women are all the same. You worry about the wrinkles and the half stone and your boobs dropping, but you don't worry about the sparkle, and that's the best bit—even for a sex maniac like me. You shouldn't let that go. I remember it fondly."

So do I, Harriet thought, and it made her sad.

It was Nick who left. "You've told him you're not coming back until tomorrow, haven't you? Better stick to it. Stay, have a lie-in, get a massage or something. I'll go home. So many women, so little time—I can't afford to waste a Saturday night here with some married bird who isn't putting out."

"Nice try, Mallory," Harriet said, as she kissed him good-bye. "Your shameful secret's safe with me. If I meet any of those girls you're talking about, your skills between the sheets are legendary, you're hung like a donkey, and you most definitely do not eat quiche."

They hugged next to the Audi.

"Thanks, Nick. I'm grateful."

"Well, if you're so grateful, how about a blow job? No one's looking . . ."

She punched his arm. He was still laughing as he drove away.

Nicole and Harriet

The doorbell rang while Nicole was still rushing around with the Clearblue stick in her hand, trying to decide how to tell Harriet. *She*'d known since last night, which had been just about twelve hours before you were legitimately supposed to take a pregnancy test. Well, she'd known since Venice, really, if gut instinct counted. Chemical confirmation was good, though. She had been supremely confident of her blue line, and had squeezed herself in a little victory hug alone there in the bathroom. A new baby, a new bond, a new start (another). She wasn't going to tell Gavin yet. Things had been lovely between them since they had come home from Venice—he wasn't working so late, and she felt as if they were holding on to the closeness they had found again. She wanted to wait for the perfect moment. The first time, with the twins, she'd been so shocked and frightened and excited when their GP confirmed her suspicions that she'd called Gavin at work and blurted it down the phone, then had to wait five hours for a hug. With Martha she'd been violently ill one morning after a dinner party they'd been to, and Gavin, hearing her, had shouted, "Didn't think you were that pissed last night, Nic—bet you're preggers again."

She had a pile of summer-holiday brochures on the kitchen table, with one open on top. A suitably slim and café-au-lait-colored couple gazed lovingly into each other's eyes over a glass of something chilled in the foreground, while their small and perfectly formed 2.4 children frolicked in the pool behind. She'd booked a villa there this morning, for two weeks in August. She would tell him about the new baby when they were being the family in that picture.

But she was going to tell Harriet today, and that made her more nervous than excited. They hadn't talked about it since that first time, when Harriet had been so hard, so very sure it was a disastrous idea. She wanted her friend not to be so hard on her now that it was too late. If she disapproved of the pregnancy, she would be disapproving of the baby, and if that was the case, Nicole couldn't imagine how things could ever again be comfortable between them. Her friendship with Harriet was the most stable relationship she had, and the most nurturing; she couldn't bear to lose it.

In the end she laid the stick beside the sink before she went to answer the door.

Harriet hugged her and came into the kitchen. Her eyes went straight to the stick. "And . . . ," she asked.

"And . . . yes."

"Something in the water, in Venice, was it?" Harriet was smiling. What else could she do? She had known for months that this was what Nicole was planning. She did think it was daft, but was it really any dafter than driving halfway across the country to *not* have a cheap affair? At least Nicole had been brave enough to confide in her—she had lied, even to her best friend, about where she had been going that weekend.

"Congratulations, Nic." She opened her arms.

Nicole came eagerly into them. "You mean it?"

"Of course I do."

"Thanks. Thanks so much. I don't think I could have stood it if you'd been cross with me."

"Why would I have been? You'd made up your mind. It's not my job to sit in judgment of you, is it? At least you're trying to make your marriage work."

That was new, Nicole thought. She knew Harriet would help her pack, change the locks and call the solicitor if she said she was leaving Gavin, so why all of a sudden was trying to stay married to him something to be commended? She realized then that Harriet looked tired and pale. Something was wrong. "What's the matter?" she asked.

Harriet sighed. There were only two ways to answer that question—tersely, with a lie, or tearfully, with the truth. She didn't want to keep on lying, especially to Nicole. She sat down heavily on the nearest chair and put her face into her hands. The tears she had been holding back for months came hard and fast now.

Nicole sat beside her for a few minutes, saying nothing, with one hand on her friend's shoulder. When she felt Harriet settle slightly, she said, in the tone she normally reserved for her children, gentle, comforting, "Tell me what's wrong, Harriet. Please."

"Everything." Harriet sighed melodramatically. "Every bloody thing." Then she raised her head. "I don't think I love him, Nicole. I can't remember if I ever did. I'm not in love with him. I don't want to make love with him, or be with him, or share things with him. And I thought I could make it all go away, and pretend it wasn't true, but I can't anymore. I honestly can't."

"Has something happened?"

"Yes, no. Well, nothing that counts. I'm not having an affair with anyone, although there was someone. But it wasn't about him. It's about me. And Tim."

Nicole didn't understand, but she didn't want to interrupt the feelings pouring out of Harriet.

"I feel like, it's like you reach a certain age, and you choose the person you're going to marry, and you marry them and get membership to this club, and it's a really nice club, and you like all the other members, and you get to have a nice house and clothes and holidays and stuff, and great friends, and you have these babies and these are like—wow—the best thing that ever, ever happened to you, and you can't believe how much you love them, but at the end of the day, when they're in bed, and your friends have gone home and you're sitting in your beautiful house, it stops being about all that other stuff and it's about that person you've chosen and only about them, and they have to be the right person, because otherwise all of the other stuff doesn't matter. And he's not, Nic. He's not that person. He's lovely and he's kind and he's good. But he's not that person."

"What person do you want him to be?" Nicole asked.

"That is so easy to answer. I want him to be the person I love more than anything else—that I love so much I would rather die than be without. That still gives me butterflies. Like Gavin."

"You wouldn't want to be married to Gavin."

"Of course not. But I want to feel about someone like you feel about him. And I don't, not about Tim. I thought I might have met someone else, only he wasn't either—it wasn't him so much as an idea of him, you know, and I just made myself look like an idiot."

"You're losing me, sweetie," Nicole said. She was a bit afraid of this Harriet. She was crying through the talk now, so that it was coming in waves from far inside herself. Nicole didn't have a clue who this someone else was supposed to be—Harriet must have been keeping secrets from her. She tried to ignore the sting—this wasn't about her. What had brought things to a head? Harriet had been moaning about Tim for months, but Nicole hadn't taken it seriously until now. Tim was a great guy, and he loved Harriet so much, loved the kids. Nicole knew better than most that heart ruled head but, on paper, at least, Tim was perfect.

She didn't mean perfect for everyone, she meant perfect for Harriet. Nicole could see the whole picture—she'd been watching them together for years and years. Tim "matched" Harriet, like she hoped Gavin and she "matched" in the eyes of the rest of the world (if not, she had to admit, in Harriet's). Harriet was ditzy and chaotic, Tim was calm and sensible; Harriet was funny and flippant, Tim lent her sincerity and, sometimes, levity. There were differences but also vast areas of common ground in the really important stuff—in warmth, caring, wanting the same things for their children. They even went together physically, Tim long and lean, Harriet smaller and rounder, but the perfect size to fit under his arm and be held.

Nicole remembered Tim telling her about their first meeting: he was a bit drunk, and his eyes had filled with pleasure at the memory. He had said, "I thought love at first sight was bollocks, and maybe it wasn't love, but it certainly wasn't lust, because she looked a fright—all tearstained and messed up—but I just knew, like a lightbulb had gone on over my head, like in a cartoon, you know—that she was the other half of me. I was born to love her— it's why I'm here, you know. It's the answer to the big question. Now they're the answer, Harriet and Josh."

Nicole had thought that, yes, she did know, that this was how it was with her and Gavin, but she had felt . . . if not jealous, ex- actly, then aware that Tim's feelings were finer, nobler, if that didn't sound pompous, than Gavin's. She thought Harriet was the luckiest woman she knew. Tim's eyes would follow her round a room, not checking up or possessively but proudly. She had never seen him flirt with anyone else—she didn't think he was capable of it, or even of registering other women. He was gone, he'd been gone from the first night he saw her.

Now Harriet poured out the story of the assignations, the lunches and the eventual disastrous weekend with Nick. It wasn't punctuated with her usual humor, or self-deprecating irony, but with shame, regret, humiliation and more tears. "I'm so sorry I didn't tell you before. I knew you'd try to stop me—I knew you'd be on Tim's side."

Nicole pulled Harriet's face up and looked into her eyes. "I wouldn't do that—I'm always going to be on your side. You're my best friend, and you've never sided against me. That's what it means."

"Even though you've been where I was putting Tim? I think that's what made me feel worst, what stopped me telling you."

Nicole imagined Tim's face, and his pain. "I would have tried to stop you, yes, not because I'm on some crusade for fidelity but because it sounds like it was always going to hurt you and Tim in the end. This Nick may not be a pantomime villain, but he clearly didn't have much regard for you or your marriage, did he?"

Harriet smiled ruefully. "Oh, I think he's probably just as screwed up as the rest of us behind that good-time façade."

"Probably," Nicole agreed. "I'm not bothered about him right now, though. I want to say something to you about Tim—and it's not that he's a perfect husband, and that you'd be mad to leave him. That isn't for me to say—only two people truly know what goes on within a marriage."

Harriet looked at her friend and recognized the barb.

"I just want to tell you that I have been your friend, both of you, for seven years, and I think you're wrong about him and you. You certainly loved him when I met you, and you loved him when Josh was born, and Chloe, properly I mean, like you're talking about. You can't fake that, and I've seen it. And he sure as hell has loved you every minute of those seven years—I know it."

Harriet was listening, and wiping her nose. Nicole knew she was on the edge of the safe zone of friendship, but she cared so very much for both of them that she took off her safety harness and jumped into the void. Once she'd started, the diagnosis poured itself out. She didn't look at Harriet, but she knew she was listening intently.

"I think you've been telling yourself all these years that Charles was the one true love of your life—because it never properly ended before you met Tim—and that you married some second-choice substitute, and that therefore you can't have truly loved him. And you hate yourself for 'settling,' and you feel guilty because you've made yourself believe you're using him. Now you're trying to talk yourself into leaving him because you think that's the best solution."

Harriet still wasn't speaking.

"And I think the thing about Charles—it's rubbish. You were so young, and it was a first love, but it wasn't real—it never got tested like real life tests you, and you fell at the first hurdle. And this Nick guy, same thing. Playing games. But don't throw away what's real. I believe in you and Tim—I truly, truly do."

Harriet knew that Nicole was right about some things, about Charles and about Nick. "Why am I feeling like this, then, if things should be so great?"

To this Nicole didn't have a ready answer. "I don't know. Call it a seven-year itch." Harriet tossed her head impatiently. "No, I don't mean that flippantly. I mean that familiarity breeds contempt and you're afraid there's something better out there that you might be missing. I think that's what Gavin feels, too, sometimes." Anger misted Harriet's eyes.

"Well, maybe that's different." Nicole steered the conversation skillfully away from the trouble spot. "I think the wedding in the spring, and being in our mid-thirties, and stuff—maybe it's watershed time. Something like that. Maybe you guys need some time away from the kids, and the day-to-dayness, you know?"

Or away from each other, Harriet thought. Nicole may have read the situation, and her mind, like a pro, but when it came to solutions, she really wasn't much help.

JUNE
READING GROUP

MY ÁNTONIA

WILLA CATHER © 1918

My Ántonia *immortalizes the beautiful, wild-eyed immigrant girl who has haunted Jim Burden all his life. For Jim, Ántonia Shimerda symbolizes the extraordinary contradictions of the American West: its harshness and untamed beauty, its blazing summers and bitter winters, its endless possibilities and vast, unconquerable horizons.*

R eady to go?"
Susan grabbed her bag from the hall table and slammed the door behind her. "My God, am I ready!" She practically skipped down the path ahead of her friend.

"Okay. So I'm guessing you loved the book?"

"The book? Hardly! Read it, didn't really get it, didn't really mind, although of course I won't admit that this evening, especially to Harriet, and I don't expect you to drop me in it. One man's meat and all that. I'm just in the mood for some fun. I want to sit on Nicole's perfect white sofa, drink a glass of perfect white wine and forget about the whole bloody lot of them."

"Who's them? Not St. Roger, surely?"

"No, not Roger. He's lovely. Obviously. My customers, for one, with their hideous taste and unreasonable demands."

"Good day at work, then?"

"Not a good day. Not at all. One of those absolute bastards, actually. Mary's been in a mood for what feels like weeks now. I think she's stressed about Clare, but that's hardly my fault, is it?"

"I must confess that I've read this before." Good-natured boos all round. Harriet put her hand up to quieten them. "But not since university, and everyone knows that children addle your brain, so I read it again for this meeting. Slowly and everything. In case I had changed, and it wasn't that good anymore. But it was. Actually, it makes me a bit nervous, because I think if you choose a book you've read before because you love it and you want everyone else to love it like you do, that's a bit risky. I loved this when I studied it. And I wanted us to be brave and read something that wasn't new, not something we chose because it was on the best-seller lists, or in the front window of Ottakar's, or because everyone else was reading it. This is a classic, and I think we're ready."

"Jane Austen, yes—although *never* ask me to read one of hers for this group. Charles Dickens, yes—but frankly the BBC does it better than he did, if you ask me. D. H. Lawrence, ahem, yes. This one, not so much. The guy in the bookshop even had to remind me how to pronounce it. How embarrassing is that? And, then order it for me. How can it be a classic if the rest of us have never heard of it?"

"Don't tempt me to answer that question." Harriet winked. "Just take my word for it, it is. It's an American classic. Which is what I was really into at college. Walt Whitman, Flannery O'Connor, Stephen Crane. All of that."

"Now you really *are* losing us."

"Yeah. I think I'm in the wrong reading group."

"No, I think Harriet's in the wrong reading group. We're all pretty much on a level. She's the intellectual one."

"Then we could read *Hello!* and Jane Green, and Wendy Holden."

"Flannery who?"

"Hang on." Nicole was remembering something now, and she sat forward excitedly. "Didn't you want to call Chloe Flannery? Is that why?"

"Yeah!" Harriet was animated. The others made faces. "Thank God for Tim."

"Absolutely. That's cruelty. Flannery. Honestly? Can you imagine calling her at soft play? Flannery! Flannery!" They were all laughing now.

"Okay, okay. And yes, I'm almost certainly in the wrong reading group, but I'm prepared to tolerate you, for altruistic reasons, of course." They knew Harriet was laughing at herself, and the fact that she did that more heartily than she laughed at them redeemed her. "But did you like it?" She looked round the room, hands out at them, palms open. God, she could be bossy. Nicole was almost expecting her to ask for a show of hands, then keep back after class anyone who said no.

Polly answered first. "I did. I didn't love it. But I did. I really like the nature in it."

"Absolutely. That incredible sense of seasons, vivid colors, the hardships."

"Come on, though, Harriet. You're the one who's always going on about passion and drama and caring. Did you honestly get that from this, or is this the kind of thing that you read on another level?"

"Oh, you get it in spades. It's all here—unrequited love, suicide, seduction, desertion, lost youth, pioneer spirit, disappointment. It all goes on."

Clare now: "I see all that, but the writing style's a bit funny. All that stuff happens, but it's not like it's the main action somehow. These major things, she writes about them like they are incidental."

"Against the backdrop they are, sort of. I think she didn't want to write some melodramatic women's novel. That's one of the points. It's the hugeness of everything."

"But it's the melodramatic women's novel you profess to like best, Harry."

Harriet was exasperated now. She didn't think they had liked it at all, and she was tempted to think that must be because they hadn't got it. Hadn't understood it. Why did they keep bringing it back to her?

Clare came to Harriet's rescue. "I loved her stoicism, Ántonia's I mean. All those terrible things happened to her—I mean, her life was an absolute drag most of the time. Her father killed himself, the man she loved got her pregnant and deserted her, but she never lost her positivity, she never gave up. And she gets a happy ending, doesn't she? I don't know if it's a *proper* happy ending. I'm not sure it is for Jim, the narrator, but it is for her, for Ántonia. She gets a husband who loves her and gives up one life for her to go and work the land, and doesn't mind that she had an illegitimate child, and she gets all those children, and they're obviously her whole life—when she talks about the oldest one leaving home, when she's grown-up and has a child of her own, the way she still couldn't bear for her to go."

Harriet looked at her. They all knew that she had left Elliot and was living with her mum, but they couldn't say anything until she told them herself. Harriet didn't think she would be in any hurry to do that. She's very pretty, and she's lovely, and her life is a tragedy. She wants what I have, she thought suddenly. She thinks I have a perfect life—a husband who loves me, and my children, who are healthy and safe. She thinks my life is untouched by unhappiness. And if I told her what my unhappinesses were, she would think I was mad. And ungrateful and wretched. It would be like complaining to a starving person that you couldn't choose between Indian and Chinese. She felt a shiver of something like shame. If Clare knew what she had done, almost done, with Nick . . . Maybe she should be talking to Clare, not Nicole. Then she might get some perspective and be able to pull herself together.

Clare saw that Harriet was looking at her. She didn't know what she was thinking, but she saw pity cross her face. She wanted to talk about it. She wanted Harriet to ask her what it felt like, to be unable to have a baby. To lose a baby you were carrying, and be so afraid, each time, that it would happen again, so that eventually you were just waiting for it to happen and joy and excitement didn't come into it. So that you could almost describe that feeling when you had the cramp, or saw the blood in the toilet, as relief, because the waiting for it was awful. And she wanted her to ask how it felt to have your marriage collapse around you because you couldn't have a baby and you had stopped knowing how to help each other accept it. She wanted to talk to Harriet about it all, but the others were there. That surprised her, somehow: she had never felt before like she wanted to talk about it, even to her mother. She couldn't stand looking at the sadness etched on Mary's face as she listened. But she could talk to Harriet. She would tell her, one day, she was sure, when she knew her a little better, when there was a chance. She smiled at her as the others chatted beside them.

Elliot

Mary had told him where Clare was. Elliot hadn't explained why he wanted to talk to her, and Mary hadn't asked. He hadn't been to his parents-in-law's house since that first night, in April, when Clare had moved out, and he had seen Mary briefly only once, when she had called round to see him on a Saturday morning, and they had had an awkward cup of tea together. Without Clare in his house, her mother's presence had seemed odd and sad, and they had both been relieved when she had stood up to leave. Reg had dropped her off, Mary said, at one of the girls' houses, she wasn't sure which. She thought they usually finished by ten-thirty or so, and that Reg would pick her up. She didn't question why Elliot would want to go and collect her, any more than she would ever question his intentions toward Clare: they had been on the same side for so long, the three of them. She called Reg downstairs to give Elliot directions to Harriet's house. They offered him a drink, to pass the time until then, they said, but Elliot thanked them and declined. If he sat with them, in the chintzy living room of a dozen Christmas mornings and a thousand Sunday lunches, he would have to tell them about the baby and about Cressida, and whether from cowardice, a sense of what was right or both, he couldn't do that now. They would hate him for it, he was sure; years of affection would be swept away by a tide of protective love for Clare. And he would miss them, but he understood.

He had spent the afternoon by the river, alone, watching the world through these new eyes he had lately, the ones which saw so much more because suddenly the old world was bustling with possibilities. Only the specter of Clare's face still hung over him, and that was why he had made up his mind to tell her tonight: the reality couldn't be any worse than what he had imagined, and he wanted to be free of both.

He had a brandy in a pub, the one where he and Cressida had had that first drink all those months ago. It was comforting to be there among the happy summer crowd. It felt so normal to say, even only to himself, "Yeah, I got together with my girlfriend in this pub. She's pregnant, you know, yeah, first baby. Cheers, yeah, we're chuffed about it." Like other people. You must feel like this if you'd just come out of prison, or if you'd had a cancer that had gone into remission. He was coming out, too, out of a bad marriage. Because that was what it had become, whatever it had once been. A marriage where two people were unhappy was a bad marriage, however much you wished you could change it back into what it once was, or even into something different. You couldn't, it was, and he was out of it. And it felt good. He was blinking in the sunlight after years underground. More than almost anything, he wanted Clare to feel the same. Maybe today would be two steps back, but he knew, or at least he believed, that there were steps forward for her to take . . . faltering ones that he couldn't help her with.

Later, outside Harriet's house, he watched the women leave. They were loud and giggling, flushed with pleasure and wine. Clare was the last out, walking down the path flanked by Susan and another woman. Her cheeks were pink; she looked pretty when she smiled. Young and pretty. She stopped short and the smile faded when she saw him through the car window. She moved forward self-consciously, almost hissed at him, "What are you doing here, Elliot?"

"I went round to yours. I wanted to see you—your dad told me where to find you. He said it was okay if I came instead of him."

She was obviously embarrassed. A little louder, evidently for the benefit of the others, she said, "But I've just offered Polly a lift home—she and I go a different way from the others."

Polly started to protest, and Susan stepped forward. "I'll drop you, Polly. No problem."

Polly accepted gratefully, kissed Clare's cheek and was gone toward Susan's car. Elliot watched her.

It was quiet in the car. Elliot's hand twitched to turn on the radio.

Clare wasn't speaking. She sat as far into the left passenger door as she could get, seeming to insinuate herself into its very fabric. And looked straight ahead. What was he doing here? What the hell was he trying to do?

Elliot was terrified by her silent reproach. He knew he could not have the conversation he was determined to have in moving traffic, but he couldn't go back to her parents' house, and he didn't want to take her to what was now only his home. A pub wasn't right either. He pulled over into a quiet lay-by and turned off the engine. They were only a couple of minutes' walk from Mary and Reg's home.

"What are you doing?" An exasperated sigh. "Elliot, I'm tired, it's late, I really don't want to sit here."

"Just listen, will you? I want to talk to you."

His tone made her listen. She honestly had no idea what direction Elliot would take. She wondered, for just a moment, what she would say if he asked her to come back, begged her to come home. She wouldn't go. This was the first time she had realized it. She didn't feel as if she was looking at the man she loved, although she had assumed, from the dull ache in her stomach every day, that she still did. Curious, because, for so long, he had been. She fixed her eyes on his mouth and watched his lips while he spoke.

Now Elliot looked at her, and just talked. It came out like the rehearsed speech it was, rushed a little for fear of interruption, a little clipped for fear of breaking down. "I know how much this is going to hurt you. I'm sorrier than you will ever know that things have turned out this way for us. We should have split up long before anything like this happened. It would have been best for both of us. We don't have the answers to each other's problems anymore, Clare. We haven't for a long time. I've made a mess of it, and I'm so, so sorry."

Clare looked right at him while he talked, not blinking, or reacting. He hadn't told her anything yet.

"I've met someone else." A kick in the solar plexus.

"We've been seeing each other for a few months." A knee in the groin.

"She's pregnant. With my baby." A clean pistol shot to the temple. Everything sounded further away after that. Elliot was rambling, from miles away. Trying to say things that would make that one thing better.

"We didn't plan this, Cressida and me." She had a name, and Clare knew who she was. She hadn't met her, but she knew.

"It just happened."

Still she didn't speak, and now Elliot could feel himself begin to squirm under her scrutiny.

"I think . . . I'm in love with her. I think she loves me . . ."

At last Clare spoke, because she wanted to drown those words. Inside she was screaming, but her words came out calmly and angrily. "Thank you, Elliot. Thank you very much. Not just for fucking someone else for months under my nose. Or for telling me about it in a sodding car. Or for getting her pregnant by accident, for Christ's sake. But for sharing with me the fact that you love each other. Thanks for that. You're a real star."

Elliot was almost relieved at her rage. Rage was so much easier.

She wanted to slap him, hard, across the mouth that had said those things. So she did. She slapped him as hard as she could. Years of anger and hurt went into the blow, and it made his head spin. She had never raised so much as a finger in anger before. He was glad she had done it.

She got out and slammed the door. Elliot wound the window down. "Clare, wait. Let me take you home. We need to talk about this."

"That's exactly what we don't need to do. This has nothing to do with me. Not anymore. Just leave me alone."

And she walked off toward Mary's house.

Elliot opened his door to go after her. But he didn't get out of the car. It wasn't fair to chase after her. To say what? There wasn't anything he *could* say. He looked at her back; her head was hunched low on her neck, and her hands were thrust into her pockets. She was probably crying; he couldn't tell. She didn't need him. She needed her mum. Still, though, he sat in the car, in the lay-by, and watched her walking.

A sort of shivery fear started to rise in him. What had he done? He had told Clare, which Cressida had specifically asked him not to do. Wasn't it the right thing to do? Wasn't it his right?

But he hadn't thought about his rights: he had just been overwhelmed by the need for it to be known. Cressida hadn't told Polly because Clare hadn't known. That was it, he was sure. He hated it being a secret, them and the baby. He was frightened now, of Cressida, and he would be afraid, later, of Reg and Mary, and Polly. But his spirit soared in the freedom of revelation.

Clare told her mum that night, and Mary told Susan the next morning, and Susan told Polly straightaway. She called her at the office, asked her to take a coffee break, drove straight down from her beautiful, peaceful hill and told her dearest friend that her daughter was pregnant not by her childhood sweetheart, a boy barely out of his teens known to Polly almost all of his life, but by a man she had never met. A man who was twelve years older than Cressida. A man who was married to a friend of theirs. It was the hardest conversation she had ever had with Polly. Maybe with anyone.

Polly couldn't believe what she was hearing. Why hadn't Cressida told her? This, when they had just got themselves back on an even keel, when she thought she had heard everything that she was going to have to get used to. Yesterday she had felt unshockable. The baby wasn't a secret anymore, not at college or out in the world—hardly could be, now that Cressida's tummy was taking on that telltale swell that started right under her bust. On her slender frame it was more obvious than it would have been on a curvier girl. Cressida loved her new belly (Polly was interested to see how long that would last, once the swollen ankles, backache and crippling indigestion set in) and wore the same short T-shirts she always wore in the summer: the expanse of flesh between T-shirt hem and trouser waistband was swelling almost weekly. Polly had watched her last week, from the doorway of the living room: she had been stroking her bump absentmindedly while she watched television, in a pose so reminiscent of Polly, twenty years ago, that it brought back a tranche of memories so vivid she could almost smell them.

But what in hell was she supposed to do with this?

She felt a surge of total rage against this Elliot. How dare he? What was he playing at? An older man, married, in a position of responsibility in an academic institution. This wasn't okay. As soon as Susan had left, and before she knew what she was doing, she had punched the number for directory inquiries into her mobile phone, had the number of the college's administration office texted back to her and called it. She asked for him by name. The quiet girl who answered said he was in a meeting. She left her name and number, and hung up.

Half an hour later she was home, and wishing she hadn't. It was Cressida she needed to talk to. Most of the anger had drained out of her, along with the energy it had generated, and she slumped onto a kitchen chair. Daniel had football practice and was going home with another boy from the squad, and Cressida wasn't home either—she had left a note on the table saying she was out with a friend and that she might drop in on Dan and Tina for supper. She had signed her name with two crosses and an *o* for hug. Polly didn't reach for the phone to demand an audience: she wanted to sit with the information for a little while. She wanted to talk to Jack too, but she didn't dare call him, not when she was feeling like this.

She was almost asleep in the living room, a large whiskey tumbler empty beside her, when the doorbell rang.

It was Elliot. He put out his left hand politely and introduced himself. "I got your message. I thought it might be better if we met face-to-face. Is Cressida here?"

"No, just me. You'd better come in." She stood against the wall to let him pass. He was brave, at least, this man who was about to make a grandmother of her.

"I suppose Cressida doesn't know you're here?"

"No."

"And does she have any idea that you were planning to drop your little bombshell last night?"

"No," he admitted.

Anger rose in Polly on Cressida's behalf. With this news he had put himself, in the clumsiest way, directly between them, and she was sure that Cressida would be furious.

Her silence egged him on. "I didn't want it to be a secret anymore. I didn't want us to have to hide away."

"Cressida's not hiding away. I'm incredibly proud of the way she's coping. I'm just not sure what role you have to play in the whole business, apart from the obvious one . . ."

That was mean. They both knew it.

"Don't say it like that. It wasn't like that at all."

"Like what?"

"You think it was just an affair to me. You say it like I'm some college Lothario who picked her up and used her."

"I don't know how it was, do I?" Polly said. "Yesterday you were a guy Cressida had met once or twice at college, married to a friend of mine. Now you're telling me my daughter's pregnant with your baby. How in hell do you think that makes you sound? Not good, from where I'm sitting."

Elliot was surprised to find himself getting angry. She knew nothing about him, yet she was judging him. He was suddenly desperate to prove to her, and through her to Cressida, what kind of man he was. The words tumbled out of him, too fast. They hadn't even been properly formed thoughts in his head until now.

"I love your daughter." He said each word slowly and distinctly. It was wonderful to say it. "I love Cressida, I do. I'm sorry it's been a mess and I'm sorry we haven't done things in the right order, but I love her and we both want this baby. I want to do the right thing, not because it's the right thing but because it's what I want. To be a family. The three of us."

Polly didn't doubt his sentiments or his intent—fervor and excitement were in every line of his face. He had one of those faces, mostly seen in children, that wore every emotion candidly: it made him seem vulnerable. Now he looked more handsome than he had only a few minutes before—that smile and those wide eyes were so eloquent.

"And what about Cressida? What does she want?"

Elliot realized too late that he didn't really know. He knew she wanted the baby, but he hadn't asked her if she wanted him too. She had said she loved him—shown it too, many times. And she was carrying his baby. Surely, she felt the same way as he did. She had to.

Polly saw that confusion and panic just as clearly. Her anger gave way to something like pity. This guy was a mess. He seemed to her like a drowning man who'd found something to cling to—and whom he might pull under with him: Cressida. She felt tired. This was another maternal battle, waiting to be fought. First there had been the baby and its fate, and now there was Cressida's future with this man. Six months ago she would have thought that Cressida getting pregnant at twenty while still at college was the worst scenario she could envisage. She wasn't sure now if that was true.

"I don't know." He couldn't give any other answer. He was utterly deflated.

The courage that had surged through him in the past twenty-four hours had fled. No more confrontations. Not tonight.

"Do you want to wait here for her? She'll be back later."

"Perhaps I should come back."

"You're probably right." She wanted to sleep (or rather lie awake) on it herself. "But tomorrow? I have to talk to her tomorrow. Now that people know."

"Okay. Talk to her. I'll be at home if she needs me."

"No way." She put her hand on his shoulder. "You'd better be here. If you love my daughter, you'll be here in the morning to explain what you've done, and to tell her how you feel. That, Elliot, is the least you can do."

Cressida

Cressida and Polly sat together, ate cereal, drank tea and talked about the forms she was filling in for the DSS—income support, child benefit, lone-parent benefit—and about Cressida needing a few "enormous" shirts for the next couple of months. When the doorbell rang, Polly answered it, ushered Elliot into the kitchen and stood beside him. Cressida was stunned to see who had come, she had been expecting Susan, or some friend of Daniel's. "What are you doing here?"

She was too shocked, Polly thought, to bluster, or try to lie.

"Your mum knows about us, Cress. I told Clare, and she told her mum, and she told her boss, evidently, who told your mum. It sounds like a bloody game of Chinese whispers, I know. I came round and talked to your mum last night, as soon as I found out she knew."

"You did what? But you promised!" she screamed, looking at Polly. "What did he say to you, Mum?"

"That you and he had been seeing each other for a few months now. That you'd been sleeping together."

Cressida colored.

"And that the baby is his."

"She had to know sometime, Cressida."

"It wasn't for you to do. It wasn't up to you."

"And I didn't. I didn't tell your mum, Cress. I told my wife." The word was hard. "I had to—I owed her that, at the very least."

Cressida didn't answer.

"But I'm not sorry that everyone knows. I'm not. I knew you'd find it hard—"

"Get out of here."

Polly and Elliot both said, "Cressida—"

She was shaking now, standing up, steadying herself on the back of her chair. Her whole body was shaking, and her voice shook. "You had no right to do that, Elliot. No right at all. Get out."

"It's not about rights, Cress," he implored her. "It's about us not having to hide anymore—I've had enough of that. Haven't you? Don't you see? I want everyone to know."

"But she's my mum." She was crying now. "I'm sorry, Mum."

Polly opened her arms, but Cressida shook herself again, rubbed her hand angrily across her face and turned back to Elliot. "I can't believe you've done this."

Elliot hung his head. "I love you, Cressida. I love the baby." The words were muffled now, spoken into his chest. They had seemed so much the reason, but now, in this anger and in his fear, they came out small.

She couldn't take that, not in front of Polly, not now. This didn't feel like love. "If you won't go, then I'll have to." She swept past them, ignoring their pleas to stop, grabbed a cardigan from the hooks by the front door and left, slamming it behind her. She could tell Elliot wanted to leave. And she didn't want him to stay.

A couple of hours later Polly was still waiting in the kitchen for Cressida when she came home. She had calmed down: she'd been walking around the neighborhood, she said. She smiled weakly at her own daftness. She'd forgotten to take her purse, so she'd come home for a cup of tea. "I'm not any good at flouncing, that's the truth."

"And that's strange, because it was one of your dad's party pieces." Polly hugged her.

"I'm sorry, Mum. Again. Am I ever going to stop saying that to you?"

"I do hope so."

Cressida smiled again.

"It was a bit of a shocker, though, Cress." What a triumph of understatement.

"I know I should have told you. But you see why I didn't, don't you?"

"It wasn't going to go away, though, honey, any more than the baby was. You didn't think you could go on pretending Joe was the father, did you?"

"I never said he was. I just let you all believe it. It seemed the best option."

"Not for Joe."

"Joe knows everything—I wrote to him. He knows I'm pregnant, and he knows it isn't his. Joe and I never even slept together, Mum."

Polly gave a little laugh. She'd been right about that. It was almost comforting. "Look, sweetheart, I'm not going to get all moral on you about Elliot."

"Mum, I know he's married, and I know that's wrong, and I never in a million years thought I was the kind of girl who could go off with someone else's husband, but . . ." Her voice trailed off. Even at twenty, she knew all the clichés. Clare didn't understand him. He was staying with her because he felt sorry for her. It didn't feel right to use them about her and Elliot. It made everything sound cheap and nasty. It wasn't like that: she knew it, and so did he. She wasn't even sure she wanted to explain it to her mum. It belonged to them.

"Hey, hey, it's okay. Honestly. I just want to say"—Polly took Cressida's hand and pressed it against her own heart—"that you can't expect him to keep a secret like that from his wife, Cress. Whatever has gone on between them, she's still his wife. He had to tell her. You mustn't be angry with him for that."

Cressida was surprised. That was the last thing she had been expecting from her mum. "You sound like you're defending him."

"He doesn't need me to either defend or attack him. He's a grown man in one hell of a mess—and I think he is honestly trying to find the best way out of it. I think you must understand that."

Cressida nodded.

"This baby is going to mean you have to grow up in lots of ways, sweetie, and not just the obvious ones either. Do you know what I mean?"

Cressida thought that maybe she did.

Elliot

It was Cressida at the door. He had hoped it would be. He opened it wide and stood with his arms by his sides. She came to him, and he held her. They didn't speak. When she lifted her head to look at his face, she said, "Sorry."

"Me too."

They didn't know what to say next. Then they both started speaking at the same time.

"I'd just had enough . . ."

"You were right, she needed to know . . ."

They laughed, nervously. Cressida made a sweeping gesture with her arm. "Enough. It's done. There's no point having an endless postmortem about it." Elliot was relieved. "How about a cup of tea?"

"Yeah."

She sat at his kitchen table and crossed her hands over the bump. He thought she looked stunning. Men who didn't like the way their wives looked in pregnancy mystified him. She looked good to him now in a completely new way. Still sexy, still his friend, still all of those things, but something new. Now her face was concerned. "How did it go, anyway?" she asked.

"Not well. How I expected, I suppose."

"It must have been awful for her."

"Yeah, but I don't think she wanted me back. It's over for her too."

"Really?" Cressida wondered momentarily if he was trying to protect her.

"I think so."

"Still, even if she had made up her mind that you two were going to stay split up, I bet this was the last thing she expected to hear."

"Probably." Elliot was uncomfortable, talking about Clare. He couldn't bear to think of her just now. It was selfish, he knew that, but he felt that in telling her he'd closed a door. He would always care for her—wasn't that what you said?—and he meant that, of course he did, but that bit was over for him now. He wanted to move forward. He wanted to talk about the future to this beautiful girl sitting at his kitchen table with his baby inside her.

That was the one thing he hadn't done since she'd told him. Maybe it was because until now Clare had been in the way, or he was frightened of the conversation.

"Can we talk about us?" he asked.

"What about us?"

"Isn't it obvious? In a couple of months you're going to have our baby, and we haven't really talked about it at all. Fair enough, it was a secret for a while, and maybe that made it difficult, but it's not now. Don't you think we should be talking about what we're going to do?"

"I don't really know what you mean."

Elliot felt himself growing frustrated. Was she being deliberately obtuse? "This is our baby."

She nodded. "Of course."

She was leaving him no choice but to lay it on the line. "I want us to raise him or her together. I want us to be a family. I know we can't do it now, I'm still married to Clare, the baby's not even here yet, but I would like to think of you and me, one day, being together, maybe being married to each other."

Christ. That was smooth. He had a vivid flashback of proposing to Clare. He'd been twenty-one, and he'd borrowed some money from his mum to take her to a posh restaurant. He'd spent most of his overdraft limit on a ring: nine-carat gold with a square-cut emerald and two tiny diamonds flanking it. He'd told her they were celebrating their graduation. He'd been going to ask her after the meal, but his nerves were so shredded he thought he might throw up if he didn't get it out, so he asked her before the starters had come. Went down on one knee by the side of the table and everything. Her eyes had shone, and she had flapped her hands in front of her face to stop herself crying. She'd said yes before he finished the question, and got down to hug him on the floor. Turned out to have been a shrewd move, doing it early, because the restaurant gave them a free bottle of champagne. The thing was, he had never considered that she might not say yes. He wouldn't have asked unless he was sure of her.

It felt very different with Cressida. No ring, no smart restaurant, no knee. He was just as sure of what he wanted, but what about her?

"Elliot . . . you're lovely." She put her arms round him so that he couldn't see her face, but he was pretty sure she wasn't trying not to cry.

Pulling back, Cressida looked at her hands. She was going to try to explain.

He wanted to let them both off the hook. "Not now. You can't know how you're going to feel, can you, when everything's up in the air? And I'm not a free man. The last thing I want to do is pressure you when you've got everything else to cope with."

She put her hand on his cheek. He didn't like it: it felt maternal, sympathetic. "Listen, Elliot. I do love you. And I promise you"—she took his hand and put it on her stomach—"this baby is yours. It always will be. Okay?"

He got off his chair, laid his cheek next to his hand where she had placed it. Next to the baby. He'd ended up on his knees after all.

Susan

"Mrs. . . . ?"

"Yes?"

"It's Giles Higson. I'm the manager at The Cedars. We have met."

"Yes. Hello." Tall and a little stooped, with damp palms and a limp handshake. "Is anything wrong?" She was held still by a white-hot ring of fear.

"Not now. Everything's fine. I just thought we should give you a ring because we had a bit of a problem with Alice this morning."

She didn't like the way he called her mother Alice, as if she was a child. "What happened?" She leant back against the desk, facing the window, and watched the trees. Mary had looked up, when the phone rang, and when she heard her ask if anything was wrong, but she left her work on the wide table and went quietly out of the room now, with the two coffee mugs they had finished a few minutes before. Susan held a curtain hook in one hand and worked it between her fingers nervously.

"One of our care workers found her in the car park. She'd packed her bag, said she was going home. She got quite agitated when we tried to bring her back inside."

"Oh, God."

"There was a taxi driver. He'd just dropped off a visitor, and she was trying to persuade him to take her to an address he didn't know. He said it wasn't anywhere local. Obviously he became suspicious, and alerted one of our staff."

He talked like an animated brochure, the one that promised you a home from home. Christ, no wonder Mum had tried to run away.

"She's fine now. She had a nice sleep, after lunch, and now she's in the lounge with the other residents."

Watching children's television, no doubt. That patronizing tone again. Why are you telling me? she wanted to ask. What's the point of me knowing?

He answered her silent question. "We'll have to report it to the GP, when he comes, and if it happens again, we may have to look at her security arrangements—for her own protection, of course."

Lock her up. Susan's mind was offering a steady simultaneous translation. "Isn't the front door secure?"

Now his tone became even more didactic. "It is, but your mother can appear to be very lucid at times." I know: those are the moments where I am afraid that I have condemned her. "She must have waited until someone came to the door who wasn't familiar with her . . . problems."

"I'll come over."

"Well, if you would like to."

She could hear his subtext: that there was no point, really, that Alice wouldn't know if she was there or not.

"We serve supper at five p.m." High tea, not supper, at tables covered with plastic cloths, to old people who dribble and suck food through their teeth. Not something you would choose to interrupt. Far better that it happens behind closed doors.

"I'll be there as soon as I can." She hung up but stayed where she was, still watching the trees.

What home did Alice think she was escaping to? Not Maple Cottage, her most recent home, certainly. Perhaps the house where Susan and Margaret had grown up. Or further back, the house Alice herself had grown up in. Susan had never been there, but it was still alive—home—in Alice's head.

With a deep sigh, Susan gathered up her handbag and shoved her mobile phone into it. "Mary?" She appeared at the door. "I've got to go and see Mum. Can you hold the fort?"

"Course I can. Everything okay?"

"I don't know till I get there. Mum tried to run away, apparently." Her voice, which had been strong, broke and wobbled. She pushed the fingers of one hand into her eyes. "They found her outside."

"Thank goodness."

Mary didn't fuss. She knew Susan well enough to know that she didn't want that, a sympathetic hug or a clucking, maternal "there, there."

She went over to the curtains she had been cutting and picked up the scissors. "I'll be fine here. I'll lock up behind myself, shall I?"

"Thanks, Mary. See you."

She drove slowly to The Cedars. It was getting harder every day to will herself to go in. She was less certain, each time, of what or who she would find. And she had pretty much given up hope of finding her mother.

Nicole

Nicole looked at Gavin. Ten out of ten for effort. If only six out of ten for appearance. Mind you, even dressed like he was, he was a good-looking bugger. She wondered if everyone else saw what she did.

At this minute he was at the far end of the games field, with its freshly painted, not entirely straight lines, wearing a lace tutu over his suit trousers and a six-year-old's school beret, waiting to do his stuff in the fathers' race at Sports Day, the first he had been to. Until now Nicole had flown the flag for the kids at these events on her own—she would watch through the camcorder lens, stopping to wipe away tears of laughter or pride, recording it all for Gavin to see later. She'd been running in the mothers' race since the twins were at nursery school, even when Martha was still a baby and her pelvic floor wasn't entirely up to it. But at breakfast that morning, Gavin had announced that he'd canceled a lunch, moved a meeting, and would be coming to Sports Day.

The boys had been so delighted they had spat Rice Krispies across the table in exultant cheers, and Martha had rushed upstairs to get dressed in her "bestest bestest shorts" to mark the occasion. It wasn't fair, was it, that fathers had to do so little to earn adulation mothers could only dream of? But Nicole didn't mind—not today. Instead of sensible trousers and flat shoes, and the prospect of her sore breasts being made more so by the exertion, she was wearing a floaty summer dress with underwear that was not suitable for running and pretty kitten heels. She was feeling wonderful. If this was atonement, and she had thought a great deal about that since the reading group had read that McEwan novel, then long might it last.

Last week he'd run the BBQ at the Summer Fayre, had donned an apron and spent several happy hours flipping burgers and drinking beer with the other mums and dads from Martha's nursery class. He used his breaks to take Martha on the pony that was lumbering from one end of the playing field to the other at a pound a go, or to watch the boys toss the welly over their shoulders.

Harriet and Tim saw her from where they were chatting to one of the teachers, waved and came over.

"Hiya!"

Nicole kissed Tim warmly. She hadn't seen him since Harriet had poured out her heart.

"Well, this is a turn-up for the books." Tim was looking at Gavin.

"I know." Nicole laughed. "I don't know what's got into him!"

"Aren't you in this race?" Harriet asked Tim. "You'd better hurry up—it looks like they're about to start." She sounded irritated.

"Okay, hold these, will you?" Tim passed her his jacket and shoes, stuffed with his socks. Harriet looked at them with distaste and put them on the ground.

"Good luck, Tim," Nicole shouted, since Harriet clearly wasn't going to.

Josh's voice rang out from the throng of his classmates: "Go, Dad, go." Tim saluted, Rocky-style, in his son's direction and trotted over to join Gavin.

Harriet turned to Nicole. "You look lovely. Is that a new dress?"

"Yes." Nicole dropped her voice. "I've bought a twelve so that nothing shows."

Just as quietly, Harriet replied, "Okay, it's official, I hate you. How many weeks are you?"

"Eight on Friday."

"Cow! I was in, oh, at least a sixteen by then. He hasn't guessed?"

"Not a thing. I can't wait to tell him. He's going to be so thrilled. Look at him—he's like a different bloke."

Not so much, Harriet thought, watching Gavin give his all to secure victory in the race.

"How are you?" Nicole asked.

"Bobbing along." Harriet nodded determinedly. "I'm okay."

"Are you looking forward to your holiday? At all?"

Harriet smiled with closed lips. "Portugal. Tim's parents' villa again. Not really. The kids'll love it, though."

"You might, too, you know, if you give it a chance."

"I know. I'll try. Watch me smile." And she made one of her comedy faces. Nicole laughed.

"You should have come with us."

"Oh, yes. Now that *is* a good idea. Love's young dream. I wouldn't get a moment's peace once Tim found out you two were having another baby."

"Might not be a bad idea, you know."

"You just want someone to suffer through bladder incontinence and toddler group with you."

"Yes." Nicole was giggling again.

"Besides," Harriet went on, "I don't think I can bear to see Gavin in a thong, not this year." Gavin had a penchant for ridiculously small swimming trunks, which he hoicked up into the crack of his bum when he was lying on a sun lounger to maximize tanning. At the thought Nicole and Harriet broke into fresh peals of laughter.

"What are you two laughing at?" Tim and Gavin were back, still breathing heavily from their race.

"Yeah, you look like a couple of naughty schoolgirls. What did I miss?" Gavin asked.

"Nothing . . . yet," Harriet blurted, and the two women were lost in new gales of laughter. The men shrugged. They were used to it. Harriet and Nicole had been like this practically from the day they met.

"Fresh air's gone to their heads," Gavin opined.

"That or the caffeine in all the lattes," Tim agreed.

Susan

Susan watched Alice watch *Ground Force*. She was smiling beatifically. The Alice who had been here last month—the one who had remembered when Susan and Margaret were little—had gone away again and left in her place the shrunken woman with skin like tissue paper gazing through the television screen into goodness knew what.

Through the safety-glass panels of the fire door, Susan could see Roger talking to Sandy Kershaw, his colleague from the practice, and the regular doctor at the home. Roger was nodding. Susan could tell that their voices were low, confidential. She wondered what Sandy was saying.

They'd been here for almost an hour. Susan had rearranged the photographs on her mother's chest of drawers, checked through her clothes in the wardrobe. She and Roger had taken Alice for a walk. It was a warm day, and the golf course behind the home was busy with middle-aged men in their Argyle T-shirts and big golf bags. Alice thought that was where Dad was. The three of them had sat on a bench with a brass plaque commemorating the life of Doris Johnson, who'd lived somewhere else but died here three years ago, a month shy of her hundredth birthday, and who had, apparently, loved this view. Alice was like a child, looking about her with a mixture of bewilderment and excitement. They had had to take an arm each when they guided her back inside. She didn't reach Roger's shoulder, and he had to stoop. She seemed actually to be shrinking, somehow.

Back in her room, she had wet herself, soaking the incontinence pad on her armchair, so they had come down to the lounge. Susan had left the window as wide open as the safety catches allowed to get rid of the smell.

Before they left she took her mother in to supper, sat her between two other ladies, who smiled and nodded, and left them all in a silence punctuated only by the sound of soup being sucked off spoons. Afterward she always felt as if she'd been through a battle, even when Alice was more lucid. That was worse, actually—those days tortured Susan with the fear that maybe Alice knew where she was, and what was happening to her. Roger told her it wasn't so. But how could he know?

Still, Ed was home. He'd been to see Alice himself a couple of times. He was a good boy, and he had loved Alice. ("Had loved": she already thought of her in the past tense.) She was surprised, and grateful, that he had been able to brave it more than once. She had asked him, last night, what he made of it.

"That's easy, Mum. I just pretend I'm in a sitcom."

Maybe that wasn't such a bad idea.

In the car, Susan asked Roger what Sandy had been saying. Was there news?

"No, sweetheart, no news. I just asked him how he thought she was getting on."

"And?"

Roger slowed the car so he could face her briefly. "He thinks she's going downhill." Susan had known that already. "Shutting down, gradually."

"Is it the home doing that?" Always the guilt.

"No." Roger was firm. "It's the illness. Her body is catching up with her brain, that's the best way I can explain it to you."

"But it might not happen if she was at home with us?" The true answer to Susan's question was that of course it was quicker at the home, accelerated by the lack of love and attention. Roger had seen it happen before. But he was determined that Susan shouldn't carry this enormous burden, real or imagined. There was no way she could cope with Alice at home. "There's no way of knowing." He settled on that. "But think about what your mum would have wanted. She wouldn't want to drag on in that way, helpless, dependent, for years and years, would she?"

"No." Susan's answer was little and quiet. She knew Roger was right. Alice would want to die.

They had a lovely meal that night, the three of them. Roger took them to the Indian at the top of the high street, and Ed told them all about this new girl he'd met. He had a picture of them, taken in one of those booths at stations: they were laughing, squashed together on that tiny revolving stool. In one they were kissing. She looked a bit like Julia Roberts, without the curls and with slightly fewer teeth, and Ed was smitten, although he shrugged off his father's accusation.

He was gorgeous, her tall, handsome son. Susan felt, as she often did when looking at him, swamped with love and pride. She remembered when she would swoop down on him while he played and scoop him up to squeeze him, get her nose into his neck and smell him. Now he was far too big for scooping, and smelt more of aftershave, and sometimes of Silk Cut, than of little boy. Everything else might change, but that incredibly physical love remained exactly the same.

That night she couldn't sleep. She lay curled on one side, watching the gentle rise and fall of Roger's shoulder as he slept next to her. She wondered if Alice, too, was lying awake, wanting to die.

JULY
READING GROUP

THE MEMORY BOX

MARGARET FORSTER © 1999

A mother leaves her baby daughter a mysterious sealed box before she dies. Years later, when Catherine opens her mother's box—the "Memory Box"—she finds it full of strange, unexplained objects, carefully wrapped and numbered, like clues to a puzzle. Catherine never knew her mother, but her idealized image, as the "perfect," beautiful and talented woman that the rest of her family remembers, has cast a long shadow over her life. As she tries to solve the mystery of the box of secrets, she is pulled into the past and her mother's story, which reveals a woman far more complex, surprising and dangerous than the family legend has allowed. And in turn Catherine, fiercely independent and self-absorbed, discovers unexpected truths about herself.

H e's a bit of a dish, Suze."

"If I was ten years younger . . ."

"Fifteen, don't you mean?"

"All right, do you have to rub it in?"

Harriet and Nicole were in the temporary end-of-term high. Nine weeks lay ahead of not having to be up at six-thirty barking orders like a drill sergeant and packing enough kit in book, boot and ballet bags to keep a small third-world nation fed and clothed. That morning they'd "done" Speech Day, floated in their pastel linens to a mothers' lunch (pretty liquid for Harriet, who winked conspiratorially at Nicole each time she turned down a glass of white wine) in the garden of the local pub, pottered around the town all afternoon—getting giggly in the swimwear changing rooms—while their offspring were cared for at various end-of-term Bouncy Castle and Laser Quest parties. Now they had offloaded the lot of them onto Cecile, driven here and thrown themselves down on Susan's capacious sofa to make weakly lascivious remarks about Ed, who had left as soon as he politely could. Although he secretly thought Nicole was a bit of a dish too, or at least he would, had the words "bit of a dish" been in his vocabulary. "Hot," maybe. For an older woman, anyway.

Harriet looked at her friend. Why, when they had spent the day in exactly the same way—bar three or four glasses of Chablis—did Nicole still look uncreased, matte and fresh, like the girl in the Flake advert? She knew from a passing glance in Susan's hall mirror that she herself looked as if she'd just come out of the spin cycle on an industrial washing machine; hot, wrinkled and damp. Her linen was turned up at the corners like day-old sandwiches, and she had a five o'clock shadow on her calves. She smacked her forehead gently. Next time get an ugly friend. Ugly friend.

Susan remembered the end of term with a mix of nostalgia and envy. University wasn't the same. You didn't see them all term, and then they showed up with a carful of laundry, rickets and an unstoppable urge to go InterRailing the next day. Long summer days of playing on the lawn, picnic teas and orange-juice lollies seemed a long time ago.

They were pretty merry, these two, so she didn't have tremendously high hopes for the evening, as far as Margaret Forster was concerned. But they were great fun when they were like this—a perfect double act, Harriet the self-deprecating clown, Nicole the elegant straight man. Their friendship reminded her of hers and Polly's ten years ago, when the kids were younger. They had a lot more money, maybe, but also, in a funny way, a lot more stress. Life had changed, and not necessarily for the better. Harriet and Nicole might have the big cars and the clothes, and not have to work, but their husbands were never home for bathtime, like Roger had been, and that lifestyle, it seemed to her, was risky. The gaps between couples could get too wide maybe—school-gate friends spent all that time together, that's what it was—in some ways you were closer to your girlfriends, the good ones, than you were to your husband. But she was glad they were here, even if the book didn't get the attention it deserved. It was nice to have some laughter and chat in the house—it had been too quiet since Alice had left. Where *was* Polly, anyway?

"I thought she loved coming. Is something wrong?"

"Is it because of Elliot? We need her, I think. It's just the four of us without her. Is that big enough? Or are we a reading club-ette now?" Harriet's first thoughts were for the group. Nicole was more interested in Clare.

Polly had intended to tell them. It was obvious they would want to know why Clare had abandoned them, and she didn't have a problem with them knowing the truth. It was just that now, sitting here, she wasn't sure how to begin. Perhaps she should have let Susan do it. Susan had poured her some wine, and now she took a huge gulp of it. She looked down at the rope soles of her espadrilles, watched a blade of grass that was hanging on one shake as she lifted her leg to cross it, then fall onto the carpet.

"She's not coming because she's found out something that makes her want to stay away."

Harriet colored, and Nicole looked at her glass of sparkling water. Was it her? Had she guessed something about the pregnancy? How could she have done? She hadn't seen her since last month's meeting, and she definitely hadn't been showing at all then. Harriet was the only person who knew, and she wouldn't have told a soul, Nicole was certain of that.

Polly went on, "She found out that the father of Cressida's baby is . . . her husband. Elliot."

This was hard to take in. No one spoke: they must be trying to join the invisible dots that made it possible for Polly's daughter to be carrying Clare's husband's baby. It was like a television plot. Polly tried to answer the questions before they were asked: "Evidently they met at college, where he works. Last autumn sometime. And apparently, got . . . together"—she didn't know how else to say it—"soon afterwards. I gather Clare had left him before she found out about Cressida and the baby. I think things had been going badly wrong for a while. Not that I'm making excuses for Cressida—she knew he was married." She paused. "And now Clare knows about the baby . . . and that's why she won't be coming anymore, I suppose. I think I understand why, don't you?"

"Um, yes, I suppose it would be difficult." Harriet looked shocked.

"I thought Cressida's boyfriend—Joe, wasn't it?—I thought he was the father."

"I thought so too." Polly smiled wryly. "Turns out, they hadn't even slept together. She broke it all off with him because of the baby."

"Poor Clare," Nicole murmured. Gavin had his peccadilloes, but a baby? That was the one thing she had over all those other women, and she prized it highly: she was the mother of Gavin's children. Clare was never going to have that; and to find out Elliot had got someone else pregnant—she must have been devastated. She could cry for her. Nicole had met Elliot only once, at Clare's house for the reading group, back in March. He'd come in, shy, waved at them. Handsome, in a small way. Everything about him had been almost apologetic. He certainly didn't look the type. Not like Gavin.

"Poor Cressida." Harriet thought she saw at once how it must have been. Her imagination was always ready to flesh out the facts with a story cobbled together from a thousand made-for-television movies, bonkbuster novels and a romantic's heart. You weren't responsible for whom you fell in love with. It wasn't Cressida who had cheated, it was Elliot. A man with a broken heart—what girl wouldn't have?

"What's she going to do?"

"Clare or Cressida?"

"Both of them, really, I suppose."

Susan interjected: "Clare's with her parents for now. I think it really is over between her and Elliot. I don't know what she'll do eventually—make a clean break, maybe. Who knows? It can't be easy living so close by."

"And Cressida? Are she and Elliot . . . ?"

"I don't know. I think she needs to have the baby first."

"But Elliot? He wants the baby?"

"Oh, more than life itself, I think. I get the impression he's been just as gutted as Clare about them not being able to have a kid."

"So you think he and Cressida might end up together?"

"I really don't know."

"Are you okay about it?"

Polly almost laughed. My twenty-year-old daughter has been having an affair with a married man, and now she's pregnant, and she wants to give up college, and maybe the future she had planned as well, and have the baby, and this man, who I truly believe cannot make her happy, wants to be with her forever. No, I am not okay about it. She shrugged. "It's not what you dream of when you look into your daughter's cot when she's six weeks old, and it's going to be pretty hard for her and me, whatever happens. But it is what it is. She's an adult. I don't get to make the decisions anymore." She smiled sadly. "I just get to deal with the fallout of the decisions she makes."

Nicole nodded. She knew about relinquished control and about floating around on someone else's tide. "We'll be fine. I'm sure we'll be fine."

The others murmured affirmation. What else could they do?

The book didn't get a fair go. Harriet and Nicole hadn't been in the mood anyway. Now they were too interested in what was going on in real life. They tried, but none of them really wanted to champion it. Polly had read, and loved, *Georgy Girl*, but the author was new to the rest of them. This one, she thought, was disappointing. She could see the craft in it, the skill, but it had left her feeling, So what? She wasn't moved. She didn't feel enlightened or connected. She thought maybe she hadn't concentrated properly. It was quite dense. It hadn't been easy, these last weeks: getting into bed at night when Jack wasn't there no longer meant a good long read. It meant listening, and wondering, and worrying, and thinking. The others weren't crazy about it either. Harriet harrumphed. "Now this one, it was written by a woman, but in a Pepsi Challenge situation I would have guessed it was a man. It's holding something back."

On this occasion Nicole was with her. "I kept waiting for the real emotion. It never came."

"I kept waiting for the big mystery. That never came either. It all fell a bit flat at the end, I thought."

"Me too. Brilliant idea, absolutely cracking. A box full of secret things, each with its own story, a flag on the landscape of her mother's past, left by a dead mother, presented to a twenty-one-year-old daughter, with the time and inclination to find out what they all meant. Trouble was, they were kind of odd, and when she did discover the reasons for the things being in there—which, incidentally, she did in a series of implausible coincidences—you didn't feel satisfied, did you?"

"I know it's been my hobbyhorse lately, but I did think—didn't the rest of you?—it had interesting things to say about mothers and daughters. About mothers before they were mothers, and how a daughter can discover that as she grows up," Susan said.

"And I liked Catherine from the beginning, when she says she can't accept the idea of her mother being perfectly happy, even though that's what is always trotted out to her."

"I thought she was a spoilt brat, to be honest. I wasn't much interested in what she discovered."

"None of us lost a mother young, though, did we?" Susan persisted. "You would have questions, wouldn't you, curiosities, particularly if everyone kept giving you a sanitized version of her?"

"I suppose. It is true, isn't it, that when you grow up and have your own kids you see your parents in a different light. You imagine them in the same situations you find yourself in. And you start to see your mother in yourself."

"Well, that's true. I remember my mum shouting at us and thinking I would never shout at my kids like that." Harriet laughed.

"Yeah! And promising I'd never say ridiculous things like 'Do you want a smack?' Now? I probably say it to Martha about once a day." Nicole thought about it and smiled. "I never do it, though. One look at that little blond head, and my hand freezes in midair. That's why she's such a monster, I suppose. She knows I don't ever mean it. My mum did. Top of the thigh, bare hand. It really stung."

"How are you doing?" Susan had just waved the others off. Polly was still in the kitchen.

"I was wishing I still smoked. I could do with a fag."

"We could walk down to the off license and get some."

"Nah. Not a good idea. Emphysema, on top of everything else?"

"No. It wouldn't help, either."

"Thank you, Mrs. GP, I know that." She smiled at her friend. "Well, that went okay, don't you think?"

"What did you think might happen?"

"I thought they might be more . . ."

"Judgmental?" Susan shook her head. "Nicole and Harriet

were just a bit shocked. You've got to admit it's a good story—if you're just hearing it, that is, not living it." Polly nodded. "I wouldn't expect them to sit in judgment, either. They're from a different generation from us, aren't they?"

"You make us sound like village elders. There's only about ten years in it."

"Ten significant years. I don't think they see the world in the same way. I don't think they view marriage as we did, for a start."

"Suze, I'm divorced."

"I know that, but you didn't think you would be, did you? You married for life. We all did. These days, I think they get married for now, hoping for the best, probably, and believing the worst half the time. I think they give it a go, basically, and you can't blame them. If they ever turn on the radio or the television, they get told the odds are that their marriage will fail. One in three, or is it even higher now?"

"Okay, so they're not surprised Clare and Elliot have split up. That doesn't mean they wouldn't have a view on Cressida having an affair with him before they did. Or about being stupid enough to get pregnant. God knows, *I* want to shake her sometimes when I think about that. It's not like she didn't know how not to, is it?"

"Accidents happen, Poll. Come on. That bit's over, so what's the point in rehashing it? She wasn't careful. Or something went wrong. There it is. Weren't you just telling them you knew you had to live with it? I don't think those two see it that way. You're looking for things that aren't there."

"What about you, Suze? As a representative of the 'older generation'? Don't you judge her?"

Susan didn't answer straightaway. Then, "I've known Cressida for most of her life—for fifteen years, anyway. I know what kind of a girl she was, and I think I've got a pretty good idea of what kind of a woman she has become. No, I don't judge her. I wish it hadn't happened to her—I think it will make a time that should be carefree and happy complicated and difficult. I think it might be disastrous for her to be with Elliot. But, no, I don't judge her. Or you. Or even him." She looked straight at Polly. "I promise you that. You're my best friend, Poll, and she's your baby, and I want to help both of you, any way I can. I promise," she repeated. She put her hand on her heart to emphasize her sincerity.

"Thank you."

"You're welcome."

Harriet

Harriet lay on the sofa, one eye on the Danielle Steel made-for-TV movie, and one on Josh and Chloe rampaging around the garden. She'd shut them out there half an hour ago. It was only two-thirty, only the second week of the summer holidays, but already she was exhausted. She felt that way all the time, to be honest. Pathetic, but true. She'd begun the holidays with good intentions—booked the children onto different courses (Josh for cycling proficiency, Chloe for pony riding), invited half their respective classes for endless play dates and been to the Early Learning Centre to stock up on paints, craft paper and the dreaded PVA glue that children could spread into the strangest places if you turned your back. They'd been to the library, to the park, to the lido, to McDonald's. Six weeks to go. They'd be away for one in Portugal—only one: she'd told Tim that the kids needed more stimulation than the villa could provide, that they were excited about their courses and their play dates.

That wasn't true, of course. They'd stay at Tim's parents' house under that yellow sun, digging in the sand, eating ice cream and turning prunish in the cobalt pool all year round if they could. It was she who couldn't face it. As it was, a week meant seven evenings alone with Tim, after her human shields had been tucked, catatonic with healthy tiredness, into their beds. Alone with no television to pretend she was engrossed in, no housework to claim had rendered her exhausted. Alone with Tim. In the Danielle Steel movie the beauty-pageant-pretty heroine had been widowed, crying perfect round tears—which didn't leave her face looking as if she had an allergic reaction—into a grave, willowy in black chiffon. The next lover was the guy standing across from the grave fixing her with loving, yet lustful blue eyes. Life was awfully convenient for Danielle Steel heroines. Marry the wrong guy? Don't sweat—he'll be dead in a few minutes, and you'll be free to love again, properly, without any scarlet woman stigma. Nothing so vulgar as adultery or—shudder—leaving a husband and children.

Was she actually fantasizing about Tim dying? She thought she might be. Tears sprang into her eyes. She wasn't sure whether she was rehearsing or crying real tears at how mean she was. Bit of both, really.

She was trying, she told herself, *really* trying. She'd been a model wife since that disaster with Nick. The kids had hung banners and balloons on the front door when she got back that Sunday. "We missed you, Mummy," they read, in Josh's irregular capitals. Chloe had drawn rainbows round the words, the colors in the exact order of the song. Harriet thought about the pot of gold. It hadn't been there with Nick, and it wasn't here. Except in the children.

She switched off Danielle Steel and stood at the French windows, watching them. Josh, always so messy, hair across his forehead, Chloe so neat, holding court at a tea party for her dolls on the blanket Harriet had laid out, talking happily to herself.

She'd be doing it to them if she left Tim, or if she made him leave. They adored him. "Family cuggle," Chloe said, pulling Tim and Harriet toward her, as Josh insinuated himself under their arms. "Family cuggle."

The bloody tears were still there. She felt so trapped.

After she'd cried with Nicole, she had gone to the doctor. Nicole said she should. She had cried there too, wanting the ground to open up and swallow her. The doctor had been brilliant. She hadn't touched her, or stared, or said anything soft. She had just passed her a box of tissues and said, as though Harriet was showing her a boil or something, "Don't worry, this happens a lot in here." And she had asked what was wrong, and Harriet had lied. How could you sit there with a virtual stranger and say that you didn't love your husband anymore, that you thought you were going to suffocate? That you felt like your life was over? She said she didn't know why she felt this way. That she loved her husband, her children and her life, and that she didn't have money, health or other worries and that she didn't understand it.

So the doctor told her about depression, that it was an illness, a chemical imbalance in the brain. That there wasn't any point in feeling guilty about having it because you couldn't help it any more than you could if you had shingles or multiple sclerosis. That she should take pills. She wrote a prescription and told her to come back in a month.

Harriet had put the pills in her knicker drawer. She hadn't taken one, and she knew she wouldn't go back. She didn't think she was depressed, because she thought there was a reason why she felt this way. A reason she hadn't told the doctor. If she had, surely she wouldn't have prescribed Prozac: she'd have sent her to marriage guidance, or to a solicitor. Part of Harriet didn't want to feel better—the guilty part.

The children saw her.

"Come and play, Mummy," Chloe cried. "Are they happy tears?" she asked, as Harriet sat down on the blanket.

She wiped her eyes roughly. "That's right, darling. Happy tears."

Chloe had already poured warm orange squash into a teacup; she required no further explanation. Children were nice like that. She handed it to Harriet. "I'm telling my friends all about our holiday, Mummy." Then she adopted the teacherlike tone she always used with her dollies. "Now, in Portugal, Daddy likes to eat hairy fish. Isn't that disgusting? I like to eat pink ice cream—that means it's strawberry flavor, you know."

"Or raspberry," Josh interjected. He'd exhausted himself kicking goals in the sunshine and was lying spread-eagled nearby.

Chloe glared at him. "And then Daddy always buries me and Josh in the sand—"

"Or cherry."

Another glare. "And do you know, the sand that's under the ground is really cold, and Daddy says that's because it's wet, and the sun doesn't—"

"Or bubble-gum flavor."

"*Muuummm!*"

Harriet missed Nicole.

Polly and Jack

"Sounds serious."

"It is. I'll see you around eight?"

"I'll bring some wine. Love you."

This was going to be hard, Polly knew that. She just prayed he was going to understand. She knew he'd done more for her in the last few months than he had ever been expecting to have to do. She hoped, oh, so very much, that he was going to do *this* for her too.

Susan had made her think of it. Watching her with Alice. How the roles had changed. If not easily, then inevitably, somehow. Susan was a member of the "sandwich generation," apparently. She had laughed when she told the reading group about it one evening after they'd finished talking about the book and moved on to the rest of the universe. She'd heard about it on *Woman's Hour*: still to be caring for her own children and also for an elderly parent made her the filling in a caring sandwich. She said she thought she was probably Spam. Nicole and Harriet had considered their own positions and agreed that it was likely to happen to them too.

Polly didn't have parents to worry about, but it had started her thinking in a new way about Cressida and the baby. She wanted to be the melted cheese on a croque monsieur, rather than a sandwich filling, spreading herself to cover the ham and the bread. And she wanted Jack to be the mustard. Now she thought she'd better leave out the food analogy for the time being: cooking him dinner looked like fifties housewife bribery. And putting out nibbles was altogether too jolly and partyish. The wine would have to do, and she put a bottle into the fridge to cool.

When he arrived Jack kissed her deeply, and she reveled in the feeling of being in his arms. He was big, and he smelt fantastic, and he loved her, and that was all good.

"So," he said, as he uncorked the wine in one easy movement and poured two glasses, "the kids are not in evidence—you want to talk?"

Polly took a gulp of wine. "I do. Let's go and sit down." Blurting it out seemed the best way. Give him all the information, then let him sift through it. Less artful that way. "I want to raise the baby for Cressida, not adopt it, or anything legal like that—he or she will always be her baby—just take care of it for now. And one day, when she's finished college, and had her adventures, got on in her career, whatever, I hope it will go and live with her. I want to be a mother to both of them, just for the first few years, that's all. I'm only forty-four, and I can do it, with some help."

Jack drank deeply, said nothing.

She went on. "It's easy enough to say, isn't it? You hear parents say it all the time—'I'd do anything for my kids.' And I would, you see, anything at all, for her to have her chances. She wants the baby, and, God knows, I understand that, but I want so much more for her alongside the baby . . ."

"Have you talked to her about this?"

"Not yet. I wanted to talk to you about it first. It affects you as much as anyone."

Jack laughed tightly. "Just a bit."

"But we can make it work, I know we can. Cressida will still be here, for holidays and weekends, and Dan'll muck in. And my friends. It's not like we'll be completely tied down. She's a kid, Jack, she's twenty years old. Think of the things we've seen and done—she hasn't done any of it yet."

"You make it sound like we're finished."

"No, no, I don't mean it that way—we've got years and years ahead of us. But she's barely finished school. I can't bear for it all to be taken away from her."

"But times have changed, haven't they? She could take the baby away with her—they have crèches and whatnot and grants and things to help girls like her."

Polly didn't like the way he said "girls like her." "But she wouldn't need to if I had the baby. She could do it all properly."

Jack looked at her. "Is this about Cressida, or is it about you?"

Polly felt herself getting impatient. "It's about both of us. Sure, I wish things had been different for me, but when you become a mother the things that have or haven't happened to you stop being so important. It's all about *them*. I'm not trying to make up for my mother, or anything like that, if that's what you're saying."

She was angry now. He wasn't understanding. He was taking something that felt pure and right and sane and making it sound disturbed and wrong. She tried another tack. "Suppose she goes off with this Elliot and gets married?"

"Like you did?"

He almost threw it back. Verbal squash. This wasn't like Jack. "Yes, exactly. Like I did. Even if it worked, and I doubt very much that it would, it would be so hard for her—she'd have to give up everything she's wanted, change her life completely."

"But she wants the baby, Poll. Maybe she even wants Elliot. Why are you so sure that it couldn't work?"

Because I won't let it, she screamed, inside her own head. "Because it's all wrong. He's wrong for her—I can see that. It wouldn't last, and then she'd have a broken marriage as well as a baby and no proper education to contend with."

Jack put a hand on hers. "Don't you think you might be being a bit, well, melodramatic about all this? You make her sound like some tragic Thomas Hardy heroine."

Polly pulled away her hand. "Don't make a joke out of this, Jack."

"I'm not trying to make a joke out of it, sweetheart. I just think you've got way, way ahead of yourself. I think you think you need to 'rescue' Cressida, not just help her. You're on some kind of crusade."

His eyes and tone were loving. He was trying to make sense of it and, she could see, failing.

This wasn't what she had wanted. She had wanted—expected—Jack to fold her in his arms and murmur into her hair that, yes, of course they could cope with a baby together, and that he would be there for her, and, maybe, love her just that bit more because she wanted to do it. He wasn't saying any of that, but he didn't want to fight with her. He was still calm, still gentle.

He took his glass to the far end of the room and looked out of the window at the back garden, still bright with the orange glow of the evening. "I've never told you much about my first marriage, have I?" He hadn't volunteered, and she had never asked.

Polly believed in second chances. And new lives. She knew

that he had been divorced years ago, and that there had been no one serious until her. He had said no one else was involved. "About why we split up?"

"You said you'd drifted apart."

"And that was true. Except that *drifted* is maybe too gentle a word. Anna left me."

"I didn't know." She didn't even know she'd been called Anna.

"Why would you? It was a long time ago, and I've stopped being hurt by it. Although I was never glad it had ended—until I met you."

Polly smiled. She loved the feeling that she had turned his life round.

"Was there someone else?" She couldn't think why he would have kept that from her.

Jack smiled. "No. We were quite young when we met. We both had grand ideas, elaborate plans—we were going to see the world, make a difference, you know. I was going to use my law degree for good, for Chrissakes." He smirked. "Standard Miss World fodder it sounds now, but it was the seventies and we were kids."

She and Dan had been like that once, before Cressida, Polly remembered.

"She changed. I suppose we both changed in the end. But she changed first. One day she realized that she wanted all the things I thought we both hated. A big house, two cars on the drive and kids. She really wanted kids, although we'd always said we'd never have them. And I never did. That's pretty much why she left me in the end. I gave in about the house and the job, and we even had two sodding cars and a bloody fortnight in the South of France once a year. But I never wanted the children she wanted to go with it all."

"Why not? You'd have made a great father."

Jack waved aside the cliché. "No, I wouldn't. I'm a selfish man, deep down." Polly shook her head, tried to interrupt. She didn't recognize the man he was talking about. "I am, believe me. I never wanted to share her. I never wanted things to change. I don't want to share *you*."

"That's a long time ago, though, Jack."

"I haven't changed."

"What about Cressida and Daniel?"

"I met you, and I fell like a stone. I didn't even find out about Cressida and Daniel until it was too late."

Polly laughed nervously. "Are you saying you wouldn't have got involved with me if you'd known about the kids?"

He leant toward her, although he didn't trust himself enough to come across the room and touch her.

"What I'm saying is that it probably mattered to me that the kids were nearly grown-up, nearly gone. I knew I'd have you to myself before too long."

Polly was shocked. Now Jack came toward her. "Don't get me wrong." Now he wanted her to understand him as much as she wanted him to understand her. "I love them, really I do. At least, I'm starting to, without even trying. Daniel and Cress—they're great. Really. I even think I was getting used to the idea of being a stepfather, you know, really being involved in their lives. I like being here with you all. A family."

"But just not that involved." Polly knew she sounded unkind, but she couldn't help herself.

Jack rubbed his head. "That's not fair. You're talking about something different. You're asking me to be a father, in effect." Polly shook her head. "Yes, yes, you are." Jack was firm. "I don't know if I can do that."

Polly looked him straight in the eye. He caught the implication. "Not even for you."

"I do know that I have to do this if she'll let me."

Checkmate.

She wouldn't beg him. She wouldn't tell him that if he loved her he would be able to do this for her. She knew it wasn't that simple. He did love her. It wasn't going to be enough. She was suddenly afraid. What the hell happened to boy meets girl and they live happily ever after? Polly wondered.

Jack kissed her when he left, a kiss full of sadness and tenderness. She clung to him, but said nothing. She hadn't really known then how they had left it.

But now, as she sat in the dark on the sofa, she knew that she was alone again.

Polly and Susan

"I don't understand," Susan was saying. Things had changed so much since the reading club's last meeting. That night had been good. They'd had one of the best discussions yet, and a nice evening besides.

Polly had seemed fine then, like everything was sorting itself out with Cressida. She'd even seemed excited, talking babies with Harriet and Nicole, laughing about being called Granny. She and Jack had set the date for the wedding, at Christmas. She and Susan had talked about finding a day to go shopping together for something for her to wear. Susan had been busy since then with daily visits to Alice and the boys flitting in and out with their insatiable appetites and endless laundry, and she hadn't called Polly as often as she usually did, and now she was confused. Polly hadn't known at the reading club in June, about Elliot. She supposed that changed everything. Although she wasn't sure why. Maybe Polly had felt more in control when she thought Joe was the father. Now that she knew he wasn't, maybe she was frightened she was going to lose Cressida. But what had that to do with Jack? How could it be over between Polly and Jack so suddenly? Susan's instinctive, characteristic reaction was guilt—had she not been a good friend? She knew it had been right to tell Polly about Elliot. What other choice had she had? She reminded herself that Polly hadn't called her either.

Tonight was their regular date, at the Italian, and it was crowded with people spilling out into the courtyard on a still, close evening, sitting bare-shouldered and open-necked at the tables under fairy lights, with candles in hurricane lamps flickering around them. Susan had booked too late to be outside—she had forgotten the date until that morning—and they were at the table toward the back, where the owners had used huge mirrors to make the narrowing of the restaurant near the kitchen less obvious. She could see them both now in the mirrors. They looked tired and pale, despite the season, and about ten years older, she thought, than the last time they had been here. Something like depression settled about her, tinged with a new worry about Polly. When you had a busy life and a crowded head, you sometimes ticked off boxes next to the names of people and things you cared about. Made them like the juggling balls in your perpetual circus act that you didn't have to keep an eye on at any particular time. Things you didn't have to worry about, not just now. Alex was ticked, he was on holiday with his good-natured crowd of medical-student friends. Ed was ticked, because he'd just been home for an overhaul, as Roger called it. Polly had been ticked off, too. Now she felt she might not have checked the status for too long.

Any parting had not been of her making, Susan could see that. She looked forlorn. A bottle of Chianti and two platefuls of doughballs later, the story had spilled out, punctuated by stealthy tears, some anger, and "You understand, don't you?"

Polly had decided she wanted to look after the baby for Cressida while she went about having the normal life of a twenty-year-old student and to have Jack help her. Jack couldn't handle it. And she did understand. And she didn't. Susan didn't know what to tell her friend, who, incidentally, didn't seem to have talked to Cressida about her plan.

"I thought I'd wait until after the baby's born."

"Do you think that's a good idea? Wouldn't it be easier for Cress—and you, for that matter—to make an objective decision about what's best for all of you if you talk about it beforehand?"

"Maybe." Susan could see that Polly was considering what she said. "But until the baby comes, she won't have the first clue about what's involved in taking care of it, the way it affects everything."

"And you think understanding that will make her more likely to hand it over to you?"

"I don't know. But you sound like Jack. I don't want her to 'hand it over.' This isn't about control, Suze, I promise you. This isn't for me—you of all people should understand. Wouldn't you want to do this for the boys?"

Susan thought about it. She knew what Polly meant, of course. She couldn't think of a mother she knew who wouldn't feel the impulse. She wanted to do it for Alice, let alone the boys. Take care of it, shoulder it all, make everything all right. She also knew that what Roger had said was right. You couldn't. "I might want to, I can see that, but that doesn't mean it's the right thing to do. Anyway, I can't imagine Cress saying yes. It just doesn't sound like her."

"I'll make her understand. She'll be the mother, she will always be that. I just want to help with the practical bit until she's ready to do it on her own."

"Had you thought about how you'd afford to do what you're talking about?" Did that sound patronizing? Polly did all right for money, Susan knew. Dan was good at his fatherly responsibilities, and Polly was very good at her job.

"Of course." Polly's face told her she *had* been patronizing. "I've been at Smith, March and May for donkey's years and the least they can do is give me a few months' leave. I know Dan would help out—he wants the best for Cress as well."

"Okay, so that's a few months and a bit of kit sorted out. What then?"

"I wasn't expecting Jack to fork out, if that's what you're thinking." Polly was afraid she sounded more defensive than she felt. She couldn't bear Susan being the second person in a row who didn't understand what she wanted to do.

Susan didn't rise to the bait. "I know, Polly. It never crossed my mind. But you do have a plan?"

"Well, yes, of course. He or she would have to go into a daycare crèche, and there's one not far from the office. One of the other girls at work has a daughter there. We'd be the same as any other family."

"But isn't that what Cressida would be doing with the baby?"

"No." Polly shook her head vehemently. "It's not the hours between nine and five that make a parent, Suze. You know that as well as I do. It's the nights and the evenings, the mornings and weekends and all the other times when they aren't in the crèche, the lion's share of their lives."

"That's true," Susan conceded.

"And those are the times that I want Cress to be free. Not just for the lectures and the tutorials—there's so much more to college than that. Look at what Alex and Ed get up to. . . . That's what she'd be missing out on. And you know Cress."

Susan felt as if she didn't really know Cressida at all now. She knew the Cressida who had gone out with a boy called Joe. He had always seemed a sweet guy, and he had been devoted to Cressida since Susan couldn't remember when. Well, she could. Since they used to sit together, but a whole person's width apart, on Polly's sofa after school, watching *Grange Hill* and holding hands, adorably chaste and childish.

She knew that Cressida was a bit wild, had her funny ways about her, but an affair with a married man? A man they all knew, if only vicariously, through the reading club. And that she had become pregnant. That still seemed to Susan the province of silly girls, often from broken families, either ignorant or horribly misguided. She knew Polly and Dan weren't together, but she couldn't bring herself to think of the home as broken, of their family as dysfunctional. And Cressida was a clever girl—too clever for this bloody awful mess.

Susan wanted to be a good friend to Polly, and to Cressida, but infidelity didn't sit well with her. She had married for life, and expected Roger to have done the same. She'd be furious with the boys if they cheated on girlfriends or wives. She didn't like even the simplest forms of dishonesty and deceit. But she wasn't naïve, and she had seen a lot. She knew that the success of her marriage was only partly down to effort. The rest was luck, and she and Roger had had that in spades. Not only did they still fancy each other after all these years, which she viewed, particularly on Roger's side, as a miracle—she seemed physically, emotionally, in every way different from the girl he had fallen in love with all those years ago—but, and this was far more significant, life hadn't pushed any tragedy in their path. Who could say, without any doubt, that their happy marriage could survive a real tragedy? Susan certainly considered childlessness to be that: the boys were everything to her, as were Cressida and Daniel to Polly. She couldn't blame either Cressida or Elliot entirely for what had happened. Suppose Elliot wanted to make a go of it with Cressida? Wasn't that option open to them? She was afraid Polly was still treating Cressida like a child, not acknowledging the massive leap toward adulthood that she was about to take, and not caring, particularly, with whom she might want to take it.

"Does everyone know, now, about the baby being Elliot's?"

Polly bristled at his name. "Pretty much, I think."

"And Jack?"

"And Jack. I saw him the day after you told me."

"Before you asked him if he'd help you look after the baby?"

It grated with Polly to hear it put that way, but that was exactly what she'd asked Jack to do.

"Yep."

"And it was this looking-after-the-baby question that made Jack walk away?"

"I suppose so, yeah. It all got a bit messy for him. I think he'd probably been trying hard to take it all onboard—the baby and Dan and everything, and this was, like, the straw on the camel's back, you know. I think my baggage got a bit too heavy for him."

She didn't sound angry—she wasn't even trying to blame him—just sad. Susan saw her love for him all across her face.

"How have you left things with him?" Susan asked.

"I don't know. He said he couldn't handle it, and then he went. I haven't heard from him since."

"Do you want me to call him, have a chat?"

Polly smiled at her friend. That was so Susan. "Thanks, really. But I don't think so. Better to find out now than later. I should never have got myself into it in the first place. I blame you." And she laughed. "You said I should say yes!" Susan wasn't fooled. She knew Polly loved Jack, and was pretty sure Jack loved Polly. That this business with Cressida was going to get between them and ruin them seemed, to her, very much like another tragedy.

She put her arm round Polly. "I'm sorry," she said.

"Me too," Polly replied.

Susan got brave, then. "You don't think, do you, that maybe there's a future for the two of them—Elliot and Cressida?"

"I don't know. I hope not. I can't tell you why, I just know it's not the right thing for her. I know it. And that's why I can't ask her before it's born. I can't get in the way, not if that's what she wants. Not if he's what she wants. I have to wait for her to come to me, tell me what she's feeling. And I don't think, right now, she has the first idea of what that is."

Later, after they had salvaged the evening, with tiramisu, an

Amaretto with coffee and talk about everything except Cressida, Elliot and Jack, when they were walking arm in arm along the road to the taxi rank at the top of town, Susan said, "I do think you ought to think about talking to Cressida before the baby comes, if you're serious."

"I'm deadly serious, Suze. This can work. When I had decided that was what I should do, I felt like the clouds had parted—everything felt like it was the right decision."

"Even if it costs you Jack."

"Even if it costs me Jack. You're a mum, Suze. Wouldn't you throw Roger into the path of a runaway train to save Ed and Alex?"

Susan laughed. She wouldn't have put it that way, but she knew what Polly meant.

"I'd throw Dan."

"You'd throw Dan in the path of a runaway train for sport, not for the kids! Admit it."

Now Polly was laughing, even if tears weren't far away. "Okay, you're right. I'd throw Jack. For Cressida. That's it."

She'd got it worked out. Susan wondered what Cressida would say, and hoped Polly wouldn't lose out in both ways.

Before they parted, Polly turned to her. "I'm sorry—I haven't asked about Alice all night. What a selfish cow. How is she?"

"She's not great. Nothing dramatic to report. She's just slowly, inexorably shutting down. There isn't anything we can do."

"Oh, Suze."

"I'm getting used to it. I'm okay. I've been going a bit less often lately. You and Roger were right—there's no point as far as Mum's concerned, and my God, it depresses the hell out of me."

"I'm glad you're being good to yourself. I know it's a cliché, but that's what Alice would want, isn't it?"

"Oh, certainly. She'd be furious if she knew what was going on."

The two women smiled at each other. They felt better for spending some time together.

When she got out at her house, Susan kissed Polly on both cheeks. "Let me know what's going on, you hear?"

"I promise. Have you finished *Eden Close* yet?"

"Haven't started, of course. You know me! But I'll have it finished for reading group, I promise!"

'Okay. See you then."

Susan was profoundly grateful, not for the first time, to be coming home, to Roger. He heard her slamming the taxi door and had opened the front door before she had had time to fumble around for her keys. That was just like him.

Harriet

It must be the Venice factor: that was why she was having a good time in Portugal. Nothing seemed so awful in this unbelievable sunshine. Even her elephantine thighs looked better brown. She had caught sight of herself in the big bedroom mirror after her shower the other night, and thought she looked all right. Was Junoesque a good way to describe it? Or Rubenesque. Whichever esque, it wasn't bad. She'd had to work at it, mind you. Judicious application of factor 15 every couple of hours, plenty of after-sun. Not like Tim and the kids, who went the color of good furniture the second they stepped outside the villa and just got darker. The other day, Tim had leant against the bathroom door to watch her shower. For once, she hadn't minded. "You shower very prettily," he told her, when she got out. "I like the way you arch your back when you rinse your hair." It made her feel nice, to think he was seeing her that way. It must be the weather.

There was a new maid this year, a replacement for the desiccated widow they had known for years. This one was young and pretty, and clearly enamored of the pool man. Each morning, after she had made the beds and changed the towels, she offered, for a few extra euros, to mind the children around the pool for a couple of hours so that Tim and Harriet could escape into the village for some peace.

The first morning, Harriet had said that she wasn't about to pay the girl to sit around in a thong, and that she didn't trust her not to let the children drown while she and the pool man flirted in Portuguese. Tim said that she was the daughter of friends of his parents and that no harm could possibly come to the kids, and that it would do all of them good. The kids had implored Harriet to go with him: the pool man had said he would teach Josh how to backflip into the pool, and Chloe had developed a four-year-old's desperate crush on both of them.

Harriet had had to give in. But she liked it, really, and they fell easily enough into a routine. They would walk down the steep hill into the village, stopping at the big undercover market to buy oranges, tomatoes or bread, and then, at the same restaurant each day, Tim had his beer and sardines and she had chicken and white wine, and they watched the locals smoke on the broad beach, gesticulating wildly at each other. It was . . . comfortable. One day Tim had tried to take her hand on the walk back up the hill, when she was complaining about the heat and the incline, and she had let him.

This morning they had made love. She had only half woken, wanting him suddenly in spite of herself, and shuffled herself into the middle of the bed, from the edge she normally hugged. There she had pressed her bottom rhythmically into his lap, until, barely awake himself, he responded. She'd gone back to sleep straight afterward, feeling surprised and satisfied, but not before she had heard him murmur into her hair that he loved her.

Susan

Roger had just finished an uneventful morning surgery and was enjoying a quiet coffee in the staff room. Summer surgery was always quiet, with so many people away; those at home were seemingly healthier for a bit of fresh air and a few salads—considerably less snotty, too. He no longer ran the antenatal clinic that had once been his responsibility—one of the new female partners had taken it on last year—and the practice nurses were doing many of the routine health jobs. He might think about cutting back his hours in a couple of years, once the boys were out of university, maybe.

Although along with the pride he felt at Alexander following his footsteps into medicine came the realization that he would be, if not financially dependent, then not entirely independent, for a few more years. Another year at Edinburgh before three years clinical, and yet another year as a houseman before he would be fully qualified and properly solvent. And properly awake.

Roger remembered his own training in the eighties as both the best and the worst of times. Academically, he was middle bottom of the class, always. But he had been good with people. He could put them at their ease, make it possible for them to confide their deepest, darkest worries, from the first time he went on the ward in his short white coat. Pretty good people skills with the nurses, too, until he met Susan, of course. He hadn't looked at another one after that, and they'd been married before he got his long white coat. General practice was perfect for him. He made a difference. Alexander, of course, was full of ambition and drive and all the arrogance of a twenty-one-year-old. They'd clashed about it at Christmas. Well, clashed as far as Susan was prepared to allow at a family Christmas. Alex had made general practice sound dull, second best, and it stung, just a bit, that he held his father's work in such low regard. Still, he had time to learn that heroes weren't always in green scrubs, brandishing scalpels. He'd be bloody proud either way—GP or surgeon. Roger just wanted his boys to be happy.

Susan had loved having them both home this summer—her only regret was that they hadn't made it back together. Still, they wouldn't dare not come home for Christmas, as usual. They'd settle for two or three days. Roger was afraid Susan would need it more than ever this year.

Sandy Kershaw, one of the other partners, came in and slumped on the old sofa, with an exaggerated sigh.

"Are you okay?" Roger asked.

Sandy grinned. "Fine. I've just come back from the weekly delight of my visit to The Cedars. It's too hot for all this running about." He weighed around twenty stones, which he joked was all haggis and whiskey left over from a childhood and youth spent in the Scottish Highlands. His broad face was bright red, and his top lip was beaded with sweat. He got to his feet again and lumbered awkwardly toward the watercooler. "Water, that's what I need, and a nice sit-down before afternoon surgery."

Sacha, the new receptionist, opened the door. "Guess what?" she asked Sandy.

"What?"

"That was The Cedars on the phone. They need you back there."

"Sweet Jesus!"

"I know. One's died." She said it like they were puppies from a litter.

"Could they not have died ten minutes sooner?" Sandy smiled ruefully. "Who was it?"

Sacha looked down at the Post-it note in her hand. "A Mrs. Barnes. Alice Barnes."

Sandy's demeanor changed instantly. He looked sternly at Sacha, warning her with his eyes, then turned to Roger. "That's Susan's mother, is it not?" Roger nodded. "Och. I'm sorry, Rog. Sooner than you expected, isn't it?"

"Who can say?" Roger answered. "She went downhill fast after the TIAs this spring. I wasn't expecting her to last into the new year, to be honest." He sighed.

"Have they called the next of kin?" Sandy asked Sacha.

"I don't know."

"Susan's out this morning." Roger was thinking. His wife was notoriously bad at carrying her mobile phone around, and when she did have it, it was rarely switched on. It was for *her* emergencies, she'd told him, not other people's. He'd rather tell her himself. "Give them a ring back, Sacha, will you? Tell them I'll inform Mrs. Barnes's daughter."

Sacha looked uncomfortable.

Sandy interjected: "She's his wife."

"Oh, my God, I'm so sorry. I didn't know." She backed out of the room.

Roger smiled at her. He didn't want her to feel bad. They all talked about death flippantly. You had to.

"Hey, don't worry—how could you? It's fine." Roger just wanted her to make the call. "Make that call, will you?"

"Right away."

"How will Susan take it?" Sandy asked.

"She's expecting it. She'll be fine. It's always sad, but not tragic at Alice's age and with her in that state."

"Aye, you've got that right. I'll get up there, certify her. I only saw her last week, so there's no problem there. Do you think Susan will want to see her?"

"I expect so."

"Okay then, I'll arrange everything. Dinnae worry." He patted Roger's shoulder as he passed him.

On the drive up to the workshop, Roger wondered how to tell her. Almost a quarter century of marriage, and you'd think you'd know how to say everything. She'd been with him when he took phone calls, late in the night, about both his own parents. His mum had died not long after Alex was born: she'd had cancer in both breasts, then in her lungs. She was only fifty-eight. She'd been in a hospice, hovering between life and death for weeks, her eyeballs rolling back, eyelids flickering with the morphine dreams at the end. He had stood by her bedside and willed her heart to stop beating.

Susan had picked a sleeping Alex, only a couple of months old, up out of his cot, after the phone rang, and put him in Roger's arms to hold and smell and feel. Pulsing, breathing life, there in his lap, fighting off the feeling of death.

His dad had died five years ago—one big stroke, and he'd been dead before Roger had even made it to the hospital.

He felt like an orphan, even at forty-five.

Susan had loved her dad, of course, but this was going to be so much worse for her. What she felt for Alice was different. He was glad it would be him who told her.

Like a 2:00 a.m. phone call, though, Susan knew something was wrong as soon as she saw him. She spotted the Volvo from the bottom of the hill as she drove back, then Roger sitting on the teak bench she and Mary ate their lunch on in the summer.

She didn't say hello. "Are the boys all right?" Always that fear.

"They're fine, love."

So it must be Mum. It must be Alice. Her face crumpled. He told her quickly. "It's your mum, Suze. She died this morning. She was sleeping, they said, so they didn't disturb her. When they went to check, she'd stopped breathing. Sandy's up there now with her."

"Was it another stroke?"

"We don't know. Possibly. She might have had a heart attack. Or she might just have stopped breathing." He put his arms round her, and she leant on him so heavily that he nearly fell backward. He moved her to the bench, and they both sat down. For minutes she didn't speak, and her shoulders heaved with big, hollow sobs. He just held her.

This bit was strange—he'd seen it happen with patients. This competent, sensible adult had been rendered back into a child. She was mourning not for the hunched old lady who had succumbed to illness in the nursing home three miles down the road but for the vibrant young mother who had thrown her across her lap and tickled her, and tucked her in at night with promises to keep the goblins away. The daughter was, at this moment, bigger than the wife and the mother, and the daughter was hurting.

Eventually, Susan sat up, with an impressive sniff, and dried her eyes on the sleeves of her linen shirt. She tucked her hair behind her ears and sat back on the bench with her arms folded, looking across the valley. "I'm glad it was you who told me."

"Me too."

"Poor Mum." A solitary tear rolled down her cheek. "She'd have been happy to go, you know. She'd have hated seeing herself in that place. So . . . undignified."

"I know she would."

"I'm glad she never had to know."

"I am, too." Roger stroked her head. "Do you want me to tell the boys?"

"Would you? I'd just cry down the phone, and that'd be no help. Thank God Alex is back from Ibiza. They'll both be able to come for the funeral, won't they?"

Roger knew his boys would be there, whatever it took. They loved their mum. "Of course. Don't worry about any of that just now. We'll fix it."

"She wanted to be cremated. She always said she'd hate to know she was in the cold ground, and the idea of us feeling we had to go there and put flowers down all the time."

Roger felt her mind racing and wanted to slow it down. "There's plenty of time for that, Suze." This next bit was the hardest. "What about Margaret? I could call her?"

Susan shook her head. "I have to do it. Mum would want me to." Then she laughed, a tearful half laugh. "That'll get right up her nose, having to come over twice in a year. Ten years nothing, then twice in one year."

Roger wondered if she was right to assume that Margaret would come, but he knew now wasn't the time to ask. He would make sure he was with her when she called her sister. There'd be more mopping up to do then, he was certain.

Susan was quiet again. The valley was very still, with just the lightest breeze making the leaves stir, alleviating the heat.

"Can I see her?" she asked.

"Of course you can. I knew you'd want to. Sandy's sorting that out now. We can go right away, if you'd like."

Susan leant over and kissed him softly. "Can we just sit here together, the two of us, for a while longer?"

"Of course we can. I'm going nowhere."

Nicole

Nicole was hot and she was cross. This was not at all how it was supposed to be. She'd been getting quietly crosser and hotter for the last two hours as she lay beside Tony bloody Brooks in the full sun he required to braise his back to the same just-slapped ruddiness (complete with fingerprints—his sun cream was applied by his odious wife, Phil, with all the care a mud wrestler might show an opponent) his front had acquired yesterday. He was lying with his face in his towel, and she was forced to ask him to repeat each remark he made, which was pretty tiresome since none of them was really worth hearing. She could hardly complain about the effect the heat was having on her without telling him about the baby, and she was buggered if she was going to tell him before she told Gavin. Who probably wasn't faring any better. In this gruesome family sharing experience, it had fallen, apparently, to Gavin and Phil to take the older kids to tennis, and to her and Tony to mind the little one, as Phil consistently referred to Martha, by the vast communal pool.

This was not Nicole's natural habitat at the best of times—she was not keen on being seen in the vicinity of fifteen-year-old girls, with their tiny hips and ridiculously pert breasts. She knew she looked good for her age, even clandestinely pregnant, but she was no fool. It was a noisy language smorgasbord, fragranced not by bougainvillea and lemon but by the burger bar at the far end. And it was too bloody hot today—she was worried about Martha's shoulders burning, and her own gradual but inexorable headache.

She'd read the same page of Michael Ondaatje at least five times now, and she still couldn't tell you anything that happened. There wasn't a lot of Michael Ondaatje around this particular pool, it had to be said. It was a gold-foil sex and serial murder type of crowd. You snobby cow, Nicole thought. That is what Harriet would call her, and she was probably right. She wished Harriet were here to save her.

My trouble, she thought ruefully, is that I'm too bloody polite. I'd rather put up with this interminable man, his grotty kid and his heinous wife—even if it's ruining the holiday—and a host of perfect moment opportunities—than tell them to get lost. The cheekbone family in the brochure didn't have another family popping out from behind pot plants in distasteful swimwear waving jugs of sangria at them all day long. They didn't invite approach— they were cocooned in their own photogenic selves, safe.

Harriet wouldn't stand for it. Nicole could see her friend, the iron fist in the velvet glove, finding infinitely polite yet completely candid ways in which to say *Piss off, you sad no mates—it's not our fault you have nothing to say to each other—don't even think about looking to us to put the color in your gray little lives.* They'd never even know she'd done it. Well, they might. But so be it— they'd be gone. Nicole just didn't have that gene. Be polite or die. What a curse.

Had Phil Brooks been a mother in their school car park, Harriet and she would have giggled about her. She was the kind of mother they avoided sitting next to at coffee mornings and mums' nights out: too slim and fit for Harriet, and too competitive for Nicole. She was constantly comparing the children's swimming distances and tennis talent, and asking how good the twins' cursive hand was, and what Nicole's thoughts were about boarding for seniors—Harriet would have oozed sarcasm answering that one. As a consequence of this relentless hothousing, Crispin, their waiflike, vaguely gray little boy, had a permanent bunny-in-the-headlights look about him and probably didn't get invited out for tea very often, which was no doubt a good thing, since play dates would almost certainly clash with Conversational Latin or Art History, and anyway, he was allergic to almost everything. The poor sod didn't even have any siblings to share the weight of the yoke with.

They had met in the departure lounge. For met, read been ambushed. Once boarded, Phil and Tony had waved manically from their seats four rows away, and Phil had come over as soon as the drinks trolley had passed down the aisle to chat relentlessly and block the path of mothers with babies to the loo.

When they picked up their hire cars from different operators and set off for the resort, Nicole thought they had shaken them off, but to her horror, when they arrived Phil and Tony were picking up the keys to a villa on the same quarter mile of La Manga. Since then, they had been "just passing," and "wondering whether you needed anything from the shop," and generally worrying at them like wasps on every corner.

"You must all come over for a barbecue!" Phil had been exclaiming, ever since the departure lounge. "So nice for Crispin to have some little playmates. So difficult, you see, with an only one. Tony makes a mean steak!"

Tony didn't have the look of a man who made a mean anything, and the boys had soon grown impatient with their puny shadow. So far they had avoided the barbecue, but there had not been one day of this first week that they hadn't spent a part of with the Brooks family. Nicole was waiting for Gavin to lose patience and insult them into going away.

She was searching for Martha's distinctive, beloved head among the human flotsam of the toddler pool and listening—she hoped it seemed intently—to another of Tony's hilarious accounting anecdotes when she saw the three boys heading toward them disconsolately.

"Mum got the time wrong," Crispin bleated as they approached.

The twins rolled their eyes in disdain. "Greg was double-booked," they confirmed.

Tony sat up. "Oh, that's a shame, fellas. Bummer."

The twins and Nicole cringed at his hip-speak.

Nicole had had occasion to speak sharply to Will last night after she had heard him whispering to Crispin, "Your dad is *such* a geek." "He is, though, Mum," Will had said later, when they were finally on their own. "He is, Mum," Gavin had added, and they had all giggled, even Martha, who at four agreed with the diagnosis conspiratorially. Christ, he was.

"Where's Dad, boys? He was going to watch."

The twins had spied a burgeoning game of water volleyball in the pool and didn't answer. They pulled their T-shirts over their heads and kicked off their trainers. "Can we have a swim, Mum?" It was a rhetorical question, shouted back over their shoulders about two seconds before they plunged in. Crispin was folding his sports socks in two and back on themselves.

Oh, bloody hell. No towels, dry shorts or euros for the drinks and ice creams they would require when they got out. No Gavin to send back to the villa to get them. Where was he? At least she had the car, and it was an excuse to escape the sun and Tony. She'd better get Martha out of the water.

Ten minutes later she was being blissfully air-conditioned: both of the dashboard vents were firing straight at her face. Martha had refused to get out of the pool—"I playin', Mum, I playin'"—and Tony had assured Nicole that he could keep an eye—"well, both eyes, naturally"—on Martha and the twins while she popped back to get what she needed. He had even sat up for the job, sacrificing vital minutes of pucing-up time. His front had been unpleasantly sweaty. But there was no way Nicole was going to leave her baby with him. She hoped she could drag the boys away after they had swum—maybe they could all drive over to the strip, where the only people they would be sharing the wide, white beach with were the Spaniards who took apartments there every July and August for their annual holidays. Martha had screamed angrily, wriggling and kicking, but within minutes she had plugged in her precious thumb and fallen asleep. Nicole decided to leave her in the car in the driveway—she looked so peaceful, and it was nice and cool. She would only be a minute. Gavin might be there already, although in her experience, he was more likely to be taking advantage of the quiet to have a San Miguel on the balcony than sorting out dry towels for the boys.

And he was. In the villa. In the bedroom. And in Phil Brooks.

They always say, don't they, that if a door is closed and you suspect there may be fire behind it you must not open it? Because the rush of oxygen feeding the fire will make it burst toward you with new intensity, a wall of flames and heat.

That was what it felt like. Exactly what it felt like. A big wall of something so intense that she thought she would melt away, or be vaporized by the shock and the suddenness and the strength of it.

It happened, as these things do, in slow motion, so that the first searing pain lasted so much longer.

They heard her. Or saw her. She wasn't sure which came first. Gavin's arse, white within his tan lines, flexing, Phil's thin legs framing it. She had cracked, dry skin on her heels. It must have scratched him. The door was parallel to the bed, so that Nicole could see where their skin made contact along their bodies. See Phil's thin, long breasts, nipples jutting out sideways, shivering with motion, her pointed hipbones. Her arms were above her head, pinned back by Gavin's hands, just above her elbows. His head was above hers, too far from it for kissing, though she was sucking at his neck, his chest in between, saying, "Fuck me. Fuck—" She stopped. Her head had thrashed right toward the door, and she had seen Nicole. Gavin turned in the same direction. As he jumped off her, hopping awkwardly on the first leg to hit the floor, his penis was bright red, and it bounced, ridiculously, against his stomach. Nicole registered that she had stopped them at the crucial moment, but it gave her no satisfaction.

They moved a lot then. She was very still. They flailed, pulling at sheets, and clothes. Nicole only tightened her grip on the door handle and stared at their nakedness, the absurdity of it. She had never seen people have sex before, except in films, where it wasn't real, and she had never heard it, except through walls in cheap hotels long ago. Films and strangers were exciting. She remembered once, a million years ago, coming in time with another couple, through a wall, spooned from behind, so that she lost track, in the moment, of who she was keeping pace with, her lover, who wasn't Gavin, or them, the anonymous couple behind the wall. She'd only seen Gavin make love to *her*, from underneath, on top of or beside him. Then he had always looked sexy to her. Now he looked vaguely comical. Except this wasn't funny.

She couldn't move forward or back, and she couldn't speak. Phil was saying, over and over, "Christ, oh, Christ," looking at Gavin but not at Nicole. Gavin was silent, looking at neither of them.

The moment felt significant. If Gavin's peccadilloes and one-night stands and office shags had landed bruising blows and deep cuts on her psyche, they had never reached the core of her. Now it had been sliced through. And it was this sudden change in her, so physically powerful, that stopped her moving.

Her dignity would have had her close the door. Her pride would have had her walk out. Her rage would have made her speak vitriol at them. But this was stronger than any of those.

She looked at him, waiting to hear what he would say. And realized that she didn't want to hear him say something mitigating. She didn't want him to implore, or dismiss Phil, or apologize, or reason. And so, suddenly, with no desire for explanation with a nook or cranny she could latch on to that would make it possible, once again, for her to stay, there was no need to stay. Not in this room, not in this house, not in this moment. And she could make her body move.

She didn't close the door. Let them get dressed in public, pulling their clothes on with none of the artfulness or passion with which they had removed them.

In the villa's white kitchen Nicole made two phone calls, the first to the agency manager on site, explaining that she and the children were needed at home—illness in the family; she asked him to book a flight for that evening and a cab to drive them to the airport. Then she rang Harriet.

"Tim?"

"Is that you, Nicole?"

"Yes. What are you doing at home?"

"Been out with a client this morning, got home early—there's nobody here, I'm afraid. S'pose you're after Harry."

"I was. Do you know where she is?"

"No idea. I'm the last person she tells anything to, you know that." Tim laughed a small, sad laugh. "Can I help?" Realization. "Aren't you in Spain?"

"Not for much longer. Tim, I need a favor."

"What do you need?" That was so Tim, instantly calm and efficient, making you feel there was no problem he couldn't sort out. She nearly cried with relief.

Don't you dare cry, she told herself. Not here, not now. She used the shorthand of intimacy, and the language of a long, close friendship. That was such a relief, not to have to say why, just when.

"Picking up. Gatwick. Tonight."

"Not a problem. Which terminal, what time?"

"Thank you. North. About eight-thirty."

"Is it all of you?" Tim's question was laden with a dozen others.

"Just me and the kids."

In five words she had given him most of the answers.

She was thanking him again, and her voice threatened to break.

"It's all right, Nic. You hold it together for a few more hours. One of us will be there for you. Okay?"

"Okay. Tim?"

"Yeah?"

"Tell Harriet I'm sorry."

"She'll tell you to shut up. So will I. You just get yourself on that plane and don't worry about the rest of it. See you later, love."

When she turned round Gavin was staring at her. She couldn't see Phil. Maybe later, when she had figured it out herself, she would explain to him what he had just done to her, to all of them.

But now she wasn't sure herself, and she found she didn't need to say anything to him.

She picked up three towels from where the maid had left them earlier that morning. "I came back for these. The kids are at the main pool, with Tony Brooks." She handed them to Gavin. She had to walk across the kitchen to do it, then retreated back to the other side. She didn't want to smell him or let him touch her. "Keep them out of my hair for a couple of hours while I pack. Give them some lunch." Instructions, not requests. It felt strange to talk to him this way.

Gavin started to speak. She didn't let him. "Don't let Martha burn."

"Nicole, what am I supposed to do, stuck here without you?"

In her head, in her best southern drawl, she quoted Rhett Butler at him. Aloud, calmly, she said, "It's four days, Gavin. Sort the villa out, work on your handicap, top up your tan. I don't care. I just don't want you in my home."

Gavin turned to leave, like a schoolboy who had just heard the headmaster pronounce his punishment.

He's got no idea what he's done, Nicole thought. No idea.

Cressida

Like period pains, just a bit stronger . . . Rescue Remedy can help you to feel calm and in control. . . . It does hurt, yes, but you feel like you're working toward something—visualization techniques can make a big difference. *Bullshit. Lies. Propaganda, put about by those bastards, who are probably men, who don't want the birth rate to fall. This hurts like hell. The only thing I can visualize is dying.*

Cressida was not happy. She had read the chapter about what would happen when it was time. Only it wasn't time. And it wasn't happening like they said it would. She was only thirty-five weeks. She wasn't ready. She hadn't packed a bag with nappies (for her and the baby) and muslin squares and little vests that tied at the side with satin ribbons, and bootees that looked unfeasibly small, and slippers and breast pads. She hadn't even shaved her legs. That had been getting harder and harder, and she'd given up a couple of weeks ago, promising herself a pedicure and shave when the due date loomed—the thought of good-looking obstetricians poking about when she looked like a monkey with pig's trotters appalled her. But there hadn't been time to do it. She remembered endless sitcoms and films in which husbands ran around like headless chickens while the contractions were ten minutes apart and calm nurses told them not to worry, that it would be hours, even days before the baby came. Hers had been painful, debilitating and strong since the first, which had come while she was letting herself out of the front door this morning. There was never more than three or four minutes between them. Long enough to stop feeling sick, to catch your breath, to find a comfortable position to sit in and then—wham—another one. "You may find time for a rest, even a short sleep between early contractions, and it is important to conserve energy at this time." So the book had said. Ha bloody ha.

She felt lost in the pain. In a way it was work. When the pains weren't happening, you could see the sense of it in a way: that you were opening up, gradually, rhythmically. Each time you promised yourself that you would relax into it, think about yourself opening up so the baby could get out, let the animal process take over, but then, when it started again, all that sprang out of your grasp, and you were lost in the pain again, disoriented and desperate.

"You've got to relax, darling," Polly was saying. "You're going to be exhausted if you don't try."

She knew Polly was right but didn't know how to do it. "I can't, Mum. It hurts." She wanted Polly to make it go away. She took her mother's hand, gripped it tightly.

"I know, darling. I know. It won't be long. I'm here." That hand was Cressida's anchor. It held her down when the pain was trying to float her away.

"And me. I'm here too." That was Elliot, on the other side, helpless and apart.

He had so wanted to be there, when the baby was born. Polly had thought it was a bad idea, Cressida knew. She hadn't wanted Dan anywhere near her when Cressida and Daniel were born. It may have been the eighties, but Polly felt she was delivered fifty years too late—she would have preferred to labor alone, with Dan pacing the corridor, cigar behind his ear in anticipation, until she could sit up in a white nightdress, legs together, and present him with a cleaned-up baby.

She thought Dan would too, if there hadn't been tremendous peer pressure in the unit where Cressida had been born. Blood and violence and gore just weren't his thing. She wasn't sure he had ever seen her the same way again—he hadn't touched her for months afterward, winced and worried more than she did when they first "resumed relations" as the nurse called it, and they had both been wordlessly relieved when he had missed Daniel's birth, caught on a train on his way back from some seminar or other.

But Cressida wasn't sure. She worried about how she would behave, how she would look. But she couldn't shut Elliot out of this. It was part of what she had signed up for when she decided to keep the baby. Whatever else was going on, she felt that this baby belonged to both of them. It had been made in love by the two of them, however corny and clichéd that sounded, and it should be born into love, and the people who would always love it the most were she and Elliot. That link between them had been created forever when the first magic explosion of chemistry had happened inside her while she lay in his arms. That earned him his place by her bed now.

Polly hadn't argued. For a moment she had wondered how she would have felt about Jack being there with her, in an alternative universe where they might have had a chid. He would have been fascinated, she thought. But that thought was painful, and she pushed it to one side. Jack wasn't here.

But for now Elliot was strangely irrelevant to Cressida. It was about her and Polly and the baby. That was all.

Polly was holding the mouthpiece for the gas and air. She never once took her eyes off Cressida's face. Each time the rising crescendo of pain expressed itself there, she fed the tube into Cressida's mouth for her to suck, and they were connected then, by their hands, and by the plastic tube, and by that endless eye contact, with which, wordlessly, Polly told her that she was here, that she understood, that she would make it okay.

Cressida's knees were aching. She had been kneeling, leaning forward, across the bed at home for an hour or more, with Polly on the other side, while they waited for Elliot to come and drive them to the hospital. There they had wanted to monitor her, and she sat up, the elastic belt round her bump, under her nightshirt. She could see her knees, with red circles bright on them. Elliot stroked her head, but she didn't want that—only Polly's hand.

"Let's have a look at you, shall we?" The midwife's face was gentle and kind, but her hands were like razor blades. Her name was Alison, and she looked at the wall behind Cressida's bed, concentrating while she felt her progress. "Crikey. You're doing brilliantly. You were four centimeters when you came in, and I'd say you're about eight now, which means you're racing along." She lowered her voice. "There's a lady along the corridor who's been at it all night, poor thing, and she's nowhere near eight centimeters." Cressida felt pretty clever. "At this rate, you'll be ready to push Baby out in an hour, couple of hours, I should think. Good girl. How are you feeling? Still coping with the pain?"

"More like the pain's coping with me."

Alison laughed. "Glad to see you haven't lost your sense of humor. It's a bit late for an epidural. Think you can make it without? We give medals, you know!"

It didn't sound as though she had a choice, but she was scared about the next bit. She remembered a story her dad had told her about her mum: how halfway through her labor with Cressida, she had turned to him and begged, "Don't make me do this today, I'll do it tomorrow, but I don't want to do it today." She had found that hilarious, when she was a child, and Polly had laughed too. It wasn't so funny now that she knew exactly what her mum had meant. "I'll try."

"Brilliant. You're my favorite kind of patient." Alison looked at the monitor. "Baby's fine, happy as Larry. I'll be back in a few minutes—call if you need me."

When she had breezed out again, Cressida looked at Elliot. "Why don't you go and grab Mum a cup of tea?" The concern on his face and his desire to touch her were beginning to irritate her—she wanted him to go away, just for a few minutes, and leave her with Polly and the machine.

"Of course. Sugar?"

Polly smiled at him. "No, thanks. But I wouldn't mind a biscuit or something, if you can find one. I never did get my breakfast!"

"Coming right up." Elliot kissed Cressida's cheek. "Don't do it while I'm gone, will you?"

"I wish," she replied.

Elliot closed the door behind him and walked to the lifts. Clare was standing there, her back to him, waiting. The down arrow had been pushed. He had forgotten this might happen. His girlfriend was having a baby in the maternity unit where his wife worked and he hadn't worked out what he would say when he bumped into her. Stupid. But when the call had come from Polly this morning, he had been more excited than he could ever remember. He had put the phone down and hugged himself, trying to keep still. Thinking, Today is the day I will hold my baby. Too happy, too excited.

Guilt hit him like a brick. She looked as if she was going off shift. He glanced at his watch. Nine-forty-five. She would have finished at eight—stayed on to finish a labor where she thought it would help the woman. That was typical of Clare. He registered something like relief that she still did it, still worked longer hours than she was contracted to work, now that she wasn't trying to avoid coming home to him. Her back looked tired.

He wanted to skulk away so that this scene wouldn't punctuate his memory of today and so that he didn't make her more sad. But it was too late. She had turned, sensing a presence behind her.

For a second she was confused—had he come to look for her?—but then it dawned on her why he was there. She had been waiting for this. Like a soldier, she had planned her defensive position. She had lain awake thinking of what she would say to the ward sister if she was asked to attend Cressida's labor. She couldn't do this, but she wouldn't know what to tell her. His being here as she was going off duty was both a surprise and what she had been expecting. She was relieved to be leaving the hospital! She wouldn't work tomorrow, or the next day. She would make excuses, invent food poisoning or a high temperature. She wouldn't come back until Elliot, Cressida and their baby had gone.

She hadn't known whether he would be here with Cressida. She hadn't spoken to him since that night in his car, and whatever her mum learnt from Susan she wisely kept to herself. She didn't know if he and Cressida were together. Most mornings, she half expected the post to contain a solicitor's letter, but it had not come. But *he* had come. He was going to watch their child be born. She had watched a hundred fathers see a hundred babies burst forth, wet, bloody and red, from a hundred grunting, heaving mothers. She had seen them in tears with broad smiles, wide-eyed with shock, dazzled with wonder—fascinated, horrified, delirious, moved. She had heard them cry, moan, laugh, swear and declare their love. She wouldn't see his face, and she wouldn't hear his voice. She wouldn't ever know which kind of new father Elliot was.

Elliot moved forward. "Hello, Clare."

"Hello."

"You're off, then?"

"Yes. I'm on nights."

"I thought so."

"Of course." It seemed a long time since she had gone home, after nights, to their house to find him dressed for work, making her tea and toast, with the bed neatly rearranged for her to slip into.

"It's today, then, is it?"

"Yup." He didn't dare say anything else. Why would she want to know any more?

"Is it . . . has it . . . ?"

"Not yet. She's doing brilliantly, though."

Clare didn't want to know. She turned back to the lift. Mercifully, its rescuing bell sounded and the doors opened for her. A crowd of strangers waited to absorb her.

"I hope it all goes well," she said, and she was gone.

Downstairs, Clare ran through the wide front doors, dodging the wheelchairs, toward the car park, searching frantically in her handbag for her keys. She got to her car, opened the door, slammed it shut behind her and laid her forehead on the steering wheel while she caught her breath. As soon as she had, and her heart had stilled enough for her to feel safe, she reversed out and drove as fast as she dared down the back road to the roundabout that would point her home.

Upstairs, Elliot fumbled in his pocket for change and tried to make sense of the signs that directed him down labyrinthine corridors to the cafeteria. He was glad she had gone. It wouldn't help any of them for her to be around.

When he got back, with the tea and some limp croissants, Alison was there again. Cressida had changed positions. She had been lying on her side, facing Polly, and the blessed gas and air; now she was sitting up, her hands gripped round her knees, knuckles white. Her cheeks were red, and puffed up with air, and she blew it out ferociously when she saw him. "Just in time. Did you go to Ceylon to get that tea? Alison says I'm ready." She was smiling, but her eyes were frightened. Polly was standing up now, the gas and air abandoned behind her. She had one arm round Cressida's shoulders and a determined expression on her face. This was it.

Oh, God. Oh, God. Oh, God. Elliot issued a silent plea: Let this be all right. Let *them* be all right. It was almost too real for him now. She might die, *they* might die, and it would be his fault. His anxiety must have shown in his face, because Polly said, "Don't worry, she's doing brilliantly."

"Right, Cressida. I can see a head, and it's got your hair, lots of it. On the next one, I want you to give me a mighty push. Your baby's almost here."

They all pushed. Polly's lips were set and white. Cressida's eyes widened as the head emerged, glistening. "*Ow ow ow ow!* It hurts. It's burning. Ow!"

"You're an absolute star," Alison was saying. "I don't think you've torn at all with the head. Don't push now, sweetheart. Pant for me, just for a minute." She was calm, holding the baby's head. "Just the shoulders now, and then Baby will be out, and you can see it."

"I need to push. I gotta get it out. I gotta get it out. Please?" This last was desperate.

"Okay. Come on, then. One more big push. Good girl."

Cressida pressed her chin into her neck, gritted her teeth and the baby slithered out almost violently onto the sheet. Cressida collapsed backward into the pillows, crying with happiness and relief and pain.

Alison turned the baby over, wiped its mouth with the corner of a clean towel, and it gave a small, wet cry. Still talking, she wrapped it up expertly, in another towel, and passed it to Cressida through her legs. "You've got a boy. Quite a big boy, considering his dates, I'd say. He looks fine."

Polly opened her mouth to say something but couldn't. Tears ran down her cheeks. To watch your baby have a baby, to be allowed to be in the room where it happened, indescribable. Love, pride, relief and the reverberations of her own labor with Cressida broke over her. She reached over and laid her palm on Cressida's cheek.

"I know, Mum." Cressida was smiling at her. "Look at him. He's beautiful. Hello, little man." She had already acquired the soft, murmuring voice every mother has—the change was that quick.

Elliot reached out one finger, smoothed it slowly across the baby's damp head. It felt warm and soft. He buried his face in Cressida's dark hair. She squeezed his hand. "Thank you," he muttered.

"Shush." She pulled at his hand so that he raised his head and looked at her. "You're welcome."

Elliot laughed. "Christ. That was the most incredible thing I have ever seen."

Alison smiled at the tableau. "I know. That's why I love this job. Every time is like the first time. A new miracle every day."

When Jack got home from work that night, the red light on his answer machine was flashing insistently. He pushed it, then picked up the pile of post his cleaning lady had laid neatly on the hall table. He stopped as he heard Polly's voice.

"Jack, it's me. Sorry. It's Polly. It's Tuesday, about lunchtime. I know you're at work. I didn't want to call you there. I—I just thought you'd like to know, well, I wanted to tell you—Cressida had her baby this morning. It's a little boy. A bit early, but they say he's fine. Weighed about five and a half pounds, so no problems there. And she's fine, too. It was pretty straightforward, fortunately. She did really well—I was very proud of her. I got to be there for the whole thing. It was amazing, Jack. Well, sorry, this message is a bit rambling. Just wanted to let you know, really. Um, she's going to call him Spencer. It's different, I suppose. I guess we'll get used to it. Me and Dan, I mean. And Elliot—he was there too. Quite a day. Anyway, I'll get off now. Like I said, I just thought you'd like to know. I hope you're well. Take care. It's Polly, by the way. Did I say that already?"

There were a few seconds' silence before the receiver had gone down, as though there were other things she had wanted to say but hadn't been able to. Of course there were other things to say. Jack knew what they were, and he wished she had said them. His fingers itched to pick up his car keys. He wanted to drive to the hospital and find her. But he couldn't.

He sent an enormous bouquet of primary-colored gerberas, Cressida's favorite, a bottle of vintage champagne and a blue card that said how pleased he was for all of them. But he couldn't call, and he couldn't go.

AUGUST
READING GROUP

EDEN CLOSE

ANITA SHREVE © 1989

When Andrew returns to his hometown in upstate New York for his mother's funeral, he does not intend to stay. But the dreams and memories of seventeen years ago persist, and in the darkened farmhouse he relives that hot, bloody night when Eden Close was blinded—by the same gun that killed her father. Eden and Andrew had been childhood companions—smoking, fishing, skating and fighting—until the day the tomboy turned temptress. Now Andrew is drawn again to this lost, blind girl of his youth, drawn to save her from the cruel neglect she has endured for seventeen sightless years without him. But first he must discover the grisly truth about that night . . .

S usan?"

"Is that you, Poll?"

"Yeah, it's me. It's not a great line."

"Are you okay? You sound weird."

"Suze . . . Cress has had the baby. She's had a little boy."

"Oh, my God, Poll, that's early."

"I know."

"That's fantastic! I can't believe it. I'm shocked. When? Where?"

"About five hours ago—I just left them at the hospital. I'm in the car now."

"Are they both okay?"

"They're fabulous. Both of them. He's a stunner, Suze. Absolutely gorgeous. Five four, so he'd have been a whopper if he'd gone to term, ten fingers, ten toes. Biggest scrotum you ever saw." Polly was laughing and crying.

Susan wanted to hug her. "Oh, Poll, I'm so happy for you. Does he have a name?"

"They're going to call him Spencer."

"Okay."

"You know how it is, don't you? You hear the name, you think, Oh, Christ, but five minutes later, he's Spencer. Like he'd been born with a name tag."

"I know. And how's Cress? How was it?"

"Quick for a first one, they said. She was amazing, Suze. I don't think I've ever been prouder of her. She did it all herself. And I was right there the whole time."

"And Elliot?"

"Him too. He can't speak. It's like he's in shock. He's with them now. I've got to get home for Daniel, but I'll go back in later. I think they'll keep her in for a couple of days, with him being so early, but he's had a feed already, clever boy, so it shouldn't be for long. Suze, he's so beautiful."

"You sound so happy."

"I feel like I've taken something. I'm euphoric."

"Guess you won't be coming to the reading group tonight, then?"

"Will you say sorry for me?"

"No apology needed, I'm sure—they'll be thrilled for you."

"Better go."

"You give them our best love, won't you?"

"I will. Come and see us as soon as we get home."

"Try stopping me! Congratulations, Poll, to all of you."

"Thanks, Suze. Love you."

"Love you too."

Harriet was the first to arrive. It didn't matter how early you got to Nicole's, you never caught the tail end of any chaos, and Harriet should know—she'd tried often enough. There was never so much as a footprint on the cream carpets (rather like Baptists, apparently the twins and Martha had taken a Ribena pledge as soon as they could talk), or a handprint on the pale biscuit walls, or a fingerprint on the highly polished kitchen granite, let alone ketchup smears on the tea towels. At Harriet's house, William and George were just as messy as Josh, Martha just as lethal with felt-tip pens as Chloe. Here, it was simply not permitted, expected or tolerated. For years now Harriet had marveled at the control Nicole exerted, almost as much as she had been horrified by it.

It was no different without Gavin. Would her own home look different without Tim? The laundry pile would teeter a little less precariously without his shirts, and there would be a smaller pile of partnerless black socks waiting in vain to be reunited. Was that all?

Nicole was different, though, and Harriet was worried about

her. She was brittle, and taut with the effort of keeping it all in. She hadn't told the kids—they presumed Dad was away, working; it wasn't unusual. She looked as if she had lost weight. The pregnancy was still hidden. Tonight, in bootleg trousers, her stomach looked almost concave.

"How are you doing?" Harriet asked.

"Oh, you know."

Harriet didn't. "You look tired."

"I am. Not sleeping brilliantly. I've got a lot to think about."

"Of course. Have you seen Gavin?"

"No. Don't worry, I'm not going to. Not until I've figured everything out. I promise."

"Don't promise me anything. It's not up to me. Are the kids okay?"

"They've barely noticed he's not here. Just goes to show how absent he was from their lives before. I haven't lied to them, it just hasn't come up." She laughed bitterly and changed the subject. She wasn't ready to talk about what she was going to do, not even with Harriet. "Did you finish the book?"

"Yeah—in Portugal. I read loads. I'll say this for Tim, he's brilliant with the kids when we're away. Like he wants to make up for all the time he misses with them while he's working. He just takes them off in the morning and I don't see them again until teatime. I get out of all those ghastly things like the water parks. Now, that's my idea of hell, wandering around all day in a swimsuit, coming down vertical drops at thirty miles an hour with your legs crossed, knowing that if you don't, you'll get twenty pints of water flushed up you."

Nicole winced at the thought. "I haven't asked you much about your holiday. Sorry. Was it good?"

"It was fine. Things are easier when you're away. Everything seems a bit better in a different place with the sun shining." She caught Nicole's eye. "As long as there isn't a floor show like the one you got." They smiled at each other.

"I can't see Tim doing that," Nicole said.

"Me neither," Harriet agreed. "While you're away, you think everything might be okay. You don't have to be back long to realize nothing's changed."

"Oh, Harry, you do know this is all in your head, don't you?"

"Is it?" Harriet looked sad.

The doorbell rang. "Saved by the bell!" Harriet went to answer it, shrugging off her melancholy. She turned back to Nicole. "I guess you don't want to tell the others about Gavin?"

"Not yet."

"Okay."

"Not because I'm going to have him back." Nicole was desperate for Harriet's approval.

"Nic! Stop. Don't tell them. I agree. Stop justifying yourself to me. You really don't have to. Okay?"

Nicole smiled gratefully. "Okay."

Polly had telephoned each of them to tell them Susan's mother had died a couple of weeks back. They felt a connection to the news they might not have if they hadn't talked about it together earlier in the summer. Obviously neither of them had met Alice, and neither of them had lost her mother, but they remembered Susan, close to tears in Harriet's kitchen, talking about how it felt, and they knew it would have hit her hard. Nicole had sent a card. Harriet had been round one afternoon and left an enormous box of chocolates on the doorstep, with a note that said she was thinking of her and that cocoa solids helped. But they hadn't seen her until tonight.

Harriet hugged her. "Hello. How are you?"

"Two pounds heavier. Thanks for the chocolates."

"Beats Prozac. I'm sorry about your mum."

"Thanks."

Nicole came into the hall, and Susan let herself be held again. She found other people's sympathy stifling. Politeness required them to talk about it to you, and then you had to answer. And because she was your mother, and not your husband or your child, and because she was an old lady, and because, let's face it, she'd lost her marbles, you were supposed to be philosophical about it. Reflective, sad, but not desolate. Desolate was how Susan felt, when other people made her think about it. She wanted to answer "How are you?" with "I'm an orphan," or "I'm all alone," or

"I miss her," or "I wasn't ready." You weren't allowed to say that, though. That wasn't what people wanted to hear. But everyone meant well. She kept saying that to herself.

Nicole didn't ask. Her embrace was eloquent enough. She was strangely sensitive, Susan thought, for someone so controlled. She was glad she had come tonight, although she had been tempted not to. "You can't hibernate," Roger had told her, and he was right. Besides, tonight she had a shield of good news.

"That's brilliant news. Ooh!" Harriet was squealing. "I love baby days. They're the happiest!"

"I love the name! Spencer Bradford." Nicole rolled it around her mouth, thoughtfully. "He sounds like your mate. Spence. Like it."

"Have you seen him yet, Susan?"

"I'm going round in the morning," Susan said. "Polly brought them home this afternoon."

"Do give them all our love, won't you? I haven't got a card or a present or anything yet. I thought we had a few weeks to go."

"Polly did, too. I think he caught everyone on the back foot."

Nicole opened the fridge and brought out a bottle of champagne. "This calls for a celebration, don't you think?"

"I love the way you just happen to have cold champagne to hand. I could just about manage flat lemonade." Harriet laughed.

"Old publishing habit. You just never know . . ."

She uncorked the bottle expertly. Harriet took three flutes down from the dresser, and Nicole poured. Full glasses for Susan and Harriet, half for herself. She held the glass round the neck, instead of at the stem, so that Susan wouldn't see.

Harriet proposed the toast. "To Polly, Cressida and Spencer." The three women raised their glasses and drank. "And Elliot, I suppose," Harriet added, as an afterthought. "Not quite sure how he fits in, but here's to him anyway."

"Exactly." Susan didn't really know either. She guessed that would be up to Cressida. And that Cressida wouldn't really know either yet.

"So, no Polly. No Clare, obviously." They exchanged glances. Harriet was dying to ask Susan what was going on there, but she didn't. "Just the three of us. Hardly seems worth it."

"Don't say that! I stayed up last night finishing the book."

"We both read it while we were away, didn't we, Harry?"

"Yeah. It was a brilliant book to read in the hot sun."

"Absolutely. She captured that incredibly vividly, didn't she, the heat of that summer? So oppressive and stultifying. Is that a word?"

"I think so."

"Polly's not here, so she can't tell us why she chose it."

"Didn't she say that Cressida had had to read an Anita Shreve for A levels, and that they'd both loved it?"

"Yeah—*The Pilot's Wife*, wasn't it?"

"And this is her first."

"Crikey. A levels have come on since I did them. What—no Chaucer?"

"Don't! Well, I loved it. I guessed the ending, but that didn't matter."

"Did you? I didn't. I mean, it was obvious that something funny had gone on, and that the murder wasn't random, but I didn't guess it was the mother. Or why she had done it."

"It would make a brilliant film."

"You always say that. I mostly hate films made of books I love. They're always disappointing, don't you think?"

"Aren't the best films of the classics? Like Jane Austen. I read her at university, and she never got me going—I couldn't see what all the fuss was about. But add Hugh Grant, or Greg Wise, bit of a soundtrack, nice scenery, and I'm her greatest fan."

"You're a philistine, Harry."

"Maybe so, but I know what I like! Now this was as sexy as hell, didn't you think? All that alfresco loving! She makes being blind sound pretty raunchy. Like all the other senses have to compensate, I suppose. Touch especially."

"It was sexy, but incredibly poignant, too, didn't you think?

There was that protectiveness about his love for her, which was incredibly tender."

"And the happy ending. I'm a sucker for a happy ending. I almost thought we weren't going to get one. That's another thing about literary fiction. Sometimes it seems like they don't think a happy ending is highbrow enough. It felt all the way through like they might be overpowered by the past, and not be able to put it behind them, but they do, don't they? The truth comes out, she's pregnant. They leave the place, and all its memories, behind them. She says—doesn't she?—right at the end, 'You have made me give up all the secrets, and I am lighter now. . . . We will leave this place and not come back, and in our dreams it will turn to dust.'" Harriet turned to Susan, who hadn't said much. She was afraid she and Nicole were monopolizing the conversation. "What did you think, Suze?"

"I don't know." She sighed. "It seems to me I can't read anything at the moment without it being sort of autobiographical. I can't concentrate on what I'm reading because I keep cross-referencing it with my own life. Like *Guppies for Tea*. And *The Memory Box*. This was the same. I know what you meant, Harry, when you said we needed to read fewer men's books, after *Atonement*, but I didn't know then that they were all going to be wringing me out emotionally, month after month. I'm almost desperate for Nic's choice this month. No offense, Nicole, but I reckon you might choose something that's going to give me a break from all this *angst*."

Nicole nodded confirmation. She had her choice for September in the study, and she was pretty sure it would satisfy Susan's criteria, if not Harriet's. Susan carried on, "Polly didn't know Mum was going to die when she chose it, but there it is—the reason he's gone back to his old home is because his mother's died. The bits where he's getting the house ready to sell, getting rid of all the memories of growing up there with her, resonated with me. Although he doesn't have the same kind of relationship with his mother as I did with mine. Full of secrets. There's that bit where he says he's trying to imagine her under the ground so that he can summon up the appropriate sorrowful emotions, which is different from me. I keep trying *not* to think about Mum so that it doesn't all seep out of me all over the place. But it's basically about mothers, and the nature of mother love, isn't it, the whole book? Again."

"He doesn't have successful relationships with women in general, does he, apart from Eden? Not with his own mother, not with Eden's, not with his ex-wife. Those relationships are all portrayed fairly flatly. Like he doesn't really come alive until he rediscovers Eden."

"And what a name that is! All those connotations. Temptation, forbidden fruit, Paradise. Eden Close."

"Oh, yeah. I only just realized that!"

"You are kidding?" Susan was delighted. Even she had got that.

"No, really."

"Hopeless."

"Shut up. We can't all be geniuses." Harriet was laughing at herself. It was pretty obvious, now that she thought of it. She must have had a bit too much sun that day she was reading it.

"I can't wait to hear what you make of my book."

I know exactly what I'm likely to make of your book, Nic, Harriet was thinking.

Nicole

"Dilation and curettage" sounded like an upmarket fashion label. It was a gorgeously opaque name for what it actually was. The word *abortion* made Nicole think about Second World War pilots in Spitfires, ejecting clear of doomed missions. *Termination*— that was the best word, if such a thing could have a best word. She had looked it up in the dictionary, last night: "*Termination*: 1. the act of terminating or the state of being terminated. 2. something that terminates. 3. a final result." It didn't say anything about babies, or murder, or wickedness, or ultimate selfishness, or playing God.

"A final result."

Nicole was sitting in her car outside the surgery where she had been registered for eight years, since she moved to the area with Gavin, where both pregnancies had been confirmed, where all her antenatal appointments had been held, where she had sat, bleary-eyed with tiredness after sleepless nights, for a hundred weigh-ins, all painstakingly recorded by the nurse in the children's red books, a dozen immunizations, countless prescriptions for antibiotics and worming tablets. The kids' medical records were, doubtless, pretty standard stuff, no terrifying illnesses or traumatic accidents so far, thank God.

Her own records probably read like a physical diary of her marriage: nothing but routine appointments for well-woman checks and the odd virus until she was pregnant with the twins, then the flurry of activity that being pregnant and newly delivered involves. The six-week check, and the chat about contraception—minipill after the twins, IUD fitted after Martha, removed a few months afterward when she didn't like the side effects, then back on the pill—all that evidence of a happy sex life within a secure, fecund marriage. Gavin's infidelities were written up too, between the lines, in the form of a script for antidepressants (a girl from the office, when the twins were a few months old), chronic daily headaches, diagnosed as stress-related (a client from some major drugs company, the summer before she was pregnant with Martha), sleeping pills (when his car was stolen from a car park several hundred miles from where he should have been, though she never knew who that was).

And now this was written down forever in those records: the request for a referral for termination. Whatever she decided, it would always be there—the fact that she had considered it. She hadn't known you still had to have a letter from two doctors, both saying that the abortion was important to your mental health. That seemed to belong to a different time, although her doctor had said it was just a formality now. She'd been dreading the appointment. She was a nice woman, Dr. Simons, had the knack of being sympathetic but not cloying, asking the right questions without making you feel vulnerable. Nicole had not told her about Gavin, of course. She hadn't told anyone, except Harriet. If Dr. Simons had guessed some of what was going on at home, she had not pushed her into confessing, and Nicole had been grateful for that. She hadn't wanted to explain. She didn't want to now, either.

Dr. Simons hadn't tried to talk her out of the abortion, or tell her it was a mistake. Perhaps if Nicole had been a kid she might have done, or even if she had seemed less composed, less sure. But she had pulled herself together before she went in, pulled herself so tight that no single drop of emotion could seep out. "I'm pregnant, and I can't be." That sounded desperate, and she didn't want to sound that way. "I don't want to be."

Dr. Simons had put down her pen and sat back in her chair. She had looked at Nicole quite hard, taking in the perfect hair and makeup, the beautiful clothes, the expensive handbag, probably remembering William, George and Martha. Who knows what she thought? What she said was, "Are you quite sure of that?"

"Yes, I am. Please believe me, Dr. Simons. I have thought this through, and I am very clear on what I want."

"What about your husband?"

She had to ask, of course, just as Nicole had to lie. "He's happy for me to do what I think is best for all of us." Something in her attitude as she sat there added, "Besides, it is my body, and therefore my decision."

These were sentiments with which Dr. Simons happened to agree. Nicole was unreadable, and the set of her jaw was determined.

"Do you want to talk a little bit about why you've come to this decision?"

"I don't. Not really. Is that okay? I mean, do I have to explain my reasons?"

"No. That's fine." Dr. Simons wouldn't push her. It was early days. She had known women to change their minds at every stage. Sometimes you didn't know how you really felt until you started doing something about it. She picked up her pen again.

"Right. How pregnant do you think you are?"

"Exactly twelve weeks." She gave the date of her last period, and Dr. Simons played with her two plastic circles to confirm that Nicole was right. She obviously knew almost to the minute when she had conceived. Which suggested all sorts of things. None of which were any of her business. She looked briefly at Nicole's notes. C of E. Thirty-five next birthday. "Have you seen someone at the practice already?"

"No, I haven't."

"So you've had no antenatal care, no bloods, no scan booked in?" She tried not to make that sound negligent.

"No." Nicole didn't know how to explain that, before Spain, she had known with complete certainty that she was pregnant, reveled in keeping her secret from everyone, and that, since Spain, she had been grappling with this decision, which had first presented itself to her on the airplane on the way home.

"But you're sure you're pregnant? I'm sorry to ask, I know you've been pregnant twice before. But you are sure?"

"I'm sure. I've taken two tests. I've missed three periods. And I feel pregnant, just like before. I've put on some weight, my breasts are sore and swollen, that sort of thing."

"Just the same, I think I'll take some bloods this morning, if that's okay with you."

As she tightened the red rubber strip around her arm and patted the inside of her elbow to raise a vein, Dr. Simons looked at Nicole and wondered. But she knew her curiosity had no place in the room. The lion's share of women she referred to the clinic were married women in their thirties who already had children within their relationships. It was one of the great myths that all abortions were performed on unmarried fifteen-year-olds who were using abortion as a form of birth control. She herself had four kids, the youngest still a baby, and most of the time she thought she would rather saw off her right arm with a blunt bread knife than be pregnant again. But if it happened she knew, or she hoped she knew, that she would be flooded once more by the love and strength you needed to cope. Yet she had seen a lot of women in here who hadn't felt that way. Women for whom the money worries, the marital concerns or the fear of losing themselves and their bodies and their minds all over again were too much. They had come to this decision painfully, with a partner sometimes but mostly on their own. Grown-up, strong, loving, intelligent women, who didn't need her opening up their hearts again, in an attempt to save the life of the baby they were carrying. The mothers were the patients, she told herself. She treated them, just as she would treat Nicole. She might hope that Nicole would change her mind, somewhere between her door and the door to the clinic in a few days—she might believe that in the long term it would make her happier, and she might know from the experience of women who had gone before her that the guilt and the sadness would be with her forever if she went ahead, but she would still make Nicole's care her priority.

She laid the dark red tubes on her desk, their labels facing down. "Those'll just confirm it for me."

"Thank you."

"How much do you know about the procedure? I take it you haven't had a termination before."

"No, and I don't know much."

"Well, it's pretty straightforward so early on. We can refer you by letter, once we've confirmed the pregnancy and established that you're in good shape overall. It's quick enough. They'll probably knock you out and do a D and C, which basically means they remove the lining of your womb, taking the fetus with everything else. You'll be able to come out the same day—you'll need someone to pick you up, though, because you'll feel a bit groggy. Afterward, it's a bit like a period—you'll have cramping, and you'll bleed like a normal period for a few days, a week maybe. That's it."

It sounded ridiculously simple.

"Will they try to counsel me there?" Nicole was afraid that each stage would be presided over by moral judge and jury, standing in her way.

"No, that's my job. Finding out whether you're sure. Once I refer you, you won't be asked anything. Although I think it's important that you recognize you can change your mind at any point if you want to. There will be people there you can talk to, if you feel that way."

"I won't do that."

Dr. Simons thought she probably wouldn't. She was sorry. She'd seen Nicole with her children. She thought she'd seen Martha, for her preschool check probably, just a couple of months ago. Nicole seemed like a lovely mum. It always seemed a bit surprising: the immaculate mums (yummy mummies, as they categorized them in the surgery) often held their children at arm's length metaphorically as well as literally, but Nicole was gentle, and tactile and very much involved.

After Nicole had left, as she wrote up the appointment in her notes, filling the thirty seconds before the next patient knocked on her door, Dr. Simons found herself hoping she wouldn't go through with it.

Nicole started the car and drove off. She had arranged to meet Harriet for lunch. She had decided to tell her today, while she still had some of the strength she had summoned for the doctor's visit. She wanted Harriet to come with her. And not to judge her.

It was a beautiful day, hot and bright, with a vivid blue sky. The children had gone back to school in their summer uniforms, moaning about having to be inside working when it was so warm outside.

They ate their sandwiches on a bench facing a rose garden. The gardens were quiet—just a few mothers, with pushchairs and bowlegged toddlers, and some pensioners, with their thermos flasks of tea. Nicole chewed slowly and listened to Harriet's cheerfully inane start-of-term chat. With Martha and Chloe safely and happily ensconced in the ample arms of Mrs. Allington, the reception-class teacher, Harriet saw a whole world of liberating possibilities opening up for her and Nicole.

"And I thought we could go somewhere to do our Christmas shopping—you know, a bit further afield?"

"You mean like Bath?"

"No, I meant like Paris."

Nicole laughed. "No, Nic, seriously, I've got the brochures and everything. You can easily do it in a day. Galeries Lafayette, Les Halles, quick plate of snails for lunch and back for bedtime. Well, practically!"

Harriet was lovely when she was like this. All smiley and exuberant. She wasn't at her best stuck at home. Nicole hoped this was the beginning of a happier time for her and Tim. Once she had got a bit of space back for herself, she might feel better about her marriage. Nicole didn't want to break Harriet's mood, but she had promised herself she would ask her today.

"Harry?"

"Yes."

"I've made some decisions. About what I'm going to do."

"About Gavin?"

"And about the baby."

"The baby?"

"I'm not going to have it, Harry. I can't. I saw the doctor this morning to get a referral for a termination." Say it out loud. Make it real.

Harriet was shocked. She hadn't computed this at all. She had been hoping Nicole would say she was throwing Gavin out for good. If she'd thought about the baby at all, it had been in relation to how much help and support Nicole would need. She'd promised herself she would be there for her. How weird to have been with her for the twins' birth and then end up with her for this baby's as well. Harriet liked babies. "Why?"

Nicole took a deep breath. Harriet wasn't Dr. Simons. She was asking, and she had a right to be told: they were friends, and God knew, Nicole had laid enough of her troubles at Harriet's door over the years.

"I just can't. I should never have got pregnant in the first place. It was very wrong of me. Stupid and wrong. You were right about that. It was never going to fix my marriage, because it was broken beyond repair a long time ago. I was just too stubborn and too desperate to see it. I could never see past him before, never contemplate a life without him in it. Whatever he did to me."

Harriet knew that was true.

"I know it sounds stupid, but catching him in bed with that woman in Spain—well, it changed things for me. I think it changed *me*. It was like I could suddenly see things clearly. Like at that moment I realized it wasn't my fault that Gavin is like he is. It isn't because I've changed, or because something's missing—it was never about me. It was about him having no strength, no willpower, no morals and, most of all, Harry, having no love or respect for me."

Harriet stroked her arm. "That's what I always hated most about it."

"I know. You've watched it all. You and Tim must think I'm totally stupid."

"We never thought that."

"But I was, you see, I *was* totally stupid. Like a color-blind person—everyone else is seeing green but you keep insisting it's red. Because you really, really believe it *is* red."

She was right, Harriet thought.

"In a funny way, I'm glad I saw what I saw in Spain. It made it impossible for me to stay blind, stay stupid. I see now with complete clarity exactly who he is. And of course, that I have to get away from him, because however much I wish I was cured, I'm not. I'm better, but I'm not strong enough to call myself cured."

Harriet saw where she was going.

"We'll always have the twins and Martha, and we'll always be joined together by them. He loves them and they love him. And I can cope with that. But not a new baby, Harriet, whose father he is. Not with all those feelings and those hormones. He'd get me again, I know he would. It would be easy."

Harriet saw something like real fear in Nicole's eyes, a haunted look.

"I have to start again with my life. I want to find out how it feels to live free of all that bad feeling. The fear, the inadequacy and the anger. I've had the happiest moments of my life with him, Harriet, but I've had the worst, lowest, most miserable times with him too—because of him. And I've paid for each of those glorious moments with years of feeling like shit. And I've finally realized it isn't worth it. I have to go with that feeling while it's strong, and make myself change."

"And you can't do that if you're pregnant with his child." Harriet wasn't asking a question, she was acknowledging a reality.

Nicole felt almost euphoric that Harriet understood her. She wanted to hug her, but she hadn't finished. "I need your help." She took Harriet's hand. "I can't do this on my own. I'm asking you to come with me. Please. For the abortion. I know it's a huge thing to ask."

"It's not such a big thing to ask."

Harriet didn't have to think about it at all. Where else would she be but with her? "You don't have to ask. Of course."

"Thank you."

"But are you sure that's what you want? Do you really believe none of what you are talking about is possible with a baby?"

"Do you?" Nicole bounced the question back to her friend.

"I *do* know that what you're talking about isn't going to be easy."

"So do I. I've sat up night after night since I got back from Spain thinking about it."

"I'm sure you have. But thinking about it is different from going through with it."

"And going through with it is going to be easier than dealing with how it feels afterward. I know that, too. I promise you, I'm not seeing it as some quick fix. I promise you that. I just think it's the only way for me."

Harriet wasn't sure. It wasn't that she thought it was wrong, not in a moral way, she was resolutely pro-choice, thought the Pope was irresponsible, could think of a thousand different circumstances where it had to be the right thing to do—for the woman, for the family, and even sometimes for the unborn child. But this was Nicole. This was as close as it had ever come to her. And she wasn't sure. Could *she* do it? She didn't think so. Whatever she felt about Tim—and she knew Tim wasn't Gavin—a baby they conceived would be another Josh, another Chloe, which would stop her getting rid of it, she was almost sure. She didn't know whether she should tell Nicole that. Ask her to think about it some more. Say she thought it might be a mistake she would have to live with for the rest of her life.

Nicole was afraid she was losing her—not her support, she felt instinctively that Harriet would support her in whatever she decided to do, but her understanding of why she had to do this. "What do you think you would do if you were me?"

Harriet wouldn't lie, so she went for a best friend's half-truth. "I don't know, Nic. I honestly don't. But I'm not you. I haven't walked the mile in your shoes, or whatever you want to say. I'm not going to tell you you're wrong."

"Thank you." Nicole's voice was small and grateful.

"How long have you got?"

"They should come back with an appointment by the end of the week, beginning of next, maybe. For the week after, I guess. I don't suppose they hang around with this kind of thing."

"No. I don't suppose they do. Well, let's you and me just sit with it awhile, then. You don't have to make any really final decisions just now, do you?"

So Harriet, too, thought she might change her mind. She wouldn't. "Okay, you're right." She'd see, in the end.

Harriet didn't tell Tim what Nicole was planning—she didn't think he'd understand. She didn't completely understand herself: she thought Nicole's explanation, which she evidently believed, was only part of the reason. It felt as though she was also punishing herself for her supposed stupidity in falling for Gavin, staying in love with him, putting up with it all and getting pregnant on purpose.

She wasn't sure she believed Nicole could go through with it. It didn't fit her. Harriet was afraid that she wouldn't be able to stop herself judging her: her best friend, the person she thought of as her soul mate, was talking about doing something that Harriet never could. In a way, it was like finding out that Nicole believed in the death penalty or went shoplifting. She suspected that it separated their moral codes: hers and Nicole's. And she was afraid it would drive a wedge into their relationship. She tried to put the situation into the context of her own life. Suppose she had gone to bed with Nick and become pregnant. What would she have done? She couldn't imagine having an abortion, even if that meant telling Tim a lie rather than telling Nick the truth.

She didn't want to be the kind of friend who judged. Nicole hadn't been unfaithful, neither as a wife nor as a friend to Harriet. She was trying to find a way out of the catastrophe of her marriage. Harriet thought about how she would feel if she had found out that Nicole had had an abortion years ago, before they had been friends. Would she feel differently about her? She didn't suppose she would. But as the days passed and the appointment came nearer, Harriet found herself hoping that Nicole would change her mind so that she didn't have to deal with how it made her feel.

They told Tim they were going out for a day of pampering. They arranged lifts home for the children so that they wouldn't have to be back for three o'clock. Harriet said she would have William, George and Martha overnight at her house, but Nicole said no. She had Cecile to help, she said, and she didn't want them to worry. They wouldn't have worried—for Nicole's children a sleepover at Harriet's house was a great treat: it had become almost a refuge for them over the years. It was so messy and warm and full of noise and children's paintings and food with additives, they felt more comfortable there, sometimes, than in their impeccable *Homes & Gardens* house. But the truth was Nicole wanted them home when she got back there. She wanted to be able to stand at the ends of their beds and watch them sleeping. She hoped she would feel she still had the right to feel full of maternal love and protection afterward. She was afraid that she wouldn't.

Nicole didn't have to tell Gavin anything about where she was or what she was doing because he was staying at the Royal Automobile Club in town. He'd been home once, straight from the airport, but Nicole had been at Harriet's, hiding. She had packed a few suits, shirts and ties and left them in the hall so that the message was clear. He had taken the hint. Probably relieved, she thought, to get off so lightly. No doubt he had assumed it was only a matter of time before she forgave him again and he could come home. He called every day to talk to the kids. He always asked for her after he had spoken with Martha, knowing that Nicole had to take the phone from the child to avoid the pain it would cause her if she refused to talk to Daddy. She hated him for that, one more piece of manipulation in what felt like a lifetime of being played. Each time he asked to meet with her to talk about it. And each time she told him that she wasn't ready to see him, that she, for once, would say when, where and if that conversation would take place. It was only part rage, though, that enabled her to keep him at a distance. There was a fear, too. A very real fear of what would happen if she saw him again. That would be the real test of what she believed now was true. And she was afraid of failing it.

Once the arrangements had been made, it was just a question of waiting. Nicole felt almost hysterical with anxiety. She became acutely aware of time passing, as she could feel the child inside her growing not just by the week but by the hour, by the minute. She couldn't keep still, because she was afraid that if she did, she would feel it somehow, see her stomach expanding. She was terrified that she would feel the baby move, although she knew it was too soon. She couldn't bear that—it would feel like communication, and she was trying to concentrate incredibly hard on not having a relationship with the baby she wasn't going to have. She couldn't keep her hands off her children when they were at home, kept swooping on them and covering them in desperate kisses. "Get off, Mum," the boys moaned, rubbing at their cheeks with the overlong sleeves of their shirts. Martha liked it, though. She had taken to climbing into her mother's bed at around two in the morning. Mummy usually seemed to be awake, and she smiled in the landing light when she saw Martha at the open door, lifting the corner of the duvet in welcome. Nicole let Cecile off all her teatime duties and made spaghetti Bolognese, elaborate fruit faces and milk shakes for them, and read them three different bedtime stories. She and Harriet didn't talk about it anymore, but she knew Harriet was waiting for her to change her mind.

And so she packed a small bag and dropped off the kids, managing not to cry as Martha said, "Have a lovely day, Mummy," and went home to wait for Harriet.

Harriet had chocolate. There weren't many problems in life that couldn't be at least alleviated by chocolate, she thought, except of course, being fat, which, since Harriet blamed most of her own problems on that—apart from poor old Tim—made it a baffling remedy as far as Nicole could see. She didn't think a few Mars bars would help today. But Harriet was trying.

Harriet was nervous. She concentrated on driving, sitting forward and close to the wheel like one of those little old ladies you see sometimes. She wanted to ask Nicole whether she was sure, but she guessed that would become obvious, so she talked about the weather, and the school committee Annual General Meeting, and whatever else she could grasp.

Nicole was calmer this morning than she had been for a couple of weeks. She was getting nearer. She knew that by this evening it would be over. She would have done it. At this point she believed that wondering about doing it was harder than coping with the aftermath would be. It felt like she had a pair of scales in her brain, with weights for and against: while she'd been thinking about it, the weights had been going on and coming off, tipping the scales this way and that. Now they were almost perfectly balanced—it was just a fraction out—and she knew that was the best she could ever hope for. A decision like this would never present itself in absolutes. She would carry those weights around forever after she had done it.

In the car park, Harriet switched off the engine and turned to her friend. "Okay, don't get mad, but I have to ask this. Are you sure you want to go ahead?"

"I'm not mad. But yes."

"Okay. If you're a hundred percent certain, I won't ask you again." Which was, of course, Harriet asking again.

"Harry, I'm sure."

Harriet pursed her lips and gave a small, decisive nod.

"Are you sure you can do it with me?"

"I said I would."

"I didn't ask you that. I'd understand, you know, if you didn't want to come in." Please, please, come in.

"Don't be daft. Course I'm coming in." Harriet opened her door. "Let's get on with it."

She didn't have to do anything much, of course. Once Nicole was in her room, with its bizarrely chintzy 1980s Laura Ashley décor, in the backless gown, which they had managed to laugh about, with her little pills in the plastic shot glass, a nurse came in with a clipboard of questions and Harriet was asked to go outside. Before she left, she kissed Nicole and held her hand. She had no idea what to say to her, so she whispered, "I love you," felt Nicole squeeze her hand in reply and almost ran out of the room, feeling her own tears rising.

Nicole appeared to have gone on autopilot. She had that ability to switch herself off from something unpleasant. She had been stoic in childbirth, Harriet remembered. And she was like that whenever Gavin hurt her. It was as if her body had its own anesthesia. She needed it now.

Harriet drank two cups of watery cappuccino from the machine in the waiting room, and tried to concentrate on the back issues of *Country Life* she found there, but she watched the big white clock on the wall above the door almost minute by minute. She was half expecting Nicole to walk in and ask to be taken home. But as ten, then twenty, then thirty minutes passed, she had to accept that she was going through with it.

Finally a young nurse appeared and approached her. "Your friend is back in her room now. You're welcome to come and sit with her, if you'd like."

"Thanks." Harriet gathered up her jacket and bag, and followed the nurse to where she had left Nicole an hour or so earlier.

Nicole looked as though she was still asleep. She was pale against the white pillow, and her hair was neat around her face. Harriet was relieved to see that she looked peaceful this way, that the anesthetic hadn't frozen her features in a grimace of pain or remorse. She sat down on the chair beside the bed to wait for her to wake up. She felt unbelievably sad for her friend and what she had just been through. Part of her wanted Nicole to wake up so that she could see she was okay. Another part wanted her to sleep on and on in oblivion. She knew that Nicole would never again wake up on a day where she hadn't done this to herself, and to this baby that didn't exist anymore, except in her imagination, and her memory.

It was another ten minutes before Nicole opened her eyes. She smiled weakly at Harriet. "Can I have some water?"

Harriet poured some into a cup, and Nicole lifted her head gingerly, frightened of a sudden movement, to sip it.

"That better?"

"Much. Thanks." Then her face crumpled. Her features distorted, as if she'd been too close to a fire and was melting. Harriet had never seen her like this before. Her face was suddenly wet with tears.

"Oh, honey, don't cry, please don't cry." Harriet didn't know how to stop her, and she wasn't sure that she should. God knows she'd have been crying, if it was her.

They stayed that way, Harriet sitting in the chair, Nicole lying on the bed, for ages, without a word spoken, because there wasn't anything to say. Harriet held her hand, sometimes crying herself, and Nicole's tears came and came, until her body was too dry and too tired to produce any more.

When they said it was okay to take her home, Harriet helped her get dressed, then took her home, and they sat in the kitchen, drinking tea, until Nicole said she thought she would try to sleep. Then Harriet took her upstairs and tucked her in, as if she were Josh or Chloe. Nicole asked her to keep the children at her house for the night. "Turns out I can't face them after all. Not tonight."

"Okay, don't worry. They'll stay with me, if that's what you want."

"It's not so much what I want. I just don't think I can handle talking to them, seeing them. Not just yet."

"So don't. I'll look after them."

"I know." Nicole held her hand and looked at her face. "You've been brilliant today. Thank you so much for everything you've done."

Harriet wasn't sure what she *had* done, but she felt pretty horrible as she shut Nicole's bedroom door behind her and went home.

There in the room, Nicole rolled over to watch the branches of the trees through her window, just beginning to turn. She brought her knees up to her chest and hugged herself with both arms. She felt cold all over, although it was a warm day and she was under the counterpane. If she had thought she had no more tears, she had been wrong. They came again now, and she wondered whether they would ever stop.

Cressida

It was still taking Cressida about ten minutes to change Spencer's nappy, even though she was no longer struggling to make sure his umbilical stump lay comfortably under the top fold and had mastered the art of tucking his tiny penis downward so that he didn't wee exultantly over his shoulder, or hers, while she fiddled with the sticky tabs. Now it took so long because she couldn't stop gazing at him, and kissing his tummy while he got his fingers tangled in her curls, and singing him little songs, and burying her head in the crease of his neck to sniff that oh-so-potent baby smell. He was like the best drug ever—she was totally addicted; the effect was euphoria, and she never came down from it. Although it had its dark side. The moments when she held him almost too close and was gripped by illogical fears of losing him. Or when she woke up, bleary-eyed, and found he had slept an extra hour. Then she went, shaking with fear, to the crib, afraid of what she might find. Or when the news broadcast its usual planetary menu of violence, famine and loss, and she felt the vicarious pain so much more acutely than she ever had before. But most of the time she was suffused with this incredible, sleepy joy, and pride and excitement. God, he was gorgeous. He had what she claimed as her own thick, dark hair, lustrous and silky. He had been a little jaundiced at birth, but now he looked as if he'd spent his first weeks in the Caribbean, sun-kissed and healthy.

He had the temperament to match. Polly had shaken her head in mock dismay with the injustice of it—Cressida had been a wailer, she said, colicky and irritable for months, but her baby was so laid-back and happy that you wouldn't know he was there—if it wasn't for the paraphernalia that now filled the house. And the laundry—a never-ending parade of tiny white garments to wash and fold, and the steaming sterilizer in the kitchen, perpetually engaged in the incessant assembly line of bottle production.

Polly was loving it. The house felt so full, and the routine of caring for such a small baby put a wonderful rhythm and shape into the days. She had missed it. He was all-consuming, this tiny lodger, and totally absorbing.

Night feeds were her favorite times. Cressida, still a carrier of the young person's sleep gene, loathed getting up. She had to turn on MTV to keep her awake while she fed Spencer at 2:00 a.m., besotted though she undoubtedly was. Polly had been woken by Nirvana one night and crept downstairs to catch Cressida three-quarters asleep with her head against the sofa cushion and Spencer wide awake, lying across her lap, intently watching Kurt Cobain gyrate as he himself struggled to get a decent burp up.

After that, by unspoken agreement, Polly did it. Cressida had Spencer in Harriet's old Moses basket next to her bed, but when Polly heard him stir, she would creep in to get him. This was her time, hers and Spencer's. She would sway with him in her arms, while his feed warmed in a jug of boiling water, then take him back to her big, empty bed and feed him there, all the while talking to him. She told him in a whisper all about her, and Dan, and his mum, and his uncle Daniel, and the house and the world. She told him, every night, how loved and wanted he was, how special. About how much she loved his mother, and how full she was of the inexpressible joy of watching her baby with a baby of her own. And then, when he'd taken all his milk, and given back his wind, and listened to her with his eyes, which were slowly turning brown, fixed wide on her face, she would hold him and rock him gently until the eyelids fell and just love him, quietly, long after she knew she should have put him down. This new love, for her child's child, was both a revelation and what she had always imagined it would be. The layering of feeling was extraordinarily rich and powerful. A friend from work had bought her a fridge magnet that said, "If I had known being a grandmother was so much fun, I'd have had my grandchildren first." People said things like "Oh, yes, and the real joy of being a granny is that you can give them back when you've had enough." They didn't know what they were talking about. It was wonderful, that was all.

Susan understood. "I know—I can't wait," she'd said. "I hope my boys marry girls whose mothers live abroad."

Part of the pleasure came from watching Cressida with Spencer. She reminded Polly of herself. She was not an instinctive, earth-mother type, but tentative, enthusiastic, frightened of doing the wrong thing but so consumed with love and tenderness that it was impossible to do other than the right thing. One day, just after Polly had brought Cressida and Spencer home, she had walked in on her daughter as she tucked her baby up, fast asleep, into the Moses basket. Polly had put her arm round her daughter, and they had stared at him for a long time, watching his tiny rosebud mouth purse in dreams. Cressida had glanced at Polly, her eyes full of tears, and a moment of pure understanding passed between them. Cressida had seemed to grasp, all at once, what Polly felt for her, and all that had happened in the last twenty years, and in the last eight months, was lit in a different way.

The first time Cressida had taken him out for a walk on her own, Polly had caught her on the garden path with the pram, with Spencer, on a day in the mid-sixties, wearing a hat, vest, Babygro with scratch mittens attached and activated, a hand-knitted woolen cardigan, a padded jacket, a flannel sheet and two blankets beneath the pram's own apron.

Elliot came almost every day to see them and spend time with Spencer. He had soon stopped asking permission, and now he just turned up, usually in time to feed or bath his son. Polly had become used to having him around, and he was sometimes really useful, to be honest. He had put up the cot for them, with Daniel's help, and figured out the extraordinarily complicated pram-car-seat-pushchair pantechnicon, and the origami sling Cressida liked to use. He handled Spencer as if he'd been doing it forever, in the confident, almost unconcerned way of doctors and health visitors. He always knew how to stop a grizzle with diversion, and it gave him an obvious thrill to be able to. He called the baby "Spence," and she once heard him call him "son."

He was a good man and he loved Spencer, but Polly still didn't believe that he and Cressida should or would be together. Elliot was clearly giving Cressida all the space he could—he hadn't asked her any big questions since the birth, just accepted that this was the way it was for the time being. They weren't "together" in the conventional sense right now—Elliot didn't sleep over, and the intimacies Polly saw exchanged between them were all about Spencer. Their eyes would meet above his head sometimes, and she saw a smile pass between them that was the preserve of new parents. He would hug her, and kiss her, but as a couple they were in a strange limbo. Polly forced herself not to ask Cressida what she was feeling about Elliot. She didn't want to pressure her. She knew that things could take on their own momentum in such circumstances, and that she would do what she could to give Cressida options. Now that she knew Elliot better, she wasn't as afraid as she had been of them ending up together, but she still believed that Cressida had more life to lead, more to discover about herself and the world, before she was ready for that kind of commitment.

Harriet

"Chloe, Martha, please don't do that. I don't mind you playing up here, but please be careful." The first time, Harriet was kinder than she might have been if it was just Chloe: shouting at other people's kids was harder. The second time she meant it—that "*now*, both of you. I mean it! You're getting the floor really wet"— although she didn't think she had the energy to follow through with any threats. She wasn't in the mood today. She felt really low, as she had for weeks. Months, really, she supposed, but especially since Nicole's abortion. Everything felt sour. If Nicole was even vaguely with it, she would tell her it was a classic sign of depression, this lack of energy and permanently crabby mood. But anything Harriet was feeling was seemingly forgotten. Maybe it seemed pretty trivial, by comparison.

She and Tim were just coexisting. Whatever détente she had declared over the summer, and whatever closeness they had found in helping Nicole, had evaporated once term began and life got back to normal. She had thought having Chloe at school all day might make her feel freer—she could make some changes in her life, learn to play golf, or paint pottery, or something—but that was rubbish. Getting out of the house didn't change the fact that the work was still there when you got back, and that Tim would still come home every night, guilty only of not being what she wanted him to be. And then she'd lost her partner in crime: Nicole was still in a dreadful state. Harriet knew it had been only a couple of weeks, and she felt selfish for even thinking it, but she missed her friend. Nicole wouldn't come out with her, or make plans to do anything. She wouldn't let herself have any fun. She'd even said she wouldn't come to the reading club next week—she hadn't had a chance to open the book. Which was blatantly untrue since she hadn't done anything but sit at home. She was like an automaton when the kids were around—desperate to make life normal for them—but she collapsed, Harriet knew, like a rag doll when the door was closed behind them. Cecile had dropped them off this afternoon, and Harriet had asked her to stay for a cup of coffee. She had been pathetically grateful, close to tears. She didn't know about the abortion, so she believed Nicole was in this mess because Gavin wasn't there.

"All she does, when the children are not there, is cry. It makes me so sad. I do not know what to do to help her."

She was barely out of her teens, and Harriet felt sorry for her. "But you do help her, Cecile, by taking care of the children and the house so that she doesn't have to worry about those things."

"It's easy enough. I wish there was more."

Harriet wished there was too.

Between them, she and Cecile were doing everything for the children, and Harriet was tired. William and George seemed unscathed, so far, by what was going on at home—they inhabited that secret, self-sufficient twin world, and they were seven-year-old boys, which was a considerable buffer in itself from the emotional frailties of those around them. But Martha was quieter than usual, and coming off worst in her everyday battles with Chloe—quicker to tears and slower to be comforted. The other night, when Harriet had put both girls (and their plastic ponies) through the bath and was dressing Martha in a pair of Chloe's pajamas, Martha had put her little hands on Harriet's cheeks to hold her face still, and said, "Is my mummy going to die, Harry?"

Harriet had closed her arms round her and pulled her down onto her lap. "Of course not, sweetie. Why on earth would you think that?"

"I think she must be really poorly. She has to stay in her pajamas all day sometimes, and I only do that when I'm really ill and I can't go to school."

Oh, God.

"And her eyes look funny all the time. All red."

"Mummy has been a bit poorly, darling, but she's getting better now. I promise. She's just very tired, and she needs to have a lot of rest, and lots of cuddles to feel all okay again. That's all. Are you looking after her?"

"Yes. Will and George aren't, but I am."

"That's a good girl. Isn't she lucky to have a nurse like you taking care of her?"

Martha smiled with pride. "Yes."

"I promise you, Martha, Mummy is not going to die. She's going to be fine, very soon now."

Martha rested her hands on Harriet's shoulders while she stepped into the pajama bottoms. Another shadow of concern crossed her face. "Can I call my daddy and ask him to come home and help me look after Mummy?"

"Not just now, darling. Daddy's busy in London. I'll help you instead, shall I? Me and Chloe?" Diversion. "We could make Mummy a cake tomorrow, if you like. That would cheer her up, wouldn't it?"

"A pink one?"

"Of course a pink one!"

The next day, of course, Martha and Chloe had remembered about the cake, so they had made one, along with all the mess in the kitchen, and the buttery sugar splatted against the walls by mishandled electric whisks, and the icing sugar trail left by little feet between the kitchen and the downstairs loo.

Tim told her she was doing too much. He didn't know about the abortion, he probably thought that Gavin would buy his way back into the house with roses and dinners and Viognier, and that the status quo would be restored, just as it had been every other time over the years.

Harriet didn't know what else to do. Having the kids made her feel that she was doing something. She had nothing to say to Nicole that might make it better.

"Could you have stopped me?" Nicole had asked her.

"I tried. You didn't want me to stop you."

"I didn't know."

"You seemed so sure."

"I was sure. But I didn't know what I was talking about. I'd put it into a box, you see. Closed the lid. Dealt with it."

"I know."

"But you don't deal with it. It deals with you. You can't close the lid, put the box away. It's there every time I open my eyes. Or close my eyes. Or do anything. And it always will be."

"It won't always feel like this, though, Nic. Things never do. You know when someone dies, the feelings don't stay the same. They recede, everyone says so. You do get better. I really believe that."

"It didn't die. I killed it."

"Oh, stop it." That made Harriet cross. "Don't talk about it like that. You're just torturing yourself with that emotive language."

"What other language can you use? Believe me, if I could think of a way to let myself off the hook, I would. You know me. I'm a coward. I must be. Couldn't face being a single parent, could I, so I just got rid of it?"

Harriet was staring at a wall of self-loathing and self-pity so thick she couldn't find a way through it.

Nicole was blaming herself in new improved ways. "I keep thinking of the people I can't face anymore. Gavin's just the tip of the iceberg. Anyone with a baby. Polly's daughter—her baby is just a few months older than mine would have been. Every time I see her I'll be thinking about it. What about Clare? She'll probably never have a baby. What the hell would she think of me?"

Harriet stood up. "I can't talk to you when you're like this, Nic. You're just refusing to take onboard anything I say to you. I can't get through to you, and it's too hard."

Now Nicole was crying. "Please don't go. I'm sorry."

Harriet knelt by her friend's chair. "Listen to me, Nicole. You have just done one of the hardest things you have ever had to do—that anyone ever does. You made a decision about your own body and your future, based on what you instinctively felt at the time was right for you and the kids. You had an abortion, Nicole.

You made that choice. I don't suppose you're ever going to feel good about it. But you did it. It's over with, and there's no going back. You can't undo it. And I don't think I'd want to be friends with a person who could make that kind of decision lightly, or without any regrets at all. That would be fucked up. This is how I'd expect you to feel about what you've done. But you have got to stop thinking of yourself as a monster, motivated by selfishness and cowardice. You were brave and strong. But this person you're allowing yourself to be now, she's not strong. Clare will never know. Polly will never know. No one will ever know, unless you choose to tell them. It's just you and me."

Harriet wanted to say more, to tell Nicole that she had children who were alive and needed her, that she should do something about Gavin—go and see a lawyer, or at least decide what she was going to tell him. But she had said enough for now. Better to let Nicole digest this first. It was incredible to her that this woman she loved, who excused Gavin so often, blamed herself for what was a bad marriage to a bad man, who had just had two of the biggest shocks a person could be expected to take in a lifetime, could still be so hard on herself. When was she going to get angry?

That had been a few days ago. Now she looked at the devastation Will, George and Josh had caused in the TV room. Every square inch of carpet was covered with videos, computer games and violent little plastic men. She thought they might be outside now, since she couldn't hear the cacophony of trainer-clad feet and banter seeping down from the landing. Chloe and Martha were standing on chairs at the kitchen sink, shampooing the Barbie dolls with washing-up liquid. They were chatting happily about which Barbie was going to marry which boy doll ("ladyboy Barbies," Tim called the unfortunate dolls Chloe selected for a sex change; they retained their 36-24-36 figures, but acquired army-issue haircuts and surprisingly gruff voices), blissfully unaware of the growing puddles on the floor.

The mess defeated Harriet before she had even gone into battle. She went over to the sofa and lay down dramatically, feeling completely exhausted. In classic Pavlovian response, the demands started.

"Mummy! We want drinks."

"I didn't hear a please." There was really no point in them saying it since she had no intention of getting off the sofa for at least ten minutes.

"Please," they chorused.

"In a minute." She heard them scrabbling off their chairs. "You girlies haven't left my tap on, have you?"

"No, Mummy."

"Can we watch *Barbie in Rapunzel*?"

"Yes. Watch it in my room, will you, though?"

"We can't work the video in your room, Mummy."

Always a reason for you to get up. Always!

"Okay, you can watch it in here, then." Two small bodies hurled themselves at her on the sofa. She wrestled them off her lap and stood up. "Oh, no you don't. I didn't say I'd watch it too. The first seventy-three times were enough for me, I'm afraid. I'll get some juice." See? They always won in the end. She was wondering whether to laugh or cry when she heard George's scream. You knew, with screams, when you were someone's mummy. You could define them—the not-sharing scream, the frustration scream, the scraped-knee scream, the bad-dream scream. She hadn't heard this one before, and her whole body went cold. Straightaway, Will's voice joined George's. She couldn't hear Josh's. Josh wasn't screaming.

She ran to the door. "You stay in here, girls." But they didn't, of course. They could pick up almost as many nuances in Harriet's voice as she could in theirs, and they had caught the terror. They were in nervous tears before they even got to the front door behind her, holding hands, not knowing why.

They'd been skateboarding. They must have been taking turns—the twins hadn't had their boards with them. They'd made an assault course, found some planks and a green milk crate.

Josh was lying motionless next to the crate. Beside him, Will and George were frenetic and loud, each telling the same story. He'd fallen, they were screaming at her. They thought he'd hit his head. On the milk crate, maybe. On the corner. Or just on the tarmac. He wouldn't wake up, they said. But he wasn't bleeding.

"Fallen off his skateboard?" If she sounded incredulous, it was because he fell off it a hundred times a day. And got straight back up again.

"Off the roof," George said.

Off the roof. The roof.

"We were just mucking about."

Her world stopped. There was just the beating of her heart, harder and faster than she could ever remember hearing it before. Off the roof.

Afterward she supposed it had been she who called the ambulance and Nicole. She didn't remember.

Later, when there was time, she asked herself, Why were they up on the roof? How did they get up there? What made him fall? But it didn't matter then and it never would.

She didn't want to go to him—she was frightened. But her legs ran toward him. She knew at once that he was unconscious. Her voice shouted, louder than George and William. Bullets of instruction. The girls were crowding round. Chloe was panicking. Martha cried along with her. "Josh. Josh. Josh." Harriet couldn't think.

"Will, George, take the girls inside. Now."

There was no blood. His limbs weren't twisted unnaturally. She had the thought she'd heard a hundred times in bad films and soap operas: he looked like he was asleep. Peaceful. If there had been blood, she'd have had something to do. If he'd been awake, moaning with pain, she'd have had something to do. She'd have walked into a burning building to pull him out, she'd have held him while a doctor stitched him. She'd have done anything anyone could have asked of her. It was already too late to do the one thing she should have done: keep him safe, keep him off the roof. Now she couldn't do anything.

He was breathing. At least, she thought he was. She didn't want to push his head back and pinch his nose and push his chest in what she thought might be the right place and the right rhythm. She was afraid that if she touched him she might do the wrong thing. She wanted to pick him up, carry him inside. But she was afraid to do that, too.

She was more frightened than she had ever been in her life, or ever imagined being. The fear felt like spilt blood seeping from the pit of her stomach into every part of her—dark red, making everything dark. She couldn't say anything, beyond barking instructions at the kids, but inside her head was a Tower of Babel— and all the voices were her own. Wake up, Joshie. Wake up for me. Please don't let him die. Why wasn't he wearing his helmet? I told him he always had to. You weren't watching him. What the hell was he doing on the roof? Where's the ambulance? I want Tim. There isn't a mark on him. I want Tim. *Please please please please.*

The ambulance took eight minutes. Nicole took nine. It felt like hours. She wasn't wearing any makeup. Harriet couldn't remember when she'd last seen her without any. She'd come, as Harriet had known she would. The ambulance had parked in the driveway, blocking her entry, so she pulled up outside and ran toward the house. George and William tore to her from the front step, with Martha and Chloe stumbling behind. She took the four of them into a tight, awkward embrace, then put them down again, on the step, and turned to look for Harriet.

"What's happened?"

"The boys—they were on the roof, I don't know why. Josh fell off. He's hit his head, oh, Nic—he's unconscious." She was sitting back from him now, on her heels, with her arms round herself, rocking a little backward and forward. Nicole sat beside her on the ground, and Harriet leant on her shoulder. Josh was obscured by the paramedics, talking calmly to each other, to him, and to her, asking how it had happened, how long ago. They spoke to George and William, trying to establish whether Josh had been unconscious before he fell, or awake at all since. The boys, looking nervously from Nicole to Harriet to Josh, answered as best they could. He'd been fine on the roof, they said. Then he'd just slipped. He hadn't woken up at all.

William asked the question that Harriet couldn't: "Is he going to be okay?" His childlike faith in the uniform and the ambulance made his face hopeful. Harriet's certainties had all deserted her.

The paramedic answered William's question in Harriet and Nicole's direction. "We need to get him to hospital. They'll find out why he's unconscious. He's breathing, though, and stable, so try not to worry. We're just going to put him on a backboard, in case he has other injuries. It's a precaution with a fall like this."

Nicole's mobile started to ring. She stood up and moved out of the paramedics' way before she answered it. "Hello? Tim? . . . Yes, I'm with them now. . . . I don't know. He's unconscious. He's had a bad fall. . . . Yes, they're here too. They're just putting him in the ambulance. . . . Yes. Yes. Course I will. You go straight there. . . . Yes. Hold on, I'll put her on." She held out the phone toward Harriet. "He's just getting on a train. He wants to talk to you."

Harriet took the phone and blurted her confession. "He's fallen off the roof. . . . The garage roof. I wasn't watching them. I didn't know they were up there. . . . Okay. . . . Yes. . . . Okay. Tim? . . . Please hurry."

The ambulance man helped her up into the back. Nicole was telling her not to worry. She'd look after the kids. She was sure Josh would be fine. Tim would meet her at the hospital. Chloe was shouting for her, and Nicole picked her up. The double doors closed, and she welcomed the quiet as she watched the gentle rise and fall of Josh's chest, trying not to look at the equipment, trying to concentrate on her own breathing.

They took Josh in through the ambulance bay, but the doors swung open on the crowded waiting room. Harriet thought of when she had been there before: once, pregnant with Josh, when she had been convinced he had stopped moving; once when Tim had cut himself with garden shears and needed a couple of stitches in his thumb. Both times she had moaned about being kept waiting, tutting with the others at the infuriating red blinking sign telling her it would be another 120 minutes, 90 minutes, 60 minutes before she was seen. How she wished she was being shown into that waiting room now, to queue for the grumpy triage nurse with the other walking wounded. The speed of the staff around Josh was the scariest thing. That, and the closed curtains, the quiet voices.

Everyone wanted to know how it had happened. Every question felt like an accusation. Yes, she wanted to scream. Yes, my seven-year-old son was on my garage roof. No, I don't know why.

The paramedics were leaving now, the ones who'd brought them in. "Don't worry, love, he's in good hands."

She felt herself going wobbly, disoriented by the sights, the smells and the speed of it all. A young nurse put a hand gently on her arm. "Come on, Mrs. . . . ? Let's sit you down a minute, out here."

She didn't want to leave him, but she let herself be led toward a chair. The nurse sat her down, told her she'd find her a cup of tea, that the doctors would be out to see her in a few minutes, let her know what was going on, not to worry. That was what everyone said. What a spurious remark it was. They should be taught, in training, never to say that, even as an act of kindness.

Harriet couldn't keep still. She stood up and paced the small corridor, reading the signs for Pathology and X-ray and Ladies' Toilets, and watching a little boy with a bandaged leg playing in the toy corner. His mother caught her eye and smiled an anxious smile, but she could barely return it.

He couldn't die, could he? She might already have spoken the last words he would ever hear her say. Given him the last cuddle, the last kiss, the last telling-off. It was too big an idea to fit inside her; she thought she might explode. It might already be finished behind that curtain. Suddenly she didn't want it to be pulled back, to read a face coming from in there, see a head shaken in defeat. As long as the curtain was closed, she could pretend they were fixing him, hard at work on giving her baby back to her. She couldn't take a deep breath. It felt like her lungs weren't expanding.

She needed some fresh air. She was afraid she would faint, although she never had before, and she didn't want to do that here, in front of everyone. She told the nurse she would be back in a minute and went through to the hospital foyer. It felt normal and surreal there. A couple of workmen were up a ladder, fixing a fluorescent strip light. They were listening to a radio; the younger one was singing along to a current hit record. This might be the soundtrack of Josh's dying, she thought.

Tim was coming through the front door toward her. She felt extraordinary relief at the sight of him. He opened his arms, and she dropped her full weight into them. "Okay. Okay. I'm here." For a full minute he held her tightly, not speaking. Then he steered her round and began to walk them both in the direction of Pediatric Casualty. "How is he?"

"I don't know. They haven't told me anything yet."

"Has he woken up?"

"No. Tim, it was my fault, I wasn't watching them. I'm so sorry." And Tim's presence somehow made it possible for her to cry for the first time since she'd heard George's scream.

Her tears had always slain him. She looked like the girl from the flat, all those years ago. Blotchy and pathetic and utterly his. "Don't be stupid, darling. You can't watch them every minute. You've been so tired. They're boys, that's all. No one's blaming you, least of all me."

"I'm so glad you're here."

"Of course I'm here. He's our son."

Everything else, all the stuff you thought about when you didn't have anything more important to do, faded away. She felt it. This was so simple, so black-and-white in the world of gray. He's our son and we don't want to live without him. Give him back to us. Give him back.

Tim got back to the house at around midnight. They had called about eight to say that Josh had been sent up for a CT scan, and that they'd know more then. Martha and Chloe had fallen asleep at more or less the normal time, wrapped up together under Chloe's quilt. Nicole had sent the boys up to the spare room after Tim's call, but they hadn't gone to sleep for a couple of hours. Nicole had tried watching television, tried flicking through a magazine, but she hadn't been able to concentrate. Instead, she had mopped the kitchen floor and dried all the Barbies, and she had worked out the mess in the television room, meticulously returning everything on the floor to its correct box. Harriet wouldn't believe it when she saw it—Nicole had never seen it so ordered. She had been about to start on the fridge, where apparently Harriet was growing a cure for leprosy on a piece of Parmesan, when she saw Tim's lights and went to meet him at the door.

"How is he?" She had her arms around him.

"No change, still in a coma. They say he might be for days."

"What about the scan?"

"His brain is bruised and swollen, but there aren't any clots."

"That's good, isn't it?"

Tim shrugged his shoulders and wiped his hand across his forehead. He looked sweaty and exhausted. "Yeah."

"I'll make you a cup of tea. Are you hungry?"

"I'm not, Nic. Tea'd be great, though." He sat at the kitchen table and put his face into his hands. When he spoke it was through his fingers. "I've got to go back in a minute. They've found a bed for Harry. She's going to stay with him tonight, and I've got to take her a few things."

"Do you want me to sort some out?"

"Would you?"

"How's she doing?"

"Oh, you know Harriet. She's in pieces, thinks it's her fault."

"That's crazy." Nicole could hear Harriet saying it.

"I've told her so." He took the mug she handed him gratefully, and drank the tea although it was still too hot. "How's Chloe? And the others?"

"They're asleep. I'll take mine home in a bit. Do you want me to take Chloe?"

"No need. Let the others sleep too. They've had a shock. Why don't you all stay tonight? We'll see where we are in the morning." Tim didn't want to be alone. Neither did Nicole.

Nicole found some things for Harriet—one of her voluminous Victorian cotton nighties and her socks with treads, which she had laughed out loud at on a dozen occasions, clean knickers, her toothbrush and hairbrushes. She put in the book she was halfway through, although she couldn't imagine her reading, and some chocolate. Harriet hadn't even taken her handbag that afternoon, so Nicole packed that, then added clean clothes for the morning. She wondered whether Josh needed anything. Then she remembered the backless gowns, and the mummylike bandage tights. She couldn't imagine Josh in them. He was never still. Even as a small baby he'd been bouncing and shuffling and lurching, always hurrying on to the next thing. He had been the first to crawl, walk and run, and always the last to climb onto a lap for a story or a rest. Don't let him die, or be damaged so that he isn't Josh anymore. She hated that idea for all of them, for Tim, Harriet and Chloe, but also for her and the boys, who adored him. For their friendship, and their parallel lives, and for so many other reasons. Please let Josh be okay, she prayed, to someone. An atheist's prayers said quietly into the ether.

"You tell her I love her," she said to Tim, as she handed him the bag.

"I will. Thanks for this." He held the bag aloft. "For all of it."

"Hey." She hugged him briefly.

"I'll see you later."

He didn't have time or room for her, beyond his simple thanks. He looked smaller, and older, as he walked toward the car. His whole world had shrunk to a small room full of machines and hope.

Susan

People you didn't expect came to funerals. With some it was hard to figure out how they had known Alice had died. Did they scan the death columns daily, looking for names they knew? Susan supposed they must, especially when they were older. A couple of weeks ago an American comedian had been joking on television about British death announcements: it must be a weird country, he said, because people only ever died "suddenly" or "peacefully"—you never read that anyone died fuming with injustice, or clamoring for another breath. No one wanted to think about that, she supposed. She wanted Alice to have died peacefully. Roger said she would have done. And that was what the paper said: "Alice, aged 71, peacefully at The Cedars, widow of Jonathan, mother of Susan and Margaret, grandmother to Alexander and Edward. No flowers, please, but donations to . . ." She'd thought about all the adjectives—she had written one embellished with much-loveds and adoreds and treasureds, but it hadn't felt right. Anyone who had known her and them didn't need telling. Anyone who didn't, didn't need to know.

The boys were here, of course, looking absurdly grown-up,

and Sandy, from Roger's practice, a few staff from the home, a few old friends. Roger, Margaret. But there were also the people she hadn't expected: the pharmacist from Alice's local chemist, the librarian, Mabel's daughter Louise, who had patted her arm when she came in, although she barely knew her. And there were some people who, she was more or less convinced, had had nothing to do with Alice—professional mourners, who frequented crematoriums as she had hovered outside the church on Saturday mornings when she was a little girl, looking for brides and bridesmaids to admire. Only this lot were looking for something else. She hoped they wouldn't be disappointed.

She had eschewed lilies for roses on top of the coffin. Alice had loved roses, and these were pink, her favorite. She knew Alice wouldn't have wanted a lot of flowers—she would have thought it a waste, except for a baby or a child, but Susan had been to the crematorium before: after the ceremony they would be herded out to look at the patch of grass headed with Alice's name, empty of flowers and probably flanked by a display of giant words in carnations—MUM, SIS—from a funeral half an hour before. She couldn't quite bear that. Alice would have been quietly cross with her for worrying. She called it "polishing the step." She knew a woman, years ago, whose house was a mess but who kept her brass front step polished so you could see your face in it—more anxious to impress strangers than she was to see to the comfort of her own family. Alice wasn't here though. Susan had told them, at the florists, to put a lot of roses in the arrangement.

They were going to sing "All Things Bright and Beautiful" and "The Day Thou Gavest." She had thought about one of Alice's favorite songs—Barbra Streisand, maybe, or Charlotte Church singing "Pie Jesu"—but good taste had prevailed over sentimentality.

They'd been laughing about it last night, she and the boys. Alex was talking about some film where a guy was cremated to the sound of the Rolling Stones' "You Can't Always Get What You Want." They had giggled themselves to where "Burn baby burn, disco inferno," with Ed, as the vicar, performing *Saturday Night Fever* gyrations coffin-side, was the funniest suggestion they had ever heard.

Alex had sobered first. "Sorry, Mum. Unbelievably sick." Susan, who had enjoyed the light relief as much as any of them, put her arm round his shoulder and pulled his head under her chin. "Nothing to be sorry about, darling." Ed came too and joined the hug from behind her chair. "Listen, boys, this is okay. It wasn't a tragedy, your gran dying the way she did. She'd had a full life, and she was suffering, I know she was, inside herself somewhere. It was time. It's sad, but it isn't a tragedy. That's a baby—or a child, like my friend Harriet's boy, who's in a coma right now, or a father with a young family to raise. Not an old woman who has lived to see her children and grandchildren grow up happy." Alex squeezed her hand.

"The waiting's tough, but that's all. Funerals, in my view, should be held as soon as possible. Muslims and Jews have the right idea. Get it over with. It's just a body, I know that, but until it's gone, you can't get on with your life."

They had been waiting for Margaret. She'd taken the news badly, apparently, burst into tears, unable to speak. She'd put the phone down on Susan, called back a few minutes later, only to dissolve again. A friend of hers, Lindy, had rung back an hour or so later, said that Margaret was too upset to speak but that she would make arrangements to come over for the funeral.

She'd decided to come for a few weeks, she said. It had taken time to sort it all out—time when Susan lay in bed at night and pictured Alice in a freezer at the funeral home, and wished she could get on with it.

Margaret wasn't staying with them. Characteristically vague, she had said something about a house swap with some English relatives of a friend of a friend. They didn't have an address, just a mobile phone number for her. Just how Margaret liked it. Susan wondered briefly whether she was hurt that her sister didn't want to be near her and the boys or relieved that her sister's sometimes malevolent and always stressful presence wasn't in her home all the time. Relief won out. Convincingly.

She hadn't seen her until this morning. And now Margaret was crying again, inconsolably, in the row opposite. Alone. Susan had gestured to her when she arrived, gently shoving Ed and Alex up to make room for her, but Margaret had given her a weak smile, a brief shake of her head, and had slid into the front row next to theirs.

Susan couldn't look at her. She had put the pad of her thumb against the pad of her forefinger, both hands, and was pushing them together as hard as she could. It stopped the tears, she didn't know why. Roger's black shoulder grazed her on one side, Alex's, taller, on the other. Both were ready to offer support, but she stood up straight.

Afterward Polly was at the house first. She looked glamorous, Susan thought, with her curls pinned back into submission and her smart black suit. She put her arms round Susan, who relaxed briefly into the embrace, then pulled back and looked around her. "Nice to see a bit of a crowd for her."

"She was a gorgeous woman," Polly replied, with a shrug. Her glance took in Margaret, apparently deep in conversation, her face still tear-mottled. "She's a strange one, your sister, isn't she? Do you think she was so upset because she wasn't around when it happened?"

"She hasn't been around for years. I've given up trying to second-guess Maggie. She's been so odd about the whole thing, from the moment Mum got ill, like she was blaming me. Mind you, she's always been odd."

"Doesn't look like a face that does much smiling."

"I think that's it. She's one of those people who's never happy. Jealous, I think. Always looking around to see who might be better off."

"Which makes her about as different from you as it's possible to be, my friend."

"Who knows? Can't be bothered with it today."

Polly shifted her attention back to her friend. "How are you doing?"

"Better now. I hated not being able to get on with the funeral. God knows how people must feel who can't bury their dead, or whatever, for months and months, like murder victims and things. It just hangs over you, such a potent image." She closed her eyes tight, opened them again. "And that bit's over now."

"You made it lovely." Polly was trying to say the right thing. They looked at each other and laughed quietly.

"Yes, the nicest funeral I've been to in ages!"

At that moment Margaret came up. Her face was stony. "What's funny?" The tone was innocuous, but the voice, with its Australian twang, and the face were hard.

"Nothing."

"I'm Polly, Susan's friend."

"Nice to meet you." Margaret barely acknowledged her with the half smile she had given Susan in the crematorium, which didn't reach her eyes. "Having a nice time?"

Oh, God, Susan thought, she's spoiling for a fight. Dread, plus more than a little anger, rose in her. "No, Margaret, I'm not having a nice time. This is our mother's funeral."

"You're in your element, aren't you, though, arranging things? Especially arranging things for Mum. Done quite a bit of that this year, haven't you?"

Polly couldn't believe the nastiness. It was like a bad scene from a soap opera. If she'd been Susan, her hand would have been itching to slap Margaret, but Susan looked as if she might cry. Polly looked around the living room, but she couldn't see Roger or the boys.

"Please don't start, Maggie, not today. If you're angry— although God knows why you should be—we can talk, but not today, not with everyone here." Her voice was imploring.

Margaret seemed to shrink back a little. She bent toward Susan, and her next words were almost a whisper, meant only for Susan's ears. "Okay, not here. But I'm around for a while now, Susan. I'm going to be there when you sort the house out. I'm a part of this, whether you like it or not, and you can't shut me out."

Now irritation rose in Susan. What the hell was she talking about? Shut her out? Who had made all the phone calls, tried to include her in all the decisions, to persuade her to share the burden of their mother's failing health? She had shut the door on Susan at every stage. The visit earlier in the year had been an unmitigated disaster—Susan had hoped that when her sister saw Alice she would understand, see that what she had done she had done for the right reasons, without a viable choice. She had thought it would make things better—but it had only turned Margaret more against her. What did she mean she was going to stay around while Susan sorted out the house? Did she want to make sure Susan didn't fleece her out of her share of Alice's meager possessions? That was a new low, even for Margaret.

"Fine, Maggie. Whatever you want. You can do the whole fucking lot if you like. It's about time you pulled your weight."

Polly couldn't remember Susan ever swearing that way before. Good for you, she thought. Poisonous cow. Margaret, too, was temporarily silenced.

Polly went into rescue mode. "Oh, I forgot to tell you, Suze. Great news! Nicole rang me last night to say that Josh is in the clear. He'll stay in for another couple of days, and Harriet with him, but then they think he can come home and he's going to be fine." Polly linked her arm through Susan's and turned her away from Margaret.

"That's fantastic news. Just brilliant." For the first time that day, tears welled in Susan's eyes, for Harriet, Tim and Josh. And for Alice.

"I just don't know what her problem is," she said later, to Roger. The last of the visitors had left an hour ago, and they had loaded the dishwasher with all the cups, saucers and glasses, hoovered the hall and living room, and straightened the cushions on the so-fas. She'd changed out of her black dress and shoes, and they were sitting together, with yet another cup of tea, her back against his shoulder.

"Don't waste any more of your energy worrying about it, darling. She's a pernicious, damaged, vindictive woman, and it's nothing to do with you. I don't know what life has dished up to her in Australia, but I'm guessing it wasn't the Utopia she dreamed of. Then again, I think Maggie has the power to poison any well where she sets up camp. Probably drove that poor bastard Greg to distraction. I'm surprised he lasted as long as she says he did. Forget about her."

"I can't, though, can I? She's my sister. She's all there is left now. And she's here. In my face. In Mum's house, no doubt."

"You *can* forget about her. And she isn't all there is—what are the boys and I? Chopped liver?"

"Course not. You know what I mean."

"I don't, sweetheart. I honestly don't. All right, so she'll always be your sister. Blood may well be thicker than water. But so what? A sister who is mean-spirited, unloving, possibly greedy and just bloody weird isn't a prize to be valued above all else. Or even a cross to be borne. You don't need it. You don't have to do it. Get the house thing over with—give her what she wants—and let that be an end to it. Sod her."

Susan slid round and put her arms around his neck. "You see everything so straightforwardly, don't you?"

He kissed her forehead. "So do you, most of the time. She's your Achilles' heel, that's all."

She sighed. "You're right."

"I love you."

"And I love you."

Polly and Cressida

It was a real Indian summer, hotter than it had been in July, the kind of hot where heat shimmers on the roads, like it does in American films, and the air is still and thick. Like it was in *Eden Close*. Spencer was lying on a blanket under a tree, nappy off, his little vest pulled up. His legs were moving continuously, like he was pedaling a bicycle, and his arms were spread wide, as if he was trying to embrace the sky. The branches kept the glare out of his eyes and the searing heat off his skin, but he was still doing a static dance of sun worship, warm, contented and panting a little.

Polly had forgotten how much she loved it here. The cottage had belonged to Dan's parents—she hadn't been to it since she and Dan had split up. She remembered arriving late on countless Friday nights after battling the traffic out of London, with fractious children and a car full of gear and food, as though there weren't any shops in Norfolk, Dan said. She'd always felt better almost the second she'd got out and stretched her travel-weary limbs, breathing in the salt sea air. Daniel had been conceived on one of those Friday nights, she was sure of it. Cressida had fallen asleep on the last hour of the journey, and they had laid her straight in her bed, watched her uncurl from her car seat fetal slumber and stretch out under the pink-and-white duvet, then taken a bottle of wine into the garden, where the grass still held the warmth of the day. They had made love under the tree where Spencer was lying now, listening to the sea, keeping time with the waves. She'd almost forgotten.

Dan had reminded her about the cottage, said she ought to take Cressida up there for a few days, if she wanted to; he would have Daniel. She hadn't been all wrong to love him like she had— it was easy to forget that.

The cottage hadn't changed. Even the furniture was the same as it had always been, sofas stained now by years of salty, lotioned legs curled up on them, and beds saggy and inviting, like lying in a cloud. When they had arrived yesterday, Cressida had been like a child again. She hadn't been there since she was very young, but she greeted the village and the house like long-lost jewels, making Polly stop the car on the little lane leading up to the house so she could collect samphire for them to steam, begging Polly to pick up some crabmeat for lunch. She'd let Polly take Spencer in the sling when they'd walked down to the sea, and she'd run up the shingle bank, feet slapping outward as the pebbles gave way beneath her, just like she had as a child.

This was the right place to talk to her.

Polly was nervous, and she didn't like that—you shouldn't feel anxious about talking to your child. She was taking a while to adjust to Cressida's new status: her child still, but also Spencer's mother. She was no longer a person for whom Polly was responsible, she was a mother just as Polly had been. Young. Scared. But not just the same—not if she would listen to Polly, let Polly do this for her.

She went into the dark cool of the kitchen and poured two tall glasses of water; then went back outside to where Cressida was sitting in an old deck chair, half an eye on a book, the other, more attentively, on Spencer.

"I want to talk to you, Cress." She sat down on the grass between her daughter and her grandson, then shuffled around so that she wasn't between them.

"What is it?" Cressida had been in the garden a great deal

since July, and she was a beautiful golden color. She looked very pretty, and ridiculously young again, without the bump of Spencer and the eye circles of late-pregnancy tiredness.

"It's about Spencer. And you. And me. Mostly about you."

Cressida looked a little alarmed, so Polly took a deep breath and just said it. "I want you to have chances I didn't have, Cress. That's why I wasn't sure, at first, that you should have Spencer." That idea felt almost evil, now, as she watched him doing his newborn ballet beside them. "And I was wrong about that, very wrong. I love him too, and I'm so glad he's here. But the mother in me still wants you to have all those chances. I want the world to be your oyster, just like every parent does, and as I know better than most, they won't come along in the same way unless you get your degree, get the right start in your career."

"I know that, Mum." Cressida's tone was patient. "I'm going to go back to college. I've said that all along, haven't I?"

"You've said you'll go back to something, but it won't be what your first choice was—it won't be what you really wanted."

"Past tense. He's what I really wanted—really want. He's arrived, and he's become my first choice, hasn't he? The rest of my life will have to fit in around him, just like it does for everyone else."

Polly shook her head. It gave her a sharp ache between the shoulder blades to hear Cressida talk that way—part pride, part despair, that her daughter should have resigned herself so calmly and seemingly happily. "Not if you let me look after him while you go to university."

Cressida was quiet for a long time. Spencer gave baby sighs.

"I've thought about it a huge amount since the spring, I promise you—it's not just some whim. I'm not trying to control things. I can have him, he can live with me, while you go to university. He'll be your son, he'll just live with me. You'll come home in the holidays, look after him then, weekends if you want. But mostly you'll be free to get on with your degree, have some fun, think clearly about what you want to do with your life."

She didn't know if Cressida would be angry with her. She made herself keep looking at her daughter.

When Cressida finally spoke she said, "Don't be daft, Mum.

You've got Daniel. You've got a job. You've got Jack, if you two sort out whatever this nonsense between you is."

Polly watched realization dawn on her daughter's face.

"I'm the thing between you, aren't I? You've told him, and he can't handle it." Panicky tears sprang into Cressida's eyes. She slid out of the deck chair to sit beside her mother, took Polly's hands. "Oh, Mum, you can't break up with Jack because of me. You can't. He's going to make you happy."

"Not if he can't understand what I need to do."

"But you don't need to do it."

"I do, Cressida. This isn't about Jack. I can stand losing Jack." Could she? "But I can't stand watching your life go wrong. That, I know I can't stand. Think about him." She gestured at Spencer. "I know he's a baby, but think further down the line. Think about him when he's your age. Think about him like I think about you. I look at you and can't believe I was a part of making something that has turned out to be so unbelievably wonderful as you are, so beautiful, and so smart, and so energetic, and so passionate and so warm. Look at him. Already you know you'd die for him, don't you? You know." Cressida was looking at him. The tears were running unchecked down her cheeks. She was nodding. Polly put her hands on each of Cressida's shoulders. "So now you understand how I feel about you." She was crying too.

Polly remembered the day Cressida had started her first period, when she was thirteen. She'd been imperious, fiercely embarrassed, private and irritable, and Polly had backed off. That night she'd found her in the bathroom, crying because she'd got blood on the towel and the bath mat, and she had climbed, naked, onto her mum's lap and sobbed. All the "grown-up" had gone out of her then, and it had now. Polly rocked her gently.

"I can't leave him behind, can I?" It was a question.

Polly felt some of the tension seep out of her muscles. She was getting somewhere. "Yes, you can. You're not leaving him. You're lending him to me for a while. That's all."

Later, Polly stood at the back door finishing a glass of wine. She felt almost excited. It was one of those days when you go to bed in a different life from the one you woke up in. They had talked for hours, and Cressida had brightened gradually, thinking of the possibilities for something she had believed was lost to her forever. She was almost girlish again by suppertime, and Polly had felt a great weight lifting, one she had been carrying since spring. They could make it work. They *would* make it work.

She locked the back door and went up the narrow stairs, switching off the lights as she went.

Cressida was in bed, with the lamp still on, lying facing her baby, with one hand stretched out as if to touch him. Spencer was asleep beside her in his carry-cot, both arms above his head in surrender to sunshine and formula-milk drunkenness. Polly bent over them to turn off the light, and Cressida opened her eyes. They looked at each other, mother and daughter, for a long moment, smiling in silent complicity and love, before Polly switched them into darkness.

Elliot

Cressida had caught the sun in Norfolk. Her face was golden, and there were freckles across her cheeks and nose. Her eyes sparkled bluer in the bright sunshine, and her curls were touched with gold. She was beautiful. He wanted to push her white shirt down over her shoulders to see where the brown met the white skin, and to smell the sun and her together.

They were in the park near her house. Spencer had been asleep in his pram, but he had woken now. They stopped at a bench, and Elliot sat down. Cressida picked up the baby and gave him to his father. He was wearing a white sun hat, too big for his tiny, downy head, and Elliot pushed it up so that he could see his face. Spencer's eyes locked onto him straightaway, in the shade.

Cressida came to him, and he put his arm round her shoulders. They sat that way for a few minutes without speaking. Elliot leant back and tried to imagine that this was it, that the three of them would be here, like this, for always. That people were walking past them, looking at them, touched by the family tableau, that middle-aged couples might take each other's hands in memory. But he already knew that they wouldn't be here, like this, for always. And the sun, as though it were intent on lighting that truth, burned at his eyelids. He pulled away first, so that she could speak, tell him what she needed to. Spencer stretched and closed his eyes. But Elliot couldn't put him down. He needed to hold him.

"I'm going away."

He was concentrating on his baby's face. He didn't move, but his heart was pounding.

She hated this. Hated saying this to him.

"I'm going to college. I'm not taking Spencer."

Elliot couldn't digest the last part. What did she mean? Something like hope flooded his lungs.

"Mum's going to look after him for me while I study. When I've got myself sorted out, afterward, he'll come and live with me, wherever that is. But I'm not going to take him with me to college. I'll come back and see him at weekends, and of course I'll be with him holidays and stuff, but I'll be away, studying, the rest of the time, term time."

Still he didn't speak.

"It was Mum's idea. I said no at first, but the more we talked about it, the more sense it made. She's taking a sabbatical from the law firm, and then he'll go to a crèche. There's a really good one near her office. Mum's sorted it all out, all the benefits and stuff, and it's going to be fine, Elliot. I love him more than I ever thought or understood, and I'll miss him, horribly, but I'm going to be able to be a better mum for him, give him a better, happier life, this way. I'm not talking about money and stuff, I'm talking about being happy myself, and fulfilled. I know that sounds selfish, maybe, to you, but I think it's the right decision. I just think I'm so unbelievably lucky that Mum wants to do this for me.

"Say something, Elliot? Please?"

"I don't figure at all, do I?" His voice was hollow.

"Of course you do." Cressida put her hand on his arm. "You're Spencer's dad. Mum knows that as well as I do. She wants you to see him, and spend time with him, and you'll be able to do that, won't you, much more easily here than if I'd gone away and taken him with me?" Her tone was imploring.

"I don't mean with Spencer. I mean I don't figure with you in your plans." How could Cressida ignore what he meant? She knew what he wanted, what he hoped for. She couldn't just pretend it had gone away.

She took back her hand and sighed. "Elliot, it's not right, you and me. I know you think that's what you want but it's not right."

"How do you know that? You haven't tried."

"I know it isn't something that you can try or not try. It's something you have to feel."

"You loved me."

"I loved you, yes. Of course I loved you. No past tense. I love you. I know you love me. But there are shades of love, Elliot. I shouldn't be telling you about them. You're the older one. You know what I mean. You love the idea of me, that's what."

He turned to her, almost angry. "Don't say that. I don't love the idea of you. I love the look of you and the smell of you and the sound of you and the feel of you. I love how you fit on my chest when we hold each other, and I love how you pull those curls on your forehead when you're thinking. I love the way you can't make a decent cup of tea. That isn't ideas. That's real."

She shook her head. "You needed me. Need isn't love either. You needed to see that there was a life beyond your life with Clare. You needed to be cared for. I came along and showed you all that. You know it now."

"Why don't you stop trying to tell me that I don't love you, and tell me that you don't love me? That's what this is about. If it was up to me, we'd be together. We'd be married and we'd be a family, the three of us. So this is about you, what you want, and who you don't want. Not me."

"Okay, I don't want this."

She couldn't have hurt him more if she had stabbed him in the neck with the broken bottle that lay by the bench. He wanted to run away. But he was still holding Spencer. And then her hand was back, across his, small and warm. "I don't want us to do this because of him. I don't want the only adult relationship I have to be one that started on the back of the wrong reasons, with deceit, lying, sneaking around and someone else destroyed by it. I do love you. You're the father of my baby. That can't change, can it? And I don't think he could have a better one. We'll always have him between us. But now is not the time for us, Elliot. I know I'm right."

"Don't do that. Don't give me hope. Don't ask me to wait for you."

"I'm not asking that. I'm saying that we're always going to be connected, and I'm saying that life is odd. That's all."

Elliot stood up, put Spencer back into his pram and covered his legs with the sheet. He watched him for a moment and laid one hand on his cheek, gently. Then he stepped back.

He couldn't argue: he knew she was right—however much he wished it was different, and he couldn't remember ever wanting anything to be different so much as he did this. But that wasn't true: he'd wanted things to be different with Clare, for him and Clare. Every time it had happened he had wanted it to be different. Suddenly he felt overwhelmed with sadness. Nothing had ever gone right, not with Clare and not with Cressida. Except for Spencer. But he couldn't think about him right now. He couldn't think at all. He wanted to be gone. He stepped a few paces further back, away from Cressida.

"Elliot?" She sat forward on the bench.

"I can't be here. I'm sorry." He turned and broke into a run. He ran awkwardly, too fast, until he was a long way from them. Then he collapsed against a tree and sank down to rest on the grass beneath it, his breath coming in great rasps, and tears falling unchecked. A young mother who was walking her Labrador and her child picked up the little girl's Tweenies scooter and carried it fast past him, the child's hand held tightly in her own.

SEPTEMBER
READING GROUP

AN INSTANCE OF THE FINGERPOST

Iain Pears © 1998

Set in Oxford in the 1660s—a time and place of great intellectual, scientific, religious and political ferment—this remarkable novel centers on a young woman, Sarah Blundy, who stands accused of the murder of Robert Grove, a fellow of New College. Four witnesses describe the events surrounding his death: Marco da Cola, a Venetian Catholic intent on claiming credit for the invention of blood transfusion; Jack Prestcott, the son of a supposed traitor to the Royalist cause, determined to vindicate his father; John Wallis, chief cryptographer to both Cromwell and Charles II, a mathematician, theologian and inveterate plotter; and Anthony Wood, the famous Oxford antiquary. Each one tells his version of what happened, but only one reveals the extraordinary truth. Brilliantly written, utterly convincing, gripping from the first page to the last, An Instance of the Fingerpost *is a magnificent tour de force.*

They didn't meet for the reading group that month. Who could concentrate? Instead they had coffee together in Starbucks early one Saturday morning. They were tired and washed-out and a bit like Omaha Beach survivors regrouping after the landings.

"Hey, Granny!" Harriet hugged Polly. "Missed you last month. Hope you've brought photographs."

Polly nodded. "Which you may only see on condition that you *never, never* call me Granny in public again."

"Okay, Nana—get them out."

"You okay?" Polly knew there weren't any words for what Harriet had been through.

"We are now. Thanks." They hugged again.

The others were already sitting down, steaming mugs in front of them.

Nicole didn't think any of them had read the book. Her choice. *An Instance of the Fingerpost*, by Iain Pears.

Harriet had only bought it the week before Josh's accident. Oh, deep joy, she had thought ironically. All my favorite ingredients—history, religion, politics, science—it's written by a man, and all in a compact and manageable 698 pages. She had wondered whether Nicole had chosen it on purpose to annoy her, although it was exactly the kind of book she would have expected Nicole to love. The morning Josh had fallen off the roof she had read the first chapter for the second time and thrown it impatiently onto the sofa, convinced she understood less on second reading than she had on first. Nicole had joked with her that she had timed Josh's accident to coincide with the reading-club meeting so that she could get out of reading something she didn't fancy. It was okay to joke about it now that Josh was all right. The sheer relief made everything funny—the stories about her mattress on the floor in the high-dependency unit, the canteen's dreadful food and the endless one-sided conversations about Arsenal. She would rather have been reading Iain Pears, with its complicated plot and layered retelling, than to have been reading *Harry Potter*, with all the imagination and enthusiasm she could muster, to a nonreactive boy. It had all turned into a chapter in Harriet's family legend, her maternal stand-up repertoire, to be told over the years in exactly the same way, like all the stories that had gone before, which she told to Josh and Chloe, the ones that started, "It was a sunny morning in May when I knew you were ready to be born," and "We didn't even know that the first tooth had come through until you bit me when I was feeding you a *fromage frais*," and "On your first day at school you told the teacher you wanted to be a dinosaur doctor when you grew up." This one started, "The day Josh fell off the roof," and she hoped, every time she told it, that it was the scariest one there would ever be.

She told her friends all about it. Nicole interjected more than once—"When I got there, they were just there, on the floor, and the other kids were crying in the doorway." Now she was saying, "Tim was brilliant."

"He was." Harriet knew she couldn't have got through it without him. From the moment he arrived, he had taken charge: calm, slow and sure, although his eyes had filled with tears when he had first seen Josh, tiny in the vast white bed. Each morning he had brought her coffee, strong and frothy from the coffeehouse outside the hospital, not the watery stuff from the canteen, and an apple Danish (she hated raisins, he never forgot). He brought her favorite magazines, the gossipy photographic ones he hated, and he remembered that she needed her eyelash curlers just to feel human. And he sat with Josh every moment he could, talking to him, about things they'd done that summer, things they were going to do when he was better. He couldn't have been more perfect. Just like always.

"He was fantastic. I couldn't have done it without him."

She drew a line under the conversation about Josh with her

tone. She didn't want to keep talking about how fabulous Tim had been. Nicole was looking at her curiously. Since the Gavin thing in Spain had happened, and then the accident, she had been even more incredulous about Harriet's ambivalence toward her husband. The worse Gavin was, the better Tim looked. Harriet thought that was what it was. It made her a bit uncomfortable. The marriages were distinct, even if the friendships were sometimes blurred, like they had been these last few weeks.

She turned to Susan. "How did the funeral go?"

"It was okay. Quite a few people turned up in the end, which helped. It's a relief to have it behind me. I've still got the house to sort out, but Margaret, my sister, is going to help me with that."

Polly snorted. The others looked at her. "Margaret has . . . let's say issues."

"What do you mean?" Nicole asked.

"She must be more traumatized about Mum's dying than I thought she would be. She's been incredibly upset ever since."

"And she's taking it out on you!" Polly loved Susan for her reasonableness, and her gentleness, but she couldn't sit there and let Susan defend Margaret's behavior on the grounds of trauma. Bollocks to that! Margaret was a monster as far as she was concerned, and didn't deserve anything approaching pity from Susan, who had shouldered the entire burden of Alice's care.

Susan didn't try to defend her sister any further. She grimaced. "Yes, she pretty much is. Still, the cottage is full of paperwork, about God knows what—Mum was a real hoarder—so two more hands, albeit attached to a moody, sarcastic sibling, are better than none."

"Can we help?" Harriet asked.

"God, no! You're all busy enough as it is. No, we'll be fine. Roger's around to lend a bit of muscle. Polly said she'd put in a weekend, didn't you, to sort her clothes out?" Polly nodded. "And there really isn't any point in being sentimental. It's just 'stuff,' most of it. What's worth selling we'll sell, what's worth giving away we'll give away. The furniture will go to a house clearer. It's Mum's paperwork that'll take the time. She's the sort who will have kept her check stubs going back thirty years, that kind of thing. That generation were all a bit like that, I think. Something to do with the deprivation in the war. But you've got to go through the whole lot, haven't you, to make sure you don't miss anything?"

"Like details of her Swiss bank account?" Harriet smiled.

"No such luck. I was thinking about insurance policies, letters of wishes, that kind of thing."

"It's horrid, isn't it?" Nicole said, remembering her father's death a few years before. He'd left everything in perfect order. There had been a file in the deep drawer on the left-hand side of his desk marked "on my death" in his green ink. It had told her mother everything she had to do, financial, practical. He'd even chosen his funeral hymns. Nicole wouldn't have been surprised if there'd been diagrams included: "changing a fuse"; "attaching the brush extension to the hose." She remembered her mother sitting in an armchair with the folder open on her lap, crying, "He loved me," as if she hadn't realized until she saw it.

"It is." Susan shrugged off the idea. She didn't want to think about it. "Come on, let's talk about something more cheerful, if we're not going to talk about the book. Nicole?"

"Well . . . I'm not sure it's exactly cheerful." She took a deep breath. Harriet knew of course, but she hadn't told anyone else before today. She felt almost shy. "But I've thrown Gavin out."

"God, I'm sorry." Susan wished she hadn't asked.

"I'm not. At least, I'm sure I'm not going to be soon." She did look pale, now that Susan really looked at her, pale and tired.

Harriet watched her friend carefully. She knew that this was an important step. She believed that the more people Nicole told, the more real it would become in her mind and the less likely she would be to take him back. Every time the phone rang Harriet was afraid that it would be Nic, to tell her she was going to give him one more last chance.

Susan and Polly were looking at Nicole with sympathetic curiosity. She hadn't spoken much about her husband over the months. It was pretty obvious that Harriet didn't like him. Polly had always thought she seemed a bit closed off about him, a bit controlled. Nicole wasn't sentimental, either, about what they read. She could be a bit hard. It obviously didn't go very deep, though: she looked like a woman who'd spent days in tears.

"He was a serial cheat. I think he probably has been all the way through our marriage. I caught him with someone on our summer holiday. In our bed." She stopped. The revelation hung in the air, stark and unchallengeable.

Susan looked at her hands. God, men could be such pigs. What did they want? Nicole was beautiful, clever—she was the mother of his children, for God's sake.

"And that was the last straw on the camel's back?" Polly wasn't really asking a question. She'd been in a marriage that had failed.

"Yep."

"And that's really it, no way back?"

Nicole shook her head slowly and took a long sip of coffee. "I don't think so. It's shifted, you know? Suddenly it's not about punishing him, or making him stop it. I don't want to do it anymore."

Polly nodded. "That's what happened with me and Dan. He wasn't a philanderer as far as I know, just a useless husband. And I battled with him for years, trying to get him to change. Until one morning I woke up and thought, You know, Poll, he isn't going to change, whatever you do. And the minute you realize that, you see the time ahead with that person as all being a waste, and you want to get out and get on, don't you? I just thought I could try something else before it was too late."

She'd got it exactly. Nicole smiled at her. "How long were you on your own, before you met Jack?"

"Ten years. Except I wasn't alone, I had the kids. And even the occasional 'man-friend.'"

Susan laughed. "And I can tell you about a couple of those sometime when Polly isn't around, if you're interested."

Polly punched her arm playfully. "Some of them were all right. You were just jealous."

Now Susan laughed harder. "Oh, that's right. Really jealous! Especially of that one—what was his name?—with the hairy neck."

"Do you mean the one with the hairy neck *and* the yacht moored at Cowes?"

"He'd have needed a lot more than a yacht at Cowes to get me past that neck."

Polly was giggling now. "You should have seen his stomach."

"We practically could. He never did his shirt buttons up, if I remember rightly. He made Tom Jones look like the soul of propriety."

"Euk!"

"Be fair. It was a long time ago. It was probably fashionable at the time."

"It was not."

When they'd all stopped laughing, Polly said, "Well, since this has stopped being a reading club and turned into a confessional, you'd better have mine, I suppose."

Nicole and Harriet looked at her expectantly.

"Susan knows all this, so apologies to her for being boring. Jack and I have split up, I think. Mutual agreement, I suppose you'd call it. I've decided to do something, and he doesn't think he can handle it, so we've gone our separate ways." She was trying to keep it light. "I hope you haven't bought your hats for the wedding because there isn't going to be one."

"Christ, we're a right lot." Nicole was surprised. Polly had seemed so in love with him. With some relationships you just believed in the love, the trust and the future of them. She'd thought she was the only one among them, apart from Clare, who hadn't had a strong one, a "banker." Even Harriet and Tim—although it felt as though she was the only person who thought so. When marriages like that fell apart, you were shocked, and it chipped away at your belief in happy endings.

"What are you going to do?" Harriet asked.

"I've decided, and Cressida has agreed, that I'm going to keep Spencer with me while she goes to college. I'm taking a sabbatical from work for a few months, and then I'll go back, and he'll go to day care—there's a really nice crèche near my office. Cressida will come back at holidays and things to be with him."

"Wow." Nicole was shocked.

"I didn't have those chances, you see," Polly went on. "I had her very young, and I wouldn't change her or her brother for the world, but I know they held me back from things. Cressida doesn't have to repeat that pattern, because I'm here, and I can help."

"You're amazing!" Harriet said.

"Not amazing. Just a mother."

"And aren't we all amazing, us mothers?" Susan asked.

"We are. To mothers." Polly raised her mug.

The others smiled and joined in. "To mothers."

Harriet looked briefly at Nicole. What must she be feeling? She looked a little as if she might cry. She put her hand under the table, found Nicole's and squeezed her fingers tightly.

Nicole squeezed back. These were the conversations she was going to have to learn to get through. She would be the best mother she could possibly be to the boys and to Martha. She could never make it up to the baby who wasn't going to be born, and at moments like this, it would come to the front of her mind for always and block out everything else, like a solar eclipse.

"And that's why things have gone wrong with Jack?"

"Yeah. He doesn't want to do the surrogate-father thing, not to a baby. And I can't blame him. A woman with grown-up kids is one thing. A granny with a baby at home? Why should he?"

Because he loves me, because he loves me, her heart screamed. *Because you love me.*

"That must have been hard for you?"

"Not really. We didn't have a screaming row or anything. We didn't argue at all. I suppose we've just drifted apart, as they say, since I told him. No big good-bye scenes."

Polly shouldn't be surprised, Susan reflected, as Harriet launched into the young-mothers' information network, promising the names of babysitters, naming the children they knew at the nursery Polly was talking about, that they had taken the news in their stride. We're all mothers, aren't we? Different stages, maybe, different problems, but the love is the same. The instinct for self-sacrifice is the same.

Polly

Polly put the phone back into its cradle on the wall and laid her forehead against it. She wasn't sure she could do this anymore. She was tired, and that, of course, magnified everything, but she was also confused and sad, even a bit angry, and that was nothing to do with fatigue.

It had been Jack, who couldn't make up his mind. Or maybe Jack, who had made up his mind but couldn't convince his heart to follow suit. Or Jack, who wasn't quite the man she had thought he was and believed that he could have his cake (child-free, chaos-free life) and eat it, and her, too, whenever he got hungry.

She was such a cliché, and she was angry with herself for it. He'd told her what he wanted—or, rather more pertinently, what he didn't want. But he kept ringing and asking to see her, and she was utterly unable to stay away from him.

The first time had been a couple of weeks after Spencer was born. He'd sent those lovely flowers to Cressida, but Polly hadn't heard anything from him—she'd felt a bit stupid over leaving the message on his answerphone, but she'd been so high when the baby was born, and she had wanted so much to share it with him. Then he'd called out of the blue, when her resistance was low (when wasn't it, where he was concerned?), and asked her to meet him for a drink. That first time she'd been foolishly full of hope. She'd bought a new dress, even though it was just a drink in the pub, and worried over her hair and makeup. She'd worn a matching bra and pants, smiling at herself as she'd pulled them on. "Hopeful dressing," Harriet would have called it.

They'd had a gorgeous time. It was a pub they'd been to often, and they sat where they always sat, and drank and talked and talked. About everything except. He'd asked about Spencer, but not much, and she hadn't pushed. They had held hands.

It could be amazingly sexy, holding hands. She'd forgotten. His hand was big and cool, and hers had felt tiny inside it, submissive. He could have led her anywhere, and she was sure she would have followed.

She knew she saw love in his eyes. They twinkled and sparkled at her when she said things that were typical Polly. He listened avidly, and laughed at her jokes, and it was lovely, exciting, to be back in the bright beam of his attention.

She couldn't believe it when the evening was over and they were outside, their cars pointing in opposite directions next to each other on the road. How emblematic was that? He was going to get into his car and go back to the life he had chosen, without saying any of the things she had been hoping to hear.

Their polite, friendly good night kiss started cheek to cheek and lingered, until nose slid across nose, lips met and parted. What was she doing? If a girlfriend, or Cressida, or someone on *EastEnders* had been doing this, she would have been shouting at her not to be so stupid. She was in her forties, for God's sake, snogging the face off a man outside a pub. A man who didn't want her. Well, that was patently untrue. She consoled herself vaguely with that thought, although it didn't get her far. A man who didn't want her *enough*. Rather, she imagined, as crack addicts promised they wouldn't call their dealers again, and alcoholics promised that each new drink would be the last, Polly promised herself (and, perhaps more important, promised Susan) that she wouldn't do it again. Social masochism, Susan called it. "You know it's going to hurt you, so don't do it."

But the next Friday she was with him again. In a restaurant, feeling the whole length of Jack's thigh against hers, their forearms touching just enough above the table to make all the hairs stand to attention. Your body could scream out that it wanted something, something it had had before and loved, and it could so easily drown out your head's protests.

He'd picked her up—Cressida had stayed in the kitchen with Spencer, so she hadn't seen him. When he'd brought her home, and they'd kissed in the car until the windows had steamed up, she wanted, more than anything, to take him inside and upstairs and into her bed. If Cressida and Daniel hadn't been there, she would have done. She didn't know if she felt relief or frustration that they were. What an idiot.

She'd pulled away from him, bracing her arms against the insides of his elbows to keep him at a distance. "What are we doing, Jack?"

He hadn't answered for a long time. He rubbed his eyes, rested his fingertips on his forehead, then punched the center of the steering wheel lightly. "I don't know, Poll."

"There's no point, is there?"

"Isn't there?" He wasn't giving much away.

"We could keep meeting like this. That much would be easy," she said.

So very easy. She felt so alive when she was with him that it was almost worth it.

"But you're asking me to be here like we were, close, and then to go inside and get on with living without you until the next time you call."

"I'm not asking for anything from you, Polly."

"Yes, you are. You've no idea. And, besides, so what if you're not? You're not asking for anything from me because you know you have no right to, and I'm not asking for anything from you because I've already asked and been turned down. Now I'm too terrified even to dial your phone number. So what's the point? It's not a relationship, is it? It's a good night out, maybe. Sex, to order, almost certainly, since whatever else is wrong with you and me, it patently isn't that."

He cringed and shook his head. It wasn't like that.

She saw what he was thinking. "It *is* like that, Jack! Don't kid yourself. As soon as you say, 'I want to be with you, but on my terms, and I'm bailing out the moment it gets difficult,' that's exactly what it's like. And, it seems to me, that's exactly what you've said."

"You make me sound like a monster."

"I'm not saying you're a monster." She put her hand up to his cheek. "I love you, Jack. I love you and I want you, and I wanted to marry you. I can't switch that off like a tap. I think I always will." He brought up his own hand to cover hers. "But I'm a wise enough old bird—and, by Christ, I should be by now—to know that this is only going to make us both miserable. You know I'm right, don't you?"

"I love you too."

"I know you do. But it's not enough, is it?"

Jack's laugh was hollow and bitter.

She talked on. Who was comforting whom? "Do you remember when you were young and daft enough to think that was all that mattered? Before you realized that loving someone was just the beginning?"

He nodded.

All she wanted to do was to sink into his arms and let him hold her. Let him do whatever he wanted with her. With a gargantuan effort, she opened the car door. "We've got to stop this, Jack. You've got to leave me alone. Please?"

He nodded, without looking at her. There wasn't anything else to say. She shut the car door behind her and walked into the house without looking back, although she hadn't heard the engine start.

Inside the house she put the chain on and leant heavily against the door.

Cressida came out of the kitchen with a bottle of formula. From upstairs, the sound of Spencer mewling and mithering floated down. "How did it go?"

"Horrendously."

Cressida's face was full of concern. "What did he say to you?"

"Nothing he can say, love. It's me who's got to say something. I've got to say no. And that's what I've just done. There's no point in seeing him. Just leaves me feeling like I've been through a mangle."

"I'm sorry, Mum." She was crestfallen. "This is my fault."

"Don't be silly. Of course it's not."

"Yes, it is. You don't have to protect me from that. If you weren't going to be looking after Spencer, this wouldn't be happening. You'd be planning the wedding, Jack would be living here with you and you'd be happy together, like you were before."

"Maybe, darling, but I'd be marrying a man who only loved me on his own terms, wouldn't I? One who was going to fall by the wayside when things got tough. Best I found that out before the wedding, don't you think? Because, believe me, there are a million different ways that being married to me could get tough." She smiled, bravely, she hoped. Suddenly she wanted to be on her own. Cressida didn't need to see her cry.

Cressida didn't look convinced, but Spencer gave a timely, indignant yell. Cressida hesitated, looking up the stairs and back at her mother. "Are you going to be all right?"

"Course I am—you get back to your boy. Give him a kiss for me."

"Here's one for you from him." Cressida kissed her cheek and ran upstairs.

Nicole

Nicole had chosen everything very carefully. It had to be in public, where she knew she wouldn't cave in. So it was smart. It was a well-dressed stage for a carefully rehearsed performance. That was the only way she trusted herself to do it.

She knew it was vain, petty and superficial, but she had taken extra care with her "costume": black, fitted, tactile. She knew from the mirror, and from Harriet, whom she had seen when she dropped off the kids with her, that she looked beautiful. She knew, from the men who'd turned to look at her as she had walked the length of the long, high bar to choose a seat, that she looked sexy. She had always made the effort—so that Gavin would look at her when he came in and want her more than anyone else in the place. Now it was testament that marriage, familiarity and motherhood hadn't changed her, that she was still the girl he had wanted so instantly and so much all those years ago in a boardroom. Today it was meant to make him look at her and kick himself for what he had lost.

She still didn't know how seriously he was taking this. She'd never thrown him out before. She'd given him the cold shoulder, she'd decamped to her mother's, she'd stayed out all hours, leaving the children with the au pair. More often she'd sulked, stormed, turned away from him at night, but she'd never packed his suitcase like she had when she got back from Spain. She wondered what would have happened if she'd done it the first time he'd given her a reason to. It was too late now, but maybe then she could have made him see what he was risking.

That first time (she could remember the date, the name, everything about it), she'd taken the twins to her mother in St. Albans. They weren't very old. She claimed she needed a rest, although her mother wasn't the kind of parent who would creep in at night and pick up a crying baby: she was more of an earplugs-and-sympathetic-smile-in-the-morning mum. Nicole wished her father was alive. He'd always been the cuddler. She didn't tell her mother why she was there. Absurdly, that was out of loyalty to Gavin. Her mother was a strident, unforgiving woman, who would never have let it go. Resentment would have permeated Christmases and birthdays for years afterward. And back then, when it had been only once, Nicole had believed in a future for her and Gavin. Through the fug of her exhaustion and misery, she had found it easy to blame herself for Gavin's infidelity: she'd found it difficult to recover from the cesarean and hadn't wanted to make love for months—she was too tired, and couldn't separate Nicole the lover from Nicole the mother, and she was worried that she didn't look or feel the same. She had always let him, of course—she didn't remember ever turning him down—but she had never initiated it, and she hadn't enjoyed it. She had been aware that he knew that, and resented it. Christ! What an idiot she had been.

She'd forgiven him in her own mind before she even got to her mother's—rationalized, blamed herself, started missing him—on the M25. She'd forced gaiety at her mother's, smiled broadly at the steady stream of neighbors and others who had paraded through to look at the boys and cried herself to sleep every night in the floral guest room.

Her mother had taken one look at the earrings Gavin had given her the day she came out of hospital (diamonds, in a Tiffany box, tucked into two dozen red roses—a dozen per son, he had winked at the midwife) and told her for the thousandth time what a lucky woman she was. Eventually Nicole had started believing it again. After two nights, she drove home promising herself that she would be a better wife. Later, after she had been up with one of the twins, she had climbed on top of Gavin as he lay asleep and made vocal, spirited love to him. That was more or less how it had been ever since.

Harriet had made it okay to see it the other way. She didn't think Nicole was lucky. She didn't like Gavin, and didn't care if Nicole knew it. There had been an incredible freedom in her friendship with Harriet—she didn't have to pretend with her. And even if Harriet thought she was insane, it never stopped her being there for her. She'd been unbelievable from the moment she had picked up Nicole at the airport that horrible day after Phil Brooks. Nicole had waited for the kids to fall asleep, exhausted after the journey, then said to her, "I can't do this anymore. It's over," and Harriet had passed her a packet of tissues and said, "Okay. We'll sort it all out."

She'd been with her to the clinic, even though she didn't agree with what Nicole was doing, and had made her feel that she understood. Nicole never underestimated what that meant. She'd helped her stay focused on a future without Gavin. Maybe without Harriet, Nicole would still have found the strength this time to leave him for good, but she knew that Harriet had made it a hundred times easier, and a million times less lonely than it would have been without her. And the reading group had helped: women listened in a way men never could, and they understood so much of your subtext, without you having to articulate it. A year ago she would have been put off by the thought of such intimacy—she had only ever had it, really, with Harriet—but now she loved its comfort and support. They had been brilliant about her going for the job. Polly had called her the night before the interview, and Susan the afternoon afterward, to see how it had gone. It was a feminine cocoon, and it was unfamiliar and wonderful to Nicole.

Now she could see how much of a man's woman she had always been: she didn't have a single girlfriend left from school or university, only the wives of her male friends. The other night she had been sorting through boxes in the loft, part of her campaign to remove all traces of Gavin from her home, and she had found three or four long, thin photographs rolled up in cardboard tubes. She had taken them down, into her bed, with a tumbler of whiskey, and pored over them. She knew she had been popular. She saw how slim and pretty she had been, how animated and happy-looking, but she was always standing between men. The girls' names were harder to bring to mind than the boys.' In the pictures she saw girls and women she wished were her friends now. She had smiled and joked with them, danced and drunk with them, then moved on, not valuing them or what they might bring to her life beyond school and college. Now, she had women in her life who mattered to her. It made her feel strong.

And here he was, the man she had loved so much for so long. He was walking toward her, with his beautiful hands and his dancing eyes, and his impeccable black suit, a vivid turquoise and cobalt blue Duchamp tie the only splash of color. Had he dressed carefully for her? He bent to kiss her, with his hand on the back of her head. She moved so that his lips caught her cheek and pushed back, just a little, so that he had to move his hand.

"You look stunning."

Oh, please. Had she been so much a patsy all this time that he thought a little flattery would be enough? She heard Harriet at her shoulder, saw her rolling her eyes, melodramatically mouthing "Yes, Yes! You have!" The thought made her smile.

"What's funny?"

"Nothing."

"You want to move, sit in one of those booths?"

"I'm fine here, thanks." Not a chance.

Gavin took a stool beside her. He raised a finger imperiously at the barman and ordered a beer for himself, another gin and tonic for her.

"Just tonic, thanks."

"Not drinking?"

"I've got the car on a meter."

Gavin exhaled slowly. She wasn't melting. He took a long swig of his beer.

"I don't want you back, Gavin." She held up her hand as he opened his mouth to speak. "Let me finish." He stayed silent, his hands up in a humorous gesture of surrender. "I need you to understand why. And I need you to understand how much I mean it. It isn't because you slept with that woman in Spain. This isn't a punishment. I just don't want to be married to you anymore, that's all. I've had enough. It's over."

"You still love me." His arrogance made her want to hit him.

"I'm learning not to."

"But you still do."

"I loved you for a long time, Gavin. I spent a lot of years believing I was lucky to have you. I don't think that anymore. You don't deserve my love, and I'm withdrawing it. Whatever I feel inside myself is for me to deal with. And, believe me, it's under way."

"This isn't you talking. You don't talk this way. This is Harriet, or those other women you've been hanging around with. Putting words in your mouth."

"Oh, it's me. If you don't believe it now, you will. It's not the me you kept in a trance all that time. The me who didn't want anyone to know what was going on, who was paralyzed by pride and fear. It's the me I was before I loved you, and the one I'm going to be after I'm done."

She saw that he was deflated, a little. When he spoke again, after another deep drink, his voice was softer, more conciliatory. "We're a family. You, me, the kids."

Thank God. Now she could be angry. "How dare you try to use our children to get round me? They weren't important to you when you were fucking that woman in our villa. They weren't important to you all those other times. I sure as hell wasn't. I don't suppose for one second you were thinking of them when you were screwing around. You never think of anyone but yourself. So don't you dare use my kids."

"I love them."

"Yeah, I know that. You love them in some egocentric, uninterested way because they make you look good—they're good for your image. Tell me something, Gav. Which is Martha's favorite teddy? What color's her ballet uniform? Who's her best friend? Who are any of her friends, apart from Chloe? What's William's best subject at school? Which football team is George playing for this term?"

His face was blank.

"You don't know, do you?" He didn't answer. "So don't tell me I can't do this because of the kids." Rage was boiling up inside her. She felt like she was vomiting her words, retching to get them out.

"You didn't even know there was another one, did you?" She hadn't known until this moment that she was going to tell him. Suddenly she wanted to hurt him—hurt him like he'd hurt her. It made her afraid, knowing she had the power to do that. She almost liked seeing his face like this, bewildered, not understanding. Gavin, who was always in control, always on top.

"What do you mean, another one?"

"I was pregnant this summer, when you were fucking some-one else in our bed."

"I don't understand." Their voices were still quiet. "What do you mean?"

"Pregnant. With your child. Conceived in Venice. I was stupid enough to think another baby might make you faithful. God, how stupid could I be? I was going to tell you on holiday."

"What, how . . . ?" He was floundering now. He'd lost all his color. "But you're not . . . ?"

"I'm not now." She looked down at her hands. The courage that had carried her this far had failed. It had fled as soon as the baby had flooded back into her mind. She didn't know what to say.

He was shaking his head, thinking fast. He reached his own conclusion. She must have lost the baby. The stress of finding him with that woman. He'd caused her to miscarry his baby: it was his fault. The loss, of something he hadn't known he had, showed instantly on his face, which crumpled in shock and gen-uine sadness. "You lost the baby. I'm so sorry. I'm so, so sorry."

And she didn't correct him. Afterward she didn't know if it was because that had been the first time he had ever apologized and she felt that he meant it, or because she was afraid of his reaction if he found out the truth, or because she just couldn't bear to say it aloud.

Maybe he didn't deserve the lie. She wouldn't even tell Harriet that she had let him go believing that of himself, although she knew Harriet would tell her that Gavin *was* responsible, whichever way the baby was lost to them. She didn't want that comforting salve. Like Briony, in the book they had read, she would atone for both sins, alone, silently, eternally. Maybe that was enough.

Harriet

Josh was playing with his computer, and Harriet marveled at his ability. Seven years old and he could do things with it that were way beyond his mother. So could Chloe, and she was only four. That was private nursery education for you. You paid thousands of pounds for your children to be educated to the point where at eight they thought you were an idiot. Harriet's understanding of the family computer extended no further than switching it on and going to instant messaging, which she loved. You could gossip through the night with no one butting in. But any problems and she was kicking the desk, hitting all the buttons and calling for Tim.

"Josh, switch the computer *off* now—it's breakfast time." No response.

A few weeks ago she would have shouted at him. All mothers had unlimited fishwife license where the school run was concerned—even the gentle, pearl-wearing ones, who barely spoke at the mothers' coffee mornings, and always called their child sweetheart in public went at it like crazed banshees between seven and eight-fifteen on weekdays. She hadn't been able to be cross with him since the accident. She had cut him so much slack, and Chloe, too, that he was pretty much in charge of the morning schedule. They'd been late for school every morning this week.

Tim was late too, today. That didn't help. He was normally gone long before the kids woke, but this morning he was still thumping around upstairs. It had been hard for him, too, she knew. Life had been different since the accident. It felt like the Bible—B.C. and A.D. Harriet had come to believe that parents who had never sat beside a high-dependency bed willing their child to live were looking at life with blinkers on, taking the ongoing health and safety of their children for granted because they hadn't glimpsed the other possibility. The thoughts that ran through your head while you sat with all that time to kill and nothing to do were mad, disloyal, nasty, hysterical and sometimes almost funny. Why my child? and not that one, who isn't as clever, or cute, or careful or loved? There were random practical thoughts about cars and bedrooms, holidays and next weekend, and all the permutations and implications of a life without them. And although the moment when Josh had opened his eyes, known her and smiled had been the best she had ever lived, nothing could ever be as it was before. The shadow of his mortality had passed across her life, and with it the knowledge that his death would have destroyed her, Tim and probably Chloe. It would never go away. She hadn't talked about it, that presence that was here and hadn't been before, not to anyone. She couldn't say so to Nicole; the timing was all wrong; she had her own ghost now. She didn't want to with Tim. It was easy enough not to; people wanted to listen to the story of Josh's accident, and to celebrate his recovery, but they didn't want to know about the shadow. The ones who knew already just knew, and the ones who didn't, well, they couldn't understand.

Alongside, in Harriet's tired brain, ran the knowledge that she had relinquished control, the cardinal sin of motherhood. These last weeks when she had looked at him and Chloe, she had felt only vulnerable, massive love. She would have to do something about it soon.

They were late again. Josh had forgotten his football boots and Chloe her show-and-tell. Double maternal failure. Chloe whimpered, and Josh railed. Harriet promised to come straight back to school with the missing articles. And they sloped off, belligerently, into their classrooms.

The car park of mothers heaved a collective sigh of relief, all except those who still had babes in arms, or strollers, to take back home. The others all made for their houses, with coffee, the *Daily Mail* and *House Invaders*, or offices, dry-clean-only clothing and adult conversations at the watercooler to look forward to, their step a little lighter, without the weight of the sports kit, lunch boxes, sundry hats and gloves, and nagging-without-breathing that had accompanied them into school.

When she got home Tim was still there. Damn.

She had had her own plans after she'd been back to school with their things, and they had involved going back to bed, alone, for a couple of hours. The kind of missing time in a day that often translated itself into a strenuous gym visit when you recounted the day, fingers crossed behind the back, metaphorically, to your husband at night.

He was strange—he had been for a few days. She knew that she had needed him, in the hospital, in the days after Josh had come back. It had united them—no one loved a child as much as its mother and father. It was not so much a tie that bound as a bloody great rope, when that child was lying in a hospital. She knew, too, that things had gone back to normal between them almost as soon as Josh was better. The accident hadn't really changed anything. Not between them. Silly to expect it might have done, probably.

He was sitting, fully dressed, at the kitchen table. The television, which Harriet had on constantly in the morning, listening to the time checks and travel news, was switched off.

"What are you doing? I thought you'd be gone by now."

"I will be in a few minutes. I'll catch the nine-fifty-two." He always knew the train times. He never said "ten to ten." He said every minute counted, if you were a slave to South West Trains.

"What's up?" She sat in a chair on the other side of the table.

"I need some time on my own, Harriet. I'm going to stay at the club for a while." He was watching her face intently.

"How long? What do you mean?"

"I don't know. I just know that something has got to change."

She hadn't been expecting this. She felt a bit sick. "I don't understand."

"I know. That's the point, really." His voice was low, sad.

Harriet's was louder, frightened. "Make me understand, then. Tell me what's going on. You can't just come in here and say you're leaving. Not without explaining why."

He looked as if he was thinking of how to say something major. He was trembling, just a little. Harriet felt an unfamiliar stab of cold fear. "Is there somebody else? Are you leaving me for somebody else?" When he didn't deny it straightaway, she almost screeched at him. "Are you?"

He put out a hand. "No. I'm not. There has never been anyone else for me. Not since I met you. You are the only woman I've ever loved, I mean really loved. That's been my downfall, really. I suppose I've always believed I could make you love me as much as I love you. Or maybe I thought I had enough for both of us and it didn't matter. But I find, now, that it *does* matter, after all. Things haven't been right for ages, longer than I want to admit, I expect. You don't love me like I need to be loved, want to be loved. For Christ's sake, like I *deserve* to be loved, Harry. I know something went on earlier this year. I don't know what or with who—I don't want to." He looked almost sick at the thought. "But I do know that while it was going on you were different. You were alive. Someone else was doing that for you. And I held my breath for weeks, months, praying you wouldn't leave me. And when you didn't I thought things might be okay, that they might get better. I believed that maybe you'd chosen to stay with me. That seemed like a good start. But nothing changed. Not really. You make me feel like you don't want me here. Like I'm just an irritant, a complication. If I'm honest with myself, I never feel really loved by you.

"When Josh had his accident, and you needed me so badly? Then I thought you might see. But you didn't. I know I can't make you. And I can't spend the next ten years waiting for you to leave me. I know you love me, I just don't think you're in love with me. And if you're not in love with me, then there's space, isn't there, in you, in your heart, and sooner or later you will be, with someone else, and then you'll leave me. I can't hold my breath every day of my life and wait for that to happen. I'd rather let you go. Get it over with. I'm between a rock and a fucking hard place, Harry. I don't want to live this way anymore. I feel so bad about myself, and I can't imagine a life without you in it. I'm in a state here. I'm drowning. That's why I'm going. I need some space. I can't think straight around you—I never bloody well could. That's why."

He hadn't watched her face while he spoke. He hadn't seen what passed across it. He was dying for her to come round the table to him. He wanted more than anything to feel her arms round him, hear her voice telling him he was an idiot, that she was in love with him, that a world without him in it would be unbearable.

It was shock that kept her quiet. She couldn't believe that he had been suffering like this and that she could have been so oblivious of it. She felt numb. She felt self-loathing.

He pushed a piece of paper across the table to her. It had an address and a telephone number. "This is where I'll be, if you need me. Tell the kids I love them. Don't tell them . . ." He couldn't finish. She would have to decide what to tell them. He didn't know how to read her silence. He badly needed to be gone. As he passed her chair, he touched the top of her head.

When he reached the front door, she said his name, once, quietly. He didn't hear.

As he got into the car to drive to the station, he thought she hadn't spoken, and his greatest fear was that silence was the most eloquent answer she could give him.

Susan

Susan was surprised that Margaret didn't want to come with her to the solicitor. She didn't think her sister trusted her. She couldn't face it, she had said, when Susan rang, but she would like to meet up, afterward, for a coffee or something, just to hear what had been said.

Roger had said he wanted to be there; since the funeral he had been terribly protective of her where Margaret was concerned. Polly had said she should choose a neutral public place, so that Margaret would have to behave herself. Susan knew they both thought she was crazy for giving her sister houseroom, with everything that had gone on this year, but she couldn't bring herself to write her off.

She was curious, mostly. Alice was dead, and the two of them were estranged. She was afraid Margaret would go back to Australia and she would never see her again. That mattered: Susan had a happy family; she didn't have broken relationships.

Now a quiet, thin Margaret was sitting on the sofa with a mug of tea. "I just wanted to say . . . I'm sorry for how I was at the funeral."

"That's okay. They're always difficult."

"It's not okay, not at all. I had no right."

"It hasn't been easy, any of it, for either of us."

"No. But it's been harder for you. I know that. And I shouldn't have taken it out on you."

"Forget it. It's fine, Maggie."

She looked abjectly miserable, and Susan was moved. In her experience unhappy people were the ones who made the trouble. Happy people were too busy living their happy lives.

Margaret didn't seem to know where to go with the conversation once her apology had been accepted. How strange that we grew up together, Susan thought, came from the same womb into the same home and lived there together for years. And now we've nothing to say. "Had you thought when you might go home?"

"No plans, really. It's an open ticket. There's not a great deal to rush back for."

"But I thought you had work, and your friend—what's her name? Lindy?"

"I gave up my job when I heard about Mum. It wasn't much of a job, not going anywhere. Gave notice on my flat—I only rented. Lindy's great, a real mate. She's got some of my stuff stored at her place. I'll stay there when I go back, while I get myself sorted out. But she's got family of her own—five kids."

"Sounds like a handful."

"It is."

"You don't sound like you miss much?" Susan's question was light. She was afraid that Margaret would bolt if she pushed her.

When she answered, her sister didn't look at her. Her hands were clasped in her lap, and she turned them over to look at the palms, then back again, while she spoke. "It's been weird, coming back here. I didn't expect it to feel like coming home, and it doesn't." She was struggling to articulate her feelings. It was clearly not something she did very often. "I feel displaced, I suppose, like I don't belong either here or there." She'd found a thread, and she sat forward. As if she had heard Susan's silent question, she said, "I'm middle-aged and I've got nothing, Susan. My parents are dead—they both died without me there, not really understanding me, I know that; I've stuffed up my relationship with my sister and her family. I screwed up my marriage. I've got no kids of my own, no career. I haven't even got my own home, for God's sake, or even my own country."

"Mum and Dad loved you."

"That's the easy part, though isn't it? I loved them too. But I would have liked them to understand me, to like me. Love, mother for child, is unconditional and involuntary. Liking has to be earned."

"They told themselves you'd be happier in Australia."

Margaret laughed. "I told myself that, too. Ten thousand

miles—seemed like far enough away. Trouble is, I took myself with me, didn't I?"

Now Susan was laughing. "Why do you give yourself such a hard time?"

"Because I'm a shitty person, Suze."

"Don't be daft."

"It's not daft. I have the Midas touch of shittiness. Everything I touch goes wrong."

"What happened with Greg—do you mind me asking?"

"No, I don't mind. I used him, I think. Ticket to Australia."

"That's not true. You loved him. I remember. It was the first time I'd ever seen you like that with a man."

"Did I?" Margaret seemed surprised. "Yeah, well, maybe I did. I don't think he loved me, though, not once he got me over there and saw me against the backdrop of his own life."

"Weren't you happy at all?"

"Oh, sure, it was easy enough to be happy to start with. We had a house of our own. I remember the day we moved in. We made love in every room."

"On one day?"

Margaret giggled. "It wasn't very big." She gazed into the middle distance, remembering. "It must have started going wrong pretty soon. I was homesick—can you believe that?—we didn't have much money, and I couldn't get a decent job. Then I got pregnant, even though we thought we were being so careful."

"You had a baby?" Susan couldn't believe that was possible.

"No. I lost it—early on, it wasn't too bad."

"I'm sorry."

"Suze, it's years ago."

"Still."

"Well, anyway, having gone crazy at me for being so stupid when I first found out, Greg went all nuts when I lost the baby. He was desperate for us to try again. He sort of hated me for not being as upset as he was. Said I was selfish."

"What?"

"Maybe I was. I just didn't see the hurry, that was all. I'd have loved to have kids, but I wanted a bit of time for myself after I lost the first one."

"That's understandable."

"Yes, well. I think Greg thought it was understandable that he should seek solace in the arms of the receptionist at his work."

"Oh, Maggie."

"It went on for about two years without me having a clue, you know? Can you believe that?"

"I suppose I can, if you didn't want to recognize the signs. How did you find out in the end?"

"I caught them together one day."

"Oh, Christ."

"No, no, not like that. Not in bed or anything. I went into his office one day—I don't remember what for. They were there, not kissing or anything, but I just knew, you know? You could tell from the way they were together. Standing too close, maybe. Don't know. That night at home I asked him about it, and he said it was true. He didn't apologize. He said he was glad I'd found out, it had been a burden, keeping it from me all those months."

"What did you do?"

"I said I was glad he'd been able to unburden himself, slapped his face and left—the house, the street, Melbourne. Never went back."

"That was brave."

"D'you think? Pretty stupid, if you ask me. He got the house, pretty much everything in it, and the receptionist. I got bugger all."

"Is that when you went to Sydney?"

She nodded. Susan remembered when Maggie had moved. She just hadn't ever told them it was without Greg.

"Why didn't you tell us?"

"Pride, I think. That and shame. I know it sounds ridiculous, but in those days I was young and naïve enough to think I'd get divorced and find someone else. I figured if I waited until I was married to another guy, you wouldn't worry about me or dwell on the failure."

"But you never did?"

"I guess he screwed me up more than I thought he had."

"I'm so sorry, Maggie."

"See, Suze? That's why I never told you. That face. I don't want pity. I don't want sympathy."

"Why not? They're part of love, Maggie, part of caring about someone else. What's so wrong with that? Do you think I show the boys sympathy when they're hurt, when they've failed an exam or been dumped by a girl they liked, or dropped from the football team?"

Maggie shrugged.

"Of course I do, and not because I see them as weak, or failed, but because I love them."

Her sister gave her a half smile that got nowhere near her eyes. "See, Suze? I told you. I'm a lost cause."

"You're not a lost cause, Maggie." She came and sat beside her.

Margaret bristled a little. "I'm not a project, either."

"For God's sake, I'm not trying to treat you like one. I'm trying to treat you like a sister, if you let me."

Margaret smiled properly this time. "We could try that, I suppose."

Susan nudged her, gently, with her shoulder. And Margaret nudged back.

OCTOBER
READING GROUP

REBECCA

DAPHNE DU MAURIER © 1938

"Last night I dreamt I went to Manderley again . . ."

Working as a lady's companion, the heroine of Rebecca *learns her place. Her future looks bleak until, on a trip to the South of France, she meets Maxim de Winter, a handsome widower whose sudden proposal of marriage takes her by surprise. She accepts, but whisked from glamorous Monte Carlo to the ominous, brooding Manderley, the new Mrs. de Winter finds Max a changed man. And the memory of his dead wife, Rebecca, is forever kept alive by the forbidding housekeeper, Mrs. Danvers . . .*

Not since Jane Eyre has a heroine faced such difficulty with the Other Woman. An international best-seller that has never gone out of print, Rebecca *is the haunting story of a young girl consumed by love and the struggle to find her identity.*

I have news about Clare, everyone," Susan said. "She's decided what to do with herself—Mary told me yesterday. Clare asked her to let us know. I think Mary half hoped she would come along and tell us herself, but I guess she can't face that."

Polly looked down at the book on her lap.

"What, then?" Nicole asked.

"She's jacked in her job at the hospital. She's going to Romania with one of those aid agencies—Save the Children, I think Mary said—to work in one of those orphanages. She trained as a nurse before she went into midwifery, of course, and they're still crying out for medical staff over there. Mary says just because it's dropped out of the world's consciousness it doesn't mean the problem's gone away. She'll be there for at least a couple of years, Mary thinks."

They could all recall what they had seen on the news—hard for anyone, let alone a mother, to forget. The rows and rows of high-sided cots with tattered bed linen occupied by thin, haunted-looking, hollow-eyed children whom no one wanted, no one loved. The sense of Clare's decision was obvious to all of them, but this didn't underestimate what it meant for her to do this. It meant she had accepted that she wasn't going to have children of her own. It meant she had recovered to the point where she could see a world outside her own misery, and could want to do something about it. It was huge, and they all felt humbled by it.

"Bloody good for her." Harriet was the first to speak. "She'll be brilliant."

"She will. Her parents must be so proud of her."

"They are," Susan said, "except that they know they're going to miss her horribly, and worry about her constantly."

"She'll be fine. She was always a lot stronger than she looked—inside, I mean," Nicole said. "It'll probably save her."

"I hope so."

"I'm glad for her."

Harriet was remembering a day about three years earlier. She'd been sitting in a coffee shop in town, having palmed off the kids on her cleaner. She'd been desperate for a break. She had a serious baby belly left over from Chloe, was wearing no makeup and had just picked up a copy of the *Daily Mail*, which someone had left on the seat beside her. She'd heard her name and turned to see a girl she knew from college—Sarah. She'd always liked her, but their worlds had only ever overlapped, and they hadn't stayed in touch after graduation. She looked fabulous, all ethnic and stylish and thin, and Harriet had wanted to hide behind the *Cosmo* guide to bikini diets and die.

Sarah had given no indication that she was appalled by Harriet's appearance, or reading material, had ordered herbal tea and sat down beside her. It turned out she worked for the United Nations in Africa, coordinated all the charity contributions. She'd been living in Mombasa and Nairobi for the last six years and was home on her annual trip to stock up on Marmite and Tampax. "And what about you?" she'd asked, all open-faced and interested. "What are you up to these days?" Harriet had pulled out the credit card holder from her Louis Vuitton handbag and shown Sarah the pictures of Josh and Chloe. That was it. Harriet had tried to tell herself that Sarah would probably swap it all tomorrow for a husband, a couple of cute babies and an Aga. She had told herself she was a Judas for denying the children, denying the joy and the fullfilment and the satisfaction of being their mother. But she hadn't even convinced herself. For years she'd been having Josh and Chloe, been making a real hash of raising them. And that was it. That was all. Didn't feel that much, that morning. And it didn't now. Not with Tim gone. Not with Clare doing this amazing, brave, selfless thing. She couldn't remember ever having been more miserable.

The red lights on the baby monitor began dancing, and

Spencer's insistent cry was broadcast into the moment. "Sounds like someone wants to join the reading group. Has he finished the book, though?" Susan said.

Polly was secretly pleased—she had hoped he would make an appearance so that she could show him off to the others. Harriet and Nicole hadn't even met him yet. He was a sociable little thing; he'd probably woken for a cuddle, reassurance. She excused herself and went upstairs.

Spencer turned his head as he heard the door open and stopped crying. Polly could hardly wait until he was old enough to stand up in his cot and hold out his arms to be picked up—that was the best welcome in the world, even at five in the morning. She held him up to her shoulder and stroked his bald little Friar Tuck patch. "Are you coming down, then, little man? Did you want to meet Granny's friends? Well, all right, then."

Downstairs, Susan was pouring more wine, and the oven timer was going off. Polly handed Spencer to Nicole, who was in the armchair nearest to the door. "Here. Could you take him while I go and switch that off?"

Harriet jumped up between them. "Me, me! I'll have him."

Nicole smiled at her but said, "You wait your turn, Harry. I'll take him, Polly."

"Thanks."

Nicole couldn't believe how small, warm and solid he felt. She couldn't conjure up the feeling of her own children when they had been this small. She put him against her neck to smell him. She remembered the fragrance. Harriet came and sat on the arm of her chair, watching her. "He's gorgeous, isn't he?"

"He is. Absolutely lovely." She didn't want to hold him anymore. She laid him flat and passed him up to Harriet. "You take him."

"Okay." Harriet stood behind her, jiggling him. He felt like heaven. Her big sister Charlotte, the one who lived in Canada, had given birth to her first child, Fergus, when Harriet was about twenty. She'd been with a girlfriend—Natalie—from college at her parents' house in Shropshire for Natalie's twenty-first birthday when he'd been born. She'd been so happy, she remembered, and she'd delighted in giving all these details—date, time, name, weight, length—to Natalie's mother. He was the first baby in the family, Harriet had said, and she couldn't imagine how he felt. Natalie's mother had wrapped Aga-warmed old-fashioned weights in a few terry tea towels, seven pounds' worth, and handed the bundle to her. "It feels a bit like that," she had said, and Harriet had sat with it on her lap, imagining the new life.

Now she looked at Spencer and remembered Tim talking about a new baby. She had dismissed the idea out of hand. First it would have meant regular sex with him for a few months, and second, she had been so sure she didn't want to go through it all again. The vast bulk of herself beforehand. The agony and indignity of childbirth, and then the leaking breasts and stitched bits. The sleeplessness. And the cycle of babyhood: lying inert, then rolling over—usually from the bed to the floor, which was how Harriet had discovered a new level of mobility in her children. Crawling. The backbreaking just-walking stage. And those were the easy bits. Screaming and rigid in pushchairs, snotty and sullen in supermarket trolleys.

Holding Spencer now, she thought she would give everything she had to be cradling Tim's baby, with him beside her.

"So how many people had read this before we just did it for group?"

The others shook their heads. "Just me?" Nicole said. "I'm surprised. Clare was a fan, I remember. I just assumed we'd all have read it as younger women—I was only about fifteen when I first read it—and I was interested in how we'd read it as older women."

"I always meant to, a bit like *War and Peace*," Harriet said. "I just never got round to it."

She wasn't her normal self this evening, Susan thought. Quiet. And she looked awful, all gray round the edges. Perhaps the shock of Josh's accident was catching up with her. She knew from Roger that it could happen like that. She'd try to snatch a chat with her later, see if she was okay.

"I've been waiting for the miniseries." Polly laughed. Under the circumstances Polly was looking pretty good. No sleep, ex-boyfriend who wasn't quite ex enough. She looked to Susan as if she had all the hormonal glow of a new mother without the jelly tummy—and didn't seem tired at all.

"Verdicts, then?"

"Loved it. It was great. It had everything. Drama, tension, mystery, rugged hero, arch villain . . ."

"You're making one of the great Gothic novels of modern times sound like a James Bond."

"Sorry, but I like something that makes me keep turning the pages. I didn't get it either, that he had killed her. Even when they found the body buried in the boat. I just thought she must have had a lover or something."

"I didn't really understand why he had married her in the first place. Did I miss something, or do you usually not marry people you can't stand, then kill them when you've had enough?"

"Artistic license, Suze, please!"

"I thought Max was cruel. And I thought there was a quite stunning lack of communication in that marriage. Not at all how a relationship would work in reality. I know she was a mouse, and that she was in awe of him, and then in awe of the house, and the lifestyle and everything, but I had trouble accepting that she was so pathetic she never asked him a single thing about Rebecca, and that he was so cruel he never told her about it, even when it was obvious that she was suffering and confused . . ."

"I know. It should be a marriage guidance–prescribed text, shouldn't it? 'The Damage That Miscommunication Can Do to a Marriage.' If they'd talked it through in the South of France, things would have been a hell of a lot simpler. I mean, they don't even do it, do they, until after he's told her?"

"I missed that."

"Me too. I rather thought they hadn't done it at all."

"And there'd have been no book. Hardly a gripping plot, is it? Man who has been unhappily married finds contentment with young second wife? I think you've got to stop applying modern values to it and enjoy it for what it is—a splendidly creepy, atmospheric story. De Winter is in a tradition of great heroes, all of them emotionally retarded, who have a bit of mystery and an edge of cruelty—like Mr. Rochester in *Jane Eyre*, Hamlet . . ."

"Here she goes." Nicole rolled her eyes and cocked her head toward Harriet.

"Seriously, though, if you're talking about what makes a 'classic,' doesn't it have to be timeless? Don't you have to be able to apply what you call modern values to it and still find something relevant and pertinent in it? Isn't that the whole point of people like Shakespeare—that once you strip away the puffy shorts and the incomprehensible language, he's talking about stuff that still applies—the biggies—love, jealousy, ambition . . ."

"And that's true here. Jealousy runs through its core. The new wife, de Winter himself, the deeply twisted Mrs. Danvers . . ."

"Jealousy is more motivational than love here, isn't it, almost?"

"Aha—but can you be jealous of things you don't love?"

"No. It always comes down to love in the end, doesn't it?"

"Stop the car!"

Harriet slammed on the brakes. "What for?"

"Because I can't stand it, that's what for. Can't stand us. Not for another minute."

"What do you mean?"

"We're doing my head in. Isn't this crucifying you too?"

"Of course it's crucifying me too. I just don't know what to do about it." Tears were very near the top of Harriet's agenda.

"Don't you cry! Don't you dare."

Harriet sniffed melodramatically.

"I'll tell you the first thing we're going to do about it. We're going to go in there and have a drink." Nicole was gesturing at the wine bar ahead.

It was smoky and trendy, and attracted a young, fun crowd, which included a couple of minor celebrities from children's cable television. Harriet looked at Nicole as if she was mad. It was ten-thirty. "Why?"

"Well, because I'm in no hurry to get back to my house, and there's sure as hell nothing for you at yours except a surly babysitter, who'll get happier with each extra fiver she earns from you staying out, so why not?"

"I'm not sure a drink is the answer."

"Yeah? Well, since you don't appear to have any better ideas, I'm prepared to give it a chance. I'm not pregnant, am I? I can drink as much as I want. So can you. We could stay there until closing and get absolutely off our faces, if that's what we wanted to do. There's no one to stop us."

Harriet still looked unsure. Nicole persisted. "We used to have fun, you and me. We used to laugh all the time. Now, we've had a fairly fucking miserable autumn, and I've had enough. I want to have a laugh with you, Harry."

"I've had two glasses already, at Poll's."

"I'll get us a cab."

"It's a school night."

"You don't go to school."

"Very cute. My children do. In my car."

"I'll take them."

Harriet knew when she was beaten. "Okay, if you insist. But I'm not promising laughs." Her face was set, grim.

Nicole punched her arm. Quite hard. "Try."

Harriet rubbed her arm ruefully, then laughed in spite of herself. "All right, you Nazi. I'll try."

It was loud inside, excited chatter with a backbeat Nicole recognized vaguely from Cecile's radio. She pushed Harriet in the direction of an empty table and went to the bar. The barman, tall and slim with a floppy blond fringe and a length of brown leather tied round his neck, looked her up and down with predatory interest. "A bottle of champagne, please. Two glasses." She took out her purse and laid thirty pounds on the bar.

He looked over her shoulder at Harriet, who was sitting hunched and uncomfortable. She hadn't taken off her jacket. "Celebrating, are we, ladies?" He was Australian.

Nicole picked up the bottle and gave him her broadest smile. "I certainly bloody hope so, mate! Keep the change."

"Champagne?" Harriet's voice said she'd rather be drinking turps. "What are we celebrating?"

"I want to drink to lots of things." Nicole poured two full glasses expertly. She'd drunk enough champagne with Gavin all these years. Too bad they'd always been celebrating him getting away with being a complete shit. She put a glass into Harriet's hand, and clinked it convincingly with her own. "Here's to the end of the Gavin era. Here's to my new job. Here's to that barman fancying the ass off me even though I'm old enough to . . . Well, I'm not old enough to be his mother, am I?" She thought for a moment. "I'm old enough to teach him a few things, I reckon, and still young enough that he'd probably let me. So here's to that."

Harriet raised her glass halfheartedly and drank.

"There's more!" She looked straight and hard at Harriet. "Here's to you getting Tim back."

The morning he had left, Harriet had been sitting in her car outside Nicole's house when she got back from the gym. She was crying and listening to Elvis Costello sing "I Want You." Harriet could certainly do high drama, but this time Nicole had seen it was real. Knowing all along that Harriet had been an idiot about Tim was no consolation in the face of this abject misery.

"It's like I woke up from some horrible catatonic state the second he left me. Because he left me. A second too late," Harriet had said, hiccuping and snorting.

Nicole knew Harriet wasn't sleeping well. She had been having nightmares. Vivid, real, graphic ones. Tim in bed with someone else, making love to her. A woman without a face. Or cellulite. She said they made her so physically, demonically jealous that she felt sick. The house was spooky, too, without him. Harriet had cleaned everywhere. She'd given up watching television and, instead, listened to old CDs. So many songs reminded her of him. She spent her evenings looking at photographs, carefully stuck down and annotated in albums—by Tim, of course. She'd complained, of course, said it was anal to be so up-to-date with your photographs, said his comments in the margins were naff. Now she pored over every one, looking intently at his face and hers. Looking for clues, maybe.

Nicole had to hope that he wasn't serious, that he wanted to scare her into realizing what he and Nicole had known all along, that they were right for each other, that they were meant to be together. Any other possibility was untenable. Nicole loved Harriet, but she knew her friend had been mean to Tim, and not just about Nick—the Nick thing wasn't all that significant in the scheme of things: after all, she hadn't gone through with it, had she? The damage she had inflicted on Tim was much more subtle than another man. It was the cold shoulder, the making him feel as if he didn't affect her, the way she ignored him all evening when they were out in a group. That was far worse. Surely he wouldn't have found someone else. Whatever else Nicole doubted, it wasn't Tim's commitment to Harriet. It had to be a game. And she guessed that on some level he was counting on her to make Harriet play it.

Looking at the limp dishrag that sat in front of her now, Nicole wondered how in the hell she was expected to galvanize Harriet into anything approaching action.

"It's too late. It must be, or he would never have left. I've blown it. If there isn't another woman now, how long will it take for him to find someone better for him than I am?"

"I can't believe I'm hearing this," Nicole said, exasperated.

"Well, it's true. I've been a complete bitch. I've got what I de-served. I'm a flipping genius, I am. I got the greatest man ever to fall out of love with me. That's it. He's gone, Nic."

"You haven't."

Now it was Harriet's turn to lose patience. Couldn't Nicole see what she had done? "Most men would have gone years ago. He lasted longer than anyone else would have done. The first night we knew Josh was going to live, the first night I came home to sleep, after we'd been so close, together every moment at the hos-pital, he wanted to make love to me. He put his arms round me in our bed, and I could feel that he wanted me, wanted to be close there, like we had been in the hospital. I wouldn't even let him kiss me, not properly. I just pretended to be sleepy, and I rolled over as soon as I could. That night, of all nights. I don't know why. It's no wonder he's left, Nicole. I wasn't giving him anything he needed that he couldn't get from a service apartment and a good PA. I wasn't being a wife to him. I haven't been a wife to him for years. Probably ever."

"But you want to be?"

"Of course I do. But he's gone, hasn't he? He's given up on me. I can't fight that."

"Yes, you bloody well can. Is this my friend Harriet talking? I can't believe I'm hearing it! Fight for him, for Christ's sake. If you're telling me the truth, and you really want him back, and you're not just afraid of being alone, then fight for him. Why aren't you up there right now?"

"It wouldn't work. Men like Tim don't leave if they don't mean it."

"That's exactly where you're wrong. I think it's a classic cry for help. I think it was the only thing he could think of that would make you sit up and take notice of him and his feelings. I think he'd have you back like a shot, if you could make him see you meant it, that it was really him you wanted."

"You think?" Harriet sat up a little.

Nicole reached across the table and took her hand. "I'm sure." She squeezed. "Harriet, I don't know much. My own marriage has been a disaster, and maybe I'm the last person who should be giving advice. But I know Tim loves you. He once told me he thought he was born to love you. He is absolutely devoted to you. I am more sure of that than I am about almost anything else in my life. I have never known a man love a woman like I think he loves you. You've hit the jackpot. He wants you, he wants his kids, and he wants this life. You just have to tell him that that's what you want too. You have to make him believe it. Tell him you've been a stupid bitch, chasing some nonexistent bloody rainbow, and that you've woken up to yourself. That's all. I'm telling you."

"D'you think?" She looked like Dorothy in *The Wizard of Oz* when the good witch tells her she can go back to Kansas. She looked as though she believed that Nicole saying it made it so. That was part of Harriet's appeal, that childlike quality of trust and dependence, Nicole realized. That was part of the spell.

"I think."

"Then I will. I'll make him come back. I will."

Nicole felt relief flood through her. In a funny way Harriet's marriage meant more to her now than her own, because hers had been bad and Harriet's was good, and if it lasted, it proved something was true, and she needed that to be the case just now. "Good. Good. So, enough of lying around mooning over photographs and listening to some truly tragic eighties pop. Promise?"

Harriet giggled. She'd drained the first glass while she was listening to Nicole and was now halfway through the second. "If I can pull this off, no more mooning. But I'll never give up my Elvis Costello, and Bruce—the Boss—he stays too."

Nicole refilled her glass and tapped it against Harriet's. "Okay, Rome wasn't built in a day. We'll work on it."

"Nic?"

"Yeah?"

"What's the quickest way to lose half a stone?"

Tim

Tim was drunk. His friend Rob hadn't seen him so drunk for years—or, rather, drunk like this. They'd been housemates at university, and best mates, he hoped, ever since, and they had certainly sunk a few thousand beers over the years, but this was different.

Tim was a fantastic, amiable drunk at college. He was tall, so he could drink five or six pints without much effect except on the dance floor, where his gangly frame became more and more loose-limbed and dangerous to bystanders. But he always got you home—you could rely on that if you wanted to get completely bladdered—because he never wore the beer goggles of most of his peers, the ones that had you roaming the front quad in search of available women susceptible enough to your charms, or drunk enough, to overlook that you would never know their last name and take you to their rooms anyway. Tim never did that. He had kept a pretty little girlfriend from the sixth form for the first two years and worked hard for his degree during the third. Class of 'eighty-six, they were. Economics graduates, with jobs in the bag and wealth in their sights. Tim had been more successful than Rob—he had gone for the flat-rate-pay safe route, training as an analyst, rather than the get-rich-quick-then-burn-out path. He had diligently sat his regulatory exams with the FSA, Financial

Services Authority, grandfathered in as a market practitioner at thirty-three, and was now an acknowledged expert in the media sector. His personal stock in the City was spectacularly high. Rob had made a lot of money, too, with his flamboyant, dare-or-die attitude to the markets, but he was ten a penny, cannon fodder in a financial war, and he knew it.

Tim had been good fun after graduation, too. They'd gone round the world together, following the well-trodden steps of a million kids from the Home Counties, then settled down in a two-bed flat near Clapham Common to real life. And, eventually, in Tim's case, with Harriet, whom Rob adored, because she was funny, and sexy, and had let Tim out to play from time to time before they had had the kids. His wife, Paula, who'd come along three or four years after Harriet, was godmother to Chloe, so Rob considered himself and Tim more family than anything. He hadn't seen much of him lately—a few snatched lunches at Corney & Barrow, but no full-on sessions for months. Now Tim was drinking alone at a table in the corner of Pavilion, looking unkempt and tired, and Rob was worried.

He was pissed, that much was obvious, but it was only seven o'clock. Rob had only been twenty minutes late—a difficult phone call from the States had come through just as he was leaving—but Tim looked like he had been here for some time.

"What do you mean, you've left her?"

"Which bit is hard to understand? Left, moved out. I've left." Tim's voice was aggressive, but his face was a picture of misery.

"Where have you gone?"

Tim almost laughed. So typical of Rob to ask where, rather than why. He loved his friend, but Rob had the emotional depth of a puddle. Maybe he should have got him to bring Paula. She might have been better at this. Then he remembered that Paula was pregnant, with a boy—they'd had the scan last month—and Rob had already asked him to be a godfather. He didn't think he could bear to see them with each other, so happy. "I'm staying at the RAC."

"Christ, that must be a bit rough." Living at his club? That was sad. All right for a night when you got too pissed or worked too late to get home, although Tim was normally a homing pigeon in that situation, but not to live. Tim stared into his glass. 'You want to come and stay with me and Paula? I mean it, mate, you'd be welcome."

"Thanks, but no. You two don't want a miserable git hanging around right now."

"Offer stands." Tim nodded acknowledgment but didn't speak.

"So, do you want to tell me what it's all about, or just sit here and get shitfaced? I'm easy either way."

Tim laughed grimly. He was clearly already well on the way to the latter.

"Has she got someone else?"

"I don't think so, although a few months back I thought there might be someone—but I think it's the *idea* of it, mainly."

"I'm not with you."

"No, and nor is she. It's like I drive her crazy, like she hates me, Rob, because I'm not someone else—some*thing* else."

Rob might have had a strategy ready for the other-guy scenario—it was in his arsenal of solutions for "normal" man problems, like deal gone wrong, wife overspending, team relegated, but he was clever enough to know that he couldn't help constructively with this one. If counseling, Prozac and lawyers might be involved, it was a case for Paula. He wished she was here.

He opted for flying in the face of what Tim was slurring. Straight denial. "No, mate. She loves you. I'm sure of it."

"You think?"

"Course I do. You and Harriet, you're watertight, Tim. Look at the other couples we know who've come apart. Nothing like you two. You've got this great life—great house, great kids, great future."

Tim shook his head dismissively. "Yeah, fucking great, except that she spends all her time worrying about what she might be missing—whether she might have been happier if she'd gone for someone else." He rubbed his hand wearily across his face. He wasn't sleeping. He missed the indentation, the sound and smell of her body next to his in the bed, and every time he woke up through the night he reached out for her.

"She doesn't even want me to touch her. I can't remember the last time she made the first move." His expression was pained.

Too much information, Rob was thinking. It might be okay for women to talk about that sort of stuff, but he had given up the blow-by-blows with one-night stands and bedpost notching. The last thing he wanted was to look at Harriet when he saw her and think she was frigid—or anything else in that department, thank you very much. "I'm out of my depth here, Tim. I don't know what to tell you, mate." He patted his friend's shoulder uncomfortably. "What I do know is that you sitting in the RAC and her in the house isn't going to make it better, is it?"

"Aha. That's the point." Tim's head was rolling in a vague figure of eight as he spoke. "Exactly the point. This is make or break, mate." He never called Rob mate when he was sober. "I've removed myself, haven't I?" He wasn't making any sense.

"How many of these have you had, Tim?"

There were two chaser glasses on the table next to his pint. "Not enough. I love Harriet. I haven't so much as looked at another woman that way since I met her—you know that as well as anyone." Rob nodded. "And I want to fight for her. I do. But I can't fight out loud, that won't get me anywhere. I have to gamble, you see. I have to give her what she thinks she wants—space from me, a life without me, her freedom back. And I just have to hope it pays off. D'you see?"

Almost, Rob thought. He was wondering whether there were any cabs outside that might take Tim if he could hold him up straight.

"And if it doesn't, I'll walk away. Lose everything. Give it all up. The kids, Harriet."

Rob was horribly afraid that he was going to cry.

"I have to know, that's all. I can't live like this anymore. It's killing me."

"Come on, you're coming home with me tonight."

Tim shook his head vigorously.

"No arguments. Come on."

Tim leant on him. He didn't have the strength to argue. The fresh air outside the pub hit him in the face, but it didn't sober him up. He had drunk far too much far too fast.

"It'll pay off, Tim, I'm sure it will. This time next week you'll be home and this nonsense will have been sorted out—I'm sure it will."

"Are you?" Tim was childlike, as if he believed that if Rob said it would be okay it would be.

"Too right. Then we'll go out and get drunk the proper way, shall we?"

"To celebrate?"

"To celebrate."

"It's like that song, isn't it? Who was it? Sting I think. You know"—and now he broke into it discordant, high-pitched—"If you love someone, set them free. Free, free, set them free . . ."

Even through the fug of his drunkenness, and the disharmony of his own singing, Tim felt a shiver of fear. That future, the one where it did work out okay and Harriet loved him again, was the only one he could contemplate, drunk or sober.

The next morning he felt like death. He just couldn't do it anymore. His body was at his desk at six-forty-five, just like always, but his stomach and his head were somewhere else. He looked awful, too, he was unsurprised to find out when he went to splash his face with cold water in the washroom. The bright white of his shirt (brighter, it had to be said, for being washed, starched, ironed and hung by the club's laundry service than when it was washed with Chloe's navy swimsuit and shown the iron briefly during *Holby City* on a Tuesday night) made his face look gray and lined. His eyes were bloodshot, and his tongue, on close inspection, looked as mossy as the patio. He suspected, too, that he smelt.

He hadn't hung around long at Rob and Paula's this morning, avoiding breathing his toxicity over pregnant Paula by kissing her bump in a gesture she clearly thought endearing. She'd rubbed his hair maternally. "It'll be all right. Rob told me. It'll pay off." She'd winked kindly, then settled down to the three rounds of toast, with honey and Marmite, that Rob had made for her.

Back at his desk, Tim rooted around in the top drawer, looking for painkillers. He couldn't find any, and he was just looking up petulantly for his PA when she came in. In one hand she had a mug of coffee and two aspirin, in the other the morning's post. That was why he adored her, called her Moneypenny and spent a hundred pounds on Chanel perfume for her every time he went through duty-free. She was better than his mother.

She put down her offerings quietly beside him and watched sympathetically while he took the pills, even though the coffee was too hot and made him wince. She looked like Julie Andrews in *Mary Poppins*, but about three stones heavier. He remembered Harriet making an excuse to come in and meet her, just after he'd employed her, about five years ago. "I want to make sure you haven't hired a babe," she had said, and was satisfied instantly by the sight of Sylvia bending over a filing cabinet to retrieve something and blocking out all the natural daylight in the room. He'd been happy she cared.

"I'll take your calls for half an hour, let those have a chance to work," she said. Then, as she reached the door on her way out, without turning round, she added, "Top letter's from Harriet."

Monday
Dear Tim

I'm writing not talking because (a) I'm not at all sure you want to see me or speak to me just now, and (b) even though I don't express myself brilliantly on paper, it's probably better than blurting and wittering and going on, and I can't say much at the moment without crying, and we both know that that just comes across as manipulative, and I don't want you to think that, so I'm going to try writing. The thing is this. You have to forgive me and come home and make our family and me complete again, because it is wrong without you here and it could never be right.

I know I've been a lousy wife. Especially lately, but probably for years. I've taken you for granted, and I've been preoccupied with obsessing that the grass is greener, and I've been selfish and stupid. Early midlife crisis, maybe. Or late adolescence. I don't know why.

But you've left me, and I can't bear it.

*Part of taking you for granted has been assuming that you
would always be here with me, sorting out my messes and
putting up with my nonsense like you have done all our lives
together, and now I'm afraid, so, so afraid, that you've had
enough and washed your hands of me.*

*I'll do anything. I'd have done it already if I'd known what
it was. I love you, Tim, all the ways I should. I promise you
that if you come home it will all be okay. Better than okay.
Just please come home to me.*

I love you.

Harriet

xxx

He waited ten minutes before he picked up the phone. Long
enough to calm down, although he had wanted to run out of the
door to her as soon as he'd read the letter. There was no question
of making her suffer. Idiot that he was, he felt the pain he had inflicted on her ten times over.

"Hello?"

"Harriet?"

"Tim. Hello." So much hope in her voice. Hope and fear. "How
are you?"

"Hungover as hell, thank you. I had a big night with Rob. How
are you?"

"Much the same, except without the alcohol, I think."

"I got your letter." Harriet didn't say anything. "We need to
talk." Was he being deliberately ambiguous? He didn't know. He
didn't want to do this over the phone. He wanted to see her, hold
her.

"I know. Do you want me to come to you?"

"No. I'll come home." He had said it. Home. It felt good.

"You're coming home?"

Her voice made him want to cry. She wanted him home. "I'll
come home to talk, Harriet."

She was eager to please now. "Okay, okay—tonight?"

"Actually, I haven't got too much on today, so I can probably
get away this afternoon."

"Great. I'll see you then." A pause. "Do you want to see the kids?"

"Just you for now, if that's okay. Can you get Nicole to have them, or something? They won't help, will they?"

"No, no, of course. I'll talk to Nic—I'm sure it'll be fine."

"Okay, then. See you later."

"See you later. Thanks . . . for calling." Strangely formal.

Two people put down phones and sat back in their chairs to wait for their hearts to stop pounding tattoos in their chests.

Harriet

She hadn't seen him for days. Weeks. She knew exactly: twenty-three days. She had only heard his voice on the telephone. Twenty-three days. Five hundred and fifty-two hours. She'd never done daft things like that about him before, counting days or hours. Like riding past his house even though it was off your route. Doodling what your married name would be. Mr. and Mrs. Tim Fraser. Mrs. Tim Fraser. Harriet Fraser. Hadn't kept his love letters, or the Post-its on the fridge that said "I love you." Now after a stupid twenty-three days without him, she couldn't remember why not. She had never wanted someone so much as she did him, now. Physically. She ached, actually *ached* for him.

Would he have his suitcase with him? Could she dare to hope that he was going to give her another chance? Or was he coming to tell her, face-to-face, that he wasn't coming back? She knew that there wasn't anyone else, that there never had been. But maybe this time away from her had shown him the possibility of a life with another person. She was frightened. Scarlett O'Hara was back in her waking dreams again—running back to Rhett after Melanie died only to hear that he'd given up on her. But this wasn't a film. This was her life.

The kids were at Nicole's. She hadn't told them anything because she didn't know what to tell them. The house was quiet without them, and unfeasibly tidy. She had showered only an hour ago. She'd spent all morning with her hair up in one of Chloe's elastics, with a pink felt bunny on it, and her pajamas on, cleaning the house. She'd changed the sheets on the bed (which weren't even beginning to be smelly yet), ironing the 100 percent cotton Deschamp set they'd been given as a wedding present that had been on the bed only once before being eschewed for the crease-free poly-cotton John Lewis ones that gave you static shock if you moved too vigorously. She'd wiped down the tacky shelves in the fridge, even dared to put in a bottle of champagne to chill. Was she an idiot to plan for the best-case scenario? She'd hovered and dusted, and arranged fresh flowers in what she hoped was a vaguely Nicole way in the big glass vase. She'd swept out the fireplace and laid a new fire, properly, instead of just shoving the *Sunday Times* Culture section at the bottom under a massive log and hoping for the best when you poked the lit match into it. Consequently, it had been burning for an hour or so now, which was fifty minutes longer than her efforts usually lasted. Everywhere looked very unnatural.

She heard his car on the driveway and ran up to the half landing, where she could see it from behind the blind. He looked nervous. Stood by the car for a few moments, looking at the house. No case. She stood back against the wall, away from the window. Her heart sank to the pit of her stomach. Then she heard the doorbell. He wasn't using his key. He wasn't even treating this place like his home, let alone planning to come back to it. She wanted to hide under one of the beds, like Chloe would have done. She couldn't bear having to go through with it now. Sit on the sofa while he told her that it was over, that he was leaving her. She didn't want to hear it.

Her tread was heavy on each stair as she went down. She stood behind the door as she opened it, suddenly shy. Nothing. She put her head round it, but he wasn't on the doorstep.

She heard the boot slam, and then he was there, with his suit carrier in one hand and a beautiful bunch, tied with raffia and woven with eucalyptus leaves, of yellow roses. Yellow roses.

And then she didn't have to hear anything. And she didn't have to say anything. They had both done enough talking for now—to each other, to Rob and Nicole, and to themselves. This was just about instinct, and certainty, and, maybe for the first time ever, about balance. He knew it, and she knew it. The seesaw of their life had found its equilibrium. He put down the case and the flowers, kicked the door shut, and then he was on her. Kissing her mouth, her face and her neck, tangling his fingers in her hair and pulling at the buttons of her shirt with one hand, pushing into her bra. They backed into the sofa and fell down on it. Harriet pushed up his sweater, feeling his warm skin. He pulled up her skirt, and they kicked off his trousers together. He was inside her straightaway, oh, so easily, one arm tight under her hips, the other at her breasts.

And because she wasn't thinking about anyone or anything else, and because that dishonesty didn't make her close her eyes, she could watch him love her, and want her, and feel her. And know that he could see, in her eyes, all of those things. It was the best feeling.

"My God!" That was the first thing either of them said. And that was simultaneous too.

"My sentiments exactly."

"Why hasn't it always been like that?"

"Do you think it was the sofa?" He was still on top of her, still inside her.

"Well, if it was, I'm never going to do it in bed again *ever*." They laughed.

"Ooh, ow, get off me. You're too heavy to laugh on top of me." She couldn't breathe.

He flipped her over, without separating their flesh, so that they lay side by side on the cushions, with Harriet cocooned against the back. "Better?"

"Better." She kissed him once, a slow, gentle kiss on his top lip. "Best." They stayed there for a long time, next to the fire. It felt like a film. She didn't remember it feeling like a film before. It started to get dark. Tim pulled a blanket from the arm of the sofa over them.

"I thought I never *fell* in love with you. I think that was it."

"Thanks a lot. Now you tell me."

She pulled gently at his chest hair. "I'm trying to explain. Ssh. I sort of rolled into it, so I had a softer landing, and I never realized where I was . . ."

He was laughing at her now, silently.

"And I think I was looking for . . ."

"Harry?"

"Yeah."

"Shut up." He slid down so that their faces were level. Her expression was momentarily indignant. "Actually"—his lips were on hers, and his hand slid slowly down her back—"I think I'm going to have to make you shut up . . ."

Susan

"Christ, it's chilly in here."

"Hang on, I'll put the gas fire on."

"I'll draw the curtains. It's almost dark anyway."

Margaret and Susan busied themselves warming the house. Alice hadn't lived there since the spring, and its heart had gone cold.

Ten minutes later, with the lights on and the fire flaring artificial orange and red, the room was brighter, but the task ahead was still daunting, and Susan's companion still frosty.

"Did you not think you should have done some of this back in the summer after she'd moved out?"

"I didn't like to, not when Mum was still alive. It would have felt like a violation, going through her stuff. I think I would have kept wanting to ask her what she wanted to do with things—too hard. Maybe I thought she might come back one day."

Margaret conceded, grudgingly. "It's going to be a nightmare now."

Susan was determinedly bright. "It won't be too bad. Mum didn't have a great deal of stuff."

They looked around. Some of the furniture made Susan ache. The highly polished gateleg table at which she had eaten a thousand meals; the gay figurines in evening dress that had been on the mantelpiece forever; the brown button-back sofa she and Roger used to hold hands on. All those memories. "Well, this stuff might be worth something. Although God knows to whom. It's pretty hideous."

Susan was glad Margaret was here. She didn't want to wallow, and she didn't think that was likely while her cynical, unsentimental sister was on the rampage. It almost made her smile. And she did have a point. Alice's interior design was circa mid-1960s.

"Okay, furniture to the house clearers, most of the kitchen contents too, although I might have a quick look through. You should, too, in case there's anything you want to take."

Margaret snorted but half smiled.

"She didn't have any jewelry to speak of, apart from her wedding ring and her watch, but we'll have a look. Her clothes are probably for the charity shop, aren't they?"

"Well, you're too big and I'm too stylish for most of them, so yes, I think Oxfam it is."

Was it possible that Margaret was being playful? Susan wondered. A crying Margaret was one thing to get used to; a joking one was another. "You're so rude."

"Do you deny the charge?"

"No." She laughed, gesturing at her frame. "But you're still so rude."

"It's the Aussie way, Suze. Tell it like it is."

"The paperwork is going to be the real job. Mum never threw stuff like that away. It was almost like she was frightened of authority, like she hung on to stuff for security."

"It's probably mostly rubbish. That won't take long."

It took ages. It was, as Margaret had predicted, mostly out of date and irrelevant, and filed in three or four big cardboard boxes in the wardrobe in the spare room. The two women sat, legs apart, on the floor, leaning against the bed with a big black rubbish sack at either side of them. What took the time was the lovely stuff, the bits that brought their mother back to life.

Margaret found the bill for their parents' honeymoon. They'd stayed at a little hotel in Bournemouth for two nights; that would have been all they could afford. The bill showed that they'd had hot milk and biscuits sent up on their wedding night.

"What about the champagne? Surely a port and lemon, at least."

"It's the sweetest thing I ever read. Can't you just picture the two of them, feeling strange in a hotel—it was probably the first one either of them went to—wanting some hot milk?"

"Last of the red-hot lovers, Dad must have been! How they ever managed to have a honeymoon baby I'll never know."

"Maggie! You don't *have* to be drunk, you know."

"But it helps! Boom boom!" Margaret smacked her thigh lightly.

There were some photos, too, of the honeymoon, just three or four. Their father sitting on a towel on the sand, looking sleepy and happy and eating sweets from a paper bag.

"That's right. Dad and his sweet tooth—I remember Mum telling us they took sweets off rationing just as they got married. Dad said it was a wedding present from the government. Do you remember?"

"Yeah!" Margaret was nodding and smiling.

She'd kept all their school reports, too. Susan's final one said that she "possesses great skill in domestic areas" ("Charming! You'd get into huge amounts of trouble if you said that now about a girl. What a nerve!") and Margaret's "that for someone who has so little ambition, it is unsurprising that she has achieved so little" ("Fair cop. I did sod all at school.").

"I need a drink." Margaret stood up and stretched her arms above her head. "Would Mum have anything drinkable in, or shall we go to the pub? I'm quite hungry, actually. Do you fancy grabbing something to eat?"

"Are you giving up already?"

"Already? We've been here for hours!" Susan looked at her watch. Margaret was right: it was seven-thirty. Now that she thought about it, she *was* hungry. "Mmm. Okay. I didn't realize it was so late." She looked at the boxes still left to sort. "Didn't think it would take so long."

"It's nice, though, isn't it, in a way?"

Susan looked at her sister. "Yes, it is. It makes the real Mum feel closer again, doesn't it?" She leant on the contents of the box to help herself up. The pile slithered under her hand, and she lost her footing. A letter fell out onto the floor, and she bent to pick it up. On the envelope, Alice had written, in her old-fashioned, even hand, "For Margaret and Susan. To be read after my death," and she had signed it, formally.

"Hang on, Maggie. Look at this." Susan handed the envelope to her sister. "It must be instructions for what to do with some of this gear, I suppose." It was fat. They sat down on the edge of the bed together and pulled out a long letter, handwritten, from their mother. Susan had never seen so much of her mother's neat handwriting in one place before. They read it together, although Margaret was faster. Susan read every word slowly, almost moving her lips in time.

March 15, 1986
Dear Margaret and Susan,

If you have found this letter, then I'm gone. Maybe I should have had something so important lodged with a solicitor, instead of tucked away, but this is a secret I've held so close to my chest for so long that I can't give it up easily. I hope you are reading it together, although I don't know how likely that is, with the directions you've both taken. I've often wondered whether I should ever tell you. Your dad said not, said there was nothing to be gained from you knowing, but I think I would have wanted to know. There've been times in your lives when I've ached to tell you, but something—I don't know what—always made me hold it back. I know I'm a coward, leaving you to find it out after I'm gone.

Today is the thirtieth anniversary of my sister Dorothy's death. She was killed in a car accident, run over. She never had a mark on her face, that was the funny thing, but it killed her anyway. She looked like she was asleep, not dead. I never talked about her when you were growing up, I know, but I loved Dorothy more than anyone. She was a couple of years older than me, and she was so beautiful, always laughing and joking. She was the sort of person people just wanted to be around, but she always chose me, even though I was younger and quieter. I still miss her every day, especially this one day in the year.

Dorothy was your mum, Susan. There isn't really any other way to say it, except straight out. I'm sorry you never knew her, I truly am. I ought to explain to you how it happened, and say that I am sorry that I won't be around to give you answers to all of your questions.

Dorothy got pregnant, and she wasn't married. Things were very different then. They make it look all romantic in films, but the reality was nothing like that. She couldn't tell our parents. They'd have had nothing to do with her. Not unless she got married to the father sharpish, and took a few weeks off her dates. They had homes for girls like that, in those days, and they'd have put her in there, and then when the baby was born they'd have taken it away. I never knew who your father was, Susan. She wouldn't tell even me. My guess is that he was someone she loved, because Dorothy wasn't a bad girl, really, and that he turned out not to love her. He must have refused to marry her, scarpered when he found out she was pregnant. I don't know, I'm afraid. Maybe she would have told me eventually, if she hadn't died.

Anyway, she ran away, basically. She went up north, to Manchester, and got herself a job in the bus station, and told them her husband had been killed. She had some savings from her job down here. Not much, though, so I'm not sure how she managed. I sent her bits and bobs when I could. I was the only one who knew where she'd gone. I went with her to Woolworth's, before she caught the coach up there, to buy a wedding ring for her. She wrote to me, told me how she was getting on. I only saw her once, after you were born, Susan. I had Margaret by then, of course; there's only eleven months between you. I felt so guilty. Me pregnant at home, excited and happy, with a husband, a good man, to share it with. And Dorothy up there all alone. She brought you down, Susan, to see me. She loved you so very much. She had no money to speak of, but you were beautifully turned out, and you were such a pretty thing. I think she'd have been a brilliant mum. We went for tea at a Lyons Corner House with you girls. Margaret was just about up and walking, I remember, into everything. That's when she asked me. She gripped my hand tightly and said to me, "You promise me that if anything happens to me, you'll look after my Susan. You're all she's got, apart from me." I said I would, of course. But she kept asking me, made me say that I promised. I didn't think about it. You don't, do you, when you're young? You think you and everyone you love are going to live forever.

She died three weeks later. I got a message from her landlady. I couldn't believe it, that Dorothy, the most alive person I'd ever known, could be dead.

Your dad was wonderful. He never once complained, even though you were another mouth to feed, and there was a whole load of lies to tell. He never once told me I couldn't do it. He knew how much I loved her, you see. He knew I had no choice.

You were only five weeks old when you came to live with us, Susan. She hadn't even registered your birth—that's why me and your dad are on your birth certificate. As if she knew she wouldn't keep you for long. We didn't see much of my parents then, and Jonathan's were both dead, so we just said you'd come along early, and got on with things. I don't suppose you could get away with that sort of thing these days— social services and the police and everyone, they'd be involved. We managed it, though. And from that day you've been our daughter, not only to the outside world but to both of us too. We've loved you just as much as if you were. Just as much as Margaret. Maybe I loved you so much that's why I didn't tell you about your other mum, your real mum.

If I've made a mess of things, then I'm sorry. I don't think I've done everything right, but I've done my best. My best by Dorothy, and my best by you two girls. I'm so proud of both of you. I hope that telling you is the right thing to do now. I love you, my girls, and I hope we meet again someday.

Your loving Mother

Margaret had slipped her hand down to grip Susan's tightly. Neither of them said anything. As she finished each page, Susan laid it neatly, facedown, on her knees. She put down the last, and was still.

"Christ!" Margaret said. Susan didn't answer. When Margaret

stood up, she let the letter slide onto the floor and curled up against the peach satin of the counterpane. She hugged her knees to her chest and lay there, still, staring at nothing. Margaret was frightened. "Susan? Sis? Talk to me?" Susan just shook her head. When she got no other response Margaret said, "I'm calling Roger."

Susan heard her sister's voice, from downstairs. She couldn't make out the words, but she could hear the urgency.

"Did you tell him?" she asked, when Margaret had come back to her.

"Of course not. It's your news to tell." She sat then, beside her, with her back against the headboard and one hand on Susan's shoulder, while they waited for Roger. Susan wasn't ready to speak, and for once, Margaret understood something and kept quiet too.

When Roger got there, Susan still hadn't formed the news into things she could say aloud, so Margaret handed him the letter. "Oh, my darling," he said, when he had finished. And then she cried. He pulled her up and into his arms, and rocked her like a baby, saying several times, "Oh, my darling. Oh, my darling." Maggie didn't want to be there with them.

"I'll wait downstairs, go and start sorting through the china," she said.

Susan didn't acknowledge her, but Roger nodded and smiled at her over his wife's shoulder. When she had calmed herself, Susan tried to explain her tears. She was frantic that they be properly understood. They weren't for Dorothy, the mother she had never known. "I'm not angry with Mum. I hate that she would have died thinking I was going to be angry with her. How could you be angry at that? What she did was extraordinary—she took in someone else's child and loved it, loved me, so much, like I was her own. I couldn't do that. I'm angry that I never knew Dorothy. I've got so many questions—they're leaping around in my head—and they're never going to be answered now, and what kills me is that Mum"—her voice caught—"didn't trust me enough to tell me."

"What do you mean 'trust?'"

"I loved my mum more than anything, Rog, more than everyone I knew loved their mum, more than Maggie did, more than Alex and Ed love me. I adored her. She can't have known. In all those years I was growing up, she can't have known how much I loved her. What more could I have done to show her?"

"I don't understand why you think that."

Susan was exasperated. "Because—because if she'd known, she would have known it was okay to tell me. That it wouldn't make any difference. That, if it's possible, it would have made me think even more of her. And that makes me mad and sad. We could have talked about it. I could have asked all those questions and got answers, and now I'll be asking them forever and they'll never be answered."

"I know, I know." Roger was stroking her back as she spoke. "It's unbelievable." He was almost talking to himself. "It's so far-fetched. I never would have thought they had it in them, Alice and Jonathan. To do all that for you. I always thought you were your mum's favorite. Well, everyone did, you were—you were so alike, you two, that's the funny thing. You'd think Maggie was the adopted one."

"Poor Maggie."

"Why poor Maggie?" Susan had gone off on another tangent, and Roger was confused again.

"Because she knew it too, that I was Mum's favorite. But don't you see? It makes sense now." Not to Roger, who was baffled.

"Yes, we were more alike, had more in common, but even that's got to be because Mum tried harder with me. She was over-compensating, trying to love me for Dorothy, and probably Dad too. She thought she didn't have to worry so much about Maggie—she was with her real parents, wasn't she?" She cried again now, softly this time, tears of frustration. It felt like she was un-raveling a great tangle that was her childhood, but when she sep-arated all the threads and tried to follow them back to their beginnings, it wouldn't be there, because it was Alice and she was gone. It was like losing her all over again. "Where is Maggie?"

"She's still downstairs, I think."

Susan stood up and wiped her eyes on her sleeves. When Roger made to stand up too, she motioned at him to stay there. "Can you just give me a minute?" He nodded and blew her a kiss.

Margaret was downstairs in the living room, sitting before the sixties veneer sideboard with brown plastic handles where Alice had kept her mismatched dinner services. She was trying to put sets together, but she hadn't got far. She looked up when Susan came in, her face full of concern. She had been crying too, Susan could see.

"Are you okay?"

"Sort of. You?"

"More or less. Bit shocked, really."

"Yeah. How did she ever manage to keep it so secret, all those years?"

"Why did she want to, I'd like to know."

"I think she must have been trying to protect me."

"I suppose." Margaret's face seemed about to crumple. "Certainly wasn't trying to protect *me*, was she?"

"Oh, Mags, please don't hate her for it."

"Hate *her*? I don't hate her." Margaret was shaking her head. "I loved her too, you know, maybe not the way you did, Suze, but I loved her. I just never stopped being eaten up with jealousy, feeling hard done by because you two were so bloody close. And all the time she was my mum, not yours. We had something between us you could never have had. And I threw it back at her. Made both of them miserable—I know I did. And then I buggered off, had the world's biggest sulk for twenty years, stuffed up my own life and came back after it was too late. It's me I hate, not her. And now it's too late." Margaret jabbed at a pile of cups she had arranged on the side table. They fell to the floor and smashed. She put her head into her hands and cried. Susan fell to her knees beside her, and that was where Roger found them when he came down ten minutes later.

Polly

Jack hadn't told her he was coming, and Polly wasn't ready to see him. She hadn't got any makeup on, and she was wearing baggy clothes that she suddenly realized were neither clean nor fragrant. She hadn't been expecting anyone today. She and Spencer had been planning a lovely lazy day. At least, she had. Spencer, apparently, had had other plans. He'd been sick down two Babygros since lunchtime, carrot purée, no less. He was still wearing the second when the doorbell rang, and Polly answered the door holding him sick side out, his back to her front and his legs dangling.

She hadn't seen Jack for a couple of weeks, and her body responded to the sight of him as it always had. He looked great. He had new glasses, wire frames instead of plastic. Her manic inner self screeched with jealousy that someone else must have helped him choose them. Her instinct was to rage at him. She had asked him to stay away, to give her a chance to recover from loving him. Yet here he was again, presumably to muck her about. She didn't want him to come in. Cressida was away, Daniel was at football practice. He wasn't supposed to be here.

He spoke first. "Hello, Poll." Don't call me Poll. I'm not your Poll anymore.

He spoke quickly, having recognized the hostility across her brow. "I know you asked me to leave you alone. I haven't come to upset you." He raised his palms in a gesture of surrender. "I've just come to say that I can't do it. Believe me, I've tried to stay in my orderly, neat life, alone. And I can't do it." He put one hand down, across his heart, in a theatrical gesture. "Good lady, I am undone."

Now she was pissed off. What the hell did he mean, coming round here in the middle of the afternoon, going all Shakespearean on her? "You can't come in," she said, aware that her voice sounded unnaturally high. "I don't know what you're here for, Jack. A bit of afternoon delight, maybe? Well, it won't work. It's not fair."

He dropped the gesture, stood straight, with his hands by his sides. "You misunderstand me, Polly. Let me be clearer. Please, can I come in?"

She stood back against the open door and let him go past her into the hall. He passed so close to her and Spencer that she could smell him, which unnerved her even more. He went into the living room. Spencer was gurgling happily under Polly's arm, but she put him in his bouncy chair, secured the buckle of the harness and lowered the row of five brightly colored plastic animals so that he could play with them. He busied himself trying to focus.

Although she could scarcely believe it, she heard her voice offering him a drink. It was intoxicating, him being here. "Tea, coffee, juice."

He shook his head, impatient to get his message out. "I don't want a bloody drink, Polly. I want you. I want us to be together." Polly sat down. "I miss you too much. I've been an idiot. I was given a second chance when I found you, and I've nearly blown it by being selfish and inflexible. And I'm sorry."

It was so tempting to run at him, with her arms open, let him hold her. She'd been so strong for so long. And that was why she couldn't. She willed herself to stand still.

Spencer was starting to complain.

"It's not that simple, Jack. You know it isn't. We're talking this around in circles. Spencer is here, and he's going to be here for years. And even when Cressida's on her feet, and he lives with her, they're always going to be the greatest part of my life. They're my children. And you don't want to share me with them. I thought you did, before all this with Cressida, but you don't. You proved that when you backed away, and that means it can't work."

She thought about what Susan had said. It had been a lot to ask. Maybe too much. But she had asked, and been denied. How could they go forward from that?

Outside in the hall, the phone rang. Polly looked at her watch. It was almost certainly Cressida—she often rang at this time. Spencer was fractious now. He was due for his sleep. "I'd better get that."

"Sure."

She went out into the hall, pulling the door behind her. Cressida didn't like to hear Spencer cry when she rang. She said it made her boobs hurt.

Jack bent down to Spencer. "You against me, little fella, that's what it comes down to, isn't it? I'm not much competition." His voice was wry, amused, almost, but soft and deep.

Spencer, who had been turning his head from side to side in protest at his abandonment, went quiet and still, and gazed,

wide-eyed, at him. His mouth worked in tiny *o*'s, as if he were trying to blow smoke rings.

Jack reached out a finger and gingerly stroked his cheek. He
could hear Polly's voice through the door. He knew she was talking to Cressida—she had a special tone of voice for her children.
He supposed he was jealous of that, too. What an idiot. Surprised
at himself, he undid the harness and picked Spencer up, one
hand spread wide under each arm. He wanted to know what he
felt like. He couldn't remember holding a baby so small before.
Spencer was warm, and Jack could feel breath and ribs. He laid
the soft cheek he had just stroked against his own, careful not to
scratch him with his beard, not so much a six-o'clock as a one-
hour-since-I-shaved shadow. Polly had liked it, his beard, scratch-
ing her when they kissed until her cheeks were red. Spencer's
hand came up to Jack's face, one finger in his nostril, the other
pulling his bottom lip down. He'd never experienced the rush of
responsibility he felt now or had an appreciation of vulnerability
and dependence. And he was curious. It wasn't love, that would
be ridiculous, but it was something instinctive, quite beyond his
control. Spencer was hurting him now; one quite sharp nail was
poking the inside of his nose, and he held the baby at arm's
length, looked at him. Spencer's legs came up to his chest, and his
head lolled. Without thinking, Jack pushed his hands, thumbs
still firmly in the baby's armpits, up to cradle his neck. When he
was stilled and steady, Spencer resumed his ravenous stare.

Jack picked up his conversation: "Hey, big guy, you trying to
draw blood now, are you?"

When the smile, uncontrolled but ready, spread across
Spencer's face, Jack felt as if he'd won first prize. He wanted to
make him smile again.

That was how Polly found them. Years afterward she would
say that she couldn't believe how quickly Spencer had cast a spell
over Jack. It didn't seem possible, this road-to-Damascus conver-
sion. She'd been gone three, maybe four minutes, and the baby
had the middle-aged man in his thrall, where he stayed, insensi-
ble and babbling, she would joke, for years. And Jack would
laugh too, his big chocolate laugh, and put his arm round her and
say that was nonsense. That he knew perfectly well nothing

melted a woman's heart like a man with a child in his arms. That it had been a cold, calculated move to get her back, and that he couldn't stand the little bugger. Which no one who watched them playing cricket in the garden, Jack patiently bowling slow under-arms at him, or coming down the big green waterslide at the leisure pool, Spencer apoplectic with excitement between Jack's thick thighs, or testing each other on capital cities, football teams or makes of car believed for a minute.

NOVEMBER
READING GROUP

THE ALCHEMIST

PAULO COELHO © 1988

This is the story of Santiago, an Andalusian shepherd boy, who dreams of traveling the world in search of a treasure as extravagant as any ever found. From his home in Spain he journeys to the exotic markets of Tangier and then into the Egyptian desert, where a fateful encounter with the alchemist awaits him. The Alchemist *is a transforming novel about the essential wisdom of listening to our hearts, learning to read the omens strewn along life's path and, above all, following our dreams.*

O kay, I seem to remember from way back that we have a rule about nonfiction."

"Hear, hear."

"And the book we chose to relax it for was this one?"

'This *is* a novel, isn't it?"

"I want a word with the twenty million people whose lives have been changed by reading this book, according to the blurb on the back."

"Me, too. Right, Susan. You chose it. Tell us why . . ."

Susan grimaced. "Because I believed the blurb on the back?" It was a question. "Nice cover, not too long, author looks a bit like Roger in the photo?"

"Not good enough. If our numbers weren't already down without Clare, I'd think we should drum you out of the group."

"Sorry."

"Hang on. Don't say sorry to Harriet. She's not the boss of us." Nicole was laughing too. "You don't have to apologize for your choices in this group. That, as discussed ad nauseam, is the whole point of reading groups. They make you read things you never would otherwise. Don't they, *Harriet*?"

Harriet's face conceded.

"Besides," Nicole went on, "I did find it extraordinary. It was definitely more of an experience than a read."

"You are kidding?" This was Polly, looking at her copy with incredulity.

"I'm deadly serious. I think you can pick things out of this book that really make you think."

"Oh, yeah, absolutely . . ." Harriet's sarcasm was heavy.

"Here's one, just off the top of my head." She was flicking through the pages, dozens of which had their corners turned down. When Harriet didn't like something, she bombarded the others with her reasons. "Yeah, here." She assumed a heavily accented, deep voice: " 'Everything that happens once can never happen again. But everything that happens twice will surely happen a third time.' That's genius, that is."

"Okay, I agree, it's a bit hard to get the message out."

Susan interrupted: "I liked the way it was written. It was like a parable, wasn't it? You could imagine it being delivered orally, centuries ago. Simple."

"Simple is right."

"What really made you think, then, Nic?"

"Okay." Nicole tried to gather her thoughts into a cohesive view that she could express quickly before the others interrupted. She clearly didn't have many allies on this one, except maybe Susan.

"I thought it had smart things to say about self-determination, and self-knowledge, which are close to my heart just now. All it is is a spiritual journey that Santiago goes on, isn't it, of self-discovery? It's about listening to your heart. There's that bit where he says, 'Why should I listen to my heart?' and the answer given is 'because you will never again be able to keep it quiet. Even if you pretend not to have heard what it tells you, it will always be there inside you, repeating to you what you're thinking about life and about the world.' "

"Fair enough—he's making some good points. Obvious ones, but fair enough. Don't you think, though, that it takes an amazingly long and complicated time to say those two or three simple bits of wisdom?"

"Yeah. I must say I did lose patience with all the fantastical stuff—the alchemist himself, all those bloody 'omens' he kept finding . . ."

"Those stupid stones he kept asking questions . . ."

"And the business about turning yourself into the wind to avoid being murdered."

"I've heard the same points made more succinctly by Hallmark. Listen to your heart. Love conquers all. Sometimes what you most want is right under your nose, and you just haven't noticed it yet."

"Maybe you're just not receptive to it right now. I think I was. When they say it's a life-changing book, maybe that means if you're in a place that needs changing."

"We've all been there, one way or another, this year, haven't we?"

The women fell silent, each thinking about the corners their lives had turned. Harriet thought about losing one Tim and finding the one she had been looking for all along. Nicole thought about rediscovering herself. Polly thought about giving up Jack because she had listened to her heart over Cressida and Spencer, and how his had sent him back to her. Maybe the book had something to tell each of them.

Their silence answered the question. Harriet broke the spell. "Maybe. I could still have done without the mumbo jumbo."

"That's the ancient art of storytelling, though, isn't it? Dressing things up in the fantastical to captivate your audience. Look at the Bible, same thing. This book is like a mini Bible: it's a list of rules for life dressed up in a bit of a fable, that's all."

"I liked the bit where he says that the world's greatest lie is that at a certain point in our lives we lose control of what's happening to us and become controlled by fate. I think he's right—I don't believe in fate either."

"I do. I blame all my big cock-ups on it." Harriet laughed. "Actually, the most interesting thing I think about fate is something I remember from university. Some author—I think it was George Eliot or someone—said your life was like a ship and that you couldn't change its course but you could move around on it while it went wherever it was going. I always liked that theory. Some things are beyond your control. It's what you do about them that can make a difference."

"Only he seems a bit confused. On the one hand he's telling you that there is no fate, because it's all up to you, then on the other he keeps going on about omens, and signs that lead you—surely that's fate?"

"Is fate the same as destiny, then?"

"I think so." Nicole hadn't been able to change Gavin. She'd tried for years. In the end, she'd only been able to change what she did about him.

"I love something he says about timing. He says he's 'interested only in the present. . . . You'll see that there is life in the desert, that there are stars in the heavens. . . . Life will be a party for you, a grand festival, because life is the moment we're living right now.'"

"Hardly original, though, is it? Live for today?"

"Other people can change your destiny, too, can't they?" Susan said. "My mum changed mine."

"What do you mean, Suze?"

"She's not my mum. She adopted me." She hadn't even told Polly. It was still so new. The statement landed like a meteor in the room.

Nicole was confused. "You never told us."

"I never knew. She didn't tell me. I don't think she told anyone, except my dad. Maggie and I found a letter last week when we were going through her things. A letter she'd wanted us to read only after she was dead."

The women were fascinated. This was infinitely more interesting, suddenly, than Santiago and his desert quest for treasure.

"I was her sister's child. She had a sister, Dorothy. She got pregnant, wasn't married, had me in secret. Then she was killed. Mum—Alice—took me in, pretended I was hers."

"Jesus, Suze." Polly, who had been sitting opposite, got up and went over to sit beside her. "What a shock that must have been."

"I couldn't take it in at first. I still haven't. Everything I ever thought about myself, where I came from, is different now. I'm not who I thought I was. At least, I don't feel like I am." Her voice was trembling.

"I'm not surprised," Harriet said. "Why did she never tell you? Did she say?"

Susan shrugged. "Not really. That's part of what's so frustrating. I'm cross with her, you know, on some level, for dying before she told me. The letter said something about being jealous of Dorothy for being my real mum, something like that. I think she was saying she loved me so much she never wanted me to know I wasn't hers."

"As if that would have made any difference, after she had brought you up and everything. It wouldn't? Would it?"

"I'd have been curious, I think. I might have tried to find out more about her, about my dad. But no. She was my mum. She was the one who had raised me. If anything, it might have made me appreciate her all the more." Tears welled in her eyes. "And I still miss her so much. She's only been dead a couple of months, and I'm still upset about losing her, especially in that ghastly way. Slowly, mind first. It was cruel. And now all this. I don't know how to feel, to be honest."

Polly put an arm round her. She'd been so lost in her own family, in the joy of having Jack back, that she hadn't called to see how Susan had got on at the cottage. She couldn't imagine how it would feel to find out that your whole life had been built on a lie. "I can't believe it," she said. "It's like something out of a Catherine Cookson novel."

"I know. It doesn't seem real, does it? We forget, I think, what it was like for women who got pregnant out of wedlock even just forty-odd years ago."

"Did Margaret know?" Polly asked.

"No, no one did. She was just as shocked as me. Just as upset too, maybe even more. Mum and I were always closer than the two of them. I think that was part of why she went away as soon as she could—she was always so jealous. I'm wondering now whether Mum was just trying harder with me because I wasn't hers."

"I don't think so," Polly said. "The two of you were so alike, so close. That wasn't affected. Anyone could see it."

"She *was* your mum, wasn't she, in everything except genetics? I'm sure that's how you should carry on thinking of her," Harriet said softly.

"I couldn't have loved her any more if she truly had been," Susan agreed. "I've always been grateful to her, for her. That was why looking after her, after she got ill, was so important to me. It was why I hated putting her in the home. It felt like I wasn't doing for her what she had done for me. Put me first. Now I know she didn't have to do that because I wasn't hers. She chose to do it. Out of love for her sister, I suppose. That makes the debt feel even greater."

"It's not a debt. That's stupid. Parents taking care of children isn't at all the same as children taking care of parents. I don't want that for my kids. Do any of you?" Harriet looked around. "I mean, I don't look after them so that they can grow up and look after me. That's not how it works."

Nicole nodded in agreement. "Don't let yourself get bogged down by guilt, Susan."

"Absolutely not." Polly was emphatic.

Susan smiled at her friends. Their support and affection was palpable, and she was glad of it. They were right, she knew. Her life wasn't built on a lie. It was built on an act of supreme kindness and love, and she would get used to this new order, to a history where Alice hadn't given birth to her, and to a future without Alice. Maybe with Margaret in it. That felt like a fitting tribute to the sister who had done so much for her own.

They all looked at their orange copies of *The Alchemist*. Real life had taken over. "Now, if this Santiago had had a brother, instead of a flock of sheep, and a hidden letter, instead of some stones with daft names, you'd have been talking good story!"

Susan laughed loudest—the peculiar laughter that was sixty percent tears. "Harriet! I love you! You're absolutely outrageous."

"I know, I know. Don't thank me!"

7:15 P.M.

"We're cutting it a bit fine."

"We've got plenty of time. It doesn't start until eight-thirty this month, does it?"

"That's right. But don't forget it's our turn to do the food."

"Forget? *Moi*? Never! I've bought chicken, and salad in a bag. No problem. No one expects homemade this close to Christmas."

"Speak for yourself. I was up until eleven-thirty last night making a sherry trifle."

"You raver!"

"Don't you dare make fun of me. You try coping with a teething baby at our age."

"Cressida's home for the holidays. Did I miss something? Shouldn't she be the one pacing the hallway in the wee small hours?"

"She should, I suppose, but she was so tired. She's been working hard, and there were a few parties and things at the end of term. I wanted to let her sleep."

"You're hopeless, Polly Bradford."

"I know. Hopeless, but happy."

Susan reached over from the driving seat and squeezed her friend's knee. "I'm so glad, sweetheart. So very glad."

"Haven't finished the bleeding book, though, have I?"

"Naughty!"

"I know, I know. There's no excuse, really."

"I think yours are better than most."

"Yeah!" Polly smiled ruefully.

"I'm coming anyway. I won't get a chance to see Nicole and Harriet again before Christmas."

"Absolutely. They'd be mad if you didn't."

"Now, how many of these bags are yours? Nearly all of them, I think." She gestured at the backseat of the car, which was crammed with carrier bags.

They'd spent the day in London, which Roger had said was madness so close to Christmas. Madness it had indeed been, but wonderful too. The city had been heaving with shoppers, irritable at their own inefficiency, shoving and jostling along crowded streets, too warm for the time of year. Both women were glad they had done their serious shopping already, Susan at a big out-of-town mall with Roger one Sunday weeks ago, and Polly, bleary-eyed, on the Internet over November nights, with Spencer hoisted over one shoulder, unwilling to return to his cot.

This had been a different kind of shopping day altogether. The kind where you go to Harvey Nichols for lunch and drink champagne. And stop at the Nail Bar for a manicure. The kind for which Polly had shaved her legs and worn nice underwear. They'd found it, too. In the first shop. The perfect wedding dress.

It was a silk sheath, long and slim-fitting, the exact color of cornflowers, to be worn under a long velvet coat just a shade darker, with wide lapels overstitched in a floral pattern with a silver thread. For her head a comb in the same silk, from which a tuft of cornflower feathers, studded with diamanté and seed pearls, sprang jauntily. In her wild curls they sparkled and twinkled. Susan had cried a little when she came out of the changing room. "You look so beautiful."

"Yes, maybe, but will baby sick sponge off?"

Polly had felt tearful too when she had turned to the three-way mirror and seen herself, because someone beautiful was looking back. It wasn't just the dress, she knew that: it was happiness that made you glow that way, made your eyes sparkly and your carriage upright so that the perfect dress looked like that on you. Okay, so maybe the unhappiness that had gone before had seen off a few pounds, which meant it didn't pull across her tummy or make her thighs look like those of a rugby player, but happiness had lent her ingredient X. She wasn't even going to look at the price tag. Whatever it cost, it was worth it. She wondered whether you could get real cornflowers in December.

She opened the passenger door and gathered up her shopping. "Thanks for today, Suze. I had a fantastic time, I really did."

"Me too, hon. I'll see you later. Jack going to drop you off?"

"Yes, he is. He's here already, I see." Jack's BMW was parked in the driveway.

"Now, don't you dare show him the dress. I know you're keeping it all low key and everything, but that doesn't mean all the decent traditions go out of the window. He's not to see it. Promise?"

"I promise." Polly laughed. Susan was very old-fashioned: she had already declared that Polly was sleeping at her house on the thirtieth, "whether you're worried about Cressida coping with Spencer or not," because she didn't trust Jack not to come round and try his luck, and she certainly didn't trust Polly not to let him.

Polly turned at her front door to wave Susan off.

"Don't show him the other stuff either!" Susan cried, before she drove away. She meant the Janet Reger nightdress she had bought Polly as a wedding gift, shell pink and lacy, quite the most beautiful thing Polly would ever have slept in (or not slept, as she hoped the case would be).

Jack had seen her on the drive, and the door opened just as Polly scrambled in her handbag for her key.

"What aren't you to show me?" He had Spencer in his arms.

"None of your business!"

They leant forward to kiss, and Jack rubbed his nose against hers. "Good day, darling? Mission accomplished?"

"Absolutely. You?"

"Fine. And this little man has been making teeth, his mummy tells me."

Polly dropped her bags against the coatrack, slouched out of her jacket and held out her arms to Spencer. "Oh, my clever, darling boy. Have you been busy while Granny's been away?"

Now Jack, handing over the baby, took in the number and size of the bags. "Not as busy as you, by the look of it. Did you find some sexy swimsuits?"

He was taking her to Barbados on New Year's Day, for a whole week on honeymoon. He'd wanted to keep it a secret, but she had tickled and kissed and teased it out of him. She'd never been anywhere remotely like that. She'd come down that morning waving the navy blue utilitarian swimsuit she had been wearing for her morning dip at the leisure center over the past three years, chlorine-bleached, threadbare around the arm and leg holes and definitely not sexy. Jack had said he thought he might take someone else on their honeymoon if that was the best she could come up with. Then he'd gone to her, while she was waiting for her toast to pop up, cupped her bottom in his hands and suggested, low in her ear, that she look for something with altogether less Lycra, in a color that didn't remind him of the fourth-form swimming gala. Spencer had been gurgling beside her, in his bouncing chair, gumming one of his rattles. Now Polly said to him, "Oh, yes, I'll look out for a hot pink thong bikini, shall I? That'll give the fish something to think about, won't it? Yes, it will." Even Spencer had giggled.

"I wonder if there'll be a glamorous-granny contest at the hotel."

"I didn't know they had Butlins on Barbados."

"Ha, ha. I promised you five-star luxury, Mrs. Fitzgerald-to-be, and that is what you shall have."

"As long as you promise me I can sleep until lunch every day, I don't care how many stars it has."

"That's not really what a chap hopes for on his honeymoon. A catatonic bride."

She went to him now, but she used the same singsong voice she normally reserved for Spencer. "Oh, my poor darling. Are you afraid you won't get enough attention, poppet?" She put her arms round his neck and pulled his face down to kiss him, pressing herself against him.

"Do you two mind? There's a baby in the room. Not to mention an adolescent with hormones that need no encouragement. And a sleep-deprived zombie." Cressida, who had just come down, gestured at Spencer, Daniel and, last, herself. She threw herself into a chair, her pajamas buttoned up wrong and her hair a mess. She was smiling.

What a strange, gorgeous family this is, Polly thought. My baby has a baby. I'm like a teenager. Jack's something important—even if it doesn't have a name yet—to Daniel, Cressida and Spencer. Thank God. We've pulled it off. It's going to be all right.

"Hiya, mum."

"Hello, love." She kissed Cressida's cheek. "How's he been today?"

"He's gorgeous, aren't you, darling? Bit sad earlier, but I think that's the teeth."

"Did you find the gel? And his teething ring? It was in the fridge. I should have told you. Sorry."

Cressida smiled at her mother. She'd come back from the kitchen with a bottle of milk for Spencer. "I found it all. Don't worry. We've been fine. You've shopped for England, by the looks of it. Did you get lots of good stuff?"

"I did." She couldn't resist a girlish shimmy. "Want to see? I've got half an hour or so before I have to leave for the reading club."

"I've got to give Spence his bottle."

"Give him to me—I'll do it. You two go. Come on, mate, we can catch the end of *Question of Sport*." Jack took Spencer from Polly and rolled his eyes, pantomime-style, at her. Cressida handed him the bottle and laid the muslin square she'd been carrying across his shoulder, smoothing it down across Jack's work shirt. On impulse she kissed him quickly. "Ta."

Polly loved the pride, belonging and love in his face as he reached for the remote control, muttering to Spencer about women and shopping, and how they didn't understand the off-side rule.

There was a card in one of the bags. Susan had said Mary had given it to her for Polly. She'd forgotten about it until now. She opened it: "November 15, with best wishes for a Merry Christmas and a Peaceful New Year." It was a Save the Children card. Clare had signed it, with a single kiss, but there was a note on the left side:

This is the right place for me to be. I can do a lot to help, and that helps me. There are so many children here who need love, and I find, here, that I have so much love to give. I thought it had all gone, but really I just hadn't started. I hope that you and Cressida and baby Spencer are doing well.

I've started a book club! But we only have one copy of each book, so it takes a while to organize a meeting. I think of you every time I pick up a book. Love to all.

God, she was brave. The whole thing, going to Romania, breaking the cycle, was brave, but this struck Polly as one of the braver moments. She was imagining quiet, passive Clare marshaling a reading group into discussion when Cressida came back in. She handed the card to her wordlessly.

Cressida read it, and when she spoke, her voice trembled. "I'm glad."

"Me too."

"I feel like I've been forgiven."

"I think you have."

Cressida dropped her head onto Polly's shoulder. "I never knew it would make me feel so lucky. Having him."

"You never know before you know."

They were quiet for a moment, sitting on the bed, with the card. Then Cressida stood up. "Great dress, Mum. You'll slay him. But if you think Spencer's wearing that outfit, think again. My son is not being seen dead in silk bloomers."

"My wedding, my ring bearer, my outfit."

"He's my baby."

They were playing now. Polly hadn't been sure about the bloomers: Susan had talked her into them. Why she had listened to sartorial advice from a woman who had kept her sons in girlie pageboy crops practically until their teens she wasn't sure. She held up her hand. "Can't argue the toss with you now. I've got a reading-club meeting."

"Oh, don't worry! It'll keep until tomorrow. Unless, of course, I burn the bloomers while you're at Susan's!"

"Don't you dare!"

"Ladies, ladies, please. There are chaps catnapping here. Move your ass, Poll, or you're going to be late." Jack was at the bottom of the stairs, waving his car keys at her.

"I'm coming!"

7:20 P.M.

"But how do the babies get into your tummy?" Chloe was naked and dripping wet on the bath mat, her frame locked in its most stubborn stance, legs apart, chubby hands on chubby hips.

Harriet pushed her hair off her forehead. One of the children at school had brought a new baby brother today. Harriet had watched the mother stagger from her car with the howling infant in its heavy car seat. She had the bowlegged walk of the newly delivered and, up close, the kangaroo-pouch stomach and unmistakable pallor of someone who was surviving on three hours' uninterrupted sleep and twelve hours of uninterrupted demand-feeding a day. Chloe's friend had pulled insistently on the car seat until her mother had put the baby on the classroom floor, whereupon twelve germ-laden four-year-olds had fallen upon him ravenous with curiosity and the uncontrollable urge to "stroke" and "cuggle" him.

As a result babies had been Chloe's theme all day, and she was clearly dissatisfied with Harriet's Mills & Boon explanation of mummies and daddies who love each other and "get" a baby together. The daddy's "seeds" and mummy's "eggs" weren't terribly successful either: last week at nursery they had sown seeds on paper towels inside eggshells: the result was something green, mildew-flavored cress, to be eaten with egg mayonnaise, not something to be rocked to sleep or dressed in tiny clothes. A promise to take her to the working farm (very "Marie Antoinette Goes Farming," all sweet lambs and piglets, no muck and silage) up the road at the weekend to show her baby animals had cut no ice. Clearly, Chloe wanted details.

Josh, fresh from the bath, at his most beautifully vulnerable with wet hair and almost too small Spider-Man pajamas, was hopping from foot to foot, giggling (and not brushing his teeth, which was what he had been asked to do). He clearly knew exactly which bits went where in order to procure issue—no doubt a golden nugget of information gleaned at his favorite after-school club, the let's-tell-each-other-disgusting-things-in-the-toilets club, and was desperate to tell Chloe. Harriet was keen to avoid this: Chloe would certainly share it, loudly, with Mrs. Bond, her teacher, in a context open to misinterpretation. Last week she had informed the checkout girl at Sainsbury's that Mummy had a hairy bottom. The week before it had been the turn of some unsuspecting man at the swimming pool. He had been wearing some ill-advisedly small, tight Lycra trunks, and Chloe, at ideal groin height, had shared with him and the surrounding bathers that she could see his willie through them. The fact that she had had a point hadn't helped. These days Harriet felt in a perpetual state of readiness to talk over her about something innocuous or, in a worst-case scenario, to grab her and run like hell from the scene of the faux pas. Arming Chloe with even the most basic facts about sex didn't seem like a wise course of action.

"Josh!"

He didn't stop giggling. Couldn't stop giggling. It was still extraordinary to Harriet just how hilarious all things bodily could be to a little boy.

Tim's key in the lock. Thank Christ for that. She just had time to throw Chloe's towel round her shoulders as she charged off down the landing screaming her mantra of happiness, "Daddy, Daddy, Daddy!" closely followed by Josh.

When she got downstairs, Tim still had his overcoat on, although Chloe, from the crook of his arm, was pulling off his scarf. "Hang on. Let me kiss your mum."

His cheeks were still cold, and his nose too, as she kissed him on the mouth.

"Mmm. You're nice and warm." He let Chloe slide down his side to the floor and wrapped both arms round Harriet, who slipped hers inside his overcoat. "You're freezing."

When she let her hands rest on his bottom, he let his do the same, lifting her up into him and kissing the place where her neck became her shoulder. He smelt of aftershave, wool and fresh air. He smelt of Tim.

Chloe insinuated herself between their legs and stuck her head between them. Harriet remembered that she was still naked. "Come on, half-pint, let's get you into some pajamas."

"I want to wear the ones with the doggies." This meant an extra ten minutes of nonsense before she relaxed into story time. Each of the cartoon dogs on the blue cotton had to be named. Harriet groaned.

"It's okay, I'll do her. Do you want to put your feet up with the paper?" He pulled the *Evening Standard* out of his briefcase.

"God, yes. You're an angel." Harriet sloped off into the living room and listened to them go upstairs, the children thundering around Tim like puppies, relating anecdotes of their day. Mercifully, Chloe had forgotten her quest for the truth about babies.

This was the time when Harriet had used to feel excluded. Like a fraud. She would have sat downstairs, pretending she needed a break, or watched from a doorway, inventing essential errands to keep herself out of the happy-family tableau. She hadn't wanted to feel like a hypocrite, to act out scenes for Tim's benefit, or for Josh's and Chloe's. She'd thought she didn't love him. She'd thought she was waiting to leave him.

The accident had been the first domino that toppled, and had pushed them all over, floored them and changed their world. It had pushed Tim. Now it seemed so obvious. How did that song go? "Don't it always seem to go that you don't know what you've got till it's gone . . ." What had she been looking for? It wasn't a Nick, and it wasn't a Charles. She'd got things all wrong. Charles had been a memory held up to a fairground mirror that distorted it. Nick had been a fantasy taken out of the forgiving soft light of imagination and put under main-beam reality. The glaring evidence of everything around her had gone unnoticed, unheeded. She never wanted to be as frightened again as she had been in those weeks while he was gone. And she understood now the nature of that fear: it wasn't the dreary domestic fear of being alone, the fuse-changing, dinner-party-circuiting, bill-paying anxiety of someone giving up a habit. She didn't want to be without Tim. Tim. The man who'd fallen in love with someone who'd been crying for so long on the floor of her flat that she had sisal rash and snot running into her mouth. The man who'd loved every ounce of the fifteen stone she'd weighed when she was pregnant with his children. The man who'd known, really, about Nick and let it happen, hoping it might help, somehow. The man who'd sat hour after hour in the hospital, reading *The Hobbit* to Josh, with voices and everything. Tim.

She had stopped looking over his shoulder to see what might be better. She'd remembered, or maybe she had never known before and was just discovering for the first time, that what she had was as good as it got. And she knew what would happen tonight, and the next night, and at the weekend and, God willing, for all the years ahead. And that was okay. It didn't suffocate you, like a pillow: it surrounded you, like a warm bath. Happiness. Contentment. Devotion. Security. They weren't the dirty words they had seemed. They were the best words.

Suddenly she didn't want to read the paper. She wanted to be upstairs with them, where she belonged.

Tim was changing. She ran her hand speculatively between

his shoulder blades to where the hair curled in the small of his back. He shivered, and she enjoyed the feeling of power. Feelings of lust on a Wednesday school night? Christ, things were better.

"You're off out tonight, aren't you?"

"Yeah, it's reading group. Last one of the first year."

"Quite a year. For all of you."

"Yes. Amazing we managed to read all those books!"

"What is it tonight?"

"*Girl with a Pearl Earring*. Tracy Chevalier. Great book."

"About?"

"Unrequited love, mainly. Although that's oversimplifying."

"Chicks' book."

"Oh, yes, my darling. No mere man could possibly understand the issues—servitude, self-sacrifice, desire, inspiration, aspiration . . ."

"Or the big words."

"Or the big words, indeed. Will you be all right here?"

"I'll survive. Got some secret Christmas stuff to do, actually, so it's just as well you're out of the way." He knew she hated secrets.

"Ooh. For *me*? What did you get?"

"No way. You'll have to wait."

"You know I hate to wait." She launched herself at him, and they fell backward onto the bed.

"Please please please!"

He laughed. "You're worse than Chloe." She fixed him with her best puppy-dog stare. "I do have one gift you can have early, if you haven't the patience to wait until Christmas morning.'

"Oh, and I most definitely haven't." She scrambled up onto her knees eagerly. She wasn't expecting the small leather box. She wondered briefly if perhaps she might wait until Christmas Day, dismissed the thought and opened it.

Tim was watching her face. It was a white-gold charm bracelet, its links delicate oblongs. From it hung five charms, each studded with a single sparkling diamond: T, H, J, C, and a daisy. As if it needed explanation, Tim said, "One for each of us, and you had daisies . . ."

". . . in my wedding bouquet."

"I didn't know if you'd remember." It hurt to hear him say

that. The hotel had provided the flowers, as part of the wedding package. She hadn't thought about them for years. "Of course I remember." For a moment she was too moved to thank him, certainly too moved to jump up and down and enthuse. It was the most perfect, beautiful, meaningful gift he had ever given her. She told him so, and kissed him.

"Put it on."

"Shouldn't I keep it, you know, for special occasions?"

"No, it's for every day, every single day. I want every day to be special for us from now on."

Chloe came raging in, with the doggy pajamas buttoned up the wrong way. "You said you would read me *The Gruffalo*, Daddy, *and you haven't*." They laughed. Chloe climbed onto her father's lap, calling for Josh. When he appeared she thrust out both arms towards him and demanded, "Family cuggle. Family cuggle."

7:25 P.M.

Coronation Street was just finishing, but Cressida wasn't really watching it. She was watching Spencer. You could waste an amazing amount of time watching a baby sleep. When he slept all his creases flattened out, and his perfect skin, with no visible pores and no marks, was smooth. The tiny veins on his eyelids made them bluish, and the lashes cast a shadow on his cheeks. His rosebud mouth, with the tiny feeding blister in the middle of the top lip, pursed and unpursed in dreams, and his chest rose and fell. You could pick up his arm, when he was like this, and it was totally floppy. In his carry-cot he lay like a silent-movie lover, with one hand across his face and the other thrown back behind his head. Every single inch was enchanting to Cressida, from the back of his head to the tiny toenails she was still terrified of cutting. When he was awake, you were always moving, like a worker bee, in his service. Warm his milk, make him stop crying, make him smile, reading his facial expressions, searching them for hunger, pain or recognition. But when he was asleep, you could just watch him and marvel at him, and let the balloon of love for him that lived in your stomach inflate until it almost hurt.

At college she had a corkboard full of photographs of him. Mum and Daniel had made it for her before she went in October, and Polly added to it whenever she had a film developed. Spencer in the bath, in his pushchair, under his play gym, in his car seat. It was by the door, and every morning, before she left for lectures, she kissed her finger and laid it on a different picture.

She missed him, of course. At first she didn't think she would be able to stay away. He was so tiny. And it was so weird. No one else here had a baby, no one she'd met anyway. They were exactly like she had been a year ago. If she and her fellow students were on life's assembly line, she felt as if she had been lifted away by the machinery and put on another, for refinements, then plonked back on the original. She had something none of the rest of them had. It didn't stop her doing everything they did—working, drinking, having fun—but it did make her different. She had a baby, and she had the father of that baby, and she had about herself now all the things she had learnt from them.

She never denied him because he didn't come up—until she got to know people well enough to have them back to her room after a tutorial or something and they saw the board. Yes, he's my son. He's called Spencer, and he's four months old and he lives with my mum while I'm studying and, no, I'm not with the father and, yes, thank you, he is beautiful, at least I think so. She never got the chance to be defensive about him because she never had to be. They all made the right noises, once they'd got over their surprise, then Cressida let the conversation move back to common ground. One girl, Amie, who was on her course, had even made her laugh. "But I've been swimming with you!"

"So?"

"So I've seen you naked."

"And?"

"And there isn't a mark on you—or a flipping tummy. Damn you! You're in better shape than me, and he's yours."

Of course, she hadn't taken a guy back. She couldn't see that happening. Too weird. Amie might think she looked untouched by pregnancy and motherhood, but she wasn't sure that that was true all the way through. Her body felt different. She hadn't slept with Elliot after Spencer was born, because it wouldn't have been right, not with all the feelings and stuff, but she hadn't wanted to either. It was too soon to worry about whether it was going to be a problem. She didn't think so. She had met Amie, early on, at a party organized by the college's social committee. She'd been washing her hands in the cloakroom when Amie had rushed in. She said afterward that she only ever went to the loo at parties because, away from the noise, sitting still on cool porcelain, you could tell how drunk you were, which, presumably, informed the choices you were about to make. Drink more? Dance it off? Go home with the handsome rugby player? That sort of thing. She'd been drunk enough, at this party, to stand beside Cressida at the sink and say, loudly, at the mirror to anyone else who was listening, "I'm Amie Gordon, and I am in *love* with Simon French." Subsequently she couldn't remember who Simon French was, or what had occasioned such instant emotion.

Amie regularly slept with men she didn't know very well, but she had a fabulous instinct for finding genuinely nice guys, who took rejection well and became devoted friends. She got invited to everything, and took Cressida along with her whenever she could be persuaded. She often was: Amie was so much fun. But the sleeping-with-men bit, Cressida reasoned, was some way off for her. There were a few she liked the look of: a quiet guy from the library, who wore wire-rimmed glasses; a postgraduate rower of at least six feet four, who often had lunch in the same café she did; the lead in the student production of some god-awful Samuel Beckett play Amie had dragged her to see. None of these had gone further than smiling or nodding, and Cressida didn't want them to. It was enough that she sensed her antennae becoming alive again. It would hurt Elliot, she knew, and she wasn't ready to do that to him just now, apart from anything else she might be feeling. He knew, really, that they weren't right for each other. It made sense to her, in a moral way she hadn't thought of before. Their relationship had begun in dishonesty and deceit, and she wasn't sure that all the love in the world could make a relationship work if it started that way. Maybe she had been the right girl at the wrong time—that might be true. But you didn't stay the right girl indefinitely, and the wrong time couldn't be changed into the right time. It had passed, for now. And Elliot knew it had.

But there was Spencer, and they would always have him between them. Even if she had decided that she wasn't ready to have him (and now the thought of getting rid of him made her shudder), the baby he might have been would always have been a private, intimate thread between them. Elliot was going to be okay. They spoke a few times each week. He let her call him, now that she was at college. They talked about Spencer, what he was doing, how he was sleeping, and that was lovely, because Cressida knew that Elliot loved Spencer just as she did. His voice would break, sometimes, when she told him something, but he was always careful to sound bright and proud, and Cressida was grateful for that. He saw Spencer once a week: his new job in Bristol meant a long drive along the M4, but he adored being with his son. Bristol was working out, too: the old friend he'd kept up with there had proved a useful contact—he'd helped him find a flat in Clifton, which he was renting while he waited for the sale of his and Clare's house to go through. It sounded nice. Elliot would come down after Christmas to see them. She believed now, after this term away and all the talking they had done, that it wouldn't be awkward. She felt lucky—it might have been so different. Clare's card, on top of everything else, felt like a line being drawn under it all. She was being forgiven by the two people she felt she had wronged most, Clare and Elliot, and although sometimes she wondered if she deserved to be, it was starting to feel okay.

And she had Spencer.

A few days ago she'd bumped into Joe. Thank God, she hadn't had Spencer with her when she'd sneaked out to do her Christmas shopping. It wasn't that she'd forgotten about Joe, just that he had been eclipsed by events. Not surprising, really, to see him. But her heart had beat faster, and she'd felt color rise in her face. He'd seen her first—she thought she might have turned and run in the other direction if she'd seen him first—but he had come up, kissed her cheek, his body held back from her.

"How are you?"

"I'm great. How are you?" She'd seen him look down at her flat stomach, reminding himself.

"Really well."

What else was there to say? Nothing, and then they both spoke at once.

"I heard you'd gone to college."

"Home for the holidays?"

They both said, "Yes." Laughed nervously.

"You're not with . . . the father?"

The question was stark, bursting out of the small talk. He had a right to know, she supposed.

"I'm not, no. He's moved away."

Joe was scanning her face to see what that meant to her.

She smiled, hoping she appeared happy, not just brave. "Mum's looking after him for me while I finish studying. She's been brilliant."

He bit his lip. "That's great."

A pretty girl with very blue eyes came to stand beside him. She'd been paying for something at the cash desk. Joe broke his stare. "This is Issie. She's a . . . friend from uni." The hesitation told Cressida all she needed to know. Issie smiled broadly, waiting for Joe to introduce her. "This is Cressida." Cressida could see that her name required no further explanation, could see at once that Issie knew everything about her. She felt a bit naked.

"Nice to meet you." Issie was looking at her flat stomach too, and glancing around for a buggy.

"I haven't got the baby with me. He's at home with Mum. Thought I'd see if I could get some shopping done."

They both nodded sympathetically, as if the problems of shopping with a buggy were completely familiar to them.

"How is . . . Is the baby okay?" Joe didn't know what to ask. He wasn't sure that he wanted to know.

Cressida smiled. "He's fine, thanks. Look, I'd better get off. Promised I wouldn't be too long. It's nice to meet you, Issie."

"You too." Cressida bet it was. A face for the name and the story.

"See you, Joe."

"Yeah. See you." He gave her a half hug before she walked away.

On the escalator she turned to look at them. They were at the doorway of the shop. Joe had put his arm round Issie's shoulders, and she had one loosely round his waist, resting on his hip. It was a gesture of physical intimacy. She's much shorter than me, Cressida thought. She's a much better fit. She ran the idea round her brain, let it fly free into all the corners, trying it out: Joe with another girl. It felt okay.

The naked feeling had gone. Joe seemed like a person she had known and loved a long time ago, when she was someone else. He had probably forgiven her too. He certainly didn't turn to watch her ascent to Children's Wear on the first floor.

And she had Spencer.

The best thing apart from Spencer was Mum. Maybe the worst thing had been when Jack and Mum had split up, and she had known it was her fault. But he was back now. He couldn't stay away. As Polly had said, it proved that he really loved her. Mum had been so happy since he had come back. And she loved Spencer so.

Cressida supposed that one of the things she had learnt about herself with all this was that she wasn't a jealous person. With Elliot she'd never been jealous of Clare. And she wasn't jealous that Polly saw the baby every day, and would probably be the person he most recognized, most wanted when he needed comfort. When she thought about it, she mostly felt grateful—that she had a mother who was prepared to give her back her life and let her keep Spencer. She felt suffused, this Christmas, with something she suspected was joy—it wasn't at all how she had thought it would work out, but she was so very glad it had.

"Cress?" It was Daniel.

She went to the top of the stairs. "Sssh. Spencer's asleep!"

"Sorry. Want some pasta? I'm making some for myself—I'll put some in for you if you like. Come and grate some cheese?"

"I'll be right down." He nodded acknowledgment. "Danny?"

"Yeah?" He was whispering now.

"Thanks."

7:30 P.M.

Heroines in bad novels were always standing naked in front of mirrors admiring themselves, ticking off the good condition of that long list of essential female attributes: high, firm breasts, taut stomachs, rounded hips and pert arses. These things, in the way of novels, rendered them worthy of successful love affairs and happy lives, once the requisite search was out of the way. These women captured the hearts of the best men, the good-looking, charming, heroic ones. Ken to their Barbie contours, Prince Charming to their Cinderella, Richard Gere to their Julia Roberts.

This was clearly bollocks. Nicole had spent enough time in the changing room at the gym, after punishing workouts, and at the spa, after equally punishing rejuvenating treatments, to know that she had the best body of anyone in there. You could serve jelly on her tits, park your bike in her bum and bounce frozen peas off her stomach. Everything was absolutely where it should be. Not a mark left on her by life. On the outside.

Now she knew it made no difference. Gavin didn't cheat in some relentless male quest for the perfect piece of ass. He had it at home. He cheated because he didn't love her enough not to. Because he genuinely couldn't help it.

She'd put on weight since the summer, only a few pounds. She blamed Harriet. It had been that weekend away over the October half term. They'd gone, with the kids and no men, to a blissfully child-friendly hotel called Moonfleet Manor in Dorset, with Xbox and snooker for the boys and a fully staffed crèche stuffed with Barbies for the girls, a pool, sauna and reflexologist for them. Nicole had had that best-body-in-the-pool moment. One woman had ankles as thick as her knees, another had a stomach you could have folded up like a sheet. Harriet was gloriously round, with a metabolism that didn't respond to stress, but skin like a peach and a bosom that Nicole imagined a certain kind of man would always want to bury his face in. This time it had depressed her. What was the bloody point? All of those women had husbands who loved them, including Harriet if she could see it. Fat, misshapen, let-go, scaly women with husbands who loved them and never once thought of looking elsewhere. What was the bloody point?

"Exactly!" Harriet had been delighted to find a potential convert to a life of dietary self-indulgence. "Let a little latte in." And Nicole had. A little latte and a little champagne at dinner in the candlelit dining room and a chocolate-truffle torte for dessert. And if she didn't feel better, she at least felt a little freer.

A few extra pounds suited her, she thought now, looking in the mirror. She looked softer, less tense.

And she was. It was a relief, Gavin not being there. There were moments, usually late at night, in bed, when she ached for him— or for someone. Their super-king-size felt too big for just her. Martha had had a nightmare recently and got in with her for comfort. Nicole had let her stay all night. With Martha breathing rhythmically beside her, Nicole had dropped off and slept well for the first time in months.

She thought about the baby a lot. She'd have been big by now, nearly eight months, feeling Braxton Hickses probably, and those awful pains in her lower belly that the midwife said were caused by ligaments stretching. She'd be getting up in the night, finding it hard to get comfortable, knocking back Gaviscon like it was water. The baby would weigh five pounds or more, have eyelashes and fingernails. Her bag would be packed and in the hall, and the voluminous blue nightshirt with the pink heart on it that she felt was charmed because she had worn it for the twins' and Martha's births, and the tape she had made of her favorite songs to labor to. Maybe not that tape: it was full of songs that belonged to her and Gavin, the soundtrack of their courtship. "Lilac Wine" had been playing in the wine bar that very first night. "My First, My Last, My Everything," Barry White—the first time they had danced, at a friend's party. "Fall at Your Feet," Crowded House: they'd been sitting in the car somewhere in Norfolk, and they'd heard that John McCarthy had been released by his kidnappers, and his girlfriend had been interviewed on the radio, and it was such a moment, somehow, a "you and me together in this big crazy happy world" moment, and that song had come on right after the news. Whitney Houston, "I Will Always Love You": the first dance at their wedding. Not that tape.

It hurt so much not to be eight months pregnant, so much more than Gavin had ever hurt her. Of course, in a strange way, that perspective helped. Most of the time she wished more than anything that she hadn't done it. She was stronger than she'd thought. She'd been strong enough to shut Gavin out of her heart, her bed and her house. She'd been strong enough to end her marriage, to do the practical things that were necessary to make that happen, to tell the children. She'd been strong enough to put herself in the job market. She'd have been strong enough to bring up a baby without Gavin. She just hadn't believed it at the time. It was never going to go away, she knew. It wasn't so much guilt—she could see that eventually she would forgive herself—it was sorrow, loss and regret. There would always be a gap, in her home, in her life, in her heart, for the baby that wasn't there. That was her scar.

She'd said that to Harriet, who had held her hand. Cue more tears. But Harriet preferred to laugh. "Well, that may be so. Good to know, then, that Gavin's not the scar. He's more like the nasty rash that the nice pink ointment cleared up."

"You are so irreverent. He was my husband for nearly ten years, you know."

"Oh, I know. And he was a shit for about nine and a half of them. Don't I just love the sound of that past tense?"

Harriet's good-riddance-to-bad-rubbish attitude was good for her, she knew. She was never once flippant or dismissive about the abortion, just about Gavin. She'd been an extraordinary friend, and Nicole would love her for it forever.

At home, she had to be nice about him: the children loved him. She didn't want to be Bitter Mummy, like so many of the school-gate crowd. That was just another kind of stranglehold, another gate on a happy future. She'd given them the *Kramer vs. Kramer* version, the "Mummy and Daddy aren't going to live together any-more but we will always love all of you, and you will see Daddy lots and lots" version; the unexpurgated one could wait until they were older. He'd wanted to be there, but she had said no. She hadn't trusted herself not to explode at his display of familial loyalty and devotion. She told them, one Sunday afternoon, over Harriet's cure-all hot chocolate and cakes in the kitchen.

"Like Stephanie's mum and dad?" Martha had been apparently unperturbed, with her butterfly mind and her goldfish memory, and slid off her chair to go in search of her Play-Doh, to make Daddy a heart for his new house. He hadn't been home for weeks, and Nicole realized that Martha had acclimatized already. She supposed that one day a stroppy teenage Martha would castigate her anew, but she had learnt from Polly and Susan that hormonal loathing was normal, not confined to single parents. Susan had told her a story, months ago, about Alex, greasy, angry and monosyllabic at fifteen. He'd been asked to choose a poem to recite in a drama showcase at school. He'd learnt by heart and delivered Philip Larkin's "This Be the Verse," which had earned him untold street cred with his classmates, an A+ for expression from his drama teacher and a week of detentions from the headmaster. This was the lot of a teenager's parent: Nicole could hardly wait.

The boys had been thoughtful, more questioning. At least, George had. He wanted to know whether either of his parents would remarry, which had surprised Nicole. "One day, perhaps, sweetheart, but if we do, either of us, it won't be for a long time, and then it would only be to someone you had had a long time to get to know, who loved you and whom you loved back."

"Not 'love' like we love you or Dad?"

"Of course not. You only have one mum and dad. But there are lots of kinds of love, aren't there? You love Harriet, and Tim, don't you? And Uncle Ian and Auntie Kate?"

"Yes." He hadn't seemed sure. "But I wouldn't want to live with them."

"Darling, don't worry. You're going to live with me, only me, for years and years. Promise." He had come to her for a cuddle.

William had always been more self-contained. Like her, Nicole realized. He had fiddled with his Game Boy and not said much. "Are you okay, my love?" she had asked, putting her hand over his.

"I will be," he had replied, suddenly seeming so adult, judging his own recovery from the news. That made her sad.

Gavin always talked euphemistically about the divorce, like people talked about embarrassing medical conditions. Maybe he still didn't believe her. She didn't much care whether he did or not: he would see. She couldn't tell whether it was his wallet or his heart that was throbbing in anticipated pain.

He didn't need to worry: she was not vengeful—not nearly vengeful enough for Harriet, who thought he should pay dearly for his crimes. She wanted to keep the house, because it was the children's home. She wanted to be able to keep them at school and in a life they were used to. That was all. His money was unpalatable to her now, as though he'd been paying her for her complicity all these years. She looked now at her engagement ring, with its quail's egg diamond, and her eternity ring, with its broad band of stones, and all her other jewelry, and doubted his motives in buying it. Like it was a quarter carat per illicit shag. Maybe she would sell it all.

He'd found a flat to rent, Gavin said, "while they waited for everything to be sorted out." It was near Canary Wharf, in a serviced building with a swimming pool, close to lots of restaurants and a cinema. It had three bedrooms, so that Martha could have a room of her own. It was a nice place to take them, and she was glad. They were what mattered to her now. She thought of the time she had wasted over the past years, when she'd been too busy thinking about herself and Gavin to lie on the floor and play, bake cakes and just waste time.

She'd found a new momentum, a new rhythm. She was willing herself forward, out of this bloody awful year into the next. Normally she didn't like New Year's Eve: it was too close to Christmas, loaded with too many aspirations and intentions. This year she could hardly wait for it: a red dress, a real Chris de Burgh special, was hanging in the wardrobe. A gorgeous chiffon size-twelve dress. She would wear her hair down. Gavin liked it up. He had never liked her in red either, so it had jumped off the rail at her when she'd gone shopping with Harriet last week.

"You look fantastic in red. No wonder he said he didn't like it. You'd have been rescued from him years ago if you'd worn red to all those stuffy dos he made you go to."

She was wearing it to the first party she had been to without Gavin in more than a decade. How sad was that? Lipstick, keys, money, Gavin. What a geisha she had been. No more. It was her friend Polly's wedding party. A friend who had never known Gavin, a friend she had made on her own. Harriet would be there, and Tim, and Susan and Roger, and lots of people she had never met. And she was going to drink and dance and talk to people she didn't know, and introduce herself as single, and it was going to be great.

7:35 P.M.

Susan loved her Christmas tree. Nothing upset her more than designer trees. One of her clients, a woman who had more frilly-knicker blinds and silly little dishes of potpourri in her house than anyone else Susan had met, had a pink tinsel tree on which hung only pink and silver balls. Susan thought it was hideous, and completely un-Christmasy. Her own, which she was sitting in front of now, rubbing her shop-weary feet, was a proper Christmas tree. Seven feet of Norwegian greenery, festooned in a thousand different colors with ornaments collected over the years, from holidays and gift shops and, her favorites, from nursery and school, carefully brought home at the end of term: the toilet-roll-and-crepe-paper angel that looked more than a little like Eddie Izzard, the doily stars that had lost all their glitter, the little pictures of Alex and Ed with tea towels on their heads, set in frames of pasta shapes spray-painted gold. Every year when she got out the boxes she sat in a reverie. She couldn't remember which years, which plays, which son, but she knew that they were part of the quilt of her family life, and she adored them all.

It would be strange this year without Alice. She glanced at the picture of her on the mantelpiece. She had taken it last Christmas, just before the film—she didn't remember which one—began on BBC One. The boys, flanking her as she sat stately in the armchair, were still wearing their paper hats, and Ed had that fluorescent string down one arm. Alice was smiling that faintly bewildered, staged smile that people of her generation always wore in pictures. She looked so well, compared to the Alice of the spring and summer, so with it, although it must already have been happening. We didn't know, Susan thought, remembering the day. We didn't know it was the last Christmas she would be here. The last time she would help me peel the sprouts and the parsnips while the boys went to the pub. The last time the whole family would be hushed to listen to the Queen's Christmas broadcast. The last time that the living room would smell of the lily-of-the-valley soap and old-fashioned drawer liners Alice liked to receive.

Roger had said they should do Christmas differently this year. He thought it might make her absence less acute. But Susan knew it wouldn't make any difference if they opened their presents before breakfast instead of after, or ate their dinner at suppertime instead of in the early afternoon. Alice still wouldn't be there. Maybe next year. Maybe they'd even go to Australia, take up Margaret on her invitation, but this year she wanted to do it like they had always done it—it would be okay to remember and miss her. She wanted the comfort of familiarity: so much had changed this year. When that picture had been taken, Alice was alive and her mum. Now she was dead, and she wasn't her mother. It didn't get much more different than that. When Alice had posed with Ed and Alex, Margaret was someone they didn't think about much, a distant, difficult sister Susan had little to do with, living with her husband in Australia. None of that was true anymore, either.

Margaret came in with two mugs of tea. "Here you go."

"Fantastic. Thanks, Mags. Just what I need." She took the mug gratefully. "Now, what's the time? About half seven. I've got a few minutes. Are you sure you won't stay?"

"Sure, thanks for asking, though. I don't think it's my cup of tea."

"Don't knock it till you've tried it. I didn't think it was mine. Actually, it's a lot of fun. I look forward to it every month now—we have a laugh."

"I've already fixed to meet up with that cousin of Lindy's—remember the one I was telling you about?"

"Oh, yes, I'd forgotten."

"Can't really see the point, we don't know each other from

Adam, but that's the Antipodean way, isn't it? It's like you're ten thousand miles from home so you have to find the nearest Australian and bond. Explains Earls Court, at least." She smiled.

"If you can't face going out, you could always cancel and hide out with Roger. He'll be home soon."

Margaret wrinkled her nose. "That'd be right. Roger's dream date—supper in the kitchen with me."

"Don't be too hard on him! He's getting his head round you. Slowly."

"And your mate Polly isn't too gone on me either, is she?"

"They'll all get used to you. The new improved you. You've got to admit, Maggie, you've never gone out of your way to make a great impression on either of them, have you?"

"No. That's true." She thought for a moment. "God, when I think about Mum's funeral I cringe. I was such a bitch, Suze."

"You were." She had been. No point softening the blow. They'd promised each other they'd only be honest from now on. Too many wasted years.

They fell quiet, looking at the tree, and the fire.

"You love Christmas, don't you?"

"Best time of the year."

"Just like Mum. Do you remember, we all used to have new outfits on credit? Took her most of the year to pay for them, and then she started all over again."

"I remember."

"You used to decorate together, the two of you."

"Did we?" Susan remembered the crepe paper they had twisted and fringed with scissors and hung crisscross in the front room, and the balloons. They didn't have a tree, in those days. There had been a big one in the town center, that was all, that they had stared at in wonder and excitement. Once or twice Alice had taken them up to London, on the train, when they had the money for it, to see the lights in Oxford Street and Regent Street. She was sure they'd been more impressive then, all different colors, and huge. These days it seemed to be all about whichever five-minute wonder of a pop group switched them on; the lights looked like an afterthought, white and sparse. Then again, maybe it was a child's memory at work. She remembered other Christmases when they hadn't gone to see the lights, when Alice had left them with their dad last thing on Christmas Eve and gone down to the market to buy the boxes of tangerines they were selling off cheap.

"Do you remember our stockings?" Dad's socks, pinned to each of the wing-backed chairs in the front room.

"Yes! And they always had a tangerine and a handful of walnuts and hazelnuts stuffed into the toes."

"That's right. I did that too, for the boys, when they were little."

"You didn't?" Margaret was laughing at her now.

"I did. Not that they ever stood much of a chance against the chocolate and sweeties. Always went back into the fruit bowl on Boxing Day, as I recall."

It was there now, on the coffee table. A bowl of tangerines and nuts, and the pewter nutcrackers they had had as children. Ineffectual in their little hands, but very pretty, each with a squirrel at the top.

Margaret was looking at it. "It made me feel left out. You two loved Christmas so much, and you both got so excited and carried away, and I always felt a bit silly. Believing in Father Christmas, and trying to pretend the presents weren't the same things we had seen in the toy-shop window and on the market for months beforehand."

"Oh, Maggie."

"I just let you two get on with it, really. Stayed out of the way."

"I never noticed."

"You never did. You were always in a world of your own. Busy being just like Mum."

Susan gave a sad laugh. "Ironic, isn't it?"

"Isn't it just? I think that was one of the things I loved about going to Australia, saying good-bye to those Christmases."

"How did you celebrate it there, you and Greg?"

"Not much. Went to the beach, usually, treated it like any other day off. He was never any good at presents and that sort of thing. I usually bought myself something on his credit card. He wasn't mean, just wasn't really into it, which suited me, pretty much."

"What about since Greg?"

Margaret grinned. "Much better. I mean, I don't think I could ever feel the way you and Mum did about it, but I go to Lindy's—she always has this huge drunken barbecue, really typical Aussie stuff. There were about thirty of us last year. We cook, and drink, and eat, and dance. And she's got these mad Greek relatives, and they all smash plates and stuff."

It didn't sound very Christmasy, but it did sound fun. Susan tried to picture a laughing, lightweight Margaret in the thick of it all. Maybe she could see it. She had a lot of unlearning to do about her sister. "I'm sorry," she said.

"About what?"

"Sorry we made you feel funny about Christmas."

"You didn't do it on purpose. That's just how you were."

They were quiet for a minute or two.

"It helps me, you know. Knowing that you weren't Mum's."

Susan didn't know how to take that.

"I don't mean that how it sounds. It's hard to explain. I mean, you and Mum were more alike than she and I were, I know that—nothing to do with biology. But now that I know how she came to be looking after you, it makes me think that maybe she tried harder with you than she did with me because she thought she had making up to do, you know?"

Susan had thought it herself so many times, since the day they had found the letter.

"It was an amazing thing that she did, wasn't it?" Maggie said.

"It was. I feel slightly in awe of her when I think of the self-lessness it took for her to do that."

"Makes you think, doesn't it? I don't know if I could do that for someone else."

"Even your own sister?"

"Especially my own sister."

Susan hit her playfully with a cushion. Then they were quiet again, thinking about Alice. These were hard things to think about, and hard things to say.

"I bet it made her sad."

"What?"

"That we didn't get along."

"She never once said so. Did she to you?"

"No." Margaret shook her head. "Not that I ever gave her the chance. I buggered off, didn't I, as soon as I had the chance?"

"I wonder if she felt guilty." Then Susan answered her own question: "Of course she did. All mothers feel guilty."

"So she never talked to you about it? I sort of thought she would have done. You two have always been so close."

"Not close enough for that I guess. She missed you, I know. And she sometimes said she didn't understand how things had gone wrong between you and her. She loved you—you know that, don't you?"

"Yes."

"She made a promise, to Dorothy, I suppose, and my God she kept it."

"I've been sitting over there in Australia all these years, eaten up with jealousy. I feel like I've wasted so much of my life, Suze."

Susan thought she might cry again. This new Margaret, with all her nerve endings on the outside, was a revelation to her. It was as if a dam had burst inside her. She wasn't sure she had the energy to cope with her, but she knew she wanted to try. She wished she was religious, because then it would be possible to believe that Alice could watch her two estranged daughters moving forward without her, more together than they had ever been. That was a nice thought, the childhood idea of Alice in white robes and halo, watching them with Dorothy from a fluffy cloud. Then again, that made it sound like she was doing it just for Alice, and that wasn't true. She was doing it for herself. She wanted to keep part of her old family, however much she understood that she, Roger, Ed and Alex were a new one, and Margaret was all that was left. She wanted to love her, and be close to her, and she was just beginning to see that that was possible. She put her arms round her sister, her cousin-sister, and held her.

DECEMBER
READING GROUP

GIRL WITH A PEARL EARRING

TRACY CHEVALIER © 1999

"As historical fiction, Girl with a Pearl Earring *convinces, but as a study of human nature, honed by hindsight, it dazzles. Chevalier brings an impressive combination of passion, outrage and perception to a novel which is beautiful and brutal."* Irish Times

I wish they would put what the book was about on the back. It's really off-putting when it's just quotes. You want to know what the story's about, not whether it's won loads of prizes or critical acclaim. That just makes it pretentious, doesn't it? This is a classic example of a book I would never have picked up if it hadn't been for the reading group."

"Me too. I'm glad I did."

"Oh, God, and me. I think it's my favorite of the whole year."

"Definitely."

"Really? It was nowhere near for me. I thought it was boring. For the first hundred pages or so, I didn't give a damn. It was so agonizingly slow. I'd never have finished it on my own."

"I can't believe you thought that! It was exquisite. I really, really believed that Griet was real—it had that authentic quality, like you were reading a real diary."

"I know. Didn't you keep flipping back to the front cover? When there was that bit about him making her pierce her other ear, even though it wasn't going to be in the painting, and even though it was agony for her, didn't you spend ages looking at the front cover wondering why?"

"No. It was obvious. He was testing her feelings, flexing his power over her. I thought he was a bit of a bastard. He knew she loved him, and he knew she would do whatever he asked her to do."

"He never tried it on with her, though, did he?"

"Wasn't that the times they lived in, more than anything?"

"I don't think so. There was more illicit shagging going on then than there is now. She did it with the butcher in the alleyway because she thought that other guy, the *patron*, was going to rape her, didn't she?"

"So that if she got pregnant the butcher would have to marry her."

"I think it was more that he just wasn't interested."

"He was interested enough to get his wife pregnant every ten months, though, wasn't he?"

"But that just shows the contempt he had for her, and for 'ordinary' women. You never saw him show her any affection. It was just physical. Functional. Like the household, which his mother-in-law had to run for him. He couldn't be doing with anything practical or base. For him it was just the painting. Do you remember it says several times that he wouldn't paint any faster, compromise his perfectionism, even though the family finances were really stretched?"

"Yeah, selfish git."

"No, real artist. That's what the author wants you to think, I think. One of those people who just isn't of this world."

"And it was Griet's sense of color and space, which she demonstrated in the kitchen with those vegetables the first time they met, that attracted him, even though she was a servant and a woman."

"I don't think that was all. I think the scenes where he's painting her are as sexy as hell."

"I agree. Completely heavy with desire, aren't they?"

"I waited two hundred and forty-seven pages for him to throw her down on the bed, and it never bloody well happened!"

"You can choose *Lady Chatterley's Lover* when it's your turn if it's dirty bits you're after. This was much more subtle than that."

"It gave me a real ache in the stomach. She knows nothing can ever come of it. She knows she has to settle for the butcher. The resignation . . ."

"Absolutely."

"She isn't cowed, though, not really. When she gets the pearls, you know, after he dies, she uses the money to buy back her freedom. No one but her will ever know she's done it, but she knows, and that's enough."

"Don't you think she sells them because she knows they belong to a different life, one she's not entitled to have? She says it, doesn't she? 'A butcher's wife did not wear such things, no more than a maid did.'"

"So, do you reckon he left her the pearls because he loved her?"

"No, out of guilt. He knew he had shown her a glimpse of a world that she could never have."

"No, he left them as thanks, and remembrance. He would never have acknowledged in his lifetime the debt he owed her—she was the one who made that painting what it is. So he did it after he died."

"Don't you think there was a big cliché running through the whole thing? Don't you think Griet was just the younger woman to the man whose wife didn't understand him?"

"No, I don't, because nothing ever happened between them."

"That's not the definition of cheating I'd use. They cheated on his wife. They spent lots of time together in a place where his wife was refused entry. And he told her things and shared things with her that his wife had no knowledge of. That's cheating. Sex is just sex. They might as well have done it."

"Do you realize that most of the women we've read about this year have pretty miserable lives? Because of men. That's the most consistent theme."

"Because of men, or because of themselves?"

"Don't be pedantic. What gets done to them—what they let be done to them. That's the same thing."

"It absolutely is not."

"I agree. I think the ones that get redemption, or even where you're left believing they will be okay—like, say, *Heartburn*, or Paula in the Roddy Doyle—are the ones who take the control back."

"You always generalize, did you know that? Every month."

"I do not. Can I help it if I see the wider picture?"

"Hah!"

"Are we turning ourselves into a feminist book group? Because if we are, I would like to state for the record that I like men. Nearly all of them. Some more than others, admittedly, but in principle I'm for them."

"Me, too. And I'm not about to start shaving my head, wearing dungarees and quoting Germaine Greer."

"Enough, already. You lot have the concentration span of squid. Who's for trifle?"

"I love this reading group." Harriet beamed at the other three.

"You love everything tonight." Susan smiled. "What's up with you? You're acting like a newlywed."

Harriet exchanged a glance with Nicole. "Something like that."

"Hey," Polly cried, "I've got dibs on all things newlywed. Seventeen days to go."

"Bloody hell, is that all? I'm never going to lose that half stone, not with Christmas to get through."

"Give up, Harriet, for God's sake!" Susan laughed. "You've been saying that as long as I've known you—it's the same seven pounds that just keeps going on and coming off. Learn to love it, I say. And buy a bigger size."

"I can't. Me and my weight have been the longest relationship of my life." She laughed and took a truffle out of the box that Susan had put on the table to eat with coffee. She passed one to Nicole, who ate it, still vaguely surprised at herself.

"But I do. I love this reading group. I think it's time to reflect— we've been together for a year now, and I've come to look forward to these Wednesday nights as much as almost anything else."

"Are you going to suggest a group hug next, because I think I may need to excuse myself if you are." Nicole was goading her. She knew exactly what Harriet meant.

"We've read some great books," Susan said.

"And some absolute turkeys," Polly added.

Harriet leant down and pulled a piece of paper out of her handbag. "I've started on a list for next year. We have absolutely got to read *Divine Secrets of the Ya-Ya Sisterhood*. I can't believe we haven't read a Margaret Atwood—you can't call yourself a proper reading group if you haven't read Margaret Atwood. There's a sequel to *Rebecca* out, by Sally Beauman, who wrote that fantastic book—do you remember?—*Destiny*. And I'm still determined to make you all fall in love with Jane Austen."

"Hang on. Isn't this a democracy? We all get to choose, don't we?"

"All except you, I vote." Harriet sniggered. Nicole looked round the table for support, but Polly and Susan were laughing as well.

"You may laugh. You'll only make it worse for yourselves when it *is* my turn to choose. I feel a bit of Salman Rushdie coming on . . ."

They all groaned.

She nodded at them, like a mother nods at a naughty child. "What about new members? Without Clare we're a bit on the minimal side."

They ran the idea round their heads. It had been a pretty weird year for all of them. When they'd first sat down at this table, with their carefully read copies of *Heartburn,* and that strange first-day-of-term feeling, they'd all been fundamentally different. Nicole and Harriet had been unhappily married; Susan had had a mother she loved and thought she knew everything about; Clare had had no future; Polly had thought that becoming a grandmother was something in her far distant future. Everything had been turned on its head, and everything was different now for all of them. Some of their lives had become simpler, some had gone through complications they could never have imagined. And through it all, there'd been this forum where they had come together, sometimes to share their secrets, sometimes to escape them, but always to listen to each other and talk about life, in the abstract or absolutely in the present. They had learnt so much more than they had expected to. This felt comfortable for them now: they knew each other. It would feel strange, wouldn't it, having other people here?

"Nah." Polly shook her head.

Susan did too. "I'm happy."

"You're happy because there are fewer people here to argue with you. Suppose we got someone really clever in. Who actually got out of bed at university to go to lectures. That'd pee on your bonfire, wouldn't it?"

Harriet lifted her nose in the air, haughtily, and looked round the table at her friends. "I just dare you to try!"

Insights,
Interviews
& More . . .

About the author

About the book

Read on

Meet **Elizabeth Noble**

ELIZABETH NOBLE was born in December 1968, in Buckinghamshire, England. She was educated in England and Canada, where the family lived for several years in Toronto.

In 1990 she graduated from St. Edmund Hall, Oxford University, with a BA (Honors) in English language and literature. But it was the diploma (Intensive Secretarial) that she was awarded by the typing school above the Italian café in Covent Garden that got her into her chosen career—publishing. Over a six-year period she worked in the editorial, marketing, publicity, and sales departments of several big publishing houses—moving every couple of years, once she had made a big enough mess in the filing (note to bewildered successors: check under *m* for *miscellaneous*). This makes her a tricky author. She speaks fluent publishing.

She took a career break—she called it retired—to have her two daughters, after her marriage in 1996. When her youngest daughter was ready to go to nursery school, and real work beckoned, she decided to try what she had been threatening to do for years, and wrote a hundred pages of *The Reading Group*.

Then it took her nine months to work up the courage to send it to an agent. *The Reading Group* was published in the UK in January 2004 and went straight to the number-one position in *The Sunday Times*'s Fiction Bestseller list. She was supposed to be signing stock in London bookshops the day the chart was announced, but she had grown bored and was trying on trousers—they didn't fit—in a ladies' clothing store when the call came. So she was literally caught with her pants down.

The book has since sold almost a quarter of a million copies in the UK. But the other day her elder daughter, Tallulah, told her she would rather she got a job in a chicken plucking factory because then she would be at home more, so she doesn't think there is much danger of her getting conceited.

She has recently finished her second novel—there were no vacancies at the chicken plucking factory—and begun her third.

She lives with her husband and their ungrateful children in a haunted vicarage in "the safest village in Surrey," England. They obviously don't know about the ghost. ∾

David Galloway

3

A Quizz with Lizz

First record: *Do You Really Want to Hurt Me?* by Culture Club. I hope you are asking about singles, not albums, because that was Olivia Newton John's *Physical,* which isn't quite as cool.

Favorite movie: I mostly only watch things once, but for Sunday afternoon purposes, *Gone With the Wind, Seven Brides for Seven Brothers, It's a Wonderful Life,* and *The Sound of Music* will do nicely. My husband may not have married me if he had known about this.

> Shoes because I have tiny feet, about which I am excessively vain—they are my only tiny bit.

Accessories: Bags and shoes. Bags because they are a non-weight-related purchase. No one ever looked me up and down appraisingly and told me they didn't have a bag in my size. Shoes because I have tiny feet, about which I am excessively vain—they are my only tiny bit.

Obsessions: Apart from bags and shoes?!

Pampering: Pedicures for the aforementioned favorite body part. Back, neck, and shoulder massages. Apparently I have the muscle problems of a heavy manual laborer. I'm a housewife with small children. I *am* a heavy manual laborer.

Biggest celebrity meeting: Margaret Thatcher. Which was surreal. And I stood next to two of the boys in *Busted* at Christmas. Does that count? It sure does with my six-year-old.

Vodka or gin, red or white: Gin. With ice

and a slice. I'm *British*. And white. Preferably Viognier. But if you really want to please me, it's a big glass of Cointreau, no ice, for me, thanks.

Carbohydrates: I never met one I couldn't eat.

Sign: December 22. Which makes me on the cusp of Capricorn and Sagittarius, an apparently lucky fact I ignore unless it says I'm going to have a spectacular day.

When I am happiest: When I am awoken with breakfast in bed by my wonderful husband and two adorable daughters after a four-hour lie-in.

If I could live anywhere: Would you believe right where I do now? Okay, then let's add a beach house in the Maldives and timeshares in Sydney, New York, Boston, Florence, and Paris.

Favorite heroine in literature: She's no glamourpuss, but that Ántonia, in Willa Cather's *My Ántonia*—she's got guts.

Favorite hero in literature: You can keep your brooding Darcys, Rochesters, Heathcliffs, and de Winter's—who needs it? I prefer a twinkle in the eye. Rhett Butler, I say.

Favorite modern author: Armistead Maupin. I read the entire Tales of the City series in about a week fifteen years ago, and I re-read them every few years. I love them more every time.

Favorite classic author: Has to be F. Scott Fitzgerald. Those books make you ache. ⌒

> 66 That Ántonia, in Willa Cather's *My Ántonia*— she's got guts. 99

5

Behind
The Reading Group

I READ A LOT. When I was young and pretentious, I read all the "should read" clever books; when I was at university I read the classics; when I had babies and my brain was porridge I read big fat funny books for comfort, and for escape; and now, in my mid-thirties, a working mother who belongs to a reading group, I read all of those—and sometimes, just magazines.

But whichever category you're thinking of, I have always felt that there is just one ingredient that a book, for me, has to have. I have to care about what happens to the characters. I have to feel compelled to finish a book, to feel that if someone took my copy away, I would need to go out and buy or borrow another copy, just so that I could get to the end. If I love a book, recommend it to friends, re-read it—it's because I care.

And I like a story. A proper story, with a beginning, a middle, and an end. Nothing annoys me more than a book where you feel like the author has lost interest and left almost mid-sentence. I don't find that thought-provoking, I find it irritating. And lazy. It's the grown-up equivalent of a child's story that ends, "and then I woke up and it was all a bad dream."

So that's what I wanted to write. I wanted to create female characters to whom you could relate. And to have them going through situations and scenarios with which you would empathize.

It was also important to me that my women characters were of different ages. One of the nicest discoveries I have made as I have grown

> ❝ I have to feel compelled to finish a book, to feel that if someone took my copy away, I would need to go out and buy or borrow another copy, just so that I could get to the end. ❞

nicest discoveries I have made as I have grown older is how much you can learn from older women, and how much pleasure you can get from their company—from the company of people who have been in your shoes, but who no longer are.

And so my heroines, if that is what they are, were born. Harriet is a wife and mother who wonders, from her comfortable world, what she might be missing. She yearns, I think, for excitement, and has stopped valuing the things that contentment and security bring. I don't think I have a woman friend who hasn't at least flirted with that emotion. Nicole is that most fascinating of women: the clever, attractive, articulate, bright woman who loves unwisely, and who goes on letting herself be hurt, knowing why it is happening, and how to stop it, but powerless to do so. We have all known someone like that. Susan characterizes the sandwich generation—still caring for her children while taking on an infirm mother. I watched my husband lose both his beloved parents to a form of dementia and the sadness of grieving for someone years before they actually die is awful, and exhausting. Polly is a strong, independent single mother, terrified of being once again made vulnerable and needy by love, but at the same time so tempted to seek that happiness. Clare is infertile. Living with that stark fact, in a generation where IVF, surrogacy, and assisted conception makes us believe that it must be possible to have a child, is almost unbearable, and it destroys relationships, and lives. And Cressida, Polly's daughter, is pregnant when she doesn't want to be.

So you have these six women—the youngest barely twenty and the oldest in her forties—dealing with these quiet dramas over the course of a year. It was important to me that they weren't huge traumas—this book was supposed to be about real women. Look at the queue in the supermarket behind you and I bet one of the women there will be experiencing one of the situations—they are all around you. ∾

About **Reading Groups**

JUST AS DOCTORS are always being shown strange rashes at dinner parties, people are always telling me their reading group stories. I met a woman who was asked to leave a group she belonged to a few years ago when her fellow members "found out" that she had not been to university. They thought she might feel "more comfortable" at another group. I met a woman who knew of a group where the members read in French in alternate months, because they can. And one woman—a bright, funny woman—left a group she had joined after just a few meetings because she found it had awoken feelings of intellectual inadequacies she thought she had left behind decades before. These, I suggest, are not good reading groups.

I have also learned that not all groups are like mine. The wine and whine type. Some are mixed—although I think men are still a minority; some are not made up of friends but of acquaintances, in groups brokered by bookshops or libraries; some have been set up to help adults in prison, or those just learning to read and write.

Whatever kind of group, what the members seem to have in common is that the group becomes incredibly important to them. Mine certainly is. We were friends first when we set up the group about four years ago. After a period of natural settling, we are now a fixed number, and we squirm with reluctance at the thought of admitting anyone else. We are cohesive; we are intimate; we are comfortable. At a library talk I did, one woman castigated me for that, and for the fact that my fictional

> 66 Whatever kind of group, what the members seem to have in common is that the group becomes incredibly important to them. Mine certainly is. 99

reading group also declines to take on new members. She argued that this was intellectually stultifying and creatively limiting. Which was probably true. But that tells you that she wants something from her reading group that I don't from mine. And *vive le difference*.

I did a radio program in the UK with an erudite and expert panel, where one social historian argued that reading groups were something like a formalization of social rituals—extra help we all need in modern life, where we are too busy, too stressed, and too superficial to really get to know people well. I'm not sure about that, but I do think reading groups are, if not quite the new cocktail party, then certainly the new quilting bee, or the new coffee circle. With an exciting, stimulating, fascinating twist. ᴄᴡ

> " I do think reading groups are, if not quite the new cocktail party, then certainly the new quilting bee, or the new coffee circle. "

How to Set Up a Reading Group
(like Harriet's)

1. It's no good if you are all great friends. Get two or three great friends, and get them to bring a couple of their own. That way there's still lots to learn about one another.

2. Take turns to choose a book. Do this religiously. Even though some of your friends always choose titles that make your head hurt.

3. Make only a few rules, but adhere to them. If you haven't read it, or certainly most of it, you *can't* come. Fake out the fakers.

4. Food and drink are good. Take turns to make, bake, and bring. But don't turn it into a gourmet cook off. It's fuel for the debate.

5. To take notes or not to take notes. There's always one who'll show up with Post-It notes throughout their copy. Don't be intimidated!

6. Don't always stick to the front table in the bookstore or the bestseller lists. The classics make great reading group books.

7. Once you're comfortable with one another, experiment. See films made of books you have covered; invite partners once a year and have a mixed reading group (top tip: choose a book with some boy stuff); it's meant to be fun.

> " If you haven't read it, or certainly most of it, you *can't* come. Fake out the fakers. "

The Real
Reading Group

"CAN YOU WRITE five hundred words on what it's like to be in the reading group with me, please?" Lizzie asked innocently following a trip to meet her publishers in New York. We were very excited! This was our big break—the chance to show our own literary talents. Our confidence wavered only slightly when Lizzie offered to write the piece herself. When we refused her kind offer she suggested a list of adjectives to include. On the evening we met over pasta and wine to discuss what we would write, she even called us to see how we were getting on. Was she worried we wouldn't tell the truth? Rest assured! This is our unabridged, unedited, unprompted account of what being in "The Reading Group" with Lizzie is really like.

It all began a few years back. Lizzie gathered together a group of women with different personalities, interests, and as we were to discover, different reading habits. The group was bound together at that stage by a thread of friendship and children of similar ages.

There's Nic, a doctor and mother of three—a self-confessed *Hello* reader who likes thin books with a good story. Nic was reluctant to join the reading group initially as she didn't "do" books but was swayed by her liking for the other members.

Maura is a former fashion buyer with four daughters who loves books with a historical setting and plenty of mystery. Her house provided the inspiration for Nicole's in the book.

Jenny is the oldest member of the group (as Lizzie constantly reminds her). A mother ▶

> 66 This is our unabridged, unedited, unprompted account of what being in 'The Reading Group' with Lizzie is really like. 99

of two, management consultant, and chair of the school Parent Teacher Association, she enjoys reading books she otherwise wouldn't choose.

Kathryn works for a charity and is mother of two. She is our wonderful conscience. She organizes us and keeps us focused on the books. She wins top points for always being first to buy the book.

And then there's Lizzie. Lizzie has a passion for reading and is very knowledgeable about books and authors, with a degree in English from Oxford University. In the early days of our reading group we confess to having been a little intimidated by her knowledge, insights, and strong opinions. However, our confidence has grown and we are all now happy to contribute our views and thoughts.

Lizzie is a people person. She is sensitive, perceptive, and caring. She remembers everything we tell her about ourselves, our lives, and our families. This interest in people translates into a deep analysis of the characters in the books we read, which can be quite enlightening! Lizzie also brings her own brand of wit and humor to our group. If any of us misses a central point she will challenge us in a humorous way. She can make a joke to lighten our moods when things get heavy, but is empathetic when the time is right.

Despite all the good things she brings, Lizzie is not always the perfect reading group member. Once we suspected she didn't read the book at all, but relied on reading a review on Amazon. In fact we recognize a lot of Lizzie in the character of Harriet from *The Reading Group*.

Although none of us have yet been

> Once we suspected she didn't read the book at all, but relied on reading a review on Amazon. In fact we recognize a lot of Lizzie in the character of Harriet from *The Reading Group*.

inspired to write a novel ourselves, we do have a good plot based on a year in the life of a first-time novelist—who confessed to eating a bowl of raw cake mix to rid herself of writer's block.

We are not a highbrow group and for various reasons we've lost some members along the way. Like the characters in *The Reading Group*, we have become great friends, and sometimes what is happening in our own lives overtakes discussion of our chosen book. So, if we've been used for research for *The Reading Group* and if sometimes Lizzie contrived to choose books she wanted to include in the novel, that's okay with us. We look forward to being involved in research for future books.

We are proud to be in a reading group with Lizzie, proud to be her friend, and proud that she has written a bestseller while looking after her lovely family, without getting big headed.

❧

> " So, if we've been used for research for *The Reading Group* and if sometimes Lizzie contrived to choose books she wanted to include in the novel, that's okay with us. "

Coming Soon from
Elizabeth Noble

SHE DIDN'T HEAR her mobile phone ring; the music was too loud. But she saw its persistent green flash from where it sat in the hands-free holder next to the stereo controls. Adrian's office number. Grudgingly, she turned Harry's song down. She hated mobiles. You could never be "unavailable" anymore.

"Hello?"

"Hello? It's me."

"I know. Caller ID."

"Of course. How did it go?" He never rang to ask her that.

"Fine." So she wasn't about to tell him.

"Can you talk?" She thought they already were.

"Yes. Traffic's really crummy. I'm going about two miles an hour. What's up?"

She heard him take a deep breath—actually heard him.

"Perhaps it better wait until we're home."

"What?"

"No . . . it's okay." Freddie was instantly irritated.

"For goodness sake, Adrian, what's wrong? You've obviously rung about something . . ."

He'd obviously changed his mind again. When he spoke his voice was louder, and stronger.

"I think you should know that I'm seeing someone. It's become rather serious, actually. I love her and we want to be together. I wanted to wait until Harry had gone back. I know it's going to be rather complicated . . ."

His voice trailed off. He'd started so well, too. You'd think once you'd told your wife you were in love with your lover it wouldn't be that much harder to tell her that you wanted a divorce, that you wanted one or the other of you out of the home you shared. But apparently it was.

Silence. She very nearly felt sorry for him. Pandora's box. Lid off. Can of worms. Opened. Cat. No longer in bag.

"Freddie? Are you there? Freddie?"

More silence.

"Freddie, come on. We have to talk about this . . ."

"No, Adrian. Apparently *you* have to talk about this. Right now. I think you'll find that I absolutely don't have to."

And she pushed the red button that cut him off. Her hand was shaking.

Freddie, Tamsin, Reagan and Sarah.

They meet at university in the heady days of the eighties: four women with little in common but an eagerness to live life to the fullest. And over romantic crises, long gossipy nights, and too many bottles of wine, they form the Tenko Club and swear they'll always be there for each other. Membership is for life.

Twenty years later, that promise is put to the test. ❧

> ❝ No, Adrian. Apparently *you* have to talk about this. Right now. I think you'll find that I absolutely don't have to. ❞